Poison and Wine

Book One in the Irish Rogues Series

Katie Ashley

Trigger Warnings

Violence
Murder
Attempted SA of FMC (Not by Hero)
Attempted Miscarriage (Not by FMC or MMC)
Assault to FMC (Not by MMC)
Sexually Explicit Scenes
Rape (Not FMC and off page)
Kidnapping/Abduction

All rights reserved.

No part of this book may be used, reproduced, or transmitted in any form or by any means, electronic or mechanical, including photocopying, recording, or by any information storage or retrieval systems, without prior written permission of the author, except where permitted by law.

Published by:

Katie Ashley

This book is a work of fiction. Names, characters, places, and incidents are products of the author's imagination or are used fictiously. Any similarity to actual persons, living or dead, is coincidental and not intended by the author.

Cover design by: Harsha Dhananjaya

Model: Epifanio Lopez

❦ Created with Vellum

About the Author

Katie Ashley is a New York Times, USA Today, and Amazon Top Three Best-Selling author of both Indie and Traditionally published books. She's written rockers, bikers, manwhores with hearts of gold, New Adult, Young Adult, and now mafia. She lives outside of Atlanta, Georgia with her daughter, Olivia, her rescue mutts, Belle and Nova, and her three rescue cats: Mama Kitty, Jake, and Joe. She has a slight obsession with The Golden Girls, Shakespeare, Harry Potter, and Star Wars.

Although she is a life-long Georgia peach, she loves traveling the country and world meeting readers. She's the most extraverted introvert you can find, and most days, she prefers books to people.

*"Your hands can heal. Your hands can bruise
I don't have a choice, but I still choose you."*

Poison & Wine.
The Civil Wars

Chapter One: Callum

Ear splitting cries of terror and agony echoed through the empty warehouse. Kneeling down onto the blood-splattered floor, I eyed the man tied to the chair. A pinkish hue stained my hands from battering his face. "I want a name, Bobby. All this can end if you just give me a name."

With disgust glittering in his brown eyes, Bobby spit out of a stream of blood onto my shoes. "Never."

Tsking at him, I shook my head. "You disappoint me."

"Fuck you, Kavanaugh."

"Since I like blondes with big tits, you're not my type," I mused.

After rising to my feet, I nodded at my brothers, Quinn and Dare. "Maybe you two can get our friend talking."

As they started pummeling Bobby's chest and abdomen, I stood back, admiring their handiwork. While some children inherit the family business of banking or medicine, my brothers and I were born and baptized in the blood of the Irish mafia.

My grandfather had risen through the ranks to become a clan leader in Belfast. He'd been blessed to actually pass on his power, rather than having it ripped from his hands through assassination or mutiny. At his death, the ornery bastard had bestowed it on his firstborn son, my father. It had been my father's dream to bring the Kavanaugh empire to the states.

Ten years ago, Hugh Kavanaugh had brought me, Quinn, and Dare to Boston while the rest of our family remained protected back in Belfast. At barely twenty, it'd been hard leaving everything I'd ever known, especially my mam. But any tears I tried to shed at her loss were beaten out of me by my father.

I could still smell his harsh, whiskey-laced breath against my face. "An Irish clan member must never show weakness, and your love for your mam is a fucking weakness."

His fist pummeling against my cheek sent blood spurting from my mouth and nose. "The love for any woman is a bloody weakness!"

My lips curled in a sneer at the memory. Fucking ironic that his disgust for the love of women was what led to his demise. Some days when I stared down at my hands long enough, I could see his brain matter and blood sprayed across my skin. I was thirty when I pulled the trigger, but when I stood beside him, I became that heart-broken twenty-year-old kid again.

Over a year had passed since that day, but his spirit still haunted us. His murder at my hands was why we currently found ourselves grappling for power. Old alliances had been burned by my act of patricide. But in spite of all we had lost, I would do it again; and all for the love of a woman.

If anyone could restore and elevate the Kavanaugh name, it would be my brothers and me. As the oldest son, I'd been the obvious choice to take my father's place. I'd spent my entire life preparing to take over. Because of our wealth, I'd attended the finest schools in Belfast, and I'd graduated with a business degree from Trinity College.

Despite all my talents, I was nothing without my brothers.

With his brute strength and towering size, Quinn made a natural enforcer. When you threw in the rippled scars that ran from his temple down the length of his right side, he oozed menace. As a true phoenix risen, Quinn had survived a car bomb that had been meant for my father.

Darragh, or Dare as we called him, was the opposite of Quinn in both appearance and personality. He was shorter, leaner, and where Quinn had been broody even before the bomb, Dare excelled at being the life of the party. Even now a cruel smile was curved on the bastard's lips as blood splattered along his hands and arms.

Glancing over my shoulder, I eyed the exit of the building where my brother, Kellan, stood guard. Unlike the three of us with our dark hair and blue eyes, Kellan possessed strawberry blond hair and green eyes like our mam.

I jerked my chin up at him. "Want me to take watch and let you have a go at him, boyo?"

After clearing his throat, he called, "I'm grand."

At twenty, Kellan remained wet behind the ears when it came to the grittier side of our work. Dad had brought him over from Belfast three years ago while our youngest siblings, Maeve and Eamon, remained with our mam. While I felt he'd never truly possess a heart for the harsher side of our business, Kellan was a whizz with numbers and served a purpose within the organization.

When my phone buzzed in my pants pocket, I ignored it. After it continued to go off, I grunted and dug it out. "This better be fucking good to interrupt a perfectly good torture session."

My father's youngest brother, Seamus, chuckled. "It is. I need to speak to you and your brothers."

"When?"

"As soon as you finish with whatever poor fucker I imagine you have strung up."

"Meet me at the house in an hour."

"See you then."

At my brother's expectant faces, I tucked my phone back into my pocket. "We need to wrap this up. Seamus needs to talk to us."

I knelt down once again in front of Bobby. His head lolled forward as blood dripped out of his mouth. "Last chance," I said.

"End me." A shudder went through his body. "If you don't, they will."

"While I normally don't take commands from traitors, I'll oblige you just this once."

After grabbing my knife from my holster, I unsheathed it. With a quick flick, I sliced Bobby's throat from ear to ear. Jabbing my knife at Quinn, I said, "Arrange a clean-up, and then meet us at the house."

As he nodded, I started over to the door with Dare on my heels. When we reached Kellan, his face paled slightly at the sight of our blood-stained clothes and hands. He recovered and handed us a bag with a change of clothes.

After stripping down to his briefs, Dare groaned. "Man, I'm starving."

Kellan shot him a look of disgust. "How can you possibly be hungry after what you just did?"

Dare flashed him a grin. "What can I say? I worked up an appetite."

Chuckling, I replied, "I'll text Lorna and tell her to have lunch prepared for us."

"I want dessert, too," Dare replied before licking his lips.

I rolled my eyes. "Whatever."

After rinsing our arms and legs with a water hose and scrubbing as best we could, we toweled off before slipping on new dress pants and slightly wrinkled dress shirts. We would need minutes under a scorching hot stream to truly get clean, but at the moment, this was the best we could do to ensure we didn't look conspicuous.

Poison and Wine

We followed Kellan out the door to a waiting SUV. Once we were all inside, I gave the driver a nod, and we began the trek from the Southside back to the posh streets of Beacon Hill. Silence hung heavy in the air except for the bass thumping from Dare's rap music.

After all the years and all the killings, you would think one would grow numb to all the violence. But for each and every one of us, there was always a price to pay.

In the front seat, Kellan's low murmuring caught my ear. "*Sé do bheatha, a Mhuire, atá lán de ghrásta.*"

Of course, he would be saying the Hail Mary in Irish to acquire absolution for our sins. Although I didn't have much use for mass or prayers, I found myself reciting the next verse in my head.

Is beannaithe thú idir mná, agus is beannaithe toradh do bhroinne, Íosa.

I didn't see how there could possibly be salvation for me with all the blood on my hands, but buried deep within me was a tiny seed planted by my mam that left a sliver of belief.

As we sped along, I couldn't help the dread that filled me from Seamus's requested meeting. Seamus had been my father's right-hand man here in the states. He could have fought my accession after I murdered his brother, but Seamus had known my father's cruel brutality just as my brothers and I had. Like my uncles in Belfast, they had been grateful to see me leading the family instead of my father. Seamus was also my top advisor.

Once we arrived home, I trudged through the backdoor into the kitchen. "Hello, Lorna," I called pleasantly. She momentarily paused in bustling around. "I hope I didn't put you out asking for lunch."

To my brothers and me, Lorna held more than just the position of cook and housekeeper. She'd been a part of our family for as long as I could remember. She was the only woman our mother had ever entrusted us with.

With her own children grown and starting lives of their own, Lorna had agreed to my father's business proposal to accompany us to Boston. Since I knew it hadn't been easy for her, I made sure to fly her back to Belfast anytime she seemed homesick.

Lorna smiled as she blew an errant strand of silver hair out of her face. "Not at all."

I smirked at her as I crossed my arms over my chest. "You're a terrible liar, Lorna."

She laughed. "After all these years, you think I would be used to your wild schedule by now."

After bestowing a quick kiss on her cheek, I said, "Just do what you can."

I then made my way out of the kitchen down the long hall. As I stepped into the living room, Seamus reclined on the sofa. He turned his tortured green eyes to me.

The last couple of years hadn't been kind to him. First, he had lost his only son and heir, Rian, in the car bomb that had scarred Quinn. Then six months later, his wife had been so overcome with grief that she had taken her life.

I'd never known the love of a wife or a child, so I couldn't imagine his suffering. I only knew from the agonized look in his eyes that I never wanted to have to experience that pain.

"Are you hungry?" I asked without a hello.

"I could eat."

"Lorna's whipping something up." I motioned to him. "Come on in the dining room while we wait."

Seamus rose off the couch to follow me. After he and my brothers took their seats, I strolled over to the bar to pour a glass of whiskey. "And to what do we owe the pleasure of your company?"

"Trust me when I say I wouldn't have called a meeting if it wasn't something truly important."

"Aye, we'd surmised as much."

After pouring myself a glass, I poured one for Seamus. I grabbed the tumblers and headed over to the table. "What's the threat this time? The Bratva or the Triad? It sure as hell better not be any other Irish around here."

"They're all a clear and present threat as our current position is still precarious. We desperately need a way to elevate the family."

Dare leaned forward in his chair. "You want us to take out more families?" His words caused a grimace from Kellan.

"I was thinking of a way that entailed less bloodshed," Seamus replied.

Quinn appeared in the doorway. "How does one possibly elevate their position or territory without bloodshed?" he countered.

"Through an alliance."

With a grunt, Dare asked, "You really think anyone willingly wants to work with us now?"

The *now* he referenced was after our father's murder.

"Alliances can be made unwillingly." Gripping his whiskey glass, he threw back the contents before he spoke. "I should be disappointed that none of you guessed what I'm speaking of, but then I have to remember none of you randy fuckers give a shite about commitment."

He nodded his glass at Kellan. "Except maybe you."

While my brows furrowed at his comment, Quinn sucked in a harsh breath. "You're talking about marriage."

"Aye, boyo, I am."

I tensed. "A marriage between us and who?"

"The Italians."

I groaned. "While an alliance between another Irish family is hard enough to swallow, the thought of mixing blood with Italians makes me want to boke."

"It could be worse," Quinn remarked.

"How so?"

"It could be the Bratva."

"True," I chuckled mirthlessly. I couldn't even begin to imagine our family aligning with the likes of them. "So, which Italians did you have in mind?"

"The Neretti's."

A growl reverberated through my chest while Quinn and Dare cursed under their breaths. "You can't be serious," I demanded.

Seamus narrowed his dark eyes at me. "If you think you can do a better job making the decisions for this family, put me to ground and see where it gets you."

I held up my hands. "I'm not knocking your judgment, Seamus. It's just of all the Italian families they're the last one I would want an alliance with."

The Neretti's had held a powerful stronghold in New York City and the boroughs since the turn of the century when their first ancestors had come over from Sicily. While the Kavanaugh's had grown their wealth through liquor and gambling, the Neretetti's dirtied their hands with prostitution and pornography. Some of the earliest snuff films were financed by the Neretti's.

In later years, they had elevated themselves to wine and dine with politicians and the elite, but their business dealings remained in a seedy underbelly.

With a shake of his head, Seamus argued, "Once again, that shows your lack of discernment. Joining forces with the Neretti's ensures we keep power and gain territory as well."

"And what do they possibly get out of the union?"

"They're an old name family, but they've lost too many men in the last couple of decades. They need the manpower that we and our allies can provide to protect their territory."

Dare glanced between us. "Just which one of us do you plan to marry off?"

Seamus opened his mouth, but I beat him to it. "Me."

The moment the words left my lips dread filled my chest. Anger soon replaced it. After everything I had seen and done, I was pissed at myself for feeling dread at the thoughts of marrying.

At thirty-one, I shouldn't have been surprised by an arranged marriage. By the time I was twenty-five, two marriage contracts had already been dissolved between myself and other Irish families. Both were because of betrayals by the girls' families.

Poison and Wine

Like many in the mafia, my father believed a man shouldn't be wed too early. He should learn the ropes of the business while also enjoying himself with as many different women as possible.

"Why you?" Dare countered.

"Don't tell me you want to get roped into this?" Seamus asked.

With a grin, Dare replied, "Fuck no."

I eased back in my chair. "Of course, it has to be me—I'm the first-born son and leader of this family."

"The alleged pick of the litter, eh?" Dare teased.

"Fuck you, third born," I threw back with a smile.

He flashed me a wicked grin. "Third born yet blessed with a third leg for a cock. I'll manage."

While Quinn and I chuckled, Seamus shook his head. "Don't count any of yourselves out of being part of a marital alliance. We need to make as many as possible."

"Just not the Bratva," Dare muttered under his breath.

Seamus's eyes narrowed at Dare. "How quickly you forget my dearly departed wife was Bratva."

"She was only half Russian."

"She was still Bratva, and she made me an excellent wife."

Dare's expression softened. "Aye, Seamus, Elena was the best. My apologies."

Kellan cleared his throat to change the subject and in turn ease the tension. "I didn't think Alessio Neretti had any daughters?"

"Caterina is his only one."

"What does she have to say about our upcoming nuptials?" I questioned.

Seamus exhaled a breath. "That's where the *unwilling* part of the alliance comes in."

"I sure as hell don't like the sound of this."

"Alessio Neretti would never dream of aligning with our family. His sons would, but he's too much of a traditionalist to go outside his Sicilian brothers." Seamus drew in a harsh breath. "But even if he did, Caterina has been unable to marry for the last two years."

"Once again, I *really* don't like the sound of this."

When Seamus remained uncharacteristically silent, I cocked my brows. "Don't hold me in any more suspense. *Why* has my bride—the daughter of a high-ranking member of the Familigia who would have unlimited marriage proposals—remained unmarried?"

"Because she's been in a convent."

Holy motherfucking shit. While Quinn's eyes bulged, laughter burst from Dare. I narrowed my eyes on Seamus. "How can you possibly marry me off to a nun? She's married to God!" I snarled.

Amusement twinkled in Seamus's blue eyes. "She's only a novice."

"She's a *nun*."

With a shake of his head, Seamus replied, "She hasn't taken final vows yet, so she's only a novice."

"Does that really make a fucking difference?"

"For our blackened souls, it does. The last thing we need on our conscience is kidnapping a full-fledged nun."

A grunt of disgust came from Kellan. "I would think kidnapping and forcing a woman into marriage is bad enough regardless of her religious status."

Seamus chuckled darkly. "I'm aware I'm a fucking hypocrite to remain a practicing Catholic considering the line of work I'm in. But I do hold some things sacred. The fact that Caterina hasn't fully given herself over to the church makes this a little more palatable."

"It sure as hell isn't palatable to me." I threw back the remaining whiskey in my glass. "My future wife is a fucking nun!"

In the past year, I'd rarely entertained the thoughts of marriage. With all the chaos following my father's murder, it had been pushed to the back burner. But whenever I did imagine it, it was always with an Irish virgin from one of our ally families. One who I had some form of common ground with.

There was absolutely nothing in me that could be compatible with an Italian nun. Her entire world revolved around her faith to where mine was often just an afterthought to keep my soul out of eternal damnation.

As an Italian, she wouldn't know any of my Irish history, the foods I loved, or the difference between good whiskey and absolute shite whiskey. She wouldn't know the folklore or superstitions or the important holidays.

When my thoughts turned to my future bride's appearance, disgust rolled through me. Images of the nuns at the Catholic schools I'd attended flickered through my mind. The thought of even trying to get my dick up for any of them was useless.

"Do I get to see the lass you've brokered for me before the ceremony, or are you keeping her appearance hidden because of undesirability?"

Seamus reached into a coat pocket to retrieve several pictures. He slid them over to me. "I would say even a blind man would be able to get it up for a body like that."

Curiosity got the better of me. Snatching up the pictures, I peered down at my future wife. With just one fleeting glance, I knew he was right. Hell, she could make a half-dead man rise to the occasion.

In the first picture, Caterina wore a tight black cocktail dress that fitted perfectly against her ample curves. Her long dark hair flowed in waves almost to her waist.

The next picture showed her at the ocean where she wore a red bikini that showcased her fantastic tits. No one who saw the pictures would've believed the young woman in them would aspire to become a nun.

With a smirk, I replied, "I suppose I can muster the strength to fuck her now and then."

Seamus snorted. "You're lucky I'm not taking her for myself."

"You're a dirty old bastard considering she can't be much more than eighteen."

"She's almost twenty-one."

"And you're fifty."

"Forty-five," he countered.

"You're more than old enough to be her father, you pervert."

Seamus laughed. "I'm giving her to you, aren't I?" He gave me a pointed look. "While I'm fully capable of satisfying a woman that young, I'm too old to raise one."

I chuckled. "Is that right?"

"Aye, I need one that's been properly broken in. A lovely widow who has raised her children and wants to focus solely on spoiling me."

"Best of luck finding that," I snorted.

Dare rattled his knuckles on the table. Jerking his chin at the photographs, he said, "Come on. Give us a look at our future sister-in-law."

I tossed the photographs across the table at him. Kellan and Quinn leaned over to get a look as well.

"Fecking hell," Dare muttered at the bikini picture. "You're a lucky bastard, Callum."

"Whatever," I chuckled.

"She's a corker," Quinn grunted. With a shake of his head, he added, "What a waste of a body to be a nun."

"She's very beautiful," Kellan added with a shy smile. Leave it to him not to sexualize my future wife but instead focus on her beauty.

Turning my attention back to Seamus, I asked, "The pictures leave me with even more questions."

"Such as?"

"Why the hell would a beautiful and sexy young woman want to become a nun?"

"From the intel I've gathered, she was escaping from an arranged marriage with a sadistic pedophile."

The mood in the room shifted at the mention of Caterina's fiancé. As the heaviness permeated the table, I knew what each one of my brothers was feeling. But there was one of them more affected than the others. My attention shifted from Seamus over to Kellan whose jaw clenched.

Poison and Wine

In my father's regime, the clan believed a husband had the right to treat his wife and daughters in any way he saw fit without any interference. They were his property. I'm sure it was the same in the Neretti family.

That archaic and bullshit ideal was one of the first fucking things to go when I took over. I might be a cold-hearted killer, but I would never be someone who physically or sexually abused women. Neither would my brothers.

Any man who thought he could take a hand up against a woman was dealt with. *Painfully.*

Clearing my throat, I tried to ease the tension in the room. "While I'm sure as hell not like her former fiancé, do you really think this runaway bride is going to want to stick around to be my wife?"

He grimaced. "Not entirely."

With a growl, I swept out of my chair. "Dammit, Seamus. This has fucking disaster written all over it!"

"It doesn't have to be. Unlike her fiancée, you're young and handsome. While you can be an ornery bastard sometimes, you're not a sadist."

"High praise indeed," I muttered.

"In the end, you can give her the worldly things she possibly misses outside of the religious order."

"Or is it maybe more possible she'll resent the hell out of me for taking her away from a life devoted to God?"

"You can always negotiate to make sure it's worth her while. Perhaps in five or ten years' time when our position is more stable, she can go back to the order."

"If she's married to me for any length of time, she won't be a virgin," I countered.

"Don't worry. The order allows you to re-devote your life to chastity."

Cocking my brows at him, I said, "You've really done your homework on this one."

"It was necessary to ensure there were no loose ends."

While I wanted to argue with him that there were infinite loose ends that could unravel, I kept my mouth shut. Instead, I resigned myself that I was about to be a married man. For better or worse, Caterina Neretti was going to be my wife and the mother of my future children.

After throwing back another shot of whiskey, I asked, "So, what's the plan?"

"We leave for Palermo in two days."

My brows shot up. "She's in Sicily?"

"Is that a problem?"

"No. I just imagined she was in a church somewhere in New York."

"Caterina joined The Sisters of the Sacred Heart, which is a missionary order. She currently serves in a clinic that doubles in medical aid as well as a food pantry in a remote village outside of Palermo."

"It sounds like she's as beautiful on the inside as out," Kellan remarked.

Dare threw his arm around Kellan's shoulders. "Sounds like you have a crush."

Kellan's face flushed. "I do not."

"Tis a sin to be coveting your brother's wife," Dare teased.

Shoving Dare away, Kellan countered, "I'm not coveting her. I just said she sounded caring."

I grinned at him. "I'd say I'd need to keep my eye on you, but I know you're far too honorable to try to put the moves on my wife."

Kellan glowered at me. "Jesus, Mary, and Joseph, I only said she sounded nice."

"And beautiful," I countered.

"Fuck off," he muttered.

Seamus chuckled. "All right, boys. Back to our plan. I've secured us a house outside Catania, which puts us on the opposite side of the country from where Caterina currently is. We should be well hidden since anyone looking for us will think we fled back to the states. You'll be married from there as well."

"Why can't we just get married here in Boston?" I asked.

"It's vital that we do not leave Sicily until you are legally wed both on paper and by a priest."

Seamus shifted uncomfortably in his chair as he dropped his gaze to his lap. "Ideally you would consummate the marriage before we leave Sicily."

The air around us once again grew thick and tense at Seamus's suggestion. As agony rippled through my chest, I knew each one of my brothers was seeing the beautiful face of our sister in their mind. But there was one of us that it pained worse than the others. Kellan started to bolt from the room, but I hurried over and grabbed him.

Staring into his haunted eyes, I pronounced, "I will not force my bride. You have my word that she won't ever suffer what Maeve did."

Although I knew he hated himself for it, tears streaked down his cheeks. "Thank you, brother," he whispered, as he swiped his face.

I squeezed his shoulders before turning back to Seamus. "If her family believes in that bloody sheet nonsense, we'll fake it."

Wrinkling his nose in disgust, Seamus replied, "I don't think they're that hardcore, but I suppose it wouldn't hurt to drive the point home to them about the legality of your marriage."

"That's fucking barbaric even for me," Quinn grunted before throwing back a gulp of whiskey.

Dare nodded. "I agree."

Although I didn't feel much like celebrating, I held out my whiskey tumbler. "Let's all pour another and raise a glass to my future bride."

"I never thought I would see the day," Quinn chuckled.

"Especially not to an Italian," I mused.

With a wink, Dare thrust his newly filled glass in the air. "To my brother and the Sexy Sister."

Chapter Two: Caterina

E ar-splitting cries of fear and agony echoed through my ears. Kneeling down onto the clinic floor, I stared into the frightened eyes of a four-year-old girl. *"Prometto che non ti farò del male,"* I crooned.

It appeared my promise not to hurt her had fallen on deaf ears. Instead of appearing comforted, she shook her head while continuing to cry. I knew it couldn't possibly be an issue with my translation since I spoke Italian as well as I did English. More specifically, I'd grown up with the same Sicilian dialect as those in the villages around me spoke.

My attention went to her mother who gave me an apologetic smile. "I've tried everything to get her to calm down," she explained.

"It's okay," I reassured her. "What's your name, sweetheart?"

"Flavia," she sniffled.

"That's a beautiful name for a beautiful girl."

With Flavia's cries waning slightly, I picked up the syringe on the table next to me. I held it out to her. "This is medicine, and it's meant to help you. You're only going to feel a little pinch. I bet you won't even realize you've had it."

When her wails started up again, I added, "As soon as it's over, I'll let you have an ice cream."

When her cries abruptly stopped, I knew I'd found the magic word. For some of the children it was ice cream while for others it was candy or maybe a toy. Almost all of them eventually had a breaking point.

"What kind of ice cream would you like?" I asked as I rubbed the alcohol swipe on her arm.

"Chocolate," Flavia sniffled.

"Mm, chocolate is my favorite, too." As I brought the needle to her arm, I asked, "What do you like on your ice cream?"

"Sprinkles."

As I injected the vaccine, I asked, "Rainbow sprinkles?"

"Yes."

I nodded. After pulling out the needle, I smiled. Just as I had predicted, Flavia barely recognized she'd been given the shot.

"Great job!" I exclaimed before putting a band aid on the injection site.

Her eyes popped wide. "It's done?"

"See, it wasn't a big deal at all, was it?"

Instead of agreeing with me, Flavia demanded, "Where's my ice cream?"

I laughed along with her mother. "You're right. A promise is a promise. I will go grab you one right now."

As I made my way out of the examining room and down the hall to the kitchen, I smiled and waved at the children in the waiting area. Many of them waved back while others threw me wary gazes. I guess I couldn't blame them. Although it certainly wasn't my intention, I was the woman who made other kids cry.

Growing up, I'd never been a big fan of shots myself. My mind flickered back to the times my nanny, Talia, had loaded my brothers and I up in the car to go to the doctor. Of course, our car was actually a bulletproof SUV, and two bodyguards accompanied us.

Just like Flavia, I would cry the entire trip. Nothing Talia or my brothers said ever seemed to soothe me. It wasn't until we swept through the doors of my favorite ice cream parlor that I would finally dry my tears. Just like Flavia, I liked chocolate with rainbow sprinkles.

An ache spread through my chest at the thought of my former life. It happened each and every time I thought about my brothers or Talia. It wasn't that I was unhappy belonging to the Sacred Heart. It was more that being a novice in a religious order at twenty-one wasn't exactly how I'd seen my life unfolding.

My shoes shuffled along the aging tile. Our facility wasn't much to look at both on the inside or outside, but it did so much for the impoverished people of the area. The work my fellow sisters did was a matter of immense pride to myself. I felt extremely blessed to be a part of it.

When I strolled into the kitchen, two large pots bubbled on the burners while two sisters stirred the contents. "Come to help us with the soup?" Sister Lucia asked with a smile.

"While I would love to lend a hand, I'm actually on a mission for something sweet," I replied as I made my way over to the freezer.

"Let me guess. This one is not for your outrageous sweet tooth, but it's another bribery for a shot?" she asked.

Laughing, I pulled out a mini container of chocolate ice-cream. "How do you know me so well?"

Sister Lucia winked. "Lucky guess."

"Any chance we have rainbow sprinkles?"

"I think there might be a jar left in the pantry," Sister Maria replied.

"Thanks."

After peeking in the pantry, I began eyeing the shelves. Today was a lucky day apparently because I found a half empty jar. Normally, the order didn't allocate funds for treats.

The money we spent went only for basic needs. But I snuck the allowance from my trust fund into the budget to ensure we had treats for the kids and even the parents.

I shoved the sprinkles into my skirt pocket and made my way out of the kitchen. As I walked past a mirror, I used my free hand to tuck back the hair that escaped my ponytail. I didn't have time to stop and redo it.

I'd been eternally grateful when I joined the Sacred Heart that their more modern rules didn't dictate that we had to wear a habit or robes. Instead, we wore black or navy calf length skirts and white or gray blouses while our hair remained uncovered.

When I arrived back at the examination room, I handed Flavia the ice cream. Then I dug the sprinkles out of my pocket. Her eyes popped wide with excitement. "Thank you, sister."

"You're welcome," I replied. After covering the ice cream with sprinkles, I smiled. "Take care."

Once Flavia and her mother exited the room, I moved on to my next patient. Anyone who presented with serious issues was moved on to the doctor. In my brief medical course with the order, I'd been taught how to take blood pressure, administer vaccines, and clean wounds. Back home, I would barely be qualified as a CNA, but here, what skills I had were very needed.

After making it through the rest of the patients, it was almost closing time. I'd just come out to the main room when Amara, a blonde girl with pigtails, approached me. "Sister Cat, will you read us a story?"

Although I had a million things to do to close down the clinic for the day, I could never tell the children no. They were truly my weakness. Besides my brothers, they were the thing I truly missed from the outside world, or I guess I should say the world outside of the Sacred Heart. Growing up in a large Italian family, I'd never been at loss for endless numbers of cousins. Before I was ten, I'd garnered the nickname of Baby Whisperer.

Smiling at Amara, I replied, "I would love to."

She shoved a book into my hand. "Read this one, please."

"Of course," I replied, as I eased down in a chair.

Amara waved over several other children who were waiting as their mothers visited the food pantry.

"Once upon a time in a faraway land, there was a beautiful princess who was locked away in a castle..."

Although my eyes focused on the words on the page, my mind became spirited miles away in another place and time. Once upon a time, I had been a princess held captive in a castle. Instead of a faraway land, I'd been born and raised in Manhattan, and my castle came in the form of a penthouse on the Upper East Side as well as a mansion in the Hamptons.

A handsome prince had never come to rescue me from my prison where we could live happily ever after.

Instead, six months after I turned eighteen, a marriage contract had been brokered with a man twenty-five years older than me. A man who I'd never seen, least of all spoken to. The first time I'd met him was when I'd been paraded in front of him in my father's office. Just the thought of that day sent a shiver of dread down my spine.

Without even a hello or a handshake, Carmine Lucero had leered at me. His lecherous gaze had first focused on my breasts before trailing down. He'd licked his lips at the sight of my legs. After smacking my father on the back, he bellowed, "You've produced quite a specimen, Alessio. With those child-bearing hips, I'm sure she'll give me many sons."

Carmine's first wife had died unexpectedly, if not somewhat

suspiciously, leaving him with three daughters to raise. Daughters who would make me an instant mother upon our marriage. One of which was only four years younger than me.

After sliding an enormous diamond on my left finger, Carmine asked to be alone with me. Although I knew better than to vocalize my fear to my father, I'd tried conveying it with my eyes. He'd merely given me a disapproving shake of his head before he left us alone.

Carmine loomed over me. I kept backing away from him until I bumped into the wall. "I'm going to enjoy breaking you in."

When he'd dipped his head to kiss me, I'd darted away from him. But he grabbed me by the arms and shoved me back against the wall. "You *will* let me kiss you."

"I'm not supposed to kiss you until we're legally married," I protested.

"Our contract is enough."

Thrashing against him, I shouted, "You will not disrespect me in this way!"

"Listen to me, you little cunt. When we are married, I will *disrespect* you in any way I see fit. I'll *fuck* you in any way I see fit, and you'll take it because you'll be my wife."

In that moment, my disgust and hatred of him overtook my fear. All of the lessons of obedience my mother had forced upon me escaped me. Rage like I'd never known possible rocketed through my veins, and I didn't stop to question my actions.

I reacted.

Rearing back, I spat into his face.

Carmine had flushed with a hideous violet fury before his meaty palm struck my cheek. "If you ever even think of doing that again, I will let every one of my soldiers fuck you before I traffic you somewhere your father and brothers will *never* find you."

At his threat of rape and trafficking, fear overwhelmed me, causing my knees to buckle. I slid down the wall. After cupping my stinging cheek, I feebly protested, "I'll tell my father what you said. He'll break the contract this instant."

Carmine's lips curled into a sneer. "Who do you think he'll believe? A well-respected Made Man like myself who brings much to the table, or the girl who is so desperate not to marry that she would say or do anything not to make it happen?"

And as I had cowered there on the floor, I knew he was right. In that moment, the old Caterina had splintered into jagged pieces. Without a handsome prince to whisk me away, I'd been forced to put myself back together again.

I had to rescue myself.

I'd refused to be nothing more than a powerful man's wife or a breeding machine for his heirs. I'd refused to live with bruises on my body from being beaten or raped by my husband. I'd refused to let my life be controlled by a man.

Instead, I'd turned to the sisterhood.

In spite of attending mass religiously, anyone who knew me would've never fathomed I could possibly join a convent. Since I reveled in loud music, designer clothes, and an occasional alcoholic drink, I wasn't what one imagined in a potential woman of the cloth.

Within a career you make personal sacrifices in order to adhere to the expectations of a company or your boss. I'd done the same thing when I'd joined the Sacred Heart.

Even though I'd come from immense wealth, I wasn't so spoiled that I couldn't take the vow of poverty. With a controlling father and an emotionally absent mother, I'd witnessed firsthand how money didn't buy happiness.

While it had been expected of me to always play by the rules, I'd never rebelled until it came to marrying Carmine. In that respect, the vow of obedience wasn't an issue either.

And as for the one so identified with being a nun, I was as chaste as they came. Like everything in my life, my virginity wasn't my own. It belonged to my future husband. To ensure that I was pure, I never had an encounter with a guy that wasn't chaperoned. I'd managed one brief kiss with a boy from school, but that was it.

I was completely untouched by men.

Two and a half years had passed since I'd escaped to the sisterhood. Some days it felt like just yesterday while others felt like decades had passed. My choice still enraged my father as well as my former fiancé.

Since the only thing my father truly feared in life was God, he hadn't dared to force me leave the order. Instead, he'd told me I was dead to him, which I felt was a willing sacrifice to make to earn my freedom.

After I finished the book to a round of hugs from the children, I followed their mothers to the door where I locked it for the night. Before I could start putting away misplaced items, my phone buzzed in my pocket. Because of our remote location, it was necessary for the four of us sisters to keep a phone.

When I dug it out, happiness rippled through me as I eyed the screen.

Once I swiped the answer button, I grinned at the faces of my three brothers. Tall, impossibly built, and devastatingly handsome was how they were described in the newspapers and social media in New York. But to me, they were the kindest and most wonderful big brothers any girl could ever ask for.

At twenty-eight, Raphael, or Rafe, was the oldest followed by Leandro, or Leo, at twenty-six, and then Gianni at twenty-five. All three had jet black hair, onyx eyes, and bulging muscles earned not just from workouts in the gym.

They were all Made Men, and each held an important rank in the Famiglia.

"Hey guys!"

"Happy Birthday!" they shouted in unison.

I couldn't help the grin that spread across my cheeks. "Thank you. You don't know how much it means to hear from family today."

Although this was the third birthday I'd experienced in the order, I still wasn't used to spending it away from the outside world. Growing up, my parents had thrown lavish birthday parties with hundreds of guests, tables of food, and outlandish party themes like an amusement park on our back lawn. But their efforts were more a show of our wealth than love for their children.

"I can't believe our baby sister is twenty-one," Raphael commented.

Gianni nodded. "It makes me feel so old."

I snorted. "Like you're so much older than me, G."

"But being twenty-one means you're not a baby anymore, Kitty Cat," Gianni replied.

"Ugh, do *not* call me by that old nickname."

The boys chuckled at my outrage. For as long as I could remember, they'd tortured me with the nickname. As a child, it was only mildly annoying, but it was the bane of my existence as a teenager.

Wanting to change the subject, I asked. "How's Mom?"

Leo rolled his eyes. "Keeping the boutiques and fine restaurants in business with her excessive shopping excursions and social lunches."

I laughed. "I guess I shouldn't be surprised."

Growing up, my mother resembled the epitome of an ice princess Mafia wife. The boys and I had always been closer to our nanny, Talia. She raised us like we were her own. Since entering the order, my mother hadn't contacted me, but I spoke to Talia at least once or twice a month.

"We have big news," Rafe pronounced.

My brows popped in surprise. "One of you is getting married?"

When a chorus of grunts and groans came back to me, I cocked my head at them. "Seriously? I can't believe Father has let you all stay bachelors this long, especially you Rafe."

With a roll of his eyes, Rafe replied, "You know how Father has always said a man shouldn't tie himself down before thirty. His sole focus should be on the Familigia."

Leo grinned at Rafe. "But rumor has it he's been in talks about your future bride."

"I have at least another two years of freedom, thank God,"

"Well, if impending matrimony isn't the news, what is it?" I asked.

"We're coming to see you," Gianni replied with a grin.

"Really?"

Rafe nodded. "We're going to be in Milan next week for business, and we thought we'd fly over to Palermo on the way home."

"Oh my God, guys! This truly makes my birthday."

Rafe winked. "We knew it would, kiddo."

I rolled my eyes. "You're so humble."

"What about tonight? Got big plans?" Leo teased.

"Totally. The sisters are taking me for drinks and dancing." Waggling my brows, I whispered, "Rumor is Sister Lucia and Sister Antonia might even take off their habits."

My brothers chuckled. "Still our smart-mouth baby sister, I see," Gianni replied.

"Yes, in more ways than one since that's *Sister* Caterina now."

Their smiles faded. Even after the last two and a half years, they still couldn't grasp my choice. More than anything, they didn't want me thousands of miles away.

"Remind me again. How long is it until you take your Perpetual Vows and become a full-fledged nun?" Leo asked.

The boys held out hope that as long as I hadn't taken my final vows, I could leave the order and return back to them. I didn't know how to get it through to them that I would never be coming back. Not as long as I still faced an arranged marriage from my father.

"Three years."

"That soon?" Gianni asked with a wince.

"Yes."

Rafe's jaw clenched. "You wouldn't have to go through with final vows if Father was dead."

"Considering he's only sixty-five and in relatively good health, I don't see that happening anytime soon," I replied.

Leo's dark eyes glittered with malice. "Accidents happen every day, especially to men in our line of work."

At Rafe's slow nod of approval, I shook my head. "I won't let you have that on your consciences."

"Let us worry about that," Gianni said.

As I stared into their earnest faces, there was a small part of me that wanted to take them up on their offer. While I was content in the order, it wasn't what I'd envisioned for my life. But at the same time, I'd made my choice, and I couldn't let my brothers kill our father just so that I could have my way.

"It's a mortal sin just talking about it, least of all doing it," I whispered.

Rafe sighed. "We would do anything for you, Kitty Cat."

Tears stung my eyes. "I know you would, and I love you all so very much for that."

"And we love you," Gianni said.

Leo smiled at me. "Dry your tears, Kitty Cat. We wouldn't have you crying on your birthday for anything in the world."

I laughed as I wiped my cheeks. "Don't worry. They're happy tears, I promise. Especially since I get to see you in a few weeks."

"Be thinking of where you'd like to go or what you'd like to see," Rafe suggested.

Leo nodded. "We'll fly you anywhere you want to go."

"I think it'll be more of where I'm allowed to go."

"Surely sisters get time off."

"They do. But I don't know how much G-rated fun you guys will be into."

With a snort, Leo replied, "Like we would take our baby sister clubbing even if you weren't in a religious order."

"You guys are no fun," I teasingly replied.

"See you soon, Kitty Cat," Rafe said while Leo and Gianni waved.

After blowing them a kiss, I hung up. Cradling the phone against my chest, I didn't bother fighting the tears. I let them flow freely down my cheeks. My shoulders rose and fell with harsh sobs.

At that moment, I didn't care about all the good I was doing through the order or my victory against my father. All I wanted was to be back home in New York, surrounded by brothers while eating one of Talia's famous cakes.

"Caterina?" Sister Lucia questioned.

Sniffling, I swiped my eyes. "Yes?"

"There's something that needs your attention in the kitchen."

"Right. Of course." Ducking my head so she wouldn't see my tears, I rose off my chair and followed her down the hall.

When I got to the kitchen, I furrowed my brows at the darkness. "Oh no. Don't tell me the electricity has gone on the fritz again," I groaned.

The lights flashed on, and "Surprise!" erupted in the room. The waterworks started again at the sight of my three fellow sisters holding a small cake with a lit candle.

"Happy Birthday, Caterina," Sister Lucia said with a smile.

A grin stretched across my face. "I can't believe you guys did this."

"It isn't every day you turn twenty-one," Sister Antonia replied in her diplomatic way.

Since the day I'd arrived in the village, she'd felt like my long-lost grandmother. Especially considering she was just as strict and stern as my Nonna had been. One of her hands weathered with age motioned for me to blow out the candle. "Make a wish."

The selfish part of me wanted to argue that as long as I lived in the order, there wasn't anything to wish for. My life didn't truly belong to me anymore. Of course, the rational side argued that I could wish for good health and happiness in my journey.

But for the first time in a long time, something felt missing.

A strange emptiness had started plaguing me. I'd tried arguing that it was because I was turning twenty-one, which was a rite of passage. Back in the states, it would've meant a party with free-flowing alcohol. In another life, it would've meant closing in on my last year of college.

Poison and Wine

When Sister Antonia frowned at my hesitation, I forced a smile on my face. "I'm sorry. I was trying to decide what to wish for."

"My child it's as simple as asking for the Lord's will to be done."

When I leaned over the cake, I shut my eyes. As I blew air from my lips, I didn't go with Sister Antonia's words for fear that voicing a wish aloud might make it not come true. Instead, I wished for my true path to be fulfilled.

Chapter Three: Caterina

While it wasn't quite the party I had teased my brothers about, I still had a wonderful time with my sisters. We ate leftover soup and drank aged wine while polishing off the cake. They'd each regaled me with stories of their own twenty-first birthdays all of which had been inside the order. We ended up chatting long past our usual nine p.m. bedtime.

When I finally trudged into my bedroom around ten, I eyed the mop and bucket beside my nightstand. I'd fully intended on finally cleaning my floors after a two-day hiatus. But as tired as I was, it wasn't going to happen tonight. Especially since it was my birthday.

After grabbing a nightgown out of the drawer, I went into the bathroom and took a shower. When I got into bed, I fell into an exhausted sleep. The clanging of the midnight church bells startled me awake.

Lying in the pitch dark, a prickly awareness filled me. It sent a cascade of shivers down my spine. Fighting my fear, I tried regulating my erratic breathing. There hadn't been a specific noise to alert me. It was just a feeling.

Someone was in my room.

With a trembling hand, I snaked my arm out from under the covers. Fumbling for the cord on the nightstand, I flicked on the lamp. I momentarily fought for my eyes to adjust to the light. My gaze bounced around the room, which thankfully I found empty.

As a sigh of relief whooshed from my lips, I fought to swallow but my mouth had run dry. Flipping the sheet off of me, I padded across the floor and into the bathroom. I turned on the faucet and bent my head over the sink. Instead of bothering with a glass, I cupped my hands and brought the cool liquid to my lips. Once I'd taken in enough, I splashed water on my face.

When I tossed my head back, I looked into the mirror. I shrieked when I found myself staring into a man's blue eyes. My body tensed as fear and horror ricocheted through me.

Before I could react, the man grabbed my waist and spun me around to face him. His tattooed hand closed over my mouth while his other hand pressed against my throat.

"Not a fucking sound, sister," he warned.

Instantly, I recognized his deep Irish brogue. It certainly wasn't an accent I heard around here. It reminded me of New York. More than anything, it made me think of the Irish families who warred against ours. Was this man one of my father's enemies? Had he somehow managed to track me down here to enact revenge on the Neretti family?

In another situation, I would've found him handsome. Jet black hair, ocean blue eyes, and finely chiseled facial features. But his beauty encompassed cruelty. His harsh gaze trailed from my face down to my breasts where it lingered momentarily before dipping lower to my hips.

"Fuck me, sister. The pictures didn't do you justice." He licked his lips. "You have a body for sin," he remarked as he pressed me tight against his hardened muscles.

At that moment, I realized his intentions were to rape me. In spite of my fear, I knew I couldn't let that happen. From the time I could walk, my brothers had taught me how to defend myself. It was a necessity for all Famiglia daughters in cases of kidnapping.

With everything I had in me, I jerked my knee up between his legs. When his hold momentarily lessened on my mouth, I reached out and chomped down on his hand, shredding the skin with my teeth until a metallic rush hit my tongue.

"Motherfucker!" he shouted before releasing his grip on me.

I dashed into the bedroom and whirled around the side of the bed. With trembling fingers, I ripped open the nightstand drawer and dug inside for the Glock my brothers had gifted me for my eighteenth birthday. While many would've been surprised to know that a sister was armed, it was a necessary evil based on our location outside of cloistered walls.

Once I had the gun in my hand, I spun around just as the man had breached the bathroom door. At the same time, footsteps echoed in the hallway. When the man lunged for me, I squeezed the trigger. Because of his movement, the bullet grazed him in the thigh instead of my intended target of his stomach.

"Fuck!" he bellowed, his face contorting in pain.

With a grimace, I steadied my hand, which was hard to do with how much I was shaking. Just as I was about to shoot again, another man barreled into me. When he slammed the two of us to the floor, the gun slipped from my grasp.

I began thrashing under the man's weight, kicking him as hard as I could in the shins. As we rolled around on the floor, the mop next to the nightstand got knocked to the ground. I reached over and grabbed it. Instead of whacking him around the head or abdomen, I jammed the hard end between his legs repeatedly.

At his howl of agony, I scrambled to my feet and raced out of the room. "Sister Caterina?" Sister Antonia called from her doorway.

Waving my hands, I ordered, "Get back in your room and lock the door!"

I knew she wouldn't want to listen to me. As the head of our group, she should've been the one going for help. But something in my steely expression registered with her.

Maybe it was the fact she knew I'd come from a dangerous past—one that gave me more survival skills than she possessed. After giving me an agonized look, she slammed the door.

I sprinted down the corridor. If I could get to the main office, there was a phone I could use to call for help. It was a windowless room, so I could barricade the door with some of the furniture. It would buy me time to hopefully have someone come to our rescue.

As I started around the fountain past the main gate, a body crashed into me, sending me flailing into the fountain's pool. As water cascaded over me, I gasped from the temperature.

Then as a body held me captive, I fought to breathe. Panic ricocheted through me as I desperately tried getting air in my lungs.

Strong hands grabbed me by the shoulders and jerked me to the surface. I gasped and wheezed to catch my breath. "Let me go!" I screeched.

"Dunk her again," a man's voice growled from my right.

"Forget that. Just fucking sedate her."

"No!" I screamed. If I was out, the men could violate me anyway they wanted to. I continued to thrash and fight, but then something jabbed into my upper arm. "No, no, no!" I cried. I kicked one last time before darkness took me under.

Chapter Four: Callum

After scaling the gates of the religious order, I'd broken my first rule: never underestimate your target. I suppose I let my guard down because everything was too easy.

No guards.

No alarms sounding our arrival or motion detectors announcing our presence.

Not to mention the ancient locks that appeared easy to pick.

Once Quinn and Dare convened with me in the courtyard, I had barked out a few orders. "Quinn, you stay here by the gate and pick the lock for us to have a clear getaway."

Glancing over at Dare, I said, "You cover my back as I head in the building. After I'm inside, move to the front room, and I'll meet up with you once I've secured Caterina."

Dare's brows had furrowed. "You don't want me to come with you?"

With a roll of my eyes, I had replied, "I'm pretty sure I can handle four unarmed nuns."

In hindsight, that was a grievous mistake. Of course, it wasn't four nuns that incapacitated not only me, but Dare as well. It was only my not so blushing bride.

She'd felt like heaven when I'd pressed against her. Her full breasts had pillowed against my chest while her round, full hips had curved against me. At that moment, I'd wanted to claim her mouth and thrust my tongue against hers.

But then that heavenly moment had turned to pure hell when she racked up my balls and then bit me. The bitch had maimed me enough to draw blood. I'd yet to have an enemy make me bleed through a bite. I'd be lying if there wasn't a small part of me that was turned on by her ferocity.

But then she had to go and fucking shoot me. The bite was nothing compared to the gaping wound in my upper thigh. I imagined without the fear and shock, Caterina probably would've been able to shoot me right through the heart. I gave thanks for small mercies, and the fact that Quinn knew how to tie a tourniquet to stop the bleeding.

I turned my attention back to Caterina. She lay limp on the edge of the fountain. Even in the dark, I could make out how her wet cotton nightgown was drawn obscenely tight against her skin—the see-through white color leaving nothing to the imagination. If it hadn't been so dark, I would've taken off my shirt to cover her so my brothers couldn't see.

She may have bitten and shot me, but she was still *mine* and only *mine*.

Quinn tossed the syringe in his hand to the ground before glancing around the courtyard. "Where the fuck is Dare?"

I opened my mouth to reply, but a grunt from over my shoulder silenced me. "I'm here," he gritted out as he limped over to us.

He held a small bag in one of his hands. I imagined it was filled with some of Caterina's possessions.

"Did she shoot you, too?" Quinn questioned.

"I think I would've fancied it more than her jabbing a broomstick repeatedly against my cock and balls," Dare replied through gritted teeth.

Quinn winced and cupped himself. "Jesus Christ."

I shook my head. "Look, we gotta get the hell out of here before the other sisters see us."

I motioned to Caterina's crumpled form. "Quinn, I need you to carry her because I don't think Dare nor I have it in us."

When he hesitated, I clapped my hand on his shoulder. "I wouldn't ask this of you if it wasn't absolutely necessary."

After staring down at Caterina for a few moments, Quinn finally nodded. Since the car bombing, he could barely tolerate anyone being too close to him or touching him. I truly hated to put him in that position.

Under my intense gaze, Quinn gently brought Caterina into his arms. I then texted Kellan to bring around the car. At the sight of us coming through the gates, Kellan hopped out of the SUV.

As he jogged around the front of the hood, he asked, "What the fuck happened to you all?"

I scowled at him. "What the hell does it look like?"

"It looks like someone beat the hell out of Dare and shot you."

"Yeah, that pretty much sums it up."

"Was there some sort of militant opposition our intel didn't include?" Kellan asked.

Dare snorted. "It was only a ripshit future nun."

Kellan's brows shot into his hairline. "*She* shot you, Callum?"

"The bullet only grazed my thigh."

"He's lucky I tackled her, or she probably would've blown his dick right off," Dare quipped.

I rolled my eyes at him. "I think I had the situation under control."

"Sure, mate," Dare replied before hoisting himself into the backseat.

Kellan winced. "Christ on a cross, Dare. You manhandled a nun?"

"It wouldn't have mattered if it was Mary Magdalene herself—she had a gun on Callum."

Shifting his gaze from Dare in the backseat, Kellan apprised Caterina in Quinn's arms. "Did you knock her unconscious when you tackled her?"

"No. We had to give her ketamine because she wouldn't stop fighting us."

As Kellan gave me a disapproving look, I jerked my chin at the passenger seat. "Save your judgment and help me in the car."

"Hell must be freezing over for you to ask for help," he quipped.

"Fuck you," I muttered under my breath.

After Kellan had helped me onto the seat, I threw a glance in the back. Quinn delicately sat Caterina in the seat between him and Dare. Once she was upright, her head lolled over onto Dare's shoulder. With a hiss, he shoved her harshly away, causing her to whimper.

Red criss crossed through my vision.

As a low growl came from deep within my chest, both Dare's and Quinn's eyes popped wide. "Do *not* hurt my future wife," I blared.

Dare held his hands up in surrender. "I'm sorry. I'm still a little pissed with her for potentially damaging my family jewels."

"It has nothing to do with you, asshole. She was merely defending herself."

"Is that how you feel about your thigh and your hand?" he countered.

"As a matter of fact, it is. She thought I was going to rape her, and that you were there to help. You can't fault any woman for trying to save herself."

A hush fell over the car. I knew each of my brothers were thinking about the same thing, or in this case, the same person. When Caterina's head once again fell against Dare's shoulder, he didn't move her away. Although I was grateful to him for showing her kindness, I didn't like how she snuggled herself against him. Like she was seeking out his warmth.

When she turned her face into his neck and pressed her nose and lips against his skin, the bastard had the audacity to wink at me. "You even remotely get off on that, and I'll cut off what's left of your balls," I growled.

Dare chuckled. "Then turn the light off in the car because I can see way too much through her nightgown. Or then again, don't turn them out. I need to make sure my cock will still rise to the occasion after her mop assault."

Before I could bark out the order, Kellan turned the interior light off. Glancing in the rearview mirror at Dare, he said, "There's a blanket in the third-row seating."

"Grab it," I ordered.

"Yeah, yeah," Dare muttered before throwing his arm behind the seat to grab the blanket. I watched him like a hawk as he draped the blanket over Caterina's shoulders and then wrapped it around the front.

When she sighed with pleasure and then snuggled up to Quinn, I turned around. Considering his aversion to touch, I knew he wouldn't be getting any enjoyment out of having a half-naked woman against him.

Any bump in the road sent searing agony through my thigh. "You want something for the pain?" Quinn asked.

Turning around in the seat again, I jerked my chin at Caterina. "I sure as hell don't want what you gave her," I mused.

Quinn chuckled before digging into his medical bag. After he pulled out a pill and a bottle of water, he handed them to me. "This will take the edge off, but not knock you on yer arse."

"Thanks."

After tossing the pill in my mouth, I gulped down the water. Leaning my head back, I closed my eyes and willed for the pain to subside.

After a silent drive, we made it to the airport in Palermo about an hour later. A jet sat on the tarmac waiting for us. To ensure our undetected escape, our pilot had logged a fake flight plan with a destination of Prague, rather than Catania.

Seamus would be waiting for us at the house he'd rented. Since I didn't know how much longer Caterina would be knocked out, I was glad our flight was merely thirty minutes.

Because she was already plastered against him, Quinn reluctantly pulled Caterina into his arms. She sucked in a harsh breath as he lifted her up and out of the car.

After we'd all boarded the jet, Quinn took Caterina over to the sofa and laid her down. Before he fixed the cover over her, he threw an uncomfortable glance at me. "She really needs to come out of that wet nightgown."

"We don't have anything else to put her in, do we?"

"There's a robe in the bathroom," Kellan replied.

I nodded at him. "Grab it."

As he went to retrieve it, I narrowed my eyes at Quinn and Dare. "You two turn yer backs."

Dare grunted. "I could give a shite less about what your bitch of a bride looks like naked."

"That's sure as hell not what you alluded to in the car," I challenged.

He laughed. "That's just because I wanted to get a rise out of you. All I want now is a drink and an ice pack for my cock."

"Then fuck off, why don't you?"

"Gladly," Dare replied before heading to the liquor cabinet.

Kellan returned with the robe. Without even having to be told, he turned his back to Caterina. "Always a bleedin' gentleman," I chuckled.

Bending over, I brought my hand to the hem of Caterina's nightgown. I jerked it up her thighs and over her hips. Silently, I gave thanks for what I would've considered Nuns Knickers—the white cotton panties that covered not only her pussy, but most of her lower abdomen.

I don't know why I was surprised. It's not like I expected her to be wearing a lacy thong.

After bringing the nightgown over her head, I tossed it to the floor. I then gently eased her arm in the robe before pulling her up against me to do the second arm. Once I was finished, I tied the lapels together. To ensure she warmed up, I added two blankets.

The pilot poked his head out of the cockpit area. "We're about to take off, so I really need you all in your seats with your seatbelts fastened." His gaze dropped to Caterina. "She needs to be belted in as well."

"She's fine as she is."

The pilot's brows furrowed. "But—"

My eyes darkened. "I said she's fine."

He dropped his gaze before mumbling, "Yes, sir." He then ducked back into the cockpit.

Looking at Dare, I said, "Make sure he never flies us again."

Tilting his head, Dare asked, "You want him never flying us or never flying the friendly skies ever again?"

"Killing him isn't necessary," I replied in a low voice.

"Sure thing, boss," he replied with a smile.

I grunted at him calling me boss. While it was the truth, I didn't like my brothers feeling any less than I was simply because I was older. For our family to not only survive but thrive, we had to be one unit.

When I shifted in my seat, pain radiated through my leg, causing me to wince.

Quinn motioned his phone at my leg. "I texted Seamus to have a doctor waiting for us at the house."

"I appreciate that."

As he surmised Caterina, he shook his head. "You sure as hell underestimated her, didn't you?"

"*I* underestimated her? I didn't hear any of you fuckers mention her potential as an assassin."

Grimacing, Quinn replied, "Aye, you're right. It's on all of us, I suppose. The girl was raised in a capo's house with three older brothers. We should've imagined she would know her way around a gun and have some self-defense skills."

Dare collapsed down into the seat next to me. After plopping an ice pack on his cock, he said, "In Callum's defense, I didn't think nuns were allowed to be packing."

"I'm sure the ones in a convent don't. I suppose it makes sense for the missionary ones to have them since they aren't under the protection of the convent walls."

With a grunt, Dare replied, "Can you imagine some of our teachers at St. Ignatius having a Glock under their robes?"

Quinn and I both snorted. "No, I can't."

At that moment, a low moan erupted from Caterina. Her head thrashed on the pillow. "Heads up, boys. The little assassin is waking up," I mused.

Chapter Five: Caterina

As I started coming in and out of consciousness, I realized I was no longer in the fountain. Instead of floating on water, I floated along like I was a cloud bobbing through the air. One minute I was tucked close against something warm and firm, and then the next I was floating higher.

The warmth that I desperately needed was gone. But then a soft heat enveloped me, and darkness took me over again. I don't know how much time passed, but eventually it felt like I was flying, rather than floating.

A shudder rippled through me like my soul had been dropped back down into my body. I realized there was light around me and muted voices. Memories flashed like jagged lighting in a summer storm through my mind.

A devastatingly handsome man with a cruel aura about him.

My shaking fingers searching for the gun in my nightstand.

My feet pounding down the tile floors of the order as I tried to escape.

Sinking into a watery grave.

A prick on my arm.

With a groan, I turned my head from side to side. The pain that shot through my skull felt like a knife stabbing my brain. Raising my arm, I palmed my forehead, desperately trying to stop the agony.

"Would you like some medicine for yer head?"

At the sound of the familiar male voice, all thought of my pain was forgotten, and fear rippled through me. I popped open my eyes and gasped in horror.

With a menacing smile etched across his face, the man from the Sacred Heart glared down at me. "I'm glad to see you're awake, Caterina."

In spite of the brass band beating in my skull, I jerked myself into a sitting position before scrambling down the length of the couch. I pressed myself against the wall of what I realized was a small jet. My frantic gaze bounced around the cabin.

Fear choked off my breath at the sight of three other men. I recognized one of them from earlier, but I didn't know where the other two came from.

At the thought that I'd been unconscious with four strange men, my stomach lurched. Although I clamped my hand over my mouth, it didn't stop my stomach from evacuating on the floor of the plane.

When I finally stopped retching, a wet cloth was thrust in front of me. "Thank you," I whispered. As I wiped my mouth, the man from Sacred Heart cleaned up my mess. Something about it surprised me. Like cleaning, especially vomit, was beneath his station in life.

Easing back in my seat, my brain once again flashed to the thought of being unconscious and alone with the men. Had I been raped? I deciphered that there wasn't an ache between my legs. If they had forced themselves on me, there would be trauma.

I would have pain...and blood.

Dipping my head, I eyed the slit in my robe and searched my thighs.

"No need to worry about that, lass. Your virtue is still intact," the man said.

I snatched the slit closed. Easing back in my seat, I eyed the man warily. "Who are you?" I croaked.

"My apologies for not making the proper introductions when we met earlier." He held out his hand to me. "I'm Callum Kavanaugh."

As the last name flickered through my mind, I gasped. Last year I'd heard my brothers mention a Boston Clan leader who had been murdered by his own son. Was this the man who had killed his father —his own blood—for his position?

After eying his hand with disgust, Callum tsked at me. "Is that anyway to treat yer future husband?"

Ice cold dread splashed from the top of my scalp down to my toes, and I shivered despite the blankets on me. "H-Husband?"

"Yes. It is my belief that a partnership between your family and mine would be very beneficial."

"My father arranged this?"

In the last three years, a fear had remained tightly embedded in my mind that my father would somehow find a way to force me into marriage. That one day a more lucrative alliance would make him forget his fear of being punished by God, and he would take me forcefully from the order.

Callum shook his head. "I haven't had the pleasure of discussing the matter with him."

The continuing agony beating through my head made it hard to comprehend what he was saying. "You don't have a marriage contract with my father?"

He quirked his brows at me. "I was unaware I needed one. After all, you are of legal age to enter into an agreement of your own volition."

Gripping the blankets tighter around me, I pronounced, "I will *never* marry you."

"I'm afraid neither you nor I have much of a choice. It's a necessary evil to further my family's position back in America."

As panic criss crossed through me, I fought to keep an icy façade. "You'll have to find another bride, Mr. Kavanaugh. I'm forbidden to marry anyone as I'm a sister of the Sacred Heart."

With a smirk, Callum countered, "Yes, I'm well aware of that fact since I just rescued you from there."

"*Abducted* me," I corrected.

"You didn't belong there, Caterina. You have too much fire and spirit to ever be a nun."

Callum echoed the same words my brothers had voiced about me joining the order. How could he possibly say those things when he didn't know me?

I despised when people tried to box me in to what they felt a sister should be. Just because of my appearance or the way I acted, they felt my heart didn't truly belong to the order. The only people who didn't doubt my true intentions were my fellow sisters.

"You don't know anything about me!" I spat.

Callum shook his head. "You are so much more than just a nun."

"Some of the bravest women I know are nuns. They work in horrible conditions and endure situations a pretty boy like you could never imagine."

Two of the men behind Callum laughed while he gave me a shark-like grin. "You think I'm pretty?" he teasingly asked.

I rolled my eyes. "I meant you've never endured a hard day's work in your life."

The amusement drained from his face. "You don't know shit about me or how hard I've worked."

"Perhaps I should've said an *honest* day's work."

"It's quite hypocritical for Alessio Neretti's daughter to be praising the virtues of honest work considering how your family built its fortune."

"Leave my father out of this. I'm talking about what *I* did as a sister of the Sacred Heart compared to you."

"And I applaud you for that. However, the point is, *sister*, you have yet to take your Perpetual Vows, which means you're able to walk away from the order without any strikes against your soul."

"You kidnapped me!" I shouted.

Immediately, I cupped my head in my hands as the pain from raising my voice overtook me. Silence echoed around me as I groaned and fought not to throw up.

"Here, lass," a voice above me whispered.

I pulled my hands away to see the youngest of the men staring kindly at me. My gaze dropped to his hands where he held a bottle of water and some Motrin.

I gave him a weak smile as I reached for the medicine and water. "Thank you."

As I threw back the pills, Callum smacked the man on the back. "Yes, thank you, brother, for taking such good care of my future wife."

"You shouldn't have injected her," he bit out.

"Trust me. If it had been your cock and balls on the line, you would've changed your mind," the man who I hit with the broom remarked.

At the sight of the ice pack on his crotch, I flushed and dipped my head.

"Regretfully, it was necessary to put her out for both her safety and ours," Callum argued.

"You might as well sedate me permanently because that's the only way I won't fight against you and your absurd plan to marry me."

His hand gripped my chin, forcing me to meet his gaze. "You will marry me, Kitty Cat."

Both anguish and rage filled me with him using my brothers' nickname. "Don't call me that!"

"Let me guess. It was a form of endearment from an ex-boyfriend?"

"Only my brothers call me that."

"Aye, I imagine my future brothers-in-law love their baby sister dearly, don't they?"

"They'll kill you when they find out what you've done."

"You think?"

I nodded. "And I'll watch them do it with a smile on my face."

Callum grinned at me before turning back to his brothers. "She has claws, doesn't she?"

The one I'd assaulted with the broom snorted. "You better sleep with one eye open on your wedding night."

"If you lay one finger on me on our wedding night, I'll make you bleed far more than I did tonight," I spat.

"Actually, I think I'll call you Kitten because you remind me more of a feral kitten who needs taming."

"Go to hell."

Callum momentarily closed his eyes. "Ooh, I look forward to taming you, Kitten." After popping open his eyes, his heated gaze trailed down my body. "Every glorious inch of you."

"You will *never* tame me," I spat back.

"We shall see," he replied with a smile.

Chapter Six: Callum

After my declaration about taming her, Caterina refused to talk to me anymore. Instead, she pulled the blankets up to her chin and stared out the jet's window.

I eased back in my chair and closed my eyes, willing the medication Quinn had given me to take affect. Within a few minutes of the silent treatment, I somehow nodded off.

It seemed I'd just closed my eyes when Dare shook me awake. "Come on, Sleeping Beauty. We're about to land."

As the boys and I started buckling up, Caterina removed her blankets and reached for her seatbelt. When she caught sight of the robe, she froze. "Why am I wearing this?" she demanded.

"You would've caught cold in your wet nightgown," I explained.

A flush filled her cheeks, and she ducked her head. Leaning over,

I placed my hand on her knee. "Don't worry, Kitten. I made my brothers turn their heads. I'm the only one who saw you naked."

Her chin trembled slightly. "Is that supposed to make me feel better?"

I don't know why her reaction bothered me, but it did. I'd fully expected her to bite my fecking head off when I told her I'd stripped her. Wounded Caterina sent feelings flooding through me, and I sure as hell didn't like it. I wasn't a man who had feelings with women.

But Caterina was different.

And not just in the fact she was to be my wife. She possessed an innocence I wasn't accustomed with. "It was a necessary evil. You have my word that I didn't touch you anywhere I shouldn't have or that would take away from your honor."

While I thought my words might ease her mind, Caterina once again proved me wrong. Jerking her gaze up to meet mine, she shook her head. "Like your word means anything."

"It means something to me and my brothers, and I state before them that I didn't touch you unnecessarily."

"Whatever," she grumbled.

When she rose off the couch, she swayed on her feet. I reached out to grip her upper arm before she could fall. "Can you walk, or would you like to be carried?"

She snatched her arm out of my grip. "I don't *need* or *want* anything from *you*."

"Considering you shot me, I'm incapable of helping you."

"Then why did you bother asking?"

"Because I was going to have one of my brothers carry you."

"I'm fine."

But the moment after she said it, she lunged to the side and almost fell against the side of the jet. "Quinn, I believe your services are needed again," I remarked with a smile.

At the sight of Quinn's scarred face and harsh attitude, Caterina's eyes widened. But to her credit, she didn't protest. Instead, she gave him a tight smile. "Thank you for the help."

A flash of surprise filled his face that she wasn't shying away from him. But as quickly as it came, he buried it. "Whatever," he grunted.

When Quinn swept her into his arms, Caterina squeaked. He did it so effortlessly that she flopped around like a rag doll in his embrace. To steady herself, she threw her arms around his broad neck.

Since Quinn hated anyone touching his damaged skin, he momentarily froze. His chest rose and fell in harsh pants.

Caterina must've noticed his reaction because she gave him an apologetic look. Pulling her arms away from his scarred neck, she then remarked, "I'm so very sorry if I hurt you. Is this better?"

Quinn remained frozen, not even blinking as he stared at Caterina. But then a slight shudder trembled through his massive body. I exhaled the breath I'd been holding.

While my brother was a ruthless enforcer, he'd never raised a hand against a woman. As a stranger, Caterina's touch could've set him off.

My eyes popped wide as I watched Quinn's usual dark expression melt to one of reverence. "Yes, lass, that's grand."

"You're very strong," Caterina complimented.

In a gravelly voice, Quinn replied, "And you're light as a feather."

The corners of her lips quirked up. "You sure know how to make a girl feel practically weightless." After appraising his unmarred bicep, she remarked, "I bet you could carry me in just one arm."

"Is that a dare?"

She giggled. "Maybe. Just don't try it as we go down the stairs in case you drop me."

"I'd never allow that to happen."

"I don't believe you would." As they started down the stairs, Quinn shifted her to where he was carrying her in only one arm. "Show off," she teased.

Dare and I exchanged open-mouthed glances while Kellan just shook his head in surprise. I couldn't remember the last time Quinn had willingly carried on a conversation with a female outside of our mother and sister. While he was far from a monk, his interactions with women had changed since the bombing.

Just when I thought nothing else could surprise me, Quinn actually smiled at Caterina. "I told you I wouldn't drop you."

"I assume you're the protector of the family?"

"I'm the enforcer."

Her brows furrowed at his words. "You enforce the laws?"

"Something like that."

"Don't tell me a capo's daughter is ignorant to what an enforcer is?" I questioned.

Caterina threw a glance at me over Quinn's shoulder. "My father and brothers always kept me out of the business."

"Then allow me to educate you. Quinn does the beating and the killing for us," I replied.

While Quinn scowled at me, Caterina's dark eyes widened. Ducking her head, she replied, "Oh, I see."

"Don't worry, lass. I never harm my family, and you will be my family when you marry my bastard brother," Quinn replied.

Caterina didn't reply. I'm sure she was probably thinking he'd already harmed her by helping in her abduction. She remained quiet as Quinn put her in the backseat of the waiting SUV. She scooted across the seat to press herself against the window. I hopped in next and took my place beside her.

We made the half hour drive to the house in silence. From time to time, I would cut my eyes to Caterina. She sat as still as a statue with her attention drawn out the window. She didn't tear her gaze away until we pulled into the driveway. Her body then tensed as if she was now on high alert.

After the driver parked, we exited the SUV. Surprisingly, Caterina didn't have to be told to get out. With her arms wrapped around her waist, she warily watched us unload the back.

As we started gathering our bags, Caterina asked, "What about my things?"

Dare held out the small bag to her. "This is what I managed to grab. Obviously, I didn't take any of your clothes since you wouldn't be wearing them anymore."

She dropped her gaze to the bag. As a sister, I couldn't imagine she would've had many possessions with her since they took a vow of poverty. Something among the contents embarrassed her since her cheeks reddened.

Glancing over her shoulder, I saw lacy bras and panties among framed photographs and a jewelry box. Narrowing my eyes, I demanded, "Was it necessary to bring those?"

Dare shrugged. "They were easy to grab."

"Of all the cheek," I grumbled before jabbing a finger at him. "Just so you know, that's the last fucking time you *ever* touch her underwear."

He chuckled. "Aye, I understand."

"Do you need any help?" Quinn asked Caterina.

She shook her head. "Although I appreciate you carrying me earlier, I believe I can walk now."

"That's fine."

After placing my hand on Caterina's upper arm, I began leading her up the drive to the house. Seamus stood in the doorway with an anxious expression on his face. His gaze dropped from mine to my leg. "How are you?"

"Fine. Nothing I haven't dealt with before."

With a nod, Seamus turned his attention to Caterina whose neck was tucked to her chest. Reaching out his hand, he patted her arm. "You have nothing to fear, lass. No one here is going to hurt you in any way."

Caterina jerked up her head and glared at Seamus. "Liar," she hissed.

Seamus's brows shot up in surprise. "I beg your pardon?"

"How can you stand there and say no one will hurt me when your nephews kidnapped and drugged me?"

At Seamus's continued shock, I rolled my eyes. "Your research was lacking when it came to the part where in spite of being a sister, she's a fecking shrew."

"I'd defy you to find any woman who would be agreeable with being kidnapped and drugged," Caterina challenged.

I gave Seamus a pointed look before tugging Caterina through the doorway. As we stepped into the living room, an older looking man with wire rimmed glasses rose off the couch. When he eyed my blood-stained pants leg, I realized he must be the doctor.

"I better have a look at that," he replied in broken English.

I shook my head. "I need to get my fiancée settled first."

"Kellan can do that," Seamus suggested.

"She's my responsibility, so I will see to her," I replied.

"I'd rather have Kellan," Caterina mumbled.

I chose to ignore her comment. Instead, I pointed to one of the men standing in the hallway. "Just in case you get the crazy idea to run away, it's not just my brothers and I you have to worry about. There are guards set up throughout the house and grounds."

Caterina's face paled momentarily, but then she quickly slid her mask back in place.

"Are you hungry?" I asked. At the shake of her head, I asked, "Do you need something to drink?"

"No," she whispered.

"Then I'll show you to our bedroom."

I didn't realize I had said anything offending until Caterina's terror-filled eyes snapped off the floor. "*Our* bedroom?" she questioned in a strangled voice.

"Don't get yer knickers in a twist, Kitten. You won't be performing any marital duties tonight," I replied with a chuckle.

I started for the stairs when Caterina's sniffle froze me. When I dared to look at her, tears streamed down her face. Just when I thought she couldn't surprise me again, she sank to her knees in front of me. Her chest rose and fell with harsh sobs.

"Please, *please* don't do this. I'm begging you to let me go."

For reasons I couldn't fathom, her anguished cries had an effect on me. My blackened heart ached in my chest. I hated that *I* was the one inflicting her emotional pain.

At the same time, the fact that I felt sorry for her enraged me. I could practically hear my father sneering in my ear about my weakness. With an angry shake of my head, I snarled, "That's not happening, so get off your fucking knees!"

"You could ransom me back to my family. While I'm dead to my father, my brothers would pay you a lot of money to get me back."

While her offer was tempting, I shook my head. "We must have a marital alliance."

The glimmer of hope in Caterina's eyes vanished at my words. She then curled into herself to weep unabashedly. Her cries felt like tiny pinpricks along my skin. But with each jab, the angrier I became that she was emasculating me, especially in front of the others.

When I glanced at my brothers, their expressions revealed pure horror. From the way they looked, you would've thought something truly terrifying, like a banshee, had swept through the room instead of a woman crying.

To prove a lass couldn't lead me around by the balls, I stalked back over to Caterina. "Enough!" I commanded.

After grabbing her by the arm, I tugged her to her feet. When she wavered, I swept her into my arms. Although the added weight caused my thigh to scream in agony, I ignored it and started for the stairs once again. Each step was torture, but I wouldn't falter. I would not allow any further weakness either physically or emotionally.

I didn't know which room had been allocated as ours, so I took the first bedroom I saw to spare my leg. After opening the door, I went over to an elaborate king-sized bed and eased Caterina down on the mattress. She immediately rolled into a fetal position and continued crying.

Without another word to her, I stalked out of the room and slammed the door. When I came back downstairs, my brothers sat around the living room in silence. They weren't drinking, watching television, or partaking in a midnight snack. They sat in an almost trance.

After eyeing them suspiciously, I asked, "What the fuck is wrong with the lot of you?"

While Kellan and Dare remained silent, Quinn gruffly replied, "Nothing."

"You're full of shite."

He exhaled a ragged breath. "It's just I feel sorry for the wee lass, that's all."

My eyes bulged. "My hearing must be failing because I'm sure my brother, the family enforcer, didn't just say he felt sorry for a spoiled mafia princess turned novice."

Quinn crossed his arms over his broad chest. "You heard me just fine."

"You don't have an empathetic bone in your body."

"That might be true, but at the same time, I feel sorry for her."

Turning from him in exasperation, I eyed Dare. After shifting the ice pack on his crotch, he said, "It couldn't hurt to be a bit kinder to her."

"She maimed your cock and balls!" I bellowed.

"Like you said, she thought I was going to rape her. And even if she didn't think that, the fact we were kidnapping her made her react that way."

Throwing my arms up in frustration, I blared, "What the hell has happened to you all? Caterina goes on one crying jag, and you all turn into bleedin' eejits."

After sharing a look with Quinn, Dare replied, "Are you that much of a plonker that you don't get it?"

"Apparently, I am since I can't fathom how the killers I call my brothers are now moping around the living room because I made my future wife cry."

"She reminds us of Maeve," Dare replied.

I frowned at him. Physically my sister and Caterina were as different as night and day. Maeve had flaming auburn hair and emerald green eyes like Kellan and my mam. She would never dream of physically defending herself or mouthing off like Caterina.

But I knew what they meant.

Not only were Maeve and Caterina close to the same age, they were both innocent pawns in our world. In their eyes, hurting Caterina was the same as hurting our beloved baby sister.

With a ragged sigh, I ran my hand over my face. "You have to leave Maeve and what happened to her out of this."

"That's impossible," Kellan protested.

"With Caterina, I have to be firm with her, or she's going to keep running over me. Can you imagine if wind got around to our enemies that Callum Kavanaugh had been fanny-whipped into submission? We wouldn't hold our ground for five minutes!"

Seamus nodded. "Callum's right, boys. At the end of the day, she'll be his wife, and she's his to deal with."

When my brothers remained silent, he then motioned for the doctor who had been waiting in the hallway. "Now get your leg seen about."

To lighten the mood, Dare teasingly asked, "Will he do an exam on my wounded cock?"

The doctor's eyes popped wide, causing the rest of us to chuckle. "I-I don't think that will be necessary. Just continue icing it," he replied before turning his gaze back to me.

After I whipped off my pants, I stood before the doctor in my briefs. He eyed Quinn's handiwork before taking off the tourniquet. He then dug gauze and tape out of his bag.

Once he'd wrapped me, he handed me a bottle of pills. "Take these for possible infection. Change the bandage morning and night for the next five to seven days."

"Thanks, Doc." I nodded to Seamus. "He'll take care of the bill."

The doctor held up his hands. "Oh no, there's no charge." With a knowing look, he added, "Just remember that I did you all a favor."

"You have our word."

In our world, we executed many transactions this way. No deed was too small to be remembered and in turn rewarded. I didn't blame the good doctor for wanting to have us in his pocket. He'd probably done favors for most of the Sicilians around us, so it made sense to have some Irish on his side too.

As Quinn led the doctor to the door, Seamus suggested, "Why don't you all take your things up to your rooms and get settled."

"Think we could get the cook to fire up an early breakfast?" Dare asked.

With a smile, Seamus replied, "I don't see why not."

After we started climbing the stairs, Kellan's voice interrupted the silence. "It might be better if you chose one of the guest rooms for tonight."

Whirling around, I pinned him with a hard stare. Apparently, my statement from earlier had fallen on deaf ears. "Excuse me?"

He flushed before ducking his head. "I just thought maybe it might be better to give Caterina a night alone to get acclimated to her new surroundings."

"*I* am her new surroundings."

Although I knew it pained him greatly, Kellan merely nodded. As Seamus directed my brothers to their rooms, I stopped at mine.

After rapping my knuckles against the door, I waited for Caterina to open it. I knocked again. "Caterina?" I called.

I exchanged a glance with Dare whose room was across the hall. He shrugged. "Maybe she's in the shower?"

With worry nagging my gut, I replied, "Or maybe she's taken the sheets and hanged herself in the closet."

He winced. "Christ, Callum."

Unable to wait another second to check on Caterina, I flung open the door. Relief flooded me when I saw her.

Across the room, she was on her knees by the bedside. At the sound of the door, her pinched eyes shot wide open.

"Didn't you hear me knocking?" When she nodded, I demanded, "Then why didn't you answer the door?"

"I was praying."

I stalked over to her. "Let's get one thing straight. When I call, you come. Understood?"

"I'm not a dog," she spat.

With her haughty tone and tense body language, it appeared she was over her emotional breakdown; her venom and spite was back.

"You are to answer to me, Caterina."

With a shake of her head, she replied, "I will not interrupt my prayers for anyone, least of all you."

Grabbing her arm, I jerked her to her feet. "The only time you should be on your knees in our bedroom is when you have my cock in your mouth."

The next thing I knew Caterina's palm connected with my cheek in a jarring slap. "Don't you *ever* say something blasphemous like that in my presence again!"

My eyes narrowed into fury-filled slits at her. "I'll say and do whatever the fuck I want. I'm the head of this fucking family and your future husband."

Caterina slung herself out of my grip. "Then say what you came to say and leave me alone."

"This is *our* room."

"You can sleep somewhere else," she commanded.

"I don't take orders, Kitten." I grabbed her by the shoulders and jerked her against me. My head dipped to press my lips against the shell of her ear. "I give orders, and people follow them."

"Let me go!" she demanded.

"I'll let you go when I'm fucking ready."

At the realization I was serious, Caterina stopped thrashing in my arms. Instead, she tucked her chin to her chest almost obediently. "While this is *our* room, I actually came to see if you were settling in all right."

"As if you really care."

"I do."

She shook her head. "If you truly cared about me, you'd let me go."

Rubbing my hand over my face, I countered, "I'm not arguing about this with you again."

"Then leave me."

"Gladly," I hissed.

After I slammed the door, Dare gave a low whistle. "She's a real corker."

"A fecking geebag."

"She's not that bad."

After glancing around the hallway, he leaned in closer to me. "When she slapped you?" He shuddered. "Christ, I got hard as a rock."

With a grunt, I shoved him back. "Shut your fucking mouth and go take a cold shower."

"Come on, man. Didn't it kinda turn you on too? I mean, think about that kinda fire but when you're fucking."

My frayed patience snapped, and I lunged at Dare. With my elbow against his throat, I pushed him against the wall. "Do not *ever* let me hear you talk about Caterina that way again. Got it?"

The bastard had the audacity to grin back at me. "Damn... she's... already... under... your skin..." he choked out.

"And if you fuck with me anymore about it, I'm going to be under yours with a sharp instrument," I snarled.

"Okay," he wheezed.

Jabbing my finger at him, I said, "Go get me a fucking whiskey and have it waiting for me after I finish my shower."

Since he was fighting to breathe normally again, he bobbed his head in agreement.

Although I sure as hell would never admit it to him, Dare wouldn't be the only one taking a cold shower tonight.

Chapter Seven: Caterina

It was the second full day of my captivity, and I had yet to leave the bedroom I'd been given. I'd barely left the bed. While Callum claimed the bedroom was ours, he had yet to share it with me. In fact, I'd barely seen him since the night he'd taken me. I'd continued to infuriate him by not speaking and refusing to leave the room.

Although there was a television and two shelves full of books, I lay in a depressed stupor the entirety of the first day. My only focus was on how to get myself out of my current hell.

Shortly after breakfast yesterday I'd come to the realization that while I had no physical weapons to fight for my freedom, I did have the ability to put an end to the madness of this proposed arranged marriage.

Over the years, I'd read in many medical books how dehydration was an easy and painless death. Death wasn't the freedom I'd envisioned for my life, but I knew I couldn't bring myself to live a life that wasn't my own.

After everything I had been through, I couldn't bring myself to obey a man. Even though Callum didn't appear to be the monster Carmine was, I wouldn't allow myself to find out.

Even after making my decision, I'd grappled with the moral dilemma of what I was doing in relation to my beliefs. But a part of me argued that I was sacrificing myself to the cause since I'd been stolen from the order and from my life of sacrifice. I spent much of the day praying for forgiveness.

It was now twenty-four hours without anything to drink, least of all to eat. While not drinking was difficult, the eating was torturous. The Kavanaugh brothers must've hired a cook because the food that was brought to me was five-star hotel level.

For lunch, I'd endured a bowl of mouthwatering Ziti on the bedside table. It had taken everything within me to refuse it, but I left it untouched.

At dinner, a different maid from lunch appeared with a tray of roast chicken, rice, and vegetables. Once again, I fought my hunger and refused to eat. If I could've opened one of the windows, I would've tossed the food out, so I would've been spared the smell.

This morning after refusing a platter of scrambled eggs, Italian sausage, and French toast, I debated flushing the food down the toilet to avoid the delicious aromas.

But I barely had the energy to make it to the bathroom, nevermind to haul a platter of food in there. I could definitely feel the dehydration setting in.

At a little past noon, my door burst open. I expected another maid with a platter, but this time Callum himself held a tray in his hands. Since I didn't want to be in bed with him in the room, I forced myself to my feet.

"I was told that you haven't been eating."

When I didn't respond, he eyed me curiously before setting the tray down on the bedside table. "Are you fasting for a religious reason or something?"

"No."

"Then why aren't you eating?" When I didn't answer, he crossed his arms over his broad chest. "Is there something wrong with the food? Like you're a vegetarian or vegan?"

I was surprised he cared enough to even enquire about my reason. After a few moments, I finally shook my head. "No. It's nothing like that."

"Is it because you're homesick for the order?"

I widened my eyes at his question. I never expected my captor to care if I was homesick. "If I tell you yes, will you let me go?" I whispered.

"Must we revisit this question again? If I've told you once, I've told you a thousand times. You are not going back to the order. *Ever.*"

I swallowed down the cries rising in my throat. I hated myself for asking him to let me go again. Deep down, I knew he wasn't going to change his mind. My future was tied to his now. At least he thought so.

"I'll ask you again. Are you not eating because you're homesick for the order?" Callum questioned.

When I apathetically shrugged, Callum huffed out a frustrated breath. "What is the fucking problem, Caterina?"

After I merely stared back at him, he shrewdly narrowed his eyes at me. "Are you protesting our impending marriage by not eating?"

"Maybe," I whispered.

"That's fucking ridiculous. We're getting married. End of story." He shoved the tray toward me on the table. "*Eat.*"

I glared up at him. "I thought as an Irishman, you would appreciate a hunger strike when you saw one."

Surprise momentarily flashed in his eyes. I'm sure he thought an Italian capo's daughter would have no idea about the Irish Hunger Strikes of 1981. What he didn't know was my father insisted that my brothers and I know the history of all the warring families. I could quote Bratva, Greek, and Triad history as well as the cartels, along with the Italian enemy families.

Callum's expression changed from shock to disgust. "What could an Italian princess possibly know of the suffering Bobby Sands and the other Northern men endured on the hunger strikes?" he growled.

"They were protesting something they believed in. Just as I'm protesting my kidnapping and this sham of an arranged marriage you are forcing on me."

He stared at me for a moment before slowly shaking his head. "I must've been fucking insane when I thought taking vows and being a novice would mean your temperament would be any different."

"Let me guess. You thought because I was in a religious order I would bend to your every whim. That I would be quiet and mousy and never speak my mind."

"As a matter of fact, that's exactly what I assumed."

"I imagine it's one of *many* things you've been wrong about."

He swept his hands to his hips. "One thing I'm right about is you're a stubborn, spoiled princess who is only used to getting her way."

"That's how you choose to see me." Jerking my chin, I added, "I know exactly who I am, and I don't care what you think of me."

His blue eyes narrowed as fury danced in them. "You will care."

"Are you threatening me?"

"Aye, princess." He jabbed a finger at the bowl of soup. "If you refuse to eat that voluntarily, I'll have one or more of my brothers hold you while I force that soup down your throat."

A strangled noise came from behind Callum. I glanced past him to see the brother who had given me medicine on the plane. I'd heard him called Kellan.

His mouth turned down in a grimace, and it was very apparent he didn't like Callum's suggestion.

"Do you not approve of my tactics, boyo?"

"Don't ask me to hold her down." Kellan's gaze shifted to the floor. "You can shoot me before I'll ever do that."

My breath hitched as I glanced between Callum and Kellan. Callum's jaw clenched before he slowly nodded his head. "Aye, you're right. That would be too harsh for more than just her."

While Kellan looked slightly relieved, the gleam burning in Callum's eyes told me I wasn't going to get off so easily.

I should've backed down, but I couldn't resist saying, "Do what you must, but I swear to you I will not voluntarily eat."

"Get this through your thick skull, Kitten. You will *not* starve yourself to death. Before I let that happen, I'll have a doctor hook you up to an IV and pump you full of nutrients. I'll even send you down the aisle to marry me with a feeding tube if necessary. Regardless of what you think you're going to accomplish, you will fail."

Although I hated myself for it, I trembled beneath his intense stare and harsh words. When I ducked my head to refuse to look at him, his fingers gripped my chin and jerked my gaze back to his.

"You *will* enter into a marriage with me, and we *will* unify our families. Understood?"

"I will *not* marry you," I replied.

Callum threw up his hands before blaring something in Irish. He then stormed from the room.

I sucked in a harsh breath to try and still my erratic breathing. When I started to slide the tray with the soup to the floor in continued protest, Kellan rushed forward. "Please, don't."

My eyes widened at his request. Since he had only ever been kind to me, I quickly removed my hands from the tray. "You're not like him, are you?"

His friendly expression darkened. "I've been inducted into this family the same as Callum. I'm loyal to my brothers and my family. That's all you need to concern yourself with."

"I wasn't doubting your devotion to your family. I just meant you have a kindness about you that he lacks. Like when you gave me medicine for my head."

When he didn't respond, I cocked my head at him. "You didn't like he was going to force me to eat."

Kellan eyed me warily. He was just as handsome as Callum, but there was an innocence to him that surprised me.

I held my hands up. "I'm sorry. I shouldn't have said anything."

"It's all right."

"Are you sure about that?" I countered.

"I am."

Sighing, I turned and started to climb back into bed, but when I lifted my leg, the world spun around me. Pinching my eyes shut, I braced my hands on the mattress to try and keep myself upright.

"Are you all right?" Kellan asked, as he hovered behind me.

"Just a little dizzy," I admitted.

"I know you've not been eating, but have you at least been drinking?"

"Not exactly." Once the world stopped spinning, I started easing back into bed. When I threw a glance at Kellan, I found him staring at me with furrowed brows. "I'm fine."

"You almost passed out."

"Don't worry about me."

After throwing a glance over his shoulder, he took a few steps closer to the bed. "Couldn't you eat just a little?"

"I'm really tired and dizzy right now..."

His gaze dropped from me to the tray with the soup. "I...I could feed you."

As I stared wide-eyed at him, he grabbed a spoon before stirring the soup. After scooping out a bite, he held the spoon out to me. "Come on, lass. Just a little."

His expression was so earnest and his kindness so endearing I didn't think I could turn him down. "Will Callum be angry if you get me to eat?" I questioned softly.

The corners of Kellan's lips quirked up. "Aye, I imagine he will."

"He won't hurt you though, will he?"

He shook his head. "He'll just be angry that for once, I could do something he couldn't."

The devious side of me wanted to piss off my future husband. I especially liked the idea that I could elevate Kellan at the same time. In the end, the groaning of my stomach outweighed anything else.

Leaning forward, I opened my mouth and brought it over the spoon. Although the soup was lukewarm, it tasted like heaven, and I couldn't help the moan of pleasure.

"Good, huh?" Kellan asked with a smile.

"It is." As he spooned another bite, I asked, "Is it maccu di fave?"

"I think that's what I heard it called."

My brows quirked in surprise. "Irish brothers know how to make maccu di fave?"

He laughed. "Seamus hired a cook from the area."

I took in another hearty spoonful. "I thought as much. Please give them my compliments."

Kellan could barely keep up with my appetite. Once I finished with the soup, I grabbed the bread off the tray and broke it apart. Without even buttering it, I brought a chunk to my lips and began devouring it.

My ravenous actions caused Kellan to chuckle. "Sorry," I mumbled around the bread.

"It's okay. I know you have to be starving."

"So much for being a hunger striker."

Kellan's face darkened. "I know this may be hard to believe, but none of us want you to suffer, Caterina. Especially not Callum."

I swallowed hard. "How can you say that when he kidnapped me?"

"He didn't have much of a choice."

"You always have a choice, especially when it comes to good and evil."

With a shake of his head, Kellan countered, "You know as well as I do that the mafia life doesn't give us many choices."

"He could've picked a girl from another family—one who wanted to be married and have children. This is not the life I wanted."

Kellan frowned. "I'm sorry, but it's the connections to your family that we need."

"We'll see," I murmured.

After an awkward silence, he asked, "Want more soup?"

"Yes, please."

He gave me a small smile. "I'll be right back."

"Thank you." I then lay back against the pillows and closed my eyes.

The longer I laid there, the stronger I felt. I knew it was probably too soon, but I swore I did.

A voice caused me to jump. "I see you finally decided to listen to me."

My eyes popped open to see Callum smirking down at me. Before I could respond, Kellan appeared with another bowl of soup and more bread. At the sight of Callum, he froze in the doorway.

With a victorious smile curving on my lips, I said, "It wasn't you I listened to—it was Kellan."

Callum's expression darkened as Kellan made his way to my bedside. "I suppose I don't need to question the validity of Caterina's statement considering you're standing there with a fresh tray of food."

"I'm sorry, Cal. I was only trying to help."

While Kellan and I waited for Callum to unleash his fury, he surprised us both by smiling. "Good for you. I'm glad someone could make her see reason."

Shock flashed across Kellan's face. Turning to me, Callum shook his head. "You may have won this battle, Kitten, but you will lose the war because you *will* be my wife."

After curling my lip at him, I replied, "Go away, and let me eat in peace."

After starting for the door, Callum turned to flash me a shark-like smile. "Yes, eat up, Kitten. I want you well fed and strong for our wedding day."

And with those words, whatever appetite I had left was gone.

Chapter Eight: Callum

Since Seamus felt we shouldn't squander our time in Sicily, he'd set up a meeting an hour outside of Catania for us to meet with two smaller families looking for American allies.

Before we headed out, I stopped to see Caterina. I found her curled into a fetal position staring at the wall. At least her breakfast tray was half eaten.

With an exasperated sigh, I stalked over to the bed. When I sat down next to her, she didn't bother scooting away from me. Instead, she just continued staring straight ahead.

"My brothers and I have to attend a meeting out of town, and we'll be gone until dinner time."

At the mention of being deprived of our presence, Caterina's expression brightened. Of course, I quickly doused her hope when I said, "But don't worry. There will be men posted throughout the house and grounds."

She huffed out t breath. "I should've imagined as much. I'm surprised they're not instructed to stand in the bathroom while I shower."

"The only reason you're allowed that privacy is because I'm the only man who will ever see you naked, Kitten."

"You're such a gentleman."

Ignoring her jibe, I added, "As for today, my men have strict orders not to let you leave the grounds, but you are allowed to go downstairs or outside for a walk if you'd like."

"How generous of you to extend the confines of my prison," she remarked. It didn't escape my knowledge that her lashes were encrusted with tears.

"It's only a prison of your making, Kitten."

"Just leave me," she sniffled.

I reached my hand out to place it on her shoulder but then thought better of myself. Instead, I rose off the bed. Giving comfort wasn't something that came naturally to a man like me.

While I loved my mother and my sister and showed them affection, it never seemed to correlate to the women I was with. The moment they showed any flicker of negative emotions I showed them the door.

"I'll see you this evening," I called from the doorway.

"I'd say be careful, but your demise only benefits me."

"Aye, with the claws, Kitten. Your words wound me only with how not Christian they are."

When she whirled around in the bed to glare at me, I winked. "I'll be sure to say a prayer for you."

With that, I closed the door and started down the stairs. When I climbed into the waiting car, I threw a wary look back at the house. "Don't tell me you're already missing your fiancée," Seamus teased.

"It's more about leaving her unprotected."

He chuckled. "Considering there's five men guarding the grounds and three in the house, I'd hardly consider her alone."

"But can we truly trust those men?"

"They're being compensated nicely for their time."

"What's stopping them from taking even more money from the Neretti's? I'm sure word has reached them by now of Caterina's abduction."

He clapped my back reassuringly. "Because all of the men on the outside are ours."

My brows popped in surprise. "When did you fly them in?"

"This morning. They relieved the Sicilians who were on duty last night."

"You think of everything, don't you?"

He flashed me a grin. "That's why I'm your unofficial right hand man."

"And I'm sure as hell glad to have you."

The meeting went well. Aligning ourselves with the Malgeri and Scavo families would ensure our safety while in Sicily as well as continued support stateside. In turn, we would ensure our connections in Boston helped their new ventures on the East Coast.

It was almost six when we returned to the house. I would be lying if I said I hadn't spent most of the day thinking about Caterina. I'd messaged several times with the head of the contingent guarding the house. After the third text, he'd started sending me hourly updates of what Caterina was doing.

Surprisingly, she had left her room. She'd taken a long walk outside before coming back in to chat up Nera, the cook. She'd spent time in the library as well as watching television. She'd also requested and been denied a trip to the local church.

As we came through the backdoor into the kitchen, surprise filled me at the sight of Caterina at the stove, rather than Nera. Guido, a bodyguard in his early fifties, stood beside her. My brows quirked at the sight of him wearing oven mitts and carrying a large dish.

"Buonasera," he said pleasantly.

"Good evening to you, too."

My gaze bounced over to take in an appreciative look at Caterina. She was a vision in a casual, yet form-fitting red dress. When I'd instructed Nera to purchase some clothes for Caterina, I never imagined she would pick something out like that. Caterina's hair was swept into a ponytail that fell down her back. She must not have been a fan of the shoes I'd provided because she was barefoot.

When she turned around to glare at me, a sly smile curved on my lips. "I suppose I should say buonasera, *una fidanzata*."

She rolled her eyes at me calling her my fiancée. She then said something in Italian to Guido. It must've been to tell him to set the dish down on the counter close to me.

As he obliged, a delicious aroma filled my nose. Motioning to the dish, I asked, "What's that?"

"I got bored with reading and the television, so I decided to cook some lasagna," Caterina replied.

I narrowed my eyes suspiciously at her. "We just happened to have the ingredients lying around?"

She shook her head. "No. Nera went to the market in town for me. Since she wasn't going to be needed, I gave her the evening off."

Dare dipped his head over the cooling dish and inhaled noisily. When he turned back to us, his eyes rolled back in ecstasy. "That smells fucking amazing."

Caterina smiled shyly. "I wasn't sure you all would like it, but I didn't know how to make any Irish food."

Licking his lips suggestively, Dare replied, "We've been known to sample a little Italian."

She rolled her eyes at his innuendo. "You're disgusting."

Crossing my arms over my chest, I countered, "Did someone watch you cook?"

"You know as well as I do that your men are all over this house."

"That's not what I meant, Kitten." Closing the distance between us, I loomed over her. "I want to know if someone was watching your hands as you prepared this very generous offering for us."

Her eyes bulged when she got my meaning. "You think I tried to poison you?"

I shrugged. "Since you can't take us out physically, it would make sense."

Smacking her hands against my chest, Caterina countered, "Newsflash, *idiota*. Not everything is about you and your brothers."

"Is that right?"

"For your information, I needed a little comfort food, and lasagna fits the bill for me."

Glancing between us, Dare argued, "I'm sure it's fine, Callum."

"Aye, so you're willing to be the tester?"

"You know I'd never pass up an opportunity to prove you're full of shite," he countered with a smirk.

After swiping a spoon out of a drawer, he scooped out a bite. As steam rose off of it, he blew a few cooling breaths over it. With one fleeting look at me, he thrust the spoon into his mouth. I dared a glance at Caterina whose expression was unreadable.

Suddenly his eyes bulged as the spoon clattered to the floor. Gasping in a breath, he staggered around the kitchen before collapsing. While I rolled my eyes at his theatrics, Caterina shrieked in terror before her hand flew to her mouth.

After a few seconds, Dare popped back up with a cheeky grin. "It's fucking delicious."

For a moment, all Caterina could do was stare in wide-eyed, wide-mouthed horror. But then slowly her shoulders started to rise and fall. When a laugh burst from her lips, it caused me and Dare to jump. "How could you scare me like that, you jerk!"

Dare laughed. "Easy with the insults there."

Caterina threw her head back and giggled in response. She fucking *giggled* at my brother. As I glanced at the two of them, a foreign feeling criss crossed through my chest. I hadn't felt it before. But the longer I stood there, the more I realized it was some form of jealousy.

I didn't like it one fucking bit that Dare had been able to illicit such a positive reaction from her. That he was the one who had made her dark eyes light up. That she had given him a smile—a genuine one at that. She had yet to give me one kind expression.

Rolling my shoulders, I tried ridding myself of the feeling. In the end, I don't know why I really gave a shite.

Caterina was to be my wife, not his. Not to mention the fact, Dare had been charming ladies long before his balls dropped, so the fact he could garner that reaction from Caterina shouldn't have been surprising. Normally, I didn't give a shit about his interactions with women, but I sure as hell did with Caterina.

As Dare started to spoon out another bite, Caterina swatted his hand away. "Wait for us to sit down."

"But it's so fucking good."

Once again, she gave him a beautiful smile. "Patience."

"Fine," Dare grumbled.

After an eternity, Caterina finally turned her attention back to me. "Will you take the non-poisonous lasagna into the dining room while I grab the salad?"

I opened my mouth to argue that I wasn't a fucking domestic, I bit my tongue instead. After accusing her of trying to kill me, the least I could do was take a dish out of the kitchen.

When I walked into the dining room, I found the table had been set with plates, glasses, and utensils along with a pitcher of water and a bottle of wine. Apparently while we were gone, Caterina had made herself at home.

After putting the lasagna in the middle of the table, I remarked, "You're fitting into your new role well."

"That's kind of you to think I do a good job of playing a kidnapping victim," she shot back with a sickeningly sweet smile.

Curling my upper lip, I replied, "That's not what I meant."

With doe-eyes, she asked, "What role were you speaking of?"

"A proper wife."

She wrinkled her nose. "I see Irish men aren't so different to Italians when it comes to adhering to traditional gender roles."

"If that means I expect you to cook and keep our home, then yes, we are alike."

Caterina swept her hands to her full hips. "My mother is a capo's wife, and she was never expected to cook and clean. I assumed since you're the Irish equivalent of that, I could expect the same."

"Well, you assumed wrong. My mother made sure there were three meals on the table for my father as well as keeping his home spotless."

"Like she had much of a choice," Dare quipped under his breath.

I jabbed my finger at him. "Stay out of this."

He held up his hands. "I was just trying to diffuse the situation."

"I don't need your help."

"Just remember. She's stealthy with round objects so protect your cock at all costs."

At Caterina's gasp, I growled, "Bugger off."

He grinned. "I'll go find the wine opener."

After he left us, Caterina crossed her arms over her chest, which emphasized her perfect, round tits. I silently cursed Nera for picking out that temptation of a dress. It molded against each and every one of her sinful curves.

"I will cook and clean for you only if I want or feel like it, and most of all, I will do it only if I feel respected. I won't be some employee you bark orders to. A marriage is about being partners."

"Your parents were partners?" I countered.

She scowled. "I would imagine that if we want any semblance of a happy marriage we shouldn't look to our parents as examples."

"Aye, I suppose you're right," I relented.

"Do my ears deceive me or did you just admit to being wrong about something?"

"Fucking hell, woman!"

Jesus, how was it possible that after only forty-eight hours, Caterina knew how to push each and every one of my buttons? This wasn't what I had envisioned when Seamus had concocted this marriage plan.

A triumphant fire burned in Caterina's dark eyes, and fuck me, if it didn't go straight to my cock. "It's fine if you won't admit it. I know that I'm right."

I threw up my hands. "You know what? You can do whatever the hell you want, and I'll do whatever the hell I want. The little we have to see or talk to each other the better."

"I agree."

It was then I realized my brothers had all come into the dining room. Their attention pinged back and forth between me and Caterina like they were front row at a tennis match.

Quinn grabbed my shoulder. "Let's eat before it gets cold."

"Fine," I grunted before taking a seat at the head of the table. The others hung back, unsure of where to sit. I tapped the seat to my right. "Sit, Caterina."

With her eyes locked on mine, she edged around the table to sit at the very end. Her brows cocked defiantly as she placed her napkin in her lap. I clenched my jaw as I pulled my hand back—a hand that was itching to pull Caterina over my knee before sending stinging slaps across both of her ass cheeks. I wanted nothing more than to see her pink-tinged skin with the imprint of my hands.

Instead, I rose out of my chair to pour a glass of whiskey. I didn't care whatever aged bottle of wine was on the table. After throwing back half a tumbler full, I returned to my seat. My brothers had started passing food and digging in while Caterina's mouth turned disapprovingly down.

When she didn't start filling her plate, I huffed out an exasperated breath through my nose. "What's wrong now, Kitten?"

"Aren't we going to say the blessing?"

My brothers froze at her question. Their expectant gazes bounced to me. "We don't normally return thanks." Smirking at her, I added, "But knowing you like I do, I imagine we're about to start."

"If you don't mind."

I motioned my hand over the table. "Be my guest."

As Caterina bowed her head, my brothers followed suit. After rolling my eyes, I tucked my head to my chest. Caterina's voice echoed through the quiet room. "Bless us, O Lord, and these Thy gifts which we are about to receive through Christ Our Lord. Amen."

"Amen," echoed around the table.

Caterina raised her head, and the corners of her ruby red lips quirked up before she reached for the salad. When she caught my eye, she suggested, "Perhaps next time, you'll want to say it since you keep reminding me that you're the boss of this family?"

"I'll pass."

She frowned. "But weren't you all raised Catholic?"

After snaring a piece of bread from the basket, Dare replied, "Aye. Our mother insisted we go through every single step from christening to First Communion."

"Callum and I were even altar boys," Quinn remarked.

Caterina's mouth gaped wide. "You were?"

With a chuckle, Quinn replied, "Not that it'll help us much in the end."

"Very true," I replied.

"Don't you practice anymore?"

While Kellan quickly replied, "Yes," I countered, "It doesn't actually align with our type of work, Kitten."

Snatching her wine goblet, she muttered, "I've been abducted by godless heathens."

I curled my lip at her. "I would argue your family isn't any better. Yer precious brothers included."

"Regardless of what they do in their business, they still attend mass."

"Hypocrites," I grumbled before shoveling in a bite of lasagna.

The moment it hit my tongue I fought the urge to groan with pleasure. It was that fucking good. Considering she was a good cook, I couldn't imagine why she wouldn't want to do it all the time. A voice in my head said, *because she doesn't want to be your fucking slave, arsehole.*

After silence fell over the dining room, Kellan remarked, "This is seriously the best lasagna I've ever had."

Caterina beamed at his compliment. "Thank you, Kellan."

"You're welcome."

When she met my glare, she sighed. Waving her fork at Kellan, she asked, "Why can't I marry him?"

While Quinn and Dare snorted laughter behind their napkins, Kellan's eyes bulged as he flushed the color of the red tablecloth. After he ducked his head, I grunted. "He's practically a kid."

"He's closer to my age than you are."

"She has a point there, Cal," Dare replied with a grin.

Ignoring my arsehole of a brother, I replied, "He's a fourth son. Why would you possibly want him?"

Caterina's soft gaze appraised Kellan. "He's compassionate."

"He gave you one fucking compliment about your cooking and that makes him kind?"

She scowled at me. "He's done more than just that. He fed me soup."

At her admission, Kellan's fork froze midway to his mouth. When he cut his eyes to mine, I quirked my brows. "It seems the two of you left that part out."

He shrugged. "She needed to eat."

Caterina nodded. "Since I was so weak, Kellan insisted I let him feed me." Giving Kellan an appreciative look, she added, "I certainly wouldn't have eaten without him."

"Well, we owe our eternal gratitude to Saint Kellan," I grumbled.

Shaking her head, Caterina said, "Why must you be such a jerk?"

"That's your opinion."

"Seriously, even marrying Chuckles at this point would be an improvement over you."

Dare threw his head back with a laugh. "Seriously, Kitty Cat? You're calling me Chuckles?"

With a shrug, she replied, "It's better than asshole, isn't it?"

Jerking his thumb at me, Dare replied, "I think that's more his moniker than mine."

All the bickering and backbiting of the past two days converged on that moment. I very rarely blew my top with my family, but I'd been pushed past my limit. I slammed my hand down on the table, causing Caterina to jump.

"OUT! Everyone out!" When Caterina dared to slide her chair back, I jabbed my finger at her. "Except you."

"Come on, man. We're hungry," Dare protested.

"Then take your fucking plates with you," I growled.

Without another word, my brothers gathered their plates and glasses. Kellan threw Caterina a fleeting look of concern before he left the dining room.

Rising out of my chair, I stalked down the length of the table before plopping down in the chair next to Caterina. She eased away from me.

"We're not leaving this room until you get some things straight, and I don't care if it takes all fucking night."

Chapter Nine: Caterina

Although I fought to keep my composure, I couldn't help trembling at Callum's outburst. I'd seen him angry, but I hadn't seen him like this. When he'd abandoned his chair and taken the one next to me, I cowered in my seat.

I didn't know this man, nor did I know what fury he was capable of. While I didn't think he would physically hurt me, the possibility was there.

Callum flicked his hand at me. "Come closer, Caterina."

The last thing I wanted to do was answer his command, least of all be any closer to him. So, I inched my chair slightly towards him.

A low growl rumbled in his chest. Reaching over, he grabbed the arm of my chair and tugged it with all his strength.

A gasp flew from my lips as my body flailed in the chair. "Must you continue to manhandle me?"

"Must you continue to disobey every command I give you?"

I jerked my chin up at him. "I answer to no man. Not even to my father."

"You *will* answer to me."

"Over my dead body," I bit out.

Callum's dark blue eyes turned almost black as he stared at me with absolute venom. When he whirled out of his chair, I flinched in fear that he was going to hit me.

Instead, he stalked past me over to the side table that held the liquor. With a shaky hand, he poured himself a rather large glass of what I imagined was whiskey.

After he downed the glass in three long gulps, Callum stared up at the ceiling. He sucked in a harsh breath before exhaling slowly. When he turned back to me, his expression remained slightly murderous.

"I don't know if it's the same for Made Men, but in my clan, we don't hurt women. They're considered innocents. They're to be protected and cared for at all costs."

He swallowed another gulp of whiskey. "But you...it's taking everything within me not to hurt you, Caterina."

"Am I supposed to thank you for that?"

Like a snake striking out at its prey, Callum lunged from the whiskey cart over to me. Grabbing me by the shoulders, his fingers twisted into my flesh.

I didn't dare give him the satisfaction of crying out. Instead, I raised my chin and stared him down.

A few tense seconds ticked by where I wondered if I'd finally gone too far. And then as he stared down at his hands on me, a look of disbelief flashed on Callum's face. He jerked away from me and spun back around to the whiskey cart.

While his back rose and fell in harsh pants, I pinched my eyes shut as I tried regulating my own breathing. The sound of his voice caused me to jump.

"Despite neither one of us wanting it, this marriage is happening. We have to find a way to coexist without killing each other."

A mirthless laugh bubbled from my lips. "What could possibly induce me into wanting to work on a marriage with my kidnapper?"

Callum turned around and shot me a pointed look. "I know the real reason why you joined the religious order."

In spite of the cold chill that reverberated down my spine, I fought to keep my body or face from reacting. "Because I had a calling to serve God."

With a shark-like smile, he then tsked at me. "Come now. It's one thing to lie before me—" He paused to point his finger at the ceiling, "but it's quite another to lie before him."

"Only he knows my heart."

Gripping the arms of the chair, Callum loomed over me, his face only inches away from mine. "I know more than you could ever imagine."

I licked my lips. "Such as?"

"You joined the order to escape an arranged marriage."

Nervous laughter trilled from my lips. "That's absurd. If I didn't want to get married, I could've just run away."

Callum shook his head. "You know as well as I do you were a caged animal, Kitten. If you had ever managed to escape, they would've dragged you right back. Even if you changed your name or your hair or even went to the extreme and got plastic surgery, they would've eventually found you and forced you back."

When I didn't respond, he quirked his brows at me. "The only choice you had at any freedom was to join the order. Even a man with a soul as black as your father's still harbors a little fear of God, and he would fear him too much to steal you from Him."

"How could you possibly know?" I whispered.

Anguish marred Callum's handsome features. "Because of my sister."

"What do you mean?"

"The reason why I killed my father was because he promised our seventeen-year-old-sister to a pedophile whose kink was beating young girls."

"He sounds like Carmine," I murmured.

"Except he didn't get the chance to actually hurt you like Oisinn did my sister."

My breath hitched in my chest. "That's why you killed your father?"

"Aye."

His fingers traced the rim of his whiskey glass. "My brothers and I tried to talk him out of the arrangement, but he wouldn't listen to reason. When Maeve threatened to run away to avoid the marriage, he ordered Dare, Quinn, and I to beat her."

I widened my eyes in horror. "That's horrible."

"It was. Of course, we refused, which only enraged my father further."

"Is that when you killed him?"

A haunted look entered Callum's dark blue eyes. "I should've done it then. If I had, it would've saved Maeve from what he allowed that bastard Oisinn to do to her."

I gasped. "He beat her in your stead?"

Agony overcame Callum's face. The emotions swirling within him must've been overwhelming because he didn't speak for several moments. The anguished whisper that came from him caused my stomach to roll.

"He destroyed her."

My hand flew to my mouth as I fought the bile rising in my throat. No, it couldn't be. A father could never willingly allow such a thing to happen to his daughter. "Your father let him..." Unable to say the word, I swallowed hard. "*Hurt* her?"

Callum gave a slight jerk of his head. "Instead of protecting her in her hour of need, the bastard held a gun to Kellan and my youngest brother, Eamon's, heads and forced them to hold her down while Oisin raped her."

Desperate agony rippled through my chest as I didn't fight the tears streaking down my cheeks. I swallowed my sobs as I couldn't even form thoughts to imagine the horrors that Maeve endured at her father's bidding.

Then I thought of sweet Kellan being forced to do such a thing, and a sob tore from my lips. My heart broke for him as well.

Callum had been made out to be a monster for murdering his father when all this time he'd merely been avenging his sister. After wiping my cheeks, I reached out with a shaky hand to touch his shoulder. At the touch, he stared at me in surprise.

"Callum, there's nothing I can possibly say, but please know I'm so very sorry. For Maeve and for Kellan and Eamon." I swallowed hard. "And for you."

He cocked his brows at me. "Does that mean you absolve me of the sin of killing my father?"

"While it's not for me to forgive, you had more than enough reasons to do it."

When I thought of the torture Maeve had endured and the potential that I faced with Carmine, I whispered, "More than that, I'm glad you did it."

"You are?"

I nodded. "I know my brothers would do the same."

Tilting his head at me, he said, "I didn't think things were so strained in your family."

"Let's just say that when it comes to my father, they're willing to do exactly what you did."

To Callum's surprise, I said, "They've always hated the idea of me in the order. They were willing to take my father out to give me my freedom."

A smirk curved across his lips. "I can imagine I just made three new enemies then by kidnapping you."

"I would imagine you have."

"After we have the chance to speak, I'm sure I can get them to see things more favorably."

"Don't count on it."

As Callum went to get another drink, I couldn't help asking, "What happened to your sister?"

"She's a sophomore at Trinity College in Dublin."

"You didn't marry her off when she turned eighteen?"

Callum's jaw tensed. "We won't be marrying her off period. If she ever decides she wants to get married, she'll do the choosing."

"That's very progressive of you. Not to mention you're allowing her to get an education."

After sliding back into his chair, Callum eyed me curiously. "Did you want to go to university?"

With my chest constricting, I glanced down at my lap. "Very much."

"What did you want to study?"

I snapped my surprised gaze back to Callum's. I couldn't help being surprised by his question. Men in the world I'd grown up in didn't appreciate educated women. "You really want to know?"

"Aye."

Chewing on my lip, I debated telling him. For some reason, it felt like I was stripping myself bare in front of him. Other than my brothers, I'd never spoken it aloud to anyone.

"At the very minimum, I wanted to be a nurse, but in my wildest dreams, I wanted to become a doctor and serve with Doctors Without Borders."

"Somehow I could see you as a nurse."

"Really?"

"You have a natural compassion about you."

"Just not with you, right?" I teasingly asked.

Callum chuckled. "In your defense, I don't bring out the best in you."

"That's true."

"Is your desire to be a nurse the reason why you became a missionary novice?"

"Yes and no. I wanted to travel to help people, but I also wanted to put as much distance between my father and the man he wanted me to marry."

"That's understandable." He then quirked his brows at me. "Would you still want to pursue a degree?"

My heartbeat accelerated at his words, and I fought the urge to pinch myself. Was he actually alluding to what I thought he was? "More than anything in the world."

With a quick nod of his head, Callum replied, "Then I don't see anything wrong with you pursuing a degree as my wife."

"Please don't tease me right now."

"I'm not."

"You would actually let me go to college?"

"Yes." He tilted his head at me. "Obviously, you would have to commute. I sure as hell wouldn't allow you to live away from me."

"I'd be fine with that."

"Then it's settled. If you willingly consent to marrying me, you may go to university. And as long as it doesn't fuck up being a supportive wife and mother, I don't see any reason why you can't pursue a career."

I blinked at him. I was too shocked to do anything else. Surely I was dreaming. Callum agreed that not only could I earn a degree, but I could work. It had to be too good to be true.

"Will you put that in writing?"

The corners of his lips twitched. "Don't you trust me?"

"That shouldn't be too shocking considering you're the leader of an enemy family who I've only known for three days."

"Fine, Kitten. I'll have our attorney draw up the necessary papers."

Although a part of me said not to press my luck, I decided to go with my gut. "There's something else I want to negotiate."

Callum scowled at me around the lip of his whiskey tumbler. "Isn't me letting you go to university enough?"

When I shook my head, he sighed. "What is it?"

"You just mentioned me being a mother."

As the words left my lips, an image of my belly swelling with Callum's child flooded my mind. After I'd joined the order, I'd buried the idea of ever becoming a mother. At the time, it had been a hard pill to swallow. But in the span of just a couple of days, the possibility was back on the table.

Of course, that meant I would have to conceive it with Callum. At the thought of doing *that* with him, my cheeks flushed.

Amusement twinkled in his eyes at what must've been my apparent embarrassment. "Yes, Kitten, I will need heirs."

Tilting his head at me, he added, "As a Catholic, I'm sure you won't object to not using birth control."

With a scowl, I replied, "There are gray areas when it comes to my faith."

"You would deny me children?"

"That's not what I meant. I love children, and before I entered the order, I always wanted to have them."

"Then what could possibly be the problem."

"I don't want to become your breeding machine."

A laugh burst from Callum's lips. "A breeding machine?"

"Don't mock me."

"I'm not."

"Are you denying that by not using birth control, you'll keep me pregnant all the time?"

With a cocky smirk, Callum replied, "You must think I'm a hell of a virile bastard if I'll be constantly knocking you up."

"I merely assumed an Irishmen's sexual drive is the same as an Italian's." Pursing my lips at him, I countered, "But I could be wrong about your abilities."

Lust glittered in his blue eyes as he closed the distance between us. "Never doubt my abilities to make you purr, Kitten."

Rolling my eyes, I tried shoving him back from me, but he didn't budge. "You're disgusting."

As Callum leaned closer to me, his breath warmed against the sensitive skin near my ear. "You won't always think that way."

His lips brushed against my ear. "Someday soon I'm going to make you beg for my cock and scream my name."

A shiver rippled through me at his words, and this time it wasn't from disgust. His words and overwhelming presence seemed to awaken long-dormant feelings. Feelings I had never imagined I would ever experience again after I entered the order.

Feigning indifference to the effect of his words, I countered, "Can we please focus?"

He eased back in his chair with a cocky smirk. "What else did you want to say about breeding?"

With an exasperated huff, I crossed my arms over my chest. "I will give you heirs, but I get to choose how many."

"Why is it only your choice?"

"Because it's *my* body going through the pregnancy, and *my* body going through the birth."

"Aye, and your beautiful cunt getting ravaged in the delivery," he teased.

My eyes bulged in horror while my hand involuntarily came up to slap his cheek. His hand caught mine. Instead of being angry, he merely winked.

"Put the claws away, Kitten. They have the opposite effect on me than you think."

I jerked my hand away from his. "You shouldn't speak that way to me when I'm still considered a sister."

Amusement twinkled in Callum's blue eyes. "Does that mean I can when we're married?"

"I would prefer you didn't."

"Sorry, Kitten, but I won't make any promises."

I fought the urge to call him a bastard. Instead, I stared down at my hands. I knew there was one more thing I desperately needed clarity on before I could ever say I do.

When I looked up, I found Callum staring intently at me. He raised a dark brow at me. "What is it you want to say to me?"

"Am I that obvious?"

"I'm just good at reading people."

I shifted in my chair. "There's one last request I need to make."

"Jesus, woman, what else can there possibly be?"

"Something that's more important even than me going to school and having a career."

Callum eased back in his chair while narrowing his eyes at me. "What is it?"

I knew what I was about to ask could potentially send Callum into a rage. While I shouldn't have cared about his reaction, I still nervously fingered the hem of my dress. I knew his response would soil all the other promises he'd made.

At the feel of his fingers on my chin, I jumped. "Out with it, Kitten."

I nodded. "If we have a daughter, I want you to promise me you'll never arrange a marriage for her. Just as Maeve has the freedom to choose, I want the same for my daughter or daughters."

Without missing a beat, Callum quickly replied, "You have my word."

Surprise flooded me. "Just like that and no arguments?"

"I would've thought you wouldn't have to ask after what I told you about Maeve."

"That was your sister where this will be your daughter. Because she belongs directly to you, her marriage would be worth more when it came to power and position."

"I will still honor her freedom."

For reasons I couldn't understand, pride bloomed in my chest. Pride that came from the fact the man who would be my husband respected his future daughter or daughters enough to care that they had freedom over their lives.

"You can't imagine how pleased it makes me to hear you say that."

"It surprises you that I would agree?"

A shy smile tugged at the corners of my lips. "Considering your reputation, it is a surprise. But a good one."

"I may be a monster to my enemies, but I'll never be the evil bastard that my father was. In spite of not having the best role model, I know I can love a child. More than that, I know I would never want to hurt my child."

"Thank you." I stared intently into his eyes. "Even though I don't know you well, I don't think you would ever willingly hurt a child either."

"Before you give too many compliments, you must know this. While I'll do everything within my power to keep them safe, our sons will be brought up in the family."

I sighed. "I imagined as much."

"And you don't object?"

"Would you change your mind if I did?"

"No."

"Then there's no point. While it's not what I would want for them, I understand what they're being born into. After all, they'll inherit it from both sides of their family."

"I'm glad you can see it that way."

With a teasing smile, I countered, "Maybe it's more that I'll be lighting candles to be blessed with only daughters."

Callum barked out a laugh. "Do what you must, Sister, but considering the amount of sons in my family, the odds aren't in your favor."

"I suppose we'll just have to wait and see."

"Speaking of conceiving children, I feel we should discuss our wedding night."

Apprehension rocketed through me. Of all the aspects of a

marriage to Callum, the physical side unnerved me the most. After joining the order, I'd never imagined sex with anyone, least of all a man who abducted me.

As someone with no experience with men, it was a matter of extreme apprehension. "W-What about it?"

"I just wanted to ease your mind that I won't be expecting us to consummate the marriage on our wedding night."

A gasp escaped my lips as surprise shuddered through me. "You're not?"

"I'm a bastard, but not that big of a bastard to force a nun into sex with a stranger."

As I processed his words, I couldn't help thinking there was more he wasn't saying. Although our families were different nationalities, rules were similar. In the mafia world, he would be my husband, and it would be within his rights to expect me to consummate the marriage. Even if I said no, it wouldn't be considered rape.

"It's about your sister, isn't it?"

His expression darkened. "What about her?"

"The reason you won't force me on our wedding night–or any night for that matter–is because of what happened to Maeve," I said softly.

"You owe more to the suffering of that poor girl than you can ever imagine," he grunted.

It hit me then. The unusual kindness he and his brothers had shown me was also because of Maeve. I swallowed hard. "I realize how indebted I am to her, and for what it is worth, I'm grateful."

"I'm glad you realize it."

An uncomfortable silence penetrated the air after the mention of Maeve. I cleared my throat. "When can I sign the contract?"

"I'll type up what we discussed and send it to our attorney tonight. I should have a copy in the morning."

"Good."

Before I could rise out of my chair, his hand came over mine. At the mischievous glint burning in his eyes, a shudder ran through me. "Until then, I know another way we could seal the deal."

"How?"

"With a kiss."

"I think a handshake would suffice."

"You never know. I might throw something in the contract about a summer study abroad if you kiss me now."

My eyes popped wide. "You're trying to bribe me to kiss you?"

"I'm a businessman, Caterina."

Leaning over, Callum slid his hands around my waist. The heat from his body singed my skin through my dress. Before I could shove him away, he rose to his feet, pulling me up with him.

His whiskey-laced breath warmed my cheek, sending a shiver rippling through me. "Surrender a little of yourself to me, Caterina."

"No! You don't get to kiss me until we're married," I protested as I fought to escape his embrace.

"Says who?" he questioned, as he kissed a moist trail down my neck.

I tried ignoring the electricity dancing along my skin that his lips were producing. "T-That's how it's done in my w-world."

Callum's lips froze on my collar bone. He then pulled away to stare down at me with eyes glittering with lust. "But you're in *my* world now, Kitten."

As I pinched my eyes shut, I pleaded, "If we're going to do this, then let's do it right. Honor my tradition."

A few moments passed where my heart threatened to beat out of my chest. At his frustrated grunt, I popped open my eyes. He glared back at me. "I should take what's mine regardless of your pleading."

"I'm not yours. Not even after we're married," I protested in a whisper.

Callum's lips hovered close to my own. A part of me wanted nothing more than for him to take what was allegedly his. I wanted to feel his lips on mine; the wet heat of his tongue against mine. I hated that I was experiencing feelings like that for him.

"You are mine, Kitten. You'll take *my* name, sleep in *my* bed, and one day very soon, you'll take *my* cock."

He licked his lips as if savoring the thought of us sleeping together. "When I put my baby in your belly, you'll even carry a part of *me* inside you."

Both disgust and longing rippled through me at his words. "Let me go."

With a smirk, he shoved away from me. "Once again, you may have won this battle, Kitten, but I'll win the war."

Chapter Ten: Callum

After Caterina tore herself out of my embrace, she sprinted out of the dining room. As I heard her feet pounding up the stairs, I remained rooted to my seat. Every fucking altercation with Caterina left me utterly and completely enraged.

But as usual, I'd been left with more than just anger. A white-hot lust and desire sent my cock straining against my zipper. Once I knew she was safely in her room, I made my way upstairs.

The last thing my sweet virgin needed to see was my erection tenting my pants. Even if it was all her fault.

Once I got inside my room, I headed straight for the shower. As I stripped out of my clothes, my need grew even more intense. It took everything within me not to stalk down the hall and barge into Caterina's room.

I wanted the smell of her pussy in my nose, its taste on my tongue, and its tight walls clenching around my cock.

Like a junkie desperate for a fix, my hand trembled as I palmed my stiff erection. As I jerked my hand up and down the length, I groaned as images of Caterina filled my dirty mind.

She's laid out before me, naked and dripping with need. Her long legs are spread wide as I bury my head between them. I grunt as I imagine the taste.

Slowly, I drag my tongue through her lips, taking my time not only to taste every inch but to drive her wild. I suckle her throbbing nub into my mouth as her thighs tremble against my ears. "Please, Callum," she whines as I drive her to the brink.

"Say it," I command.

With a whimper, she shakes her head. "Say it, Kitten, or I'll stop eating your sweet pussy."

Her dark eyes shimmer with lust as she stares down at me. "Fuck me, Callum. Fuck me *hard*."

I replace my tongue at her entrance with my cock. I slam into her, causing both of us to groan with pleasure. Her arms encircle my neck as her nipples pebble against my chest. I drive into her over and over again. Our pants of pleasure and the sound of my balls slapping against her ass echo through the room.

My hand grasps her throat, squeezing gently. "I'm coming!" she cries before she arches her back off the bed. As my hips piston faster, my release explodes. Dipping my head, I bite into Caterina's neck, eliciting a moan. I mark her both inside and out.

In the shower, I barked out a cry as my cock jerked, and I came in a rush, sending ropes of cum across the glass shower wall.

When I finished coming, I grunted in disgust that at thirty-one fucking years old, I'd jerked off in the shower to my future wife. Considering Caterina's virginal state and her continued loathing, I had a terrible suspicion I would be jerking off daily for the foreseeable future.

After drying off and throwing on a pair of briefs, I fell into bed and an exhausted sleep.

My sleep was plagued with dreams of Caterina. Some were illicit while others were darker where I was having to save her from an unknown assailant. Just before I could take a bullet for her, I seized up in bed with my heart beating out of my chest.

As I tried regulating my breathing, I slowly shook my head. I had never dreamed about giving my life for a woman. Even when everything had happened with my father and Maeve, I had never dreamed of her. I couldn't begin to imagine after just a few short days, why I would be dreaming of giving my life for this one.

Part of me argued that the dream was somewhat predictable. In my line of work, women and children were innocents who were to be protected at all costs.

As my future wife, I would be expected to lay my life down for Caterina. Even though she drove me insane, I wouldn't allow anything bad to happen to her.

Although my still jet-lagged body called for more rest, I rose out of bed with the sun. After a quick shower and shave, I threw on some clothes and headed downstairs. Nera was at the stove cooking up some eggs. At her questioning look, I shook my head.

After pouring a cup of coffee, I bypassed Quinn and Kellan at the table. I didn't bother asking where Dare was. He'd taken two bodyguards and gone into town last night. I was sure he was waking up in the local hotel next to a piece of ass.

Truthfully, when he'd texted me after I'd gone to bed, I'd been tempted to join him. Caterina had me wound so tight, and I needed relief that didn't involve jerking off in the shower. While it had been over a week since I'd last fucked, I didn't know how long of a dry spell lay ahead of me before Caterina consented to consummate our marriage.

There was a part of me that said it didn't matter when I fucked my wife. Just because we were married, I didn't have to be faithful. My father sure as hell hadn't. The only man I'd ever witnessed be faithful to his wife was Seamus.

I caught sight of him standing on the terrace watching the sun rise. From his stance, I knew something was weighing on him. When I stepped outside, he turned around.

"*Buongiorno,*" he pronounced with a smile.

"Don't you mean *maidin mhaith?*" I countered.

"I thought I'd adhere to the old adage when in Rome. Or I suppose I should say Sicily," he quipped.

"I prefer Irish, thank you very much."

"Since your wife is Italian, I would think you should learn the language."

I scowled around the mouth of my cup. "Caterina is Italian-American, and she speaks perfect English."

"It might come in handy to learn a little." He gave me a knowing look. "Especially when she's conversing with her brothers."

"Is this your way of telling me you've signed me up for an Italian language course?"

He grinned. "A private tutor would be more beneficial."

"Is she young and sexy?"

"*He* is middle-aged and balding."

"You're no fun," I grumbled.

"When we get back to Boston, you'll have a very *young* and very *sexy* wife at home, so you won't need an attractive tutor."

Poison and Wine

"An attractive tutor might be a lot more accommodating than my virgin bride."

"It can be very pleasurable breaking them in," Seamus argued with a gleam in his eye.

Groaning, I swept my hand over my face. "Can we not allude to your sex life, you dirty old bastard?"

Seamus chuckled. "Once again, I'm only forty-five. You act like I'm on a walker and wearing adult diapers."

Since my cock didn't want me focusing on breaking in Caterina, I decided to change the subject. "Did you have something to tell me besides the fact I'm about to learn Italian?"

"After the initial trouble of finding a local trustworthy priest, I finally resorted to flying one in from Belfast."

"Which one?"

"Leahey from St. Benedicts."

"I suppose he'll do."

"In the end, I think one of our own will be better. That way we don't have to worry about anything being lost in translation with a Sicilian one."

"That makes sense."

"When will he arrive?"

"On the eleven a.m. plane. I'm sending Quinn with a bodyguard to collect him."

I chuckled. "That's quite a message sending the family enforcer."

"While Leahy's proven he's trustworthy, it never hurts to give a reminder."

With Leahy arriving, the proverbial noose tightened around my neck. "So today is my wedding day?"

"Aye. And a lovely one at that."

"It might as well be storming," I grumbled.

Shaking his head, Seamus countered, "It's not as bad as all that."

"And it's still not too late for you to marry her."

"She's meant for you, Callum."

"We can barely stand each other."

"You can't fault her for fighting you like a caged animal. The poor girl was spirited away in the night and taken away from everything she knew. She's also coming to grips with the fact she's about to be married to a man she doesn't know."

"Even when I try to make sacrifices, she fights me every step of the way. Like last night, I made a bargain with her to go to university and to have a career. I even promised not to marry off any daughters we had. But was that enough for her? Feck no."

"Be patient with her."

I sucked in a sharp breath. "She tests my patience with every breath she takes."

Seamus laughed. "Beautiful women tend to do that."

"Then I wish she was ugly as gobshite."

"You lie. You'd have my arse if I'd brokered you an ugly bride."

I laughed. "I suppose you're right." Glancing over my shoulder, I eyed Caterina's bedroom window. "I guess I better go tell her the priest is coming."

"It's still early. Let her sleep."

"You're no better than my brothers when it comes to her." With an angry shake of my head, I replied, "Too fucking soft."

"Everyone needs a soft place to fall." He shot me a pointed look. "Perhaps once you're wed, you can be that person for her."

"There's not much softness about me, Seamus."

"Even among the hardest of men, you'll find a tenderness that they only show to the woman they love."

"That sure as hell wasn't something my father would've believed."

Seamus's expression darkened. "You should never want to align yourself with your father's beliefs. He made cruelty his religion and worshiped at an altar of sadistic malice. When I think of what he did to his own daughter..." Seamus swallowed hard. "The worst parts of hell aren't good enough for him."

"Aye, I agree."

"Thankfully, you aren't him, Callum."

"I sure as shite don't want to be."

"Then open your mind and your heart to Caterina."

I scrubbed my eyes with a grunt. "Why is this love bullshit worse than fighting the Russians or the Triad?"

"Because matters of the heart are always infinitely more painful than the physical ones."

"Tell that to my thigh."

"You're a fecking lost cause," Seamus grumbled.

I held up my hands. "Fine. I'll try, okay? Will that make you happy, old man?"

"I'm only fifteen years older than you."

"But you look at least forty years older than me."

"You know if I dragged you over the side of this terrace, my life would be a lot easier."

"Dream on."

Seamus chuckled. "Is there anything you'd like me to do around here before the ceremony?"

It shouldn't have surprised me that our wedding would take place at the house. We were trying to keep a low profile.

"Considering her faith, I'm sure Caterina will be disappointed not to be married in a church."

"Then find some ways to make it up to her."

I grimaced. "You want me to be romantic?"

"Don't tell me you're incapable of wooing your future bride?"

"I can woo the fucking nun's knickers right off of her." I raised my brow at him. "Have you ever known me not to have any woman I wanted?"

"Romance and lust are two very different things."

"Give me pure and unadulterated lust any day."

"It's not going to work with your untouched bride."

Since I was never one to stand down from a challenge, I cocked my head at Seamus. "You want romance? I'll give you fucking romance. Stand back and watch the master work.

With a chuckle, Seamus replied, "Oh, I look forward to this."

After the three phone calls with Guido translating and almost an hour spent in one of the shops, I'd gone farther for Caterina than I had for any other woman outside Mam and Maeve. I suppose I'd expected to feel differently about what I'd done. Like I would be repulsed by my actions.

If my father were still alive, I'm sure he would've had something to say about it. He'd probably use his hands to express his disgust.

But in the end, a peculiar sense of pride filled me. I hadn't backed down when Seamus had called me out for being unromantic. Even though it was about proving a point to him, there was also a part of me that wanted to prove it to Caterina.

To show her I was more than just the mafia criminal who'd kidnapped her. Although it was still too soon, I wanted her to want me. I wanted her to reach a point where she could be grateful I'd swooped in to save her from a life she wasn't truly destined for.

When I returned home with an enormous white garment bag thrown over my shoulder, Quinn and Dare exchanged curious glances.

"What the fuck is that?" Quinn questioned.

"None of your damn business."

Quinn tilted his head. "While it looks like a bodybag, I can't imagine anyone choosing white ones."

"It's not a fecking bodybag."

Dare flashed Quinn a grin. "Ooh, it's something for Sister Sassy I'd wager."

With a roll of my eyes, I replied, "Stop calling her that."

"I will if you'll tell me what's in the bag."

Kellan snorted. "You're completely daft if you don't know what that is."

"Okay, smartass. Enlighten me."

Crossing his arms over his chest, my shit of a little brother replied, "It's a wedding dress."

Both Quinn and Dare's jaws unhinged at his comment. "You actually bought her a dress?" Quinn asked.

At the same time, Dare questioned, "You went to a wedding dress shop?"

"They're called bridal shops," Kellan corrected.

"Have you lost your balls along with your self-respect," Dare asked Kellan.

"Fuck off," Kellan replied.

"Why don't you *all* fuck off!" I growled.

Dare slowly shook his head back and forth. "I never thought I'd live to see the day you'd do something so...."

Taking a step towards him, I growled, "What?"

"Nice," Dare replied.

"Thoughtful," Kellan added.

"Decent," Quinn said.

"Are you all insinuating I'm an arsehole?"

Quinn cocked his brows at me. "When it comes to women? Absolutely."

"Suck my cock," I spat, as I started for the stairs.

"It's a good thing, Callum," Kellan argued.

Ignoring him, I'd gotten halfway to the landing when he added, "It's good because it means you aren't him."

I froze.

Although I shared everything with my brothers, I'd never shared with them my fear of becoming my father. Deep down, I knew it was an unspoken fear for all of us.

While I welcomed the bloodlust and venom of my father's DNA

when it came to running the family, I never, ever wanted to be him when it came to women. My father was incapable of love, and I didn't want to ever be imprisoned by being unable to give or receive love. I didn't want that to be my legacy.

After taking the stairs two at a time, I made it to Caterina's door and knocked with my free hand. "Who is it?"

"It's me, Kitten."

I heard the rustling of bed covers before feet scurried across the hardwood floor. When she threw the door open, I was surprised to find she hadn't put a robe over her nightgown.

It only came halfway down her thighs and showed off her exquisitely long legs. Not to mention the thin straps and plunging neckline gave me an excellent view of her tits, which caused me to groan inwardly.

When she cleared her throat, I drew my eyes up to hers. "Good morning," I pronounced.

With a suspicious look, she replied, "Good morning."

"I wanted to let you know the priest will be here at noon."

Caterina's expression grew grim. "Oh, I see," she murmured.

I tried not to let it bother me that she was so visibly disappointed that her days as a single woman were up. I wouldn't allow my ego to be bruised over such things. While she might not want to be my wife today, there would come a time very soon that she would be grateful. Especially after all I'd bartered with her.

"My apologies for being the bearer of such bad news," I mused.

She scowled at me. "It's not like I didn't know it was going to happen."

"You just hoped for more time."

"Maybe." Crossing her arms over her ample chest, she asked, "What about the contract?"

"You still don't trust me, do you?"

"Call me jaded, but no."

"It's downstairs. We have to sign it together with witnesses."

"Let me throw on my robe, and we can do it right now."

Poison and Wine

With a smirk, I said, "Look at you being all eager to join forces with me."

"My only eagerness is in ensuring you don't try to deny what you've promised."

It was then she appeared to notice the white garment bag in my arms. "What's that?"

"Your wedding dress."

Her eyes bulged. "Seriously?"

"You didn't expect to get married in yoga pants in a t-shirt, did you?" I teasingly asked.

"Actually, I hadn't given it much thought."

"I'm sorry you couldn't pick it out for yourself, but we couldn't run the risk of you being seen." When she remained staring at the bag, I said, "Here let me bring it inside for you."

She stepped out of the way before watching wordlessly as I strode across the bedroom to the closet. After I had hung it from the door, I unzipped the bag.

"Want a little peek?"

Caterina stared between me and the dress. I could only imagine the thoughts swirling in her head. I knew a part of her wanted to see the dress very much, but another railed against anything that was a symbol of what she was being forced into.

"Don't tell me you're not even slightly curious about what it looks like?"

"I think it's more fear than curiosity driving my thoughts at the moment."

She then scooted me out of the way. After she worked the dress out of the bag, she gasped at the sight of yards of creamy white satin on display.

"Oh, my," she murmured.

"Does that mean you like it?"

"It's exquisite."

"Really?"

She nodded her head before staring at me in almost disbelief. "It's exactly what I would've picked, and everything I would have wanted in a wedding dress."

She frowned. I knew she had to be angry with herself for admitting that. "I'll make sure to write a thank you note for the sales lady who picked this out."

"I didn't have a saleslady pick it out."

Her brows furrowed. "Then who—"

"*I* picked it out."

Caterina's eyes grew comically wide while her perfect red lips formed an "o" of surprise. After a few moments of staring at me, she questioned, "*You* picked out a wedding dress?"

"Aye." At her continued disbelief, I said, "What about me makes you think I would be incapable of picking a dress for my future wife?"

"I would think the part where you're an Irish mobster."

I barked out a laugh at her summation. "I suppose men like me don't often patronize bridal shops."

Caterina smiled. "I would've given anything to be a fly on the wall to see the expressions of the workers when you walked in."

"I think they already knew I was a commanding presence considering I paid to close the shop just for me."

Her jaw jutted stubbornly forward. "Did it ever escape your mind that perhaps *I* would've liked to pick out my own dress?"

"Sorry, love, but like I told you before, we couldn't run the risk of you being seen in the village."

"I could've worn a disguise," she protested.

Planting my hands to my hips, I bellowed, "Maybe you should just be thankful I got you an arsing dress at all."

Instead of cowering at my tone, Caterina merely rolled her eyes. "Don't get your knickers in a twist."

"Since when do you say knickers?"

Jerking her chin up defiantly, she countered, "Since I'm going to be an Irishman's wife."

With a smirk, I replied, "Perhaps I'll have to teach you Irish."

Poison and Wine

"Are you sure? Once you teach me, then I'll know what you're saying to your brothers about me."

I snorted. "I'm sure."

After nibbling her bottom lip for a moment, she said, "Thank you for the dress, Callum."

"You're welcome." With a grimace, I said, "Now that I think about it, I probably shouldn't have delivered it to you myself."

"Why not?"

Scratching the back of my neck, I replied, "You know, because it's bad luck on account of seeing you before the wedding."

A laugh bubbled from her lips, which hit me straight below the belt. Fuck me if I didn't love the way her laughter sounded. She so rarely did it in my presence.

"After kidnapping me from a religious order, are you really worried about luck today, Callum?"

"A real man makes his own luck, which is why I'm marrying you." When the amusement started to fade from her eyes, I added, "But I want our union to be blessed."

"You just want me not to drive you crazy."

I shot her a cheeky grin. "Only in the bedroom will I appreciate that, love."

"As if anything is going to happen between us in the bedroom," she shot back.

"Already talking like a true wife," I replied with a wink.

"I'm sure I'll feel more like one when I put on this dress," she lamented.

As she ran her fingers over the satin, I said, "I suppose in the end, it only matters that I haven't seen you in the dress yet."

"That's probably right." After she tore her attention away from it, she motioned her hand to my side. "What's in the bag?"

"Oh, the stuff to make your face up with."

"Cosmetics," she replied with a slight smile.

"Aye, that's what the woman called them."

I handed the bag over to her. "I know you probably weren't

allowed to wear any in the order, but I thought you might like to now."

She cocked her brows at me. "Are you sure that it isn't you who would like me to wear it?"

I threw up my hands. "I could give a shite less if you wear any of it. I think you're the most stunning woman I've ever met just as you fucking are."

My compliment sent pink streaking across Caterina's cheeks. "Thanks," she murmured.

"You're welcome, Kitten."

After gazing back into the bag, her expression turned suddenly sheepish. "The truth is I adore makeup. Before I entered the order, I was ridiculously vain, and I had drawers upon drawers of lipsticks, mascara, and eyeliner."

It was hard to imagine her being that Caterina. The woman before me didn't appear to have a vain bone in her body. "I'm glad I got some for you."

When she pulled out a bottle of what the saleslady had called foundation, her brows rose. "But how did you—"

"I showed the lady a picture of you. She said if the colors weren't right we could bring them back."

After turning over a few of the tubes and boxes in her hands, Caterina smiled at me. "I think they'll work just fine."

With a nod, I replied, "Good. I'm glad to hear it."

After setting the bag down on the dresser, Caterina turned her attention back to the dress. As she nibbled on her lip, I knew there was something she dared not ask. But there was nothing to stop me from bringing it up.

"While I might've picked out the dress, the saleslady got together the intimates you would need."

Instead of seeming grateful that I hadn't been pawing through her potential underwear, she had the nerve to appear angry with me. "Was there something wrong with that?"

"You seriously have to ask if there's something wrong with getting me lingerie?"

"I didn't order you any bleedin' lingerie."

"You said you did."

When I realized what she meant, I grunted and rolled my gaze to the ceiling. "Christ, woman, I meant the right bra and knickers to wear with the blasted dress."

Caterina blinked at me in surprise. "Oh," she murmured.

"That's all you have to say after biting my head off?"

"What would you have me say?"

"Maybe that you're sorry for implying that I was some randy bastard who wanted you showing your tits and ass off in some scraps of lace."

With a scowl, she replied, "Fine. I'm sorry for jumping to conclusions."

"Don't act like it killed you to apologize."

"And you shouldn't get used to it because I won't be doing it again."

Fucking hell, this woman was going to be the death of me. She had me half-mast and wanting to beat the hell out of someone.

Placing my hands in front of my bulge, I barked out, "Be ready and downstairs at noon!"

I'd stalked halfway back to the door when her voice stopped me. "Um, I'll need someone to help me get dressed."

When I whirled around ready to blast her for being a spoiled princess, she held her hands up. "It's not that I'm helpless. The back of the dress has a lot of buttons."

Fuck me. The last thing I needed to do was to be anywhere near Caterina when she was half naked. Just me thinking about her exposed breasts and pussy was making me even harder than before.

With me out of the count, I realized there was no way in hell I would allow any of my brothers, not even Saint Kellan, to be near her.

"Since she's the only woman in the house, I'll send Nera."

"Thank you."

With a nod, I escaped out of the bedroom and ran into Quinn. "Easy, man, where's the fire?"

Before I could respond, his gaze honed in on the bulge in my pants. His expression darkened. "What were you doing with Caterina for that to happen?"

I rolled my eyes. "Not a fucking thing."

At his skeptical look, I threw up my hands. "What do you want me to say? That I'm a masochist who gets off on riling up my future wife? Or that just being in the general vicinity of Caterina makes my cock hard, like a randy teenager?"

Quinn crossed his arms over his chest. "As long as you're not laying a finger on her, then I don't give a shite."

"Just as I promised Caterina, out of honor to Maeve nothing sexually will happen between us until she comes willingly to my bed." At Quinn's nod of approval, I added, "I'm sure my dick will rot off from lack of use before she ever does that."

A chuckle rumbled from Quinn's chest. "Aye, that's a definite possibility."

Chapter Eleven: Caterina

After the last three days, I didn't think there was anything else that could possibly rock me to my core. But Callum delivering me a wedding dress that *he* had handpicked obliterated me.

Every time I thought I had him figured out, he did something else to confuse me. And that confusion led to twinges of feelings I hated myself for.

One minute he could be kind and considerate, and then the next he was an unimaginable bastard. I found myself caught between wanting to wrap my arms around him or smack him. Well, I suppose I had already done that. But I was certainly tempted to do it repeatedly.

Of course with my extremely limited experience with men, I didn't know if this was normal. Did all couples drive each other crazy while simultaneously having moments of enjoyment?

At the same time, I imagined that if it were Kellan or Dare or even Quinn as my groom, it would be different.

After Callum had left me this morning, I'd taken a long and luxurious bath. Then I'd unearthed a somewhat archaic looking curling iron in the back of the closet. Thankfully, it still worked, and I was able to do my hair in flowing waves.

It was the first time in almost three years I'd really done anything to my hair. The prideful part of me reveled in how beautiful it looked.

Disgusted with myself, I turned away from the mirror and started going through the makeup. I'd just finished with everything from mascara and eyeliner to foundation when a knock came at my door.

After exiting the bathroom, I called, "Yes?"

"*Signorina, è Nera. Sono qui per aiutarla.*"

My heartbeat accelerated. Callum had come through and asked her to help me. I opened the door with a smile. "*Grazie, Nera,*" I replied.

I was glad she was the one who was working today. We'd had a nice chat yesterday before I let her have the evening off for me to cook lasagna. It was also nice having someone else to speak Italian with besides the guards.

Nera's eyes widened at the sight of me. "You are a vision."

A nervous laugh bubbled from my lips. "In my bathrobe?"

She giggled and swatted my arm playfully. "Yes, even in your bathrobe."

"Thank you," I motioned for her to come inside the room.

As I went over to get the dress, Nera followed me. When I turned around, she wore an expression of wonder. "What a breathtaking dress," she mused in a low voice.

"Callum has good taste."

Nera swept a hand to her chest. "The boss picked this out?"

"Yes."

"All on his own?" At my nod, she replied, "Oh my."

With a giggle, I said, "Yes, that's exactly what I thought."

She shook her head slowly in disbelief as she took the dress off the hanger. She held it out for me to step into and she asked, "This is an arranged marriage, no?"

"It is." I tentatively placed one foot and then another into the pool of satin. "I only met him three days ago."

Nera murmured something under her breath as she slid the dress up my thighs and over my waist.

"I'm sorry?" I asked.

She peered up at me with a shy smile. "I said he doesn't look at you like it's an arranged marriage."

Her words sent a flutter through my chest. "He can be kind and thoughtful. I'm grateful for that. I suppose it could be much worse."

At the thought of Carmine, I shuddered. "Much, much worse," I whispered.

"And he's awfully handsome," she prompted before waggling her brows.

Warmth flooded my cheeks as I pushed my arms through the sleeves. Even in my limited experience with men, I realized how good-looking Callum was. Just looking at him made me weak in my knees.

"I suppose he is."

"I normally don't like men who aren't Italian, but for him, I could make an exception," she teased.

I laughed. "Hey now, that's my future husband you're talking about."

As she started buttoning up the back, Nera said, "I think it's a good match between you and the boss."

Glancing at her in the mirror, I asked, "But how can you possibly know?"

"I can just tell."

Nibbling my lip, I debated asking her what was on my mind. More than anything in the world, I wished Talia was here with me. I wouldn't have had any problems unburdening myself to her.

When Nera finished with the last button, I decided it was now or never. I didn't know when I'd have another opportunity with a woman I trusted.

"How can the boss and I be a good match if we always fight?"

With a knowing smile, she replied, "The best loves are the ones that are fiery and passionate."

I furrowed my brows at her response. It was hard even fathoming falling in love with Callum. I'd come to accept that I would have to tolerate his presence, but to imagine feeling a deep and abiding love for him was incomprehensible.

After almost three years in the order, I'd given up the notion of being in romantic love with any man.

Nera patted my back. "Don't worry, *cara*. It will all work out."

"I hope so." I squeezed her hands. "Thank you so much for the help. It means so much."

"It was my pleasure." With a sigh, she added, "I'm so sorry that none of your family could be here today, especially your mother."

I gave her a tight smile. The truth was I wished for only my brothers and Talia today. I would've loved to have Rafe walk me down the aisle while Leo and Gianni looked on.

As for my mother, she would've made the day about herself as well as nit-picking every detail. Talia would've been the one with tears shimmering from her eyes while she told me how beautiful I was.

Nera brought me out of my thoughts by saying, "Come. It's time to go."

Chapter Twelve: Callum

A fter eyeing the clock above the mantle, I winced. It was almost noon. From the anxiety overtaking me, it felt like high noon at the OK Corral from the old Westerns our grandfather had watched. In spite of being the best shot in the west figuratively speaking, I somehow felt Caterina was nailing me straight through the heart.

Outfitted in the best suit I'd come to Sicily with, I paced around the living room while inwardly trying to talk myself down from a ledge. The feeling escalated as I glanced down at the contract I clutched in my hand.

The steely conviction that I'd fought Caterina on us being married had begun to wane, and I wondered what the hell was I doing agreeing to this alliance. At the very least, I was marrying a woman outside my nationality.

Worse than that, I'd agreed to let my future wife get an education and to have a career. Both of which were unheard of in mafia circles. I'd even agreed to let her determine the number of our offspring, which also was never, ever done.

My father's evil chuckle echoed in my ear. *I never thought a son of mine would become utterly fanny whipped.*

My father was right. I'd handed my balls on a silver platter to Caterina in exchange for a somewhat peaceful union. But if she was already able to emasculate me this quickly, what the fuck was to happen when we'd been married five or ten years?

Better yet since it appeared she already had me fanny whipped, what was to happen after I actually got a taste of said fanny? Would I hand over everything to her?

As he sat in a chair by the fire, Quinn eyed me curiously. "Are you all right, boyo?"

"I'm fine," I croaked.

He snorted. "From the looks of it, you need to rub another one out."

"Fuck off."

Dare shook his head. "He's not sexually frustrated; he's scared out of his bleedin' mind."

I skidded to a stop in my pacing. "The feck I am."

"Don't lie to us. You're about to piss yer fucking pants at the very thought of marrying Sister Sassy," Dare replied with a grin.

With a growl, I launched myself at him. For the second time in a matter of days, my feelings for Caterina had me fighting Dare. After shoving him against the wall, I brought my hand to his throat.

"I'm not afraid, motherfucker. I don't fear anyone or anything. Least of all a woman."

Although Dare's face began to turn crimson, he chuckled. "You. Fear. Her," he choked out.

Before I could argue that I would end him if he ever said that again, Quinn and Kellan came charging over and shoved me away. "What the hell is your problem?" Quinn questioned me.

While I said, "His fucking mouth!" Dare coughed out, "Nerves." The bastard then had the nerve to wink at me.

"You're full of shite, mate," I shot back.

A throat cleared above our heads. Whirling around, my gaze took in Caterina standing at the top of the stairs.

Fucking hell.

She was an angelic vision in her white dress.

Her dark hair cascaded in waves over her shoulders. Although she hadn't been professionally fitted for the dress, the satin bodice clung to her breasts and her waist like a second skin.

She was everything I could've ever wanted in a bride and so much more. And I wasn't just speaking of her physical beauty. Although her strength was often a thorn in my side, I still could admire her for it. It was the same steely reserve my mam possessed, and without it, she couldn't have endured the demands of a clan leader's wife.

As she slowly descended the stairs, my feet moved forward of their own volition. It was as if I couldn't wait to touch her to ensure she was real and not just some dream. At that moment, I wasn't a man ensuring an alliance to further my family's standing. I was a man who was truly enthralled by a woman for the first time in my fucking life.

Instead of being alarmed by my feelings—ones my father would have considered weak—I embraced them. When she met me at the bottom of the stairs, my hand automatically went to her cheek.

"You are stunning," I pronounced.

As red tinged her cheeks, she bit down on her full, lower lip. "Thank you, Callum."

"It is me who should be giving thanks that yer to be mine."

When my words about possession caused a momentary flash of

anger in her dark eyes, I shook my head. "Don't fight it, Kitten. You're mine, and I'm yours. We'll possess each other until our last breaths."

"You'll never own me," she protested.

I frowned at her. "Why is it so wrong for me to be possessive of you? To be so devoted to you that I would threaten to maim or murder another man for simply looking at you."

She shook her head. "But I don't want to be possessed or owned. That's not who I am."

"Don't be so sure about that, Kitten. It's only been a few days, but you're well on your way to owning me. I've done more and gone farther for you than I have for any other woman."

When triumph tinged her expression, I shot her a shark-like smile. "In the same token, one might say you've done more and gone father for me than any other man."

"That's only because I wanted to make the best of this situation."

"Exactly." Taking her hand in mine, I led her over to my brothers. They stared at Caterina in wide-eyed reverence. "Isn't my bride stunning?"

"Aye," Dare replied while Quinn and Kellan merely bobbed their heads in agreement.

She smiled genuinely at them. "I look forward to having you as my brothers."

"You'll never want or need for anything, lass," Quinn proclaimed.

Tilting her head, she teasingly asked, "Does that mean you'll knock Callum around for me every once in a while?"

As my brothers chuckled, I gritted out, "Dream on."

Caterina grinned. "You can't blame me for trying."

"Come, let's meet the priest and get this show on the road," I instructed.

After she slipped her hand in mine, I began leading her over to the terrace doors. Although I hated myself for it, I couldn't stop the racing of my heart. The rational side of me argued it was only normal since I was about to bind myself to a woman I barely knew while vowing to love, honor, and keep her until death parted us.

Of course, in my line of work that wasn't always that long.

Motioning to the glass doors, I explained, "I thought it might be nicer to have the ceremony out here."

At the sight of the newly decorated terrace, her mouth gaped open in surprise. Under my directions, the stone patio and railing overflowed with vibrant wildflowers. The path to the makeshift altar was littered in red and pink rose petals.

The self-respecting mafia boss within me couldn't believe I'd given such ridiculous orders. I commanded men to kill and torture not festoon fecking altars with flowers.

If any of my enemies got wind of such a thing, I'd be fighting to keep my territory. I'd even gone so far as to lie to my brothers that it was Seamus's idea.

All the regret faded when Caterina stared up at me with a beaming smile. "It's beautiful."

"It's all for you."

Eyeing me skeptically, she asked, "You really did all of this for me?"

Nodding, I replied, "I knew that with your faith, you would be disappointed not to be married in a church, so I tried to make up for it."

Caterina's expression softened. "That's very kind of you, Callum."

"You're welcome."

At the makeshift altar, Seamus stood with Father Leahy. At Caterina's surprised expression, I could only imagine she wasn't expecting a very Irish looking priest with red hair that was practically orange and bright blue eyes.

Turning to me, she asked, "Where did he come from?"

"You know as well as I do that Sicilians can have red hair and blue eyes."

"Not hair like that," she huffed.

I laughed. "Aye, lass, you're right. After the initial trouble of finding a trustworthy priest, Seamus finally resorted to flying one in from Belfast this morning."

I knew she didn't bother arguing with me that not all priests were trustworthy. She knew as well as I did that crooked priests were often bought by mafia families.

At the sight of us in the doorway, Seamus and the priest ceased talking.

Seamus walked over to us. "You look lovely, Caterina," he said with a smile.

"Thank you, Mr. Kavanaugh."

He shook his head. "Please call me, Seamus. I won't be pretentious in asking you to call me uncle, but I certainly hope you will look at me as one."

"I would like that," she replied. I couldn't hide my surprise at her words to him. Especially after the way she'd spoken to him on her first day.

Motioning to the table, I said, "I have the contract for you."

An appreciative look filled her eyes as she made her way over. Once she'd read through the points she'd requested, she picked up the pen. "Once again, I can't thank you enough for doing this, Callum."

"You're welcome."

Intensity burned in her dark eyes. "I'll make sure my father and brothers understand how generous you've been, so they can do the same."

Considering the fire that burned within her, I didn't believe for a second she was capable of keeping her word of peace. But I wouldn't let her know that. I would allow her to think she had scored a major victory when in truth,

I knew it was me who had won.

With her in school and having a career, her mind would be occupied to where she wouldn't be sniffing around my business. She wouldn't be sitting around wondering where I was and nagging me to be home with her.

"I would appreciate that."

After clearing his throat, the priest asked, "Since we're all assembled, shall we get started?"

I nodded. "We're ready." Squeezing her hand, I asked, "Aren't we, Kitten?"

"As ready as I'll ever be."

And I knew exactly how she felt.

Chapter Thirteen: Caterina

As Callum and I took our places before the priest, my heart thrummed wildly in my chest. When I glanced over my shoulder at Seamus and Callum's brothers, they gave me reassuring smiles.

It did little to steady my racing pulse.

The logical side of my mind tried reasoning that marrying Callum wasn't the end of the world. It wasn't like he was holding a gun to my head, or he'd beaten me into submission.

"Since this isn't occurring in a church or before a large congregation, I'm going to cut down the vows to a minimum," Father Leahy pronounced.

"As long as it's still considered a true Catholic wedding," Callum replied.

"Of course." Father Leahy then cleared his throat. "Callum and Caterina have you come here to enter into marriage without coercion, freely and wholeheartedly?"

At Father Leahy's question, I fought to breathe.

I certainly wasn't entering into this bond without coercion or freely. Despite the promises Callum made to entice me into marriage, I couldn't overlook that I was being forced against my will.

My attention was brought back into the moment by Callum reaching for my hand. His calloused fingers trailed over mine.

Cutting his eyes to me, Callum replied, "I have."

Since I knew it wasn't worth fighting, I quickly murmured, "I have."

When I dared a peek at Callum, he smirked back at me. "I'm surprised you managed to keep yer trap shut, Kitten," he whispered.

"As if it would do any good," I shot back.

Nodding, Father Leahy continued. "Are you prepared, as you follow the path of marriage, to love and honor each other for as long as you both shall live?"

As Callum and I both echoed, "I am," I wondered what thoughts were circling through his mind at that moment.

Was he conflicted about whether he could ever love me? Did he feel the weight of the words 'as long as you both shall live' as heavily as I did?

When I stared curiously into his blue eyes, I only saw conviction, not confusion.

I guess I shouldn't have been surprised. Callum was a man. Marriage didn't mean the same thing for him as it did for me. He wouldn't be imprisoned by his vows the same way I would.

Father Leahy's words brought me back into the moment. "Are you prepared to accept children lovingly from God and to bring them up according to the law of Christ and his Church?" Father Leahy questioned.

Poison and Wine

Warmth flooded my cheeks at the thought of what bearing children entailed. "I am," I squeaked as Callum also answered. I was thankful for the small mercy that Callum was a young, very attractive man. The thought of his hands on my body was actually enticing.

Unlike Carmine, he would never force me, and when we finally consummated the marriage, he would be gentle when it came to taking my virginity.

"Since it is your intention to enter the covenant of Holy Matrimony, join your right hands, and declare your consent before God and his Church," Father Leahy instructed.

He stared down at our hands that were already joined. "Right. Let us continue on then."

When it was time for Callum to repeat the vows, my breath hitched. In a clear, resounding voice, he stated, "I, Callum Kavanaugh, take you, Caterina Neretti, to be my wife. I promise to be faithful to you, in good times and in bad, in sickness and in health, to love you and to honor you all the days of my life."

Swallowing hard, my frantic gaze darted between Father Leahy and Callum.

This was truly it.

There was no going back now.

Once I said the words, I'd be bound to Callum for life. Regardless of what man's laws could annul, I would be his wife in God's eyes.

With the enormity of the moment bearing down on me, I swayed on my feet. Callum dropped his hand from mine to slip his arm around my waist to steady me.

His head dipped for his lips to graze my ear. "Are you all right?"

"Yes," I whispered. I peered up into his questioning eyes. "I'm sorry."

He gave me a terse nod. I don't know how much time passed before I could find my voice again. "Yes, please, continue."

Father Leahy dabbed his handkerchief to his forehead. "Right, yes. Repeat after me, I, Caterina Neretti, take you, Callum Kavanaugh, to be my husband. I promise to be faithful to you, in good times and in bad, in sickness and in health, to love you, to honor you, and to obey you all the days of my life."

I jerked out of Callum's grasp. "No."

"Excuse me?" Father Leahy questioned as Callum's jaw clenched.

I shook my head. "I won't say I'll obey."

A low growl came from Callum. "Say the damn vow, Caterina."

"If you like it so much, you say it."

"Stop acting like a petulant child."

"These are archaic vows that no one uses anymore. I sure haven't heard them in any Italian ceremonies."

Father Leahy opened his mouth to protest, but I held my hand up. "I took one oath to obey God, and that's the only one I'm keeping."

Glaring at Callum, I said, "I'm not one of your men to command. I'll be your wife, but I expect to be your equal."

Jerking his hand through his dark hair, Callum paced around the altar. He jabbed a finger at Seamus. "You better be right about this marriage. It sure as hell better bring us everything and more for me to have to put up with her."

Seamus merely laughed. "Oh, boyo, you're in for a wild ride." At my indignant glare, he appeared momentarily sheepish. "My apologies, Caterina."

"All can be forgiven, *Uncle* Seamus, if you tell him to remove obey," I countered sweetly.

"All right, lass."

He placed a hand on Callum's shoulder. "I don't think it will hurt anything if we omit the obey."

Callum glowered at Seamus. "You should back your leader."

"I didn't have Elena say to obey in our vows, so why should you?"

"I'll never win with you when it comes to her, will I?"

"It's nothing personal. It's about keeping our alliance happy."

Callum's silence was long and calculated. After a long exhale, he nodded at Father Leahy. "Fine. Let's get on with it."

I couldn't hide the triumphant smile that lit up my face. Without prompting from Father Leahy, I recited, "I, Caterina Neretti, take you, Callum Kavanaugh, to be my husband. I promise to be faithful to you, in good times and in bad, in sickness and in health, to love you, and to honor you all the days of my life."

Father Leahy, who was beyond rattled by all that had transpired, stared at me for a moment before shaking his head. "May the Lord in his kindness strengthen the consent you have declared before the Church and graciously bring to fulfillment his blessings within you. What God has joined, let no one put asunder."

As he began to bless the rings, Callum continued glowering at me. When I glanced down, I gasped.

An enormous diamond glittered up at me while my wedding band sparkled with diamonds, rubies, and emeralds.

When I stared up at him in surprise, he said, "I chose the emeralds for Ireland, and the rubies for Italy."

My heartbeat accelerated at his admission. I couldn't believe he had done something so thoughtful. How was it possible such a brutal and heartless man could be so endearing?

"It's stunning."

He eyed me warily as if any moment I had the ability to make him go off again. "I'm glad you like it."

Although I shouldn't have, a feeling of regret entered me. "I'm sorry I don't have anything meaningful about your band."

Surprise filled his expression at my admission. "It doesn't matter."

After sliding the ring down his finger, I repeated Father Leahy's words. When I finished, he said, "With the power vested in me, I pronounce you husband and wife."

Beads of sweat glistened on his forehead. From his reaction, I'm sure he was as glad the ceremony was over as I was.

"I think you forgot a part, Father," Callum remarked.

Although Callum was officially my husband and had held up the promise I'd asked of him, I still wasn't ready to kiss him. I wasn't ready for any physical aspect of our marriage.

At what must've been my look of horror, Callum said, "I'm sorry, Kitten, but I think for all the bullshit you've put me through, I at least deserve a kiss."

A squeak of alarm escaped my lips as Callum's hands shot out to grip my waist. While my first instinct was to push him away, I froze under the intimate feeling of his hands on me. When he dragged me against him, my senses became overwhelmed by the nearness of him.

The woodsy smell of his cologne that held an aura of power.

The lust burning in his blue eyes.

The strength of his arms around my waist.

To my surprise, he didn't slam his lips to mine and take what he was owed. He brought his hands to cup my face. With his thumbs feathering along my jawline, Callum tenderly brushed his lips against mine.

At first, fear froze me. I'd only had one other man kiss me, and it had been hurried and clumsy. But Callum wasn't an inexperienced teenager.

He was a man who exuded sexual prowess.

After a few seconds of tenderness, he crushed his lips to mine. A pleasant jolt hummed through my body at the feeling of his mouth on mine. When Callum thrust his tongue into my mouth, my fear short-circuited into desire, sending a shudder through my body.

My arms, which had been frozen at my side, encircled his waist. As Callum's tongue swirled along with mine, I gripped the back of his suit jacket, tugging him closer against me.

This surge of desire and intense emotion at the feel of his kiss was extremely pleasurable. I had no idea it would be like this. That I could enjoy kissing Callum.

As our tongues battled against each other, the heat building between my legs turned into an inferno. I hadn't desired a man sexually since I entered the order.

But I did now.

Even though he had kidnapped me and forced me into marriage, I wanted Callum.

I wanted his fingers and tongue on my body.

I wanted his cock buried inside me.

I wanted him to claim every part of me.

The sound of whistling and appreciative male laughter broke through the spell, dousing whatever desire I'd felt. I pulled my arms away from Callum's back and brought them to his chest. As I tore my lips from his, I shoved him away.

At the sight of his cocky smirk, my fingers itched to slap him. His arrogance was not what I wanted to see after we'd shared such an intimate moment. I wanted what I was feeling to be reflected in his face.

"Did my lips deceive me, or were you kissing me back just now?" he teased.

My reaction frustrated me both with myself and him. Since I didn't want to give him any satisfaction, I refused to respond.

With his lips next to my ear, he added, "Since I had you practically purring from just a kiss, Kitten, I can't wait to see what you do when I put my mouth on your pussy."

"Don't flatter yourself, pig."

"You know you liked that kiss."

He jerked his thumb at Seamus and his brothers. "Hell, even *they* know you liked that kiss."

Embarrassment overwhelmed me at the thought of the others witnessing our kiss. Although part of me wanted to sprint inside to escape the humiliation, I held my ground. "Can we please sign the registry and be done with this?"

"Of course, Kitten." With a wink, Callum added, "After a kiss like that, I'm at your mercy for the rest of the day."

Chapter Fourteen: Caterina

With both trepidation and a peculiar sense of anticipation, I watched as the ink dried on the marriage license bearing both Callum's and my names.

When I tore my gaze from the document to Callum's, he gave me a genuine smile. "Ready to go home?"

I knew he referred to Boston, not New York. After I'd joined the order, New York was no longer home for me. It possessed too many bad memories as well as monsters who could hurt me.

For the second time that day, I repeated, "Ready as I'll ever be."

"Go get changed. Nera and the guards have been packing up for us. We'll leave in the next hour or two."

I nodded before heading up the stairs. When I got into the bedroom, Nera was closing a suitcase that Callum must've purchased for me.

At my appearance in the doorway, she smiled. "I left out a dress and a pair of shoes for you."

"Apparently my new husband likes me in dresses since that's all he bought for me," I mused.

"The boss said to buy them because he wasn't sure if you'd been allowed to wear pants for a long time."

She gave me a knowing look. "He wanted to make sure you were comfortable."

"That was kind of him," I replied softly.

Once again, it was hard imagining the man who had kidnapped me and forced me into marriage could be thoughtful and compassionate. As much as I hated to admit it, he'd been more considerate than cruel.

"It was."

Turning my back to her, I asked, "Would you do me the honors again?"

"It would be my pleasure."

Just as Nera started with the first button, Callum burst through the door. At my sharp intake of breath, he barked, "We have to go. Now!"

"What's happened?"

"Your father and some of his Sicilian relatives are on the way."

As my eyes widened, Nera's hand came over her mouth. "Are my brothers with my father?" I asked.

"No. They're in Palermo."

That simple fact told me everything I needed to know about what awaited me should my father catch us. While I rushed to the doorway, Callum grabbed my luggage off the bed.

Talking directly to me, Nera said, "Tell him I know a way out of town that will buy you some time."

Callum shot a questioning look between me and Nera. "What's she saying?"

"She knows a way for us to get out safely."

His harsh gaze narrowed on Nera. "Do you think we can trust her?"

After translating to Nera, I strode back over to grab her hands in mine. "We can trust you, can't we?"

She nodded. "I have no love for your father's relatives in Sicily. We align with the Malgieri's, and I heard this morning they've aligned with the Kavanaugh's."

"Caterina, now!" Callum barked.

"You'll need to come along with us to show us the way. We don't have time to write anything down."

As Nera chewed on her bottom lip while wringing her hands, I added, "Please. I'll make sure that you and your family are rewarded."

After a quick nod of her head, I grabbed her arm. "She's coming with us."

"Then let's go. Now."

Nera and I hurried out the bedroom door with Callum close on our heels. Considering her age, I felt bad pushing her to go faster down the stairs. But with each step I took, I could feel my father's hot breath on my neck.

An even larger SUV than the one we took from the airport sat waiting right outside the door. Oddly, I couldn't help lamenting all the beautiful flowers it had crushed along the pathway before I refocused on the task at hand. All of the Kavanaugh men were inside the SUV, and they were all armed.

After Nera got into the front seat with the driver, Callum grabbed my arm. "How do I know you two aren't plotting against me?"

"You don't. You're going to have to trust me."

"Don't disappoint me, Kitten."

"I won't."

Callum's hands came to my waist before hoisting me up onto the seat. Once I was in, he slid in beside me. "Drive," he commanded.

Chapter Fifteen: Callum

If there was one thing I despised, it was not being in control of a situation. I didn't like relying on anyone other than my brothers, and sometimes I didn't even want to rely on them. I wanted complete and total control in any situation.

Maybe it was the control freak in me, or maybe it was part of being a leader.

I despised having that control in the hands of a woman I didn't completely trust even less.

Or I suppose I should say *two* women.

When it came to trusting Nera, she claimed to have no love for the Sicilian Neretti's. But she had to know that by aiding us she could face repercussions. As long as she came through for me, I would make sure to have the Malgieri's give her and her family protection.

If she double crossed me, I'd blow her brains out right in front of Caterina to drive home the point. You *never* double-cross a Kavanaugh, especially me.

Deep down, I knew Caterina had more to lose if her father was to capture her. I doubted even a fear of eternal damnation would keep Alessio from forcing another marriage on Caterina just as soon as he could annul ours.

A lesser man—a true bastard—wouldn't have been wasting this time on escape. He would've been forcing himself on Caterina to consummate the marriage to where its legality couldn't possibly be questioned.

While I was a bastard, I would never be that level of a bastard.

With a snarl, I imagined it would've been something my father would've done. But I could never do that. Even if I could, my brothers wouldn't have allowed me to force myself on Caterina.

After one of my soldiers, Fionn, gunned the engine, we sped down the driveway to the main road. Nodding at Nera, I asked Caterina, "Where do we go first?"

After Caterina translated, Nera replied while wildly gesticulating with her hands. "She says to turn right out of the driveway."

Considering it was the opposite direction we usually took upon leaving, I tried not to order against it.

Instead, I nodded at Fionn.

Just as we reached the end of the driveway, a black SUV tore down the road towards us. Before we could get into position, gunfire erupted around us, blowing out the rear window. Both Nera and Caterina screamed as glass shards rained over the backseat.

Grabbing Caterina by the arm, I flung her into the floorboard. "Stay down."

"You could've just told me to move instead of manhandling me!" she shrieked.

Rolling my eyes, I replied, "Stop arguing with me when we're in a fucking gunfight."

"Whatever," she grumbled.

Poison and Wine

I turned in my seat and leaned against the door. After rolling down the window, I leaned out. I sent a hail of gunfire into the bottom of the SUV. While it appeared the outside was bulletproof, the tires weren't.

At the pop of the rubber, I shouted, "Got one!"

"Good. That will buy us some time," Quinn replied, his head buried in our weapons bag.

"This shortcut better do the trick," I replied, as I gave Caterina a pointed look.

"I'm sure it will," she countered.

Although she sounded convinced, I couldn't help noticing how she wrung her hands in her lap and chewed at her bottom lip.

Since we'd been tearing down the tree-lined main road without any further instructions from Nera, I was growing wary. The two-lane country road with rolling grass and emerald fields to the sides reminded me of the ones back home outside of Belfast.

It sure as hell didn't look like we were anywhere near civilization, least of all the airport.

Leaning forward in my seat, I started bringing my gun up from my lap. Just as I was about to point it at Nera's head, she waved her hand at the windshield and began furiously speaking to Caterina.

"Stop!" Caterina shouted.

"What the fuck is the problem?"

While Nera motioned out the window, Caterina replied, "She says to turn here."

"Here?" Fionn and I questioned in disbelief.

"Yes."

"There's not even a fucking road here!" I protested, as I stared at the waist high grass to the right of us.

Although it hadn't rained since the first day we arrived, I had no idea if there was a muddy bog we might get stuck in or God knows what else we might encounter.

At Nera's continued talking, Caterina replied, "She swears it reconnects with a road down the path."

Fionn cocked his brows at me. "We doing this, boss?"

"Fuck," I muttered under my breath. I sure as hell didn't like this. With a final glance at Nera's imploring face, I ordered, "Take the path."

After whipping the steering wheel around, Fionn lurched the SUV off the road and into the grass.

The SUV rocked and rolled over the uneven terrain. As Caterina tried repositioning herself on the floor, we lunged over a bump, which sent her body careening between my open legs.

Her face landed right in my crotch.

Smirking down at her, I replied, "Now's not the time, Kitten."

She jerked away from me. "Bastard," she hissed.

"Such language from a former novice," I tsked.

She scowled at me, causing me to chuckle. Before she could go off on me again, Nera started speaking. Caterina rose up and leaned closer to Nera.

Nodding her head, she said to Fionn, "Take a left past that apple tree. The road we need to take should come into view."

Since it hadn't been me who gave him the order, Fionn glanced at me in the rear-view mirror. "Do what the lass says," I instructed.

Caterina scowled at Fionn before shooting me a look over her shoulder. "Does this mean your men will never listen to me?"

"Aye, it does."

"That's...bullshit!"

The amusement drained out of me. With the stress of the moment bearing down on me and one of my men hanging on to every word, I grabbed her by the arm and yanked her to me.

"You need to remember who you're talking to, Kitten. You also need to remember the world you grew up in for eighteen years. Just like with your father, my men answer *only* to me. Just as you do. The sooner you get that through your thick skull, the easier it will be for all of us."

From her venomous expression, it appeared Caterina wanted to tear into me, but she bit her tongue.

My attention was torn from Caterina at Nera's screech of, "Vedere!"

Although it hadn't been me who gave him the order, he obliged. Just like Nera had said, I saw the road. Even though I knew it would take some time to fix the tire, it didn't stop me from constantly glancing over my shoulder to make sure Alessio wasn't on our tail.

Once we were on the main road, Caterina translated for Nera that we were just a few minutes from the airfield. "Tell her once again how grateful we are and how we will show our gratitude," I said to Caterina.

After hearing Caterina's translation, Nera bobbed her head. "Grazie."

"Prego," I replied.

My gratitude expanded even further when I saw the air field's tower. She hadn't screwed me over.

More than that, my bride hadn't screwed me over.

But I wouldn't fucking admit it. Not now in front of my brothers and Fionn. Only weak leaders admitted they were wrong.

When we wheeled up at the airfield, our jet sat on the tarmac. Normally, it would've been a welcomed sight, but considering the two black SUV's on either side, I knew we weren't out of the woods yet.

"Tell Nera to get down on the floorboard," I commanded as I reloaded my assault rifle.

"*Salire sulla pedana,*" Caterina commanded.

Nodding, Nera shakily unbuckled her seatbelt before slipping onto the floor.

With my rifle reloaded, I turned to Quinn. "What do we have to take them out?"

"A rocket launcher and two grenades."

Caterina gasped. "We've been riding around with all of that weaponry in the car?"

"Among other things," Quinn replied tersely.

After paling slightly, she murmured, "I don't want to know."

Nodding, I pointed at Dare. "You take the second SUV out with the grenades."

Cutting my gaze to Quinn, I instructed, "Use the rocket launcher on the first. Seamus and I will cover you. Then Kellan, while everyone is distracted, I want you to get Caterina on the jet."

With a shake of her head, Caterina held out her hand. "Give me a gun."

"You're kidding me."

Her expression darkened. "I have every right to protect myself."

"You're trembling like a leaf. How the hell do you expect to protect yourself?"

"You know as well as I do I'm a decent shot."

"Kellan and I will be protecting you."

"We're outnumbered. We need all the ammunition and firepower we can get."

"Forget the fact we need all hands on deck. I wouldn't trust you with a gun against me."

She rolled her eyes. "Do you really think after everything we've been through in the last couple of days, especially the last half hour, I would seriously shoot you or one of your brothers?"

Deep down, I knew she wouldn't.

With the parameters of our contract, I was giving Caterina the life she'd dreamed of in spite of being forced to be my wife. At the same time, I wasn't a man who would allow women to defend themselves. As long as I had breath within me, I'd lay down my life for her.

"I'm not risking it."

Crossing her arms over her chest, she huffed, "I'm a good shot."

"We don't have time to argue about this." I turned back to my brothers. "Let's do this."

The moment the SUV doors opened, gunfire erupted on the tarmac. Using the driver side door as a shield, I began rapid firing my rifle. Across from me, Seamus began doing the same thing on the passenger side.

As Quinn and Dare got into position, I nodded at Kellan who had a very reluctant Caterina by the arm. I texted the pilot to taxi the plane slowly down the runway towards our vehicle. Once the jet was in motion, I gave the signal to Quinn and Dare.

The force of the simultaneous explosions jolted me back against the driver's seat, knocking me into Fionn.

Once I repositioned myself, I trained my gun on the SUV to the left. Kellan and Caterina crept out the back and then around to the front of the car. Although Kellan was armed, I held my breath that we'd taken out all the threats.

The fear dwelling within my chest was a surprise. It wasn't directed at Kellan but at Caterina.

It was more than just not wanting anything to happen to her because she was a woman.

It was about the depth of my growing feelings for her.

Turning to Fionn, I said, "Once we're on the plane, you get the hell out of here. Don't bother taking her back to the house. Just get her safely back to Catania."

"Sure thing, boss."

"I'll have Seamus text you flight plans to get you and the others back to Belfast."

As he nodded, I met Nera's terrified eyes, I said, "Grazie."

"Prego," she replied, her voice barely audible over the jet's engine.

I wish I knew how to communicate with her how well I was going to compensate her family. Hopefully, my look of gratitude coupled with my position was enough for the moment.

Without any return fire, I motioned for Seamus to start for the plane. I don't know how the hell my crazy plan had worked, but miraculously it had. The minute I got on the jet, Quinn shut and locked the door for the pilot.

I barely had time to take a seat before we were rocketing down the runway. I would have to thank the pilot for not wasting any time. When I glanced out the window, I knew the answer for the rush.

Alessio's SUV had wheeled up.

Jerking my chin at the window, I said to Caterina, "Your father made it just in time to say goodbye."

She paled. Her legs must've given way because she sank into a seat. "I never thought he would take it this far," she said in a whisper.

"Truth be told, I didn't either."

Tearing my gaze from Caterina's, I eyed Seamus. "Did you?"

He nodded. "This was one of the scenario's I envisioned happening. Obviously, it wasn't the one I was hoping for."

"Somehow I don't think this is all about a father swooping in to save his kidnapped daughter," I said.

Caterina shook her head with a rueful smile. "It's not."

"I suppose the best thing to do is let him cool off while reaching out to Caterina's brothers," I suggested.

"I would agree," Seamus replied.

Once we were safely in the air and had left her father far behind, Caterina finally relaxed.

Or I suppose I should say she relaxed as best she could in her wedding dress that overflowed the seat. She twisted several times while wincing. Since we had a long flight, I hated the thought of her being uncomfortable.

Rising out of my seat, I went over to her. When I took her by the hand and pulled her to her feet, surprise flooded her expression. "What is it?"

"Come to the bedroom with me. We need to get you out of that dress."

Caterina's eyes bulged before she snatched her hand from mine. "E-Excuse me?"

I rolled my eyes. "That wasn't a come-on, Kitten. I was just stating facts."

"Oh, right," she murmured, as pink tinged her cheeks.

With a knowing look, I added, "You're uncomfortable, aren't you?"

"I am."

"Did you seriously expect me to fuck you on this plane with my brothers within earshot?"

The flush crept down her neck. "No, but..."

"But what? You think car chases and explosions get me so hot I would abandon all my honor to ravish you?"

"With my father chasing us, I didn't know." She swallowed hard. "I didn't know what you might *have* to do. You know, to make the marriage more legal."

Bringing my fingers to her chin, I tipped her head up to look at me. "Regardless of whatever bullshit your father pulled, I would never do that. *Ever.*"

After staring at me intently, she nodded her head. "Thank you, Callum."

"Come," I ordered. After grabbing her bag, I then led her into the bedroom off the cabin.

When I closed the door behind us, she jumped. "Easy. I'm only going to unbutton your dress."

The moment my fingers touched the first button Caterina flinched. "Seriously?" I demanded gruffly.

"I'm sorry. It's not like I'm used to men taking my clothes off."

At the illicit picture her words formed in my mind, I groaned.

I wanted to do more than just take her clothes off. After ripping the dress from her body, I wanted to press her down onto the bed.

I wanted to bury my face in her pussy until her need dripped down my chin.

Then I wanted to bury myself inside her slick walls, driving into her over and over until she cried out my name.

"Callum?"

"Huh?"

"Why did you stop?" she questioned softly.

"Sorry. I have a lot on my mind," I muttered as I continued working my way down the row of intricate buttons. "Christ, if I'd known about all these buttons, I would've picked a different dress."

Caterina's soft laughter rippled through me. "I'm glad you didn't know because this one was perfect."

"I'm glad you liked it." Gazing down at the dirt and stains, I said, "I'll make sure our housekeeper sends it to be cleaned."

"Thank you. I appreciate that."

When the last button was undone, the sides of the dress opened up, revealing a sexy white bustier and a lot of Caterina's skin.

I flattened my palm at the base of her neck.

Although I should've resisted, I couldn't. She was a beautiful temptation standing before me in the warm flesh. Slowly, I ran my hand down her skin.

When she shivered beneath my touch, I swallowed down my groan.

Caterina twisted her neck to stare at me. "A-Are you finished?"

I fought the urge to lie, so I could stay close to her longer. There was nothing more in the world I wanted than to continue standing there with my hand on her delicate flesh.

To feel the rise and fall of her breath beneath my fingertips.

What the hell was happening to me?

Snatching my hand away from her, I took a step back. "Finished. Go ahead and get dressed," I replied gruffly before starting for the bedroom door.

"Thank you, Callum," she called.

"You're welcome," I replied before I ducked out of the door and made my way to get a drink.

Or two.

Chapter Sixteen: Caterina

Once I'd slipped into one of the dresses Nera had packed, I folded up my wedding dress as best I could before I left the bedroom and went back to the main cabin.

Callum and Quinn were deep in conversation with Seamus, so I took a seat away from them. After the insanity of the afternoon my energy depleted rapidly and I dozed off.

I don't know how long I'd been sleeping when I was gently shaken awake.

When I opened my eyes, I stared into Callum's. "What's wrong?"

"Nothing. You were snoring."

My eyes popped wide at his accusation. "I do not snore."

His lips quirked. "Yes, Kitten, you do."

When I stared past him to Quinn for confirmation, he merely shrugged. "It's a wee snore compared to ours."

As embarrassment warmed my cheeks, Callum chuckled. "Don't worry, Kitten. That's not the reason why I woke you up."

"Then what?"

"It's time for you to check-in with your brother."

I tore my gaze from the phone to Callum. "Are you sure?"

He nodded. "We're almost an ocean away from him and back in our territory."

"After what happened with my father today, I'm not sure if that matters."

"I have a feeling your father's attack was without Raphael's knowledge. I might not know your brother well, but somehow I don't think he'll appreciate that."

I swallowed hard. "I'm pretty sure my father's actions were motivated by something sinister."

"I agree. He would be a fool not to at least hear us out before attacking." He gave me a pointed look. "Unless he thought he had a better option on the table."

I furrowed my brows. "You think he had a potential marriage contract for me with another family?"

With a grimace, Callum nodded. "I received intel that Carmine's last marriage contract fell through."

My stomach lurched in my throat. "You mean after all this time he still hasn't remarried?"

Disgust rippled across Callum's face. "The delay was in waiting for his bride to come of age."

I covered my mouth with my hand. "Oh God."

"The sick bastard entered into a contract with a sixteen-year-old girl."

Although I hated showing weakness in front of Callum, I couldn't stop my body from trembling at the thought of Carmine.

Callum immediately picked up my distress because he drew me closer to him, pulling me onto his lap.

As his hand ran wide circles across my back, he pronounced, "You're safe, Kitten. You're my wife, and I won't ever let that bastard lay one finger on you. I swear."

"But what if something happens to you?" I whispered.

"My brothers will protect you in my absence." He cocked his brows at Quinn and Dare who were curiously eyeing my position on Callum's lap. "Won't you protect Caterina in my absence?"

As Dare nodded, Quinn replied, "You don't ever have to fear that bastard."

Tears threatened my eyes at their compassionate resolve. "Thank you," I murmured.

When the tremors finally stopped echoing through me, I expected Callum to move me off his lap. Instead, he remained absently stroking my back.

And for reasons I couldn't possibly understand, I enjoyed the feel of his strong arms around me and the gentle touch of his hand.

Before I could get completely carried away with my feelings, I cleared my throat. "What should I say to Rafe when I call him?"

"Let him know you're all right and invite him, Leandro, and Gianni to our reception on Saturday."

"We're having a reception?"

"It's more of a party to announce our wedding to our Irish allies on the East Coast."

Curiosity got the better of me when I asked, "Will we be taking a honeymoon afterwards?"

Callum smirked at me. "I didn't think you'd be ready to consummate our marriage so fast."

I scowled back at him. "I'm not. A honeymoon usually follows a reception."

"Not in our case."

"I wouldn't have minded a little time away. Maybe a trip to the shore."

He eyed me curiously. "How long has it been since you've been to the ocean?"

"Almost three years."

"Perhaps if you behave yourself and play nice, I can convince Seamus to let us use his house on Center Beach."

"You'll only take me to the beach as a reward?" I huffed.

"Aye, if you're a good girl."

"Forget it," I grumbled.

Ignoring his laughter, I started dialing Rafe's number. When Callum ended the call, I demanded, "What is your problem?"

"You need to call him on video. He'll want to see your face to ensure nothing has happened to you."

"Oh," I murmured.

I then redialed and eased the phone up in front of my face. The image reflected of myself was one of both apprehension and excitement. With my hair and makeup done, I hoped Rafe wouldn't immediately lose his shit thinking I'd been tortured or worst of all raped.

He answered on the third ring. "Caterina?" he questioned in disbelief. My heart ached at the sight of his disheveled hair and the dark circles under his eyes.

"Hey, Rafe," I said, as I fought my tears.

"Oh Kitty Cat," he choked out.

As tears streaked down my cheeks, I reassured him, "It's okay. *I'm okay.*"

"You can't imagine how worried I've been. How worried we've all been."

"I'm sorry. I should've called you sooner."

His expression darkened. "I wouldn't imagine you would have been at liberty to call us."

Guilt flooded me that I hadn't requested Callum to at least let my brothers know I was alive and being taken care of.

"I'm so sorry that I didn't demand to speak to you."

Callum's hand came to grip my knee. "The time wasn't right for a call."

Malice lit up Rafe's face at the sound of Callum's voice. "Are you too much of a coward to show your face, Kavanaugh?"

I gasped. "How did you know who took me?"

"Leo secured an informant this morning. A woman from a bridal shop in Catania."

Callum chuckled. "I should've known showing your picture to the saleslady would be a grave mistake."

"You don't sound too regretful, motherfucker!"

Leaning in, Callum's face appeared on the screen along with mine. "Thankfully, my desire to make Caterina a stunning bride didn't fuck up my plans since we were married by a priest two hours ago."

As Rafe's eyes bulged, a string of Italian cursing and lamentations erupted from his lips. He shot out of the chair he'd been sitting in and began pacing the room. His free hand tore maniacally through his hair.

I winced as he painfully tugged the long strands that he usually wore pulled back. My relief at his hand leaving his hair was short-lived when he began snatching and throwing anything in his path.

The camera began to spin and bounce with his erratic movements. One of the bodyguards that had rushed in the room at his screams was thrown to the floor when he tried stopping Rafe.

With an amused smile, Callum said, "I imagine he's calling me every name in the book while threatening to chop off my cock."

I blushed both at his summation and at the words coming from Rafe. "Yes, he's referenced your..." I swallowed hard. "Manhood."

"What else?"

"He's detailing all the ways he's going to torture you."

At the sight of Rafe bleeding from broken glass, Callum jerked his chin at the screen. "Calm him down."

"If a three-hundred-pound bodyguard couldn't stop him, how can I?"

"When I've truly lost my mind, there's no one except my mam

and Maeve who can talk me down. I imagine for Rafe, you are the same balm for his soul."

After exhaling a long breath, I stared at the chaos before me. "Rafe, stop!" I called. When he couldn't hear me over his ranting, I screamed his name into the phone.

He froze. His broad shoulders rose and fell in harsh pants. The sweat-slickened strands of his chin-length hair stuck to his face. Finally, his haunted gaze locked on mine.

Tears stung my eyes as I fought to find my voice. "Your Kitty Cat needs you to sit back down, and listen to me."

Anguish replaced the rage on his face. "Please, Rafe," I cooed.

"Christ, Caterina," he groaned.

"I need you to take a few deep breaths while repeating that I'm okay."

"How can you possibly be okay? You've been forced into a marriage after fighting so hard to escape."

"Everything is not what it seems."

"Were you not forced?"

I stole a glance at Callum. "At first it might appear that way. But Callum found a way to make marriage very palatable to me."

Rafe's eyes pinched shut. "Did he or did he not kidnap you from the order and force you into marriage?"

"You're not listening to me," I argued.

"I'm hearing everything you're saying, and the only explanation is you're apparently suffering from Stockholm syndrome."

I rolled my eyes with exasperation. "If that were the case, I would be saying I was in love with Callum, which I can assure you I'm not."

With a smirk, Callum replied, "You wound me, Caterina."

"Shut up!" I snapped.

Rafe watched our interchange curiously. "Then why would you willingly marry him?"

"Because he offered me something no man ever had before."

A strangled growl came across the line. "Don't fucking tell me he laid one finger on you."

When I realized his insinuation, I threw a hand over my eyes in embarrassment while Callum had the nerve to chuckle.

"Oh my God, Rafe, I wasn't talking about *that*."

"Then what?"

"Callum agreed in a signed contract to allow me to get an education and have a job."

My revelation stunned Rafe into silence. "He did?" he finally questioned incredulously.

I nodded. "In that way, he gave me freedom."

Feeling Callum's heated stare, I turned to look at him. To my utter surprise, a genuine smile curved on his lips.

"But what about your vows and the order?"

My stomach twisted at his mention of the order. I'd spent the last few days swimming in a sea of guilt about abandoning my vows. The voice that had been creeping into my subconscious the last few months argued that I could still serve God without being in an order.

At the same time, I would obviously be fighting an uphill battle when I was married to a mafia man.

"While I may no longer be a part of the order, I won't be abandoning my faith. I will still serve by volunteering and helping those in need."

"You will?" Callum asked with a curious look.

"Of course." Raising my brows at him, I asked, "Do you have a problem with that?"

"As long as it doesn't interfere with your ability to be my wife or with raising our children."

With a roll of my eyes, I replied, "I think I can manage."

"Then I don't have a problem with it."

When Rafe cleared his throat, I turned my attention back to him. "I don't know what to say," he replied.

"Say that you'll give my marriage a chance." With a pointed look, I added, "Say that you'll give Callum a chance."

Rafe shook his head furiously. "You can't ask that of me. Not yet at least."

"We're having a wedding reception Saturday. I'd like for you to be there."

"Was the invitation your idea or his?" When I nibbled on my bottom lip, he grunted. "Kavanaugh, why don't you be a man and ask me to a business meeting rather than being a pussy and putting my sister up to it?"

While I expected Rafe's remarks to anger Callum, he surprised me by merely laughing. "I've always heard you get more bees with honey than vinegar. I didn't think you would possibly tell your sweet sister no."

"I don't suppose you've extended an invitation to my father?"

Callum sneered. "I have nothing to say to the man who tried to sell his daughter in marriage to a pedophilic abuser, not to mention attacking us this morning."

Rafe's dark brows shot up into his hairline. "He attacked you?"

"You weren't aware?"

"Do I fucking look like I was aware?"

Callum and I exchanged a look. He'd been right when he said that Rafe hadn't had a part in my father's attack. "Alessio and some of your Sicilian relatives attacked our SUV as we were leaving for Boston. They ambushed us at the airport as well, but thankfully, we were able to reduce the threat," Callum replied.

"My father fired on an SUV carrying my sister?"

"Yes, he did."

Rafe's expression turned menacing. "That fucking bastard."

Callum chuckled. "My sentiments exactly."

"And mine," I piped up.

This time both Rafe and Callum chuckled. "Oh Kitty Cat," Rafe mused.

"Well, it's the truth," I huffed.

Callum cleared his throat. "Anyway, after everything that has transpired, I felt it was better speaking with you, rather than your father."

"I would remind you I'm not the head of the family," Rafe said diplomatically.

"No one looks to Alessio for good decisions anymore. They know the future of the family lies with you, Raphael. Come to our reception so we can discuss how beneficial Caterina's and my marriage will be for both of our families. If we are united, your father will have no choice but to condone the alliance."

Before he could answer, I added, "Please, Rafe. I really want my brothers to be there and to be united with us."

The corners of Rafe's lips quirked up. "They say women are a weakness, and Kitty Cat, you certainly are mine. And the same can be said for Leo and Gianni."

I laughed. "I love you."

I knew Rafe wouldn't repeat the endearment to me in front of Callum. It was a silly alpha thing that Made Man never show emotional weakness.

"I'll speak to the others. In the meantime, I suppose it wouldn't hurt if you texted me the address of the reception."

At my squeal of delight, Rafe chuckled. "I'll see you Saturday."

"Bye, Kitty Cat."

Pursing his lips, Callum countered, "No goodbye for me?"

Rafe narrowed his eyes. "Fuck off, you thieving bastard."

And with that, he hung up. "Did that go well?" I asked.

He laughed. "Aye. It went well."

"If you say so," I murmured as I fell back into my seat.

Chapter Seventeen: Callum

After we landed and exited the plane, I finally felt like I could breathe. We were home and once again on our territory. The constant feeling of being on edge melted away.

Once I met with all the Neretti brothers and ironed out the parameters of our alliance, we could begin to move forward.

Since stepping on American soil, Caterina appeared to be overwhelmed with nervous energy. Even though it was almost eleven at night, she bounced in her seat while leaning from left to right to peer out the windows and take in aspects of the city.

"I've never been to Boston before," she remarked after I gave her an exasperated look.

"Never?"

She shook her head. "It was out of our territory, so I wasn't allowed."

"I'll be sure to have one of your bodyguards give you a tour."

She looked at me. "My bodyguards?"

"Yes, Kitten, you won't leave the house without at least one bodyguard. Until things are smoothed over with your brothers, you'll take two."

"I'm well aware of having bodyguards."

"Then what's the question?"

She glanced down at her hands in her lap. "I just wondered why you weren't taking me."

"While I'm touched you're bereft about being without my companionship, I must remind you that I have a job to contend with. One that I've been away from for the last week."

Her gaze snapped to mine. With a glare, she countered, "Excuse me for thinking you might take some time off to ensure your wife gets acclimated to her *new* life in a *new* city."

"She has you there, Cal," Dare replied with a grin.

"Fuck off," I snapped.

After riding along in silence for the next few minutes, Caterina's squeal caused me to jump out of my skin. "Ooh, McDonalds!"

"What about it?" I muttered as I rubbed my chest over my shirt.

"Can we stop? I'm starving."

Wrinkling my nose in disgust, I countered, "You actually like that greasy shite?"

She nodded. "I *love* it. And I haven't had any in almost three years."

I chuckled. "You sound like you've just been busted out of prison."

"Please, can't we just go through the drive thru?"

With a roll of my eyes, I muttered, "Fine."

After leaning forward in my seat, I said to Harvey, "Change of plans. Stop at McDonald's for some greasy shite for my wife."

Quinn and Dare chuckled behind me. "I wouldn't mind some myself," Kellan replied.

"Anyone else?" I questioned tersely.

"I've been a week without Lorna's cooking, so I'll wait," Quinn replied.

Dare grinned. "I'll go for both." With a waggle of his brows, he added, "You know my large appetite."

"Ew," Caterina muttered, which caused Dare to laugh.

After Harvey rattled off our order of burgers and fries, we made it through the drive through. He turned in his seat to hand the bags to Caterina. She stuck her head in one of the bags.

"Oh my God, that smells amazing!" she moaned.

"Hey, don't be sniffing all over my food," Dare protested.

She brought her head out of the bag to roll her eyes at him. "This happens to be my order." After a brief glance in another bag, she handed it to Kellan.

For the last bag, she said to Dare, "This must be yours."

As soon as the food was dispersed, Caterina tore into her Big Mac like someone who had gone days without food. Her appreciative moans shot straight to my dick, causing me to shift in my seat.

"What?" she questioned through a mouthful of Big Mac at what must've been my pained look.

"Pace yourself."

"You don't know what it's like to go without something you really, really love."

"Actually, I do."

She held a hand up before pinching her eyes shut. "Please don't turn this into something sexual."

I chuckled. "I wasn't about to."

Her eyelids peeled open to peer curiously at me. "So what was it you had to go without?"

"Supermacs in Belfast was my equivalent to your McDonalds."

Caterina swallowed her bite. "And why did you have to go without eating there?"

"Because I was in prison."

She lowered the Big Mac to her lap. "You've been in prison?"

Dare snorted around his milkshake straw. "I'd hardly call it prison."

I narrowed my eyes at him. "Oh, were you the one serving the time?"

"You were there to serve a six month sentence, which Da and Seamus got you out of after three."

"Fuck off."

"What was it for?" Caterina asked curiously.

"What do you think, Kitten?"

"There's so many possibilities for an Irish gang member," she teasingly replied.

"I hate to disappoint you, but it was actually for public indecency."

A laugh burst from her lips. "You're joking."

I shook my head with a grin. "I was seventeen and got utterly and completely pissed. In my inebriated state, I decided it was a good idea to take a leak right in the middle of the street. The cop who arrested me didn't have any idea who I was. My father was so angry that I'd been nabbed for something so foolish that he allowed me to sit in there and stew for a while before he lent a hand."

After chewing a thoughtful bite of her burger, she said, "You certainly didn't tell me you're an ex-con."

I laughed. "Aye, it certainly tarnishes my squeaky clean image."

"Very true," she mused.

Leaning over, I brought my thumb to the corner of Caterina's lip. "You have a little ketchup."

Her cheeks flushed. "Oh," she murmured as I swiped the glob off.

She watched with wide eyes as I brought my thumb to my mouth rather than wiping it on a napkin. "I thought you said you didn't like it?"

"I can handle a little ketchup."

Poison and Wine

She grinned before holding out the box of french fries. "Want some fries with your ketchup?"

"I think I'll pass."

"Suit yourself," she replied.

Just as Caterina finished her food, we turned onto Beacon Street. As we pulled up to the house, Caterina peered curiously through the SUV's window.

"I know it's hard to see in the dark, but what do you think of your new home, Kitten?"

Her eyes bulged wide. "It's... beautiful."

"Thank you."

"I didn't dream you lived somewhere like this."

I smiled. "Don't tell me you thought I resided in some shithole?"

She laughed. "Of course not. This is just so historic and classic. I guess I saw you in something more modern."

"Wait until you see the view from the rooftop."

Her eyes widened. "The rooftop is yours?"

"Yes, we have the 4th and 5th floors of the penthouse. The rooftop has gorgeous views of the neighborhood along with the Charles River."

"And you all live here?"

I nodded. "Since arriving in the states, we felt there was strength in numbers."

"That makes sense." Caterina smiled. "Of course, I can't imagine my brothers living in the same house."

"That's because they've lived and reigned in New York all their lives. We're starting from the bottom."

"That's true."

Harvey parked on the street to let us all out. While my brothers and a few bodyguards handled the luggage, I took Caterina on ahead.

After we entered the lobby, we took the elevator up to the main floor. I led Caterina into the foyer.

Walking to the edge of the living room, I said, "The kitchen and dining room are just across the hall while the master bedroom and bath are down the hall."

"Where's my bedroom?"

I gave a slight shake of my head. "We only have four bedrooms. You'll be sleeping with me."

Caterina's eyes bulged. "No. I won't," she countered.

"Yes, Kitten, you *will*. You're my wife, and wives sleep with their husbands."

"Not always."

"In our case, you will."

"I could give her my room," Kellan suggested.

I jabbed my finger at him. "Mind your own business."

After holding up his hands, Kellan pushed past me to climb the circular staircase to the second floor. Caterina tracked his movement up the stairs.

Once he was out of earshot, she argued, "You didn't have a right to turn him down. That should've been my decision."

"It's my home and my decision."

"Stop being such a caveman."

"We have to form some sort of intimacy. If not, we'll never consummate our marriage, and we'll never produce an heir."

"Surely there are other ways to do it without sleeping in the same bed with each other."

"*Enough!*" I thundered, which caused Caterina to jump. "You and I will share a room, a bathroom, *and* a bed."

With a huff, she rolled her eyes to the ceiling. "Fine. But I won't like it."

"I'm sure with your continued line of bullshit I won't like it very much either."

Taking her by the arm, I led her across the hall to the kitchen. "I want to introduce you to Lorna."

At the mention of another female, Caterina tensed. "Why do I need to meet her?" she questioned suspiciously.

"Because she's our cook and housekeeper. She basically runs this house and us."

A flicker of relief flashed on Caterina's face. I fought the urge to laugh that she could've possibly thought I had a live-in mistress. Growing up with a father like hers, I'm sure Caterina was used to Alessio shuffling women around.

I'd seen the same thing happen with my own. Keeping faithful was another way I planned to end yet another generational curse.

"You didn't tell me you had a full-time housekeeper."

"My apologies that I didn't deem it as important as saving your ass from gunfire."

She rolled her eyes. "I thought you expected me to do all that as your wife." She turned her head to me. "The whole 'my mother put three meals on the table a day' thing."

"When university starts, I know you'll be busy with your classes, so it's best that Lorna keeps running things around here."

"That makes sense."

"There's also the fact that Lorna takes care of my brothers along with me. As my wife, you'll only be expected to take care of me."

While I thought she might protest, Caterina shook her head. "I don't mind doing things for your brothers. They've been exceptionally kind to me considering the situation."

The mention of her taking care of my brothers sent an unusual feeling slashing through my chest. A green rage of jealousy blinded my eyes at the very idea she might be giving more to them than me.

"You are *mine*, Caterina."

She stared into my eyes before slowly shaking her head. "Why don't you beat your hands on your chest to drive home the point?" she suggested.

With a smirk, I replied, "If that's what it takes to get it through your head, then maybe I will."

"Lucky me," Caterina muttered.

Just as I expected, I found Lorna in front of the stove. I'd texted her we would be arriving late, and she could leave some food out for us. I should've known she would've insisted on staying to ensure we were all fed.

At the sight of me, she smiled. "Welcome home."

"Thank you."

Glancing passed me, Lorna stared at Caterina with interest. "And who is this?"

"This is my wife, Caterina."

Lorna's green eyes bulged comically wide. "Your *wife?*"

I couldn't help grinning at her reaction. "Aye, as of today."

Taking a tentative step forward, Caterina offered Lorna her hand. "It's nice to meet you."

Lorna eyed it somewhat contemptuously before she pulled a shocked Caterina into her arms. "It's so very, very nice to meet you."

Peering over Caterina's shoulder, Lorna demanded, "You left five days ago without even a girlfriend to speak of, and now you're coming back with a wife?"

With a laugh, I replied, "It's an arranged marriage."

Lorna pulled away to peer at Caterina. "The angels sure were shining upon you to be blessed with such a beautiful wife."

As red flushed Caterina's face, she replied, "Thank you."

"You're welcome, lass." Although she let Caterina out of her embrace, Lorna kept her hands in hers. "Aren't the two of you going to make some stunning wains together?"

At Caterina's furrowed burrows of confusion, I said, "Wain is Northern Irish slang for a child."

"Oh, I see," she replied, with a shy smile.

"You can't imagine how happy I am for the two of you. This house has needed a woman's touch for such a long time."

"I hope you'll be willing to help me. I don't know much about running a house."

"Of course you don't, sweetheart. You're so very young." Lorna gave me a stern look. "Aren't you a little old for her?"

For fuck's sake.

"There's barely ten years between us," I argued.

Poison and Wine

What the hell was Lorna's problem? Acting like I was some dirty old man just because there was an age difference between Caterina and me.

"Why, she's practically a wain herself." With a wink, Lorna added, "But I suppose her age will work in your favor when it comes to getting up the pole."

"Excuse me?" Caterina asked.

Before Lorna could respond, I replied, "It's Irish slang for getting pregnant."

Caterina squeaked before flushing pink. Since I knew she was desperate for a subject change, I said, "Caterina has some culinary skills."

"Is that right?" Lorna asked.

With a nod, Caterina replied, "I would love to help you cook sometimes."

Lorna grinned. "And I would love to have some help. The Kavanaugh men certainly go through the food."

"I can only imagine."

Wagging her finger, Lorna said, "But for now, you need your rest. Callum, take your lovely wife to bed."

While Caterina's face flushed at the insinuation, I jerked my chin at the stove. "I'll get Caterina settled and then come back for a plate."

With a knowing smile, Lorna replied, "Take your time."

Placing my hand on the small of Caterina's back, I guided her out of the kitchen. As I led Caterina down the hall to my bedroom, she dragged her feet as if she was a lamb being taken to slaughter.

Cutting my eyes over to her, I growled with a mixture of anger and frustration. "Stop it."

"What?"

"Stop acting like I'm about to throw you on the bed and take your virtue."

"I know you aren't," she replied softly.

"Then why are you acting so frightened?"

Refusing to meet my gaze, she merely shrugged. "Don't tell me you're that nervous about sharing a bed with me?"

She jerked up her chin defiantly. "I'm sure it's hard for someone like you to imagine, but yes, I am nervous. I've never shared a bed with a man. Not even my brothers."

Before I could open my mouth to reassure her, she shook her head. "Let's also not forget it's my first night in my *new* house in a *new* city after a day where my own father shot at my vehicle on the pretense of kidnapping me to force me into a marriage with an abuser."

When her chin trembled, I felt like an unimaginable bastard. I ran my hand over my face with a ragged sigh.

"I'm sorry, Kitten. I should've realized how overwhelming all this was for you. Just like you're not used to being around men, I'm sure as hell not used to having a woman around."

Her mouth dropped open in surprise. "You've never lived with a woman?"

"Not since my mam and Maeve."

"You haven't had women here?" she questioned softly.

"You'll be the first woman to share my bed." When her eyes bulged in shock, I added, "My bed in my home."

"Oh," she murmured.

"If I'm honest, it's been awhile since I've shared my bed overnight."

"You could make it a little easier for me by spending the night on the couch," she said

"Not on your fucking life," I countered.

She rolled her eyes. "Why am I not surprised," she muttered before going over to her luggage that had been brought up.

After grabbing her suitcase, she hurried over to the bathroom and disappeared behind the door. At the sound of the shower turning on, I headed back to the kitchen.

Lorna handed me a heaping plate of my favorite Shepherd's pie with a giant slice of soda bread. With my stomach rumbling, I practically inhaled the mouthwatering food. Lorna huffed at my clean plate. "Did you even chew?"

I laughed. "I've missed your food that much."

She grinned. "I'll make you another one."

With another plate filled to the brim, I said, "I'm going to eat this in my room."

"Aye, can't leave your blushing bride for too long, can you?"

"I was going to see if she'd like to try some."

"Sure you were," Dare said around a mouthful of food.

I gave him the middle finger before starting down the hall. When I got there, Caterina was still in the bathroom. Despite what Dare said, I had planned on getting Caterina to try the pie.

When I tried the door, I found it locked. I pounded my knuckles into the wood.

"What?" Caterina called.

"I had some food for you to try."

"I'm not hungry."

Of course she wasn't. "Also, I just want you to know that no lock will keep me out."

Her huff of frustration could be heard through the door. "You're such a brute!"

I couldn't help chuckling at her outrage. "One might argue that as my wife I have every right to see you naked. I should just break down this door."

"You wouldn't dare."

"You're right."

I went over to the nightstand and grabbed the key. After I returned to the door, I called, "I'll use the key instead."

"Callum!" she shrieked.

When I jerked open the door, Caterina stood in a pair of silky pajama shorts that hit mid-thigh. Her arm draped her pajama top across her breasts.

As her chest rose and fell, a mixture of rage and mortification resided in her eyes. "How dare you!"

I put my hands on my hips. "How dare I enter one of the rooms in my own home?"

"That's not what you were doing, and you know it. I should have a right to my privacy."

"I needed to get ready for bed," I replied as I began to unbutton my shirt.

"You could've gotten ready in the bedroom or waited until I was finished."

After pulling off my shirt, I argued, "I'm exhausted and ready to sleep."

"I would assume that this isn't the only bathroom in the house. You could've gone to–" Caterina's voice cut off when I unbuckled my belt.

Her eyes popped wide when I stepped out of my pants and stood before her in my briefs. With a flush on her cheeks, she ducked her head.

I joined her at the sink. She remained frozen as I started brushing my teeth. I jerked my chin at her. "Aren't you going to put your top on?"

"Not with you in here."

With a smirk, I replied, "Would you like some help?"

"Why are you being such a jerk?" she demanded.

"It's just part of my charm, Kitten," I replied with a wink.

After bending over the sink, I spit out some of my toothpaste. When I righted myself, Caterina gave me a death glare in the mirror. "Seriously, Kitten, after that first night of seeing you in a *white*, drenched nightgown, I promise I've already seen everything you have to offer."

"You're still a jerk."

"Yes, I am because I'm seriously enjoying this."

After meeting my gaze in the mirror, something dangerous flickered in Caterina's eyes.

Almost immediately the hairs rose on the back of my neck. I'd been trained on how to read people, and I could read that my wife was just about to react.

And it wasn't going to be good.

With bated breath, I watched her as she removed her arm and the pajama top from covering her breasts. A low groan reverberated through my chest at the sight of her bare tits.

Normally, I would've expected her to hurriedly put her top on. But I'd known from her change of expression to be prepared for the unexpected.

My kitten was about to bare her claws.

And fuck me did Caterina bring the unexpected. She went one step farther to torture me.

Taking her sweetass time, she examined the fabric of the top, picking off invisible lint and turning it inside out. All the while her fabulous rack magnetized my attention, causing my cock to rise.

When it pounded in my briefs, I gritted out, "Aren't you going to put your top on?"

I never knew how devious my wife was until she had the audacity to grab a lotion bottle out of her suitcase.

With my toothbrush frozen in my mouth and toothpaste oozing over my lips, I watched as she began to lotion up her arms and upper chest.

It sent a shimmering sheen across her skin. All the while her tits bounced with her ministrations, causing my cock to throb.

Just when I thought I might come in my pants like a horny teenager, she quickly threw her top over her head.

Caterina once again met my gaze in the mirror. "All done," she replied with a sickeningly sweet smile.

I thought she couldn't possibly have any more cheek, but then her hip brushed against my crotch as she walked out of the bathroom, causing me to hiss.

There were two ways I could handle this: one would be to jerk it out in the shower, which was incredibly creepy with Caterina just a few feet away, or I could just get in bed and wait for my traitorous dick to go back down.

I chose the second option.

After rinsing, I stalked back into the bedroom. Caterina already lay against the pillows watching me curiously. Her eyes trailed down my body to my crotch. With a grunt, I threw back the covers and climbed inside the bed.

"Goodnight," Caterina said softly.

"Goodnight," I huffed.

After turning out the light, I rolled away from her onto my side. The moment I fanned the covers Caterina's intoxicating smell invaded my nose.

With a groan, I rolled my eyes to the ceiling and willed my dick to go down.

But it didn't.

Being so close to a beautiful and sexy woman had it pulsing with need.

I don't know how long I lay there, aching and frustrated. Finally, after what felt like an eternity, I slung back the covers with a frustrated grunt. Rising out of bed, I grabbed a pillow.

Caterina's voice echoed through the dark. "What are you doing?"

"Going to the fucking couch."

"But I thought–"

I laughed mirthlessly. "Don't act innocent, Kitten. We both know you brought out the claws with your little peep show in the bathroom. So, enjoy your victory."

I could practically hear her smiling in the dark. "Sweet dreams," she replied.

I bit my tongue from telling her to fuck off. Instead I ignored her and stormed out of the bedroom. I didn't know how, but one day, I would pay her back.

Chapter Eighteen: Caterina

When I woke up on my first morning in Boston, it took me a moment to realize I wasn't in my bed at the order. Since the night I'd been taken, I'd been fighting the confusion when I woke up.

Once I realized I was in Boston in Callum's bed, I immediately remembered my victory from the previous night.

Mortification shortly followed the victorious feeling because I'd let Callum see my breasts. Not only that, but I'd given him an epic peep show. I groaned as I remembered lotioning up my arms and upper chest and how my actions had incited desire in him.

What had gotten into me?

It hadn't even been a week since I'd been abducted. Not even seven days since I'd belonged to the order and practiced chastity. Yet last night I acted as a brazen fallen woman.

How was it possible that I'd managed to do such a personality shift in just five days?

The thought that I was losing myself so quickly and so easily sent fear ricocheting through me.

I knew the first order of business for today would be to get to church ASAP. More than just making it to church, I would need to make it to confession. With another groan, I brought my hand over my eyes.

What was I possibly going to say to a priest?

Forgive me Father for I have sinned. It's been six days since my last confession. A week ago I was Sister Caterina of the Sacred Heart. Now I'm married to an Irish mobster who I tempted by baring my breasts so he wouldn't sleep in bed with me.

With a huff, I rolled over right into a warm, hard body.

Shrieking, I jumped back, kicking my legs to push myself away. Unfortunately, one of those legs connected with an appendage that I deduced was not arms or legs.

"Fuuuuck!" Callum grunted.

At that moment, I knew for a fact it was *definitely* not arms or legs. "Oh, my God, I'm sorry."

"Why do I doubt yer sincerity?" Callum gritted out as he cupped himself.

"I really am sorry. You scared me."

"Who the hell did you expect?"

"Certainly not you after you said you were going to the couch."

"Yeah, well, the couch didn't turn out to be that comfortable."

"Maybe you need to invest in a new one," I suggested.

His expression turned murderous. "There will be no need for that since I will never fucking sleep on it again." He glared at me. "Understood?"

"Does that mean you'll be sleeping with Quinn or Dare?"

With a growl, Callum reached across the mattress to grab me. As his arms encircled my waist, I squealed and tried to get away, but he was too strong.

After he pulled me against him, Callum flipped me onto my back before getting on top of me. His thick thighs pressed against mine as he loomed over me.

He smiled. "You are entirely too cheeky, my wife."

"That's your opinion."

"Perhaps I should teach you a lesson and remind you who is the boss in this house."

As my head spun in a sensory overload, I tried to fight the feelings rising in me. God forgive me, but I liked the feel of him on top of me.

I liked it very much.

I'd never been this close to any man before.

My chest heaved while heat bloomed between my legs. "W-What are you going to do to me?"

"Something devious."

"Is that necessary?" I gasped.

"I think so."

As I searched his eyes, I swallowed hard. "Please."

Callum's jaw clenched. "Oh, Kitten, the sound of that word on your lips wrecks me."

The next thing I knew Callum dipped his head before crushing his mouth against mine.

Instantly, I froze.

A kiss was to be my punishment?

I guess that couldn't be too bad. As long as he didn't try anything else I suppose it would be okay.

As his tongue delved into my mouth, an ache burned its way through my core. I never realized you could get so worked up from just a kiss.

To my surprise, Callum's hands remained respectfully around my back as his mouth worked over mine. As his chest rubbed against mine, my nipples hardened.

My hands tentatively left his shoulders to sweep through the strands of his hair, causing him to groan.

When he thrust his hips against mine, his erection rubbed against my center. Although it felt amazing, alarm bells went off in my head, and fear replaced any passion I was feeling.

This was too much, too soon.

I couldn't sleep with a man I barely knew, even if he was my husband.

I tore my lips from his. Staring into his lust-filled eyes, I shook my head. "I can't."

With a groan, Callum pulled away to flop over on his back.

When I dared to peek at him, he was staring up at the ceiling, breathing heavily. "I'm sorry," I whispered.

He turned his head to look at me. "It's me who should be sorry, Kitten. I let my teasing go too far."

I licked my swollen lips. "For what it's worth, the kissing was very nice."

Callum groaned again before rubbing his hands over his face. "You'll be the death of me."

"I'm sorry. Not just about today, but I feel terrible for teasing you like I did last night."

His brows arched in surprise. "You do."

I nodded. "So much so I want to go to church first thing."

The corners of his lips twitched at my admission. In a high-pitched voice, he teasingly said, "Forgive me, Father, for I have sinned. I tempted my husband in the worst possible way. I gave him a wee glimpse of the promised land before cruelly slamming the door in his face."

After smacking his arm, I huffed, "Don't be blasphemous."

He didn't need to know I'd envisioned a similar conversation in my head. Of course, I hadn't planned on alluding to my body as the promised land.

Grinning, Callum replied, "All right, my little temptress. Once you're ready, I'll have Owen and Shane take you to whatever church you'd like."

"You will?"

"Of course."

I leaned over and kissed his cheek. "Thank you."

"Will you light a candle for me while you're there?"

My breath hitched. "Would you like for me to?"

"Aye. I need all the prayers I can get to be able to be strong enough to keep my hands off of you."

"You're hopeless. Absolutely hopeless," I huffed before throwing the covers back and leaving Callum alone in the bed.

Chapter Nineteen: Caterina

For the next couple of days, I fell into a somewhat predictable routine. In the mornings after breakfast, two bodyguards would be by my side as I attended mass.

Once that was over, I spent two to three hours volunteering at St. Francis's. Serving others helped to make my life not seem so upended.

In the afternoons, I began exploring Boston. I did all the corny tourist things like the hop on and off trolley tours and seeing the Boston Tea party ships at the shore. I planned on guilting Callum into taking me on a day trip to Salem in the next few weeks.

Then I would come home in time to help Lorna with dinner. She began teaching me how to make several of Callum's favorite Irish dishes. Between six and seven, all of the Kavanaugh men would begin trickling in the house. We usually sat down for dinner at seven.

Afterwards, Dare and Kellan would try to catch me up on some of the movies I'd missed in the last three years. The two were apparently quite the cinefiles.

After he'd finished with all his business, Callum would come and join us, usually when the movie was halfway over. He always scooted his brothers out of the way, so he could sit by me.

Usually he pulled my legs onto his lap where he would then begin massaging my feet and calves. He never said anything about it—it was almost as if he was doing it unconsciously. I didn't ever protest because I liked the nearness of him—the feel of his fingers on my skin as they worked my muscles.

When it came to the sleeping arrangements, Callum and I were sharing a bed. Although I started the night clinging to the far edge of the mattress, somehow by morning I found myself snuggled against him.

Callum continued to be a gentleman by keeping his hands to himself. He must've been vying for sainthood since usually every morning I felt something digging into my hip or lower back.

It remained an elephant in the room since Callum would just get out of bed and shower.

Saturday dawned bright and beautiful for our reception. Even though I was the bride, I hadn't been consulted about anything. When I'd asked, Callum assured me that his mother and aunts were taking care of everything.

A part of me resented not having a voice. I hadn't had one in my wedding and now I wasn't in on my reception either. Not that I would've had any idea how to plan an Irish wedding reception, but I could've learned.

I'd been surprised it would be held at the house on the expansive rooftop terrace. Caterers arrived at noon to begin setting up the food and drinks.

Poison and Wine

At three, Callum had two bodyguards accompany me to a spa where I was given my facial and massage. It was the most decadent thing I'd ever had. I was seriously becoming spoiled in my new life as a mobster's wife.

Once my pampering was finished, someone from the spa did my hair and makeup for the reception. I didn't bother protesting why I needed someone to do it. Apparently, Callum wanted to put our best foot forward when it came to me meeting his relatives.

At a little before six, we arrived back home, and I went to the bedroom to get dressed. After the debacle at the airfield, my wedding dress had been professionally cleaned and repaired.

I slipped into it just as Callum came into the bedroom in a suit with sexy suspenders. I couldn't help doing a double-take.

"Like what you see?" Callum teasingly asked.

I rolled my eyes. "You're such an egomaniac."

His arms encircled my waist, drawing me against him. "Aw, Kitten, can't you give your husband one little compliment?"

"Fine. You look very handsome and distinguished."

A sexy smirk curved on his lips. "Thank you, wife. As usual, you are stunning."

"Thanks to you, too." Jerking my head over my shoulder, I asked, "Will you button me up?"

"It would be an honor."

As he began making quick work buttoning up my back, he said, "My mother should be here in a few minutes."

Nibbling nervously on my lip, I replied, "Do you think she'll like me?"

His fingers halted for a moment. "Since she lives in Belfast, why do you care?"

"Because she's your mother. One day she'll be the grandmother of my children."

Callum kissed the top of my bare back, causing me to shiver. "Aye, she'll like you. Especially when you start popping out babies."

I couldn't help the flush that colored my cheeks. While we

might've made out, that was as far as we had taken any marital relations. I was grateful Callum was willing to take it slow and wasn't expecting too much from me.

At the same time, I loved when he took charge.

When the last button was done, Callum turned me around. "Ready?"

"As I'll ever be."

As we made our way out of the bedroom, Callum took my hand in his. When we reached the foyer, Callum's face lit up at the sight of a very attractive woman in her late fifties coming towards us. I knew it had to be his mother, Orla, from both his reaction and the fact her face was a mirror reflection of Kellan's.

My heart sank at her disapproving expression.

It was quite evident she wasn't too thrilled to meet me. I guess I couldn't blame her.

My mother wouldn't have been too thrilled finding out about my wedding after the fact, not to mention the fact it was to an Irishman.

I'm sure Orla had her heart set on Callum marrying within the Irish clans and producing pure Irish grandchildren.

With his arms open, Callum stepped forward to hug her. "Mam, I'm so—"

Orla interrupted him by sending a stinging slap across his cheek, causing me to gasp in horror.

"What the hell was that for?" Callum bellowed as he rubbed his face.

She pointed her finger at me. "For kidnapping her from a convent."

As Callum scowled at his mother, I bit down on my lip to keep from laughing. "She wasn't in a convent. It was a religious order," Callum argued.

"Like that makes much of a difference when it comes to your immortal soul," she protested before making the sign of the cross.

I was starting to *really* like my new mother-in-law. I don't know why I'd imagined her being meek. So many mafia wives were. I should've realized that raising five sons would've killed her if she hadn't been tough.

With a smile, I held out my hand to her. "It's nice to meet you, Ms. Kavanaugh."

"It's lovely meeting you, my dear. Please accept my apologies for my son's behavior." She shook her head. "I suppose I should say *all* my sons since they helped him kidnap you."

With a laugh, I replied, "It's okay. In spite of the kidnapping, they've really treated me very well and with more care and kindness than I could ever have hoped for."

Orla's worried brow faded at my declaration. "I must say after what I'd heard about your abduction, I wouldn't have expected to see you standing so willingly at Callum's side. I was afraid I might have to coax you out of the bedroom."

"While I still have reservations and guilt about leaving the order, I've come to embrace that I might have another calling in life as a wife and mother," I replied.

And that's how I truly felt. I wasn't trying to make things sound better for my mother-in-law.

Callum smiled at his mother. "See, it's not so bad. You should be happy for us."

Orla didn't return his smile. Instead, she narrowed her eyes at him. "Only if Caterina's happy with the situation, then I'll be happy."

"Wouldn't you reconsider moving to Boston?" I asked while throwing Callum a teasing smile.

At Callum's roll of his eyes, Orla laughed. "As much as I would love to come and help you keep the boys in line, my heart and home belong in Belfast."

"Well, you always have a home here when you're ready." I elbowed Callum playfully. "Doesn't she?"

He shot me a pointed look before replying, "Aye, of course."

"The only thing that'll make me change my mind is when my first grandchild is born."

As I gasped, Callum spewed out the drink he'd just taken. "We haven't even been married a week."

After making the sign of the cross, Orla replied, "That hasn't stopped me from praying for you to be fruitful."

"We need time, Mam. Caterina and I just met."

"I barely knew your father when we were wed, and you were born nine months and three weeks after our wedding," Orla challenged.

Callum's expression darkened. "You can rest assured I'll be a hell of a lot more respectful of my bride than Da was of you."

While Orla nodded, I gave Callum an appreciative look. "For that I am very grateful."

"Just looking at the two of you together, I'm sure you will be blessed with many happy years," Orla pronounced.

When neither Callum nor I responded, Orla winked. "Now that I've met my new daughter-in-law, I'd love a nice strong whiskey."

Callum chuckled. "You can find one at the bar on the roof."

"I'll see you both later."

As she started up the stairs, I couldn't help grinning at Callum. "I think I love your mother already."

He snorted. "You only love her because she gives me shit."

"That's not the only reason," I protested.

"Sure it isn't."

"She genuinely cares about my happiness. I think that's a trait all women would like in a mother-in-law."

With a shake of my head, I added, "It's not even a trait my own mother possesses."

"Then I'm happy to share her with you," Callum said with a smile.

"Make way, make way!" a voice shouted behind us.

When we turned around, I did a double take at the sight of what appeared to be Dare's twin in both looks and personality striding towards us. Except this twin appeared to be considerably younger than Dare.

Callum rushed forward to grab the young man in his arms. "It's fucking grand to see you, Eamon."

And then I knew the young man was Callum's sixteen-year-old brother and the baby of the family. Once he slid out of Callum's embrace, Eamon turned to me.

A low whistle escaped his lips. "Fuck me, this stunning woman can't possibly be your wife, Cal," he proclaimed.

Callum responded by smacking the back of Eamon's head. "Watch your mouth."

Eamon gave me an apologetic look as he extended his hand. "Sorry. I was just calling it as I saw it."

I laughed as I shook his hand. "It's nice to meet you."

Before I knew it, Eamon was bringing my hand to his lips for a kiss. "It is exceptionally nice to meet you."

With a grunt, Callum rushed forward to extract my hand from Eamon's. "That's enough bullshit. Where's your sister?"

"She's outside with the bodyguards walking Murphy."

At what must've been my questioning look, Callum replied, "Murphy is my sister's dachshund."

"Oh, I love wiener dogs," I pronounced, which elicited a snort from Eamon.

Callum jerked his thumb to the stairs. "Go up and see your brothers."

"Fine," Eamon grumbled.

After he started up the stairs, I shook my head with a laugh. "I can't imagine this house containing him and Dare."

"It'll be a tight fit with the egos."

It was then that the front door opened and a gorgeous redhead came walking in. Right behind her, an older bodyguard wearing a surly expression held a dapple colored dachshund.

At the sight of her brother, Maeve rushed forward and dove into his arms. Knowing her tragic history made the moment even more emotional for me, and I could barely contain my tears.

Seeing Callum and Maeve together made me think of my own

brothers, and I stared expectantly at the grandfather clock, hoping they were soon to arrive.

When she pulled away, Maeve turned her attention to me. "Hi, I'm Caterina," I said.

Maeve gave me a warm smile before reaching out to hug me. "Welcome to the family."

"Thank you."

When she pulled away, her smile faltered. "Although I do have to say, I'm sorry for the way you had to join it."

I gave her a genuine smile. "It's okay."

After glaring at Callum, she countered, "Believe me when I say, it is not okay. My mam and I are horrified that he would do such a thing."

I laughed. "Yes, your mother let her feelings be known by slapping Callum."

With a grunt, Callum said, "Excuse me while I go greet our other guests and miss out on you both talking shite about me."

Once he stalked off, Maeve laughed. "He hates it when he disappoints Mam and me. Trust me, the two of us were fit to be tied when we got wind of what happened."

With a sly smile, I said, "Don't worry. I plan on making your brother pay for his transgressions each and every day."

"He certainly deserves it."

"Truthfully though, he's treated me far better than I could've ever hoped for in such a situation."

"That is some comfort to us."

"I hear you're at Trinity College."

Maeve's beautiful face lit up at the mention of school. "Yes. I've got one more year."

"What's your major?"

"Accounting."

"I admire you for that. I'm terrible with math."

"I must admit I'm a terrible nerd when it comes to numbers. I think I like it most because math is standard no matter what part of the world you're in."

"Have you thought of coming to live here in Boston?"

Maeve paled slightly. "Oh no, I can't imagine living here in the states. Even though I grew up in Northern Ireland, it's not so very different in the South."

"Since I have three overbearing older brothers, I can only imagine it's quite freeing not being in the same city as yours," I teased.

With a smile, Maeve replied, "Aye, it's been nice having my freedom." Sadness flickered in her eyes. "At the same time, I couldn't imagine what I'd ever do without them."

"I know exactly what you mean."

"Speaking of my brothers, I better go say hello to the others," Maeve said

"It was so nice meeting you."

She gave me another quick hug before she started up the stairs to the roof. Callum came back from wherever he had gone. "Looks like you and Maeve are getting along well."

I smiled. "It's nice having another woman around."

He smirked at me. "Let me guess. Maeve told you she didn't approve of your kidnapping."

"I don't think you'll find many women who would agree with what you did."

"I suppose not."

When the door opened again, my breath hitched in my chest at the sight of my brothers. Just like Maeve had with Callum, I rushed forward to throw myself at them. They encircled me in a giant hug.

"It's been so long," I murmured against Leo's chest.

"Now that you're out of the order, it won't ever have to be so long again," Leo replied.

I pulled back to smile over at Rafe. "I'm assuming my brothers will give me leeway to enter their territory in New York."

Rafe's gaze moved past mine to Callum. "That will all depend on how our meeting goes."

Rolling my eyes to the ceiling, I huffed out a frustrated breath.

"You're seriously telling me that because I'm married to Callum I wouldn't be welcome in New York?"

When he looked back at me, Rafe's gruffness faded. "There's never a time you wouldn't be welcome in New York."

"And the same can be said of Boston. Right, Callum?" I asked.

Callum cocked his brows with a smirk. "Aye. As long as your brothers play fair."

Leo's jaw clenched while Gianni tensed. When my gaze shifted to Rafe, his expression was venomous. "Quite hypocritical for you to be talking about playing fair after what you did to Caterina," he remarked through gritted teeth.

"Rafe," I warned.

"This isn't your business, Kitty Cat," Leo said.

I shoved away from him. "Excuse me? This became *my* business the moment I was kidnapped to form an alliance."

"Unfortunately, you're only a pawn in all of this, Caterina. It's up to us men to make the decisions," Rafe replied.

"That's such..." I stared into their expectant faces. "Bullshit!" I pronounced.

My brothers all stared at me with the same disbelieving expression. I hadn't raised my voice to them since entering the order. I'd also never cursed at them before either.

"This is *my* life and *my* future, so you can sure as hell believe *I'm* going to have a part in it."

When they realized I wasn't going to budge, Callum suggested, "Perhaps you would like to take this into my office?"

Before anyone could argue about my place in the meeting, I marched across the hallway and threw open the office door.

Turning back to them, I motioned with my hand, "Gentleman?"

Chapter Twenty: Callum

So far, my meeting with the Neretti brothers wasn't going as expected. While I was used to pivoting when the unexpected occurred, I hadn't planned on my wife being part of that pivot.

"You're actually going to allow her to sit in on this meeting?" Rafe questioned as he took a seat across from my desk.

I eased back in my chair. "Normally, I would've forbidden it, but after seeing your interactions with her, I would wager her presence is very much needed. At least for now."

"That's a very emasculating statement, don't you think," Leo challenged with a smirk.

"I would suppose it is for *you* since apparently you need a woman to keep you under control."

Leandro shot out of his seat. Before he could lunge across my desk, Rafe threw out his arm to stop him. "Sit. Down," he bit out.

With a snarl, Leo flopped back down in his chair. His arms gripped the sides until his knuckles turned white. "Fine. Continue," he hissed.

Rafe exhaled a harsh breath. "The only thing I'm going to address to my sister is this, and then I will not acknowledge her presence in this meeting again. I came here to speak to the head of the Kavanaugh family, not his wife."

"You're being such an unimaginable asshole," Caterina spat.

I couldn't hide my chuckle at her cursing at Rafe. From the reaction of her brothers, I knew it had rarely if ever happened.

Rafe turned to Caterina. "I'm sorry. But it's the way things have always been done."

Caterina crossed her arms over her chest. "Say what you want to say, and then I'll leave, so the big, bad men can have their meeting."

Rafe's lips momentarily twitched like he was fighting a smile, but then his expression grew serious. After leaning forward in his chair, he took Caterina's hand in his. "It's still not too late, Kitty Cat. Say the word, and we will take you away today, annul the marriage, and put you under our protection."

While Caterina gasped in shock, I rose out of my chair. Jabbing my finger at Rafe, I growled, "You've got fucking balls to come into my house and threaten to take *my* wife."

Rafe ignored me and continued staring earnestly at Caterina. "I mean it. Just say the word, and we'll do it."

Caterina jerked her hand out of Rafe's while furiously shaking her head. "If I was to leave now, it would bring war upon you, Rafe. It's one thing to defy Father when you're aligned with the Kavanaugh's and quite another if you aren't. Too many people could get hurt or killed if you had war on every side."

"I'll live with the repercussions. Don't think you have to sacrifice yourself," Rafe argued.

I came around the side of the desk to stand before him. "Considering we were married by a priest, I'm not sure how you claim you can annul the marriage."

With a sneer, Rafe replied, "On the grounds it hasn't been consummated."

"Who says it hasn't?" Caterina countered.

After my incredulous gaze snapped to hers, I quickly masked my shock before the others noticed. When I dared to look at Rafe, his face paled. Both Leandro and Giovanni stood up.

With a pained groan, Rafe said, "Kitty Cat, you don't have to lie to me."

My breath hitched as I waited for Caterina's response. After drawing her shoulders back, she pronounced, "I'm not."

Rafe lunged at me. "You fucking bastard."

"Stop it, Rafe!" Caterina shouted as Leandro and Gianni pulled him away.

She placed her hands on his shoulders. Staring into his eyes, wild with rage, she said, "On my word, he didn't force me."

His dark brows raised in surprise. "He didn't?"

"No. I wanted to consummate our marriage."

Inwardly, I groaned at the elicit images flooding my mind. Although her words were lies, it still did something to me hearing her say that she had willingly come to my bed.

That she had wanted sex with me.

More than anything in the world, I wanted to bury myself inside her, marking her as mine.

When her brothers remained silent, Caterina sighed. "Like I told you on the phone, Callum is giving me the opportunity for a future I never dreamed possible. I wanted to do everything I could to ensure that the alliance was successful."

"You really want to be his wife?" Leandro questioned in disbelief.

I stared expectantly at Caterina for her response. After she met my gaze, her cheeks flushed before she stared down at the floor. "I do."

After staring between Caterina and me, Rafe finally sighed defeatedly. Leo and Gianni exchanged horrified looks. "Then I suppose I should offer my congratulations."

Caterina jerked her head up. "Really?"

He nodded and looked at his brothers. "Right, guys?"

"Yes," they agreed in unison.

A beaming smile lit up Caterina's face. "You all make me so happy."

"As long as you're happy, that's all that matters," Gianni replied before his gaze locked with mine. "And she will remain happy, correct?"

For reasons I couldn't possibly articulate, I wanted to see Caterina happy. I liked the feeling her smile elicited, and I liked being the one to put the smile on her face.

I wasn't ignorant to think that it would be easy keeping my little hellcat happy. But I was willing to put the work in not just for what it would mean for my family, but what it meant for the two of us.

"I will do everything within my power to ensure her happiness," I replied.

When I met Caterina's gaze, she gave me a shy smile before eyeing her brothers. "So, we're good?"

"Yes, Kitty Cat, we're good," Rafe replied.

Caterina nodded. "Then I'll leave you boys to it."

As she started past me, I reached for her hand. Her eyes popped wide with surprise when I brought it to my lips. "Go have some fun. We won't be long."

"Try to behave," she instructed.

Smirking, I replied, "I'll try."

She rolled her eyes before walking out of my office.

Once we were alone, Leandro clapped his hands together. "Now that's out of the way, I suppose we should get to work."

Gianni nodded. "Kidnapping Caterina along with your airfield pyrotechnics has kicked up a fucking firestorm."

With a smile, I replied, "So let's figure out how to put the fire out. Together."

Chapter Twenty-One: Callum

With our meeting finished, I showed the Neretti brothers upstairs. The party was in full swing with the band playing traditional Irish folk music. Couples twirled around the makeshift dance floor to the tunes coming from the guitar, mandolin, and fiddle.

There was nothing that made me feel like home the way the music of my homeland did.

At the expression on the Neretti brothers faces, I couldn't hold back a laugh. "I don't suppose I can interest you in a jig later?"

Rafe rolled his eyes. "I need a fucking drink."

"Only the finest Irish whiskeys await you at the bar."

He shook his head and he made his way over there with Leandro and Gianni on his heels. I scanned the crowd for Caterina. I found her being led around by my mam for introductions.

I could tell she felt out of her element by the way she kept biting her bottom lip and shifting on her feet. I might not have known her for long, but I knew how to read her.

I decided to put Caterina out of her misery. As the music changed over from an upbeat tempo to a ballad, I made my way over to her.

Relief flooded her expression at the sight of me. "The meeting is over?"

"Aye."

"And everything is still okay?"

I motioned across from us where her brothers were drinking at the bar. "They're grand."

"I'm glad."

Holding out my hand to her, I asked, "May I have this dance?"

"I would love that."

I nodded at Mam. "Excuse us."

She smiled. "Enjoy yourselves."

Once I got Caterina on the dance floor, I pulled her tightly against me. With my hand at the small of her back, a small sigh escaped her's lips.

With our bodies pressed against each other, I kept thinking of the statement she'd made to her brothers.

As I stared intently into her eyes, I asked, "Why did you lie about consummating our marriage?"

"It was the right thing to do."

At what must've been my continued shock, Caterina said, "I wasn't just thinking about me. I was thinking about the repercussions for both of our families."

"But you had a chance to be free of me," I protested.

"At what cost? The chances of my brothers living through a war of that magnitude were slim. Then I would've been at the mercy of my father." She shuddered. "Not to mention the threat it would've brought to you and your brothers."

"As I told you before, you never have to worry about your father again, Kitten."

"You don't know how much I appreciate that."

"I'm not going to lie. You shocked the hell out of me."

Caterina giggled. "I wish you could've seen your face."

"It takes a lot to surprise me, but you fucking floored me."

"You did a good job of masking it after the initial shock and horror," she teased.

"I'm just glad it was believable to your brothers."

"I think you sold it pretty well."

"Thank you." As I stared into her beautiful face, my hand dipped to the curve of her delicious ass. "In the end, I wish you had been telling the truth."

She blinked her eyes at me in surprise. "About us..."

"Yes."

When I pressed my lips against the shell of her ear, she shivered. "I want to consummate our marriage, Kitten."

Pink bloomed across her cheeks as she tensed in my arms. "I-I can't."

"Why not?"

"I don't know you well enough yet. It's only been a week since we met."

"Is time truly a measure of knowing someone? Some people can know everything about another within hours while some spend years without ever truly knowing them."

"But I still know so little about you as a person."

"How can I fix that?"

She nibbled her bottom lip. "I don't know."

"Let's start with the basics. Do you want to know my favorite color?"

"Um, okay."

"It's red." I waggled my brows. "For blood."

Amusement twinkled in her eyes. "That doesn't surprise me."

"What's your favorite color?"

"Blue like the ocean."

I grinned. "Was that a subtle plug for me to take you to the beach?"

"Maybe."

"You have my word that as soon as things calm down, I'll take you."

"I'm going to hold you to it."

With a laugh, I replied, "I'm sure you will."

As the song came to an end, Seamus took over the microphone. "Good-evening to all my Kavanaugh friends and family!"

A raucous roar went up over the crowd. "We're so happy that you all could make it on such short notice to celebrate the nuptials of Callum and the lovely Caterina."

As appreciative whistles and catcalls echoed across the roof, Caterina's cheeks flushed pink. "Before we all get plastered out of our fecking minds, let's go ahead and raise our glasses in a toast to the new couple."

Seamus paused to raise his glass. "*Comhghairdeachas agus le deaghui to Caterina and Callum.*"

"Let me guess. That means congratulations and best wishes in Irish," Caterina said.

"Look at you. It won't be long, and you'll be speaking in full sentences," I replied with a wink.

She laughed. "I think it was more of a lucky guess."

After everyone had taken a sip from their glasses, the men began chanting, "*Póg í! Póg í!*"

When Caterina paled slightly, I laughed. "They're telling me to kiss you."

"That's all?"

I snorted. "Don't tell me you thought they wanted me to fuck you right here in front of everyone?"

"Of course not," she huffed, her face turning crimson.

After gripping her by the waist, I jerked her against me, causing her to squeak in surprise. "I think we should oblige them, don't you?"

"It doesn't look like you're leaving me much choice, you brute."

Grinning, I ducked my head before bringing my lips to hers. Fuck me, she tasted even sweeter since she must've had some of our wedding cake.

The crowd erupted in cheers when I dipped her in my arms. Although I didn't look, I'm sure at least three people weren't enjoying the show, and that was the Neretti brothers.

My hand traveled from Caterina's waist up her back to tangle my fingers through the long strands of her hair. When I tugged gently, she moaned into my mouth, which caused my dick to jerk.

When I finally released her mouth, both of our chests heaved in desperation. "Here's another thing to know about me, Kitten."

"What's that?" she questioned breathlessly.

"I fucking love the taste of you."

Despite the blush on her cheeks, she did grin up at me. "I like the taste of you, too." With a knowing look, she added, "Just your lips for now."

"Woman, you'll be the death of me."

A throat cleared behind us. Glancing over my shoulder, Leandro stood eyeing me with disdain. "Might I dance with my sister?"

"Of course."

Just to spite him, I laid another long, lingering kiss on Caterina before I pulled away. Leandro's disgust was apparent. "Have fun," I said with a grin.

While Caterina danced with Leandro, I walked off the dance floor and over to the table where Maeve sat alongside Eamon. While my youngest brother looked bored out of his mind with the couples dancing, Maeve stared longingly at the fray.

I held out my hand to her. "May I have this dance?"

She rolled her eyes playfully. "I don't want a pity dance, Callum."

"Why would I dance with my baby sister out of pity?"

Maeve shot me a pointed look. "You know why."

With a grimace, I eased down in the chair beside her. "I'm sorry, love. If there was any way I could take away your pain, I would."

"I know." A haunted look flashed in her eyes. "I just want to be a normal girl. Not poor, broken Maeve."

"We don't look at you that way."

"But you do. All of you do." She swallowed hard. "Kellan still can't look at me without tears in his eyes."

"He's wracked with guilt."

"I know he is just as much as I know there was absolutely nothing he could've done that night."

She shook her head before lowering her voice to a whisper. "My rape is the first thing everyone thinks when they see me."

"Maeve—"

"It's okay, Callum. The only time it matters is when I'm back with the family. At school, no one knows any of it. I can just be me without the baggage."

I sighed. "I'm so fucking sorry, love. Once again, I mean it when I say if there's anything I could do—"

"You already went above and beyond for me, Cal."

I'd never come out and told her that I'd killed our father for her. I didn't want her harboring one scrap of guilt after all she'd been through. I'm sure she'd heard all kinds of stories through the rumor mill. Maybe Mam had told her.

When I visited her that night in the hospital, I told her I'd kill the man who'd hurt her.

And I did.

We'd strung up the bastard who raped Maeve and tortured him for two days. Everytime it looked like our beatings and stabbings might end his life, we'd pumped him full of adrenaline to keep him going. He begged for mercy for twelve straight hours, but he never received it.

With my father, we didn't have time to indulge in torture. It had to be quick before his men could rise up against us. In the end, it was

Poison and Wine

just mere seconds for him to look me in the eye and recognize that his firstborn and heir was to be his killer.

Then with a smile, I blew his brains out.

I took her hand in mine and squeezed it. "I'd burn the world down for you if you asked me."

Despite the tears shimmering in her green eyes, she smiled. "You know your devotion and adoration has ruined me for any future men."

With a laugh, I replied, "Just know that whoever you choose will have to answer to the five of us."

She rolled her eyes. "Like any man will want to take me up on that."

At that moment, Raphael strolled up to our table. The bastard gave us a warm smile. "I noticed your beautiful sister wasn't dancing, and I thought I would ask for her hand."

Before Maeve could respond, I shook my head. "She doesn't care to dance."

Rafe's dark eyes regarded me coolly before he flicked his gaze to Maeve. "Is that true, Ms. Kavanaugh?"

When Maeve started to speak, I cut her off. "I'm the head of her family, so I speak for her."

"She is of age, is she not?"

"Aye, but the answer is still no."

"Callum, stop," Maeve interjected.

Rafe's expression darkened. "Your refusal insinuates that I'm not good enough to dance with your sister."

"It has nothing to do with you."

He raised a brow. "I'd love to believe that. But one might argue with your prior behavior towards my sister, you give me reason to believe that despite today's meeting, you do not respect me or my position."

"I don't give a shite what you believe," I growled.

With his jaw clenching, Rafe spat, "Perhaps we should settle this outside."

"If that's how you want to handle it."

Before I could stand up, Maeve shot out of her chair. Thrusting her hand out to Rafe, she said softy, "I would love to dance, Mr. Neretti."

Both Rafe's and my eyes popped wide. Once he'd recovered, Rafe gave her a smooth smile. "Please call me, Raphael or Rafe," he instructed.

"I'm Maeve." Her cheeks flushed. She replied, "Just in case you didn't know."

When she started around the table, I grabbed her free hand. At her startled look, I said, "You don't have to do this."

"It's okay." When I continued staring questioningly in her eyes, she squeezed my hand. "I'm fine, Cal."

Unable to trust my voice, I merely nodded. As Rafe led Maeve onto the dance floor, I moved out from behind the table to stand to the side. I wanted to be ready in case she needed me.

More than anything, I wanted to be nearby in case Neretti tried anything. I didn't care if it ruined the alliance. I wouldn't allow him to hurt one hair on her head.

I was so focused on the two of them that I didn't notice Caterina had appeared at my side. "What's wrong?" she asked.

"Your fucking brother."

Tilting her head, she surmised Rafe and Maeve. "They look good together."

"He forced her to dance," I growled in protest.

She shook her head. "Rafe would never do that."

"I'm sorry to tell you, but your most perfect brother did."

Caterina looked at me. "Just like I know Rafe would never force a woman to dance, you would never allow him to do that to Maeve."

Damn. She already knew me too well. "She chose to be a peacemaker by dancing with the cheeky bastard."

With a knowing smirk, Caterina countered, "She looks like she's enjoying herself."

I watched as Maeve smiled at something Rafe said. As he grinned down at her, a laugh escaped her lips, which she tried to hide by ducking her head. At my continued appraisal, the bastard's embrace was almost reverent.

"She is stronger than you think, Callum," Caterina said softly.

"I know." I swallowed hard. "But she's still my baby sister."

Caterina took my hand in hers. "You're such a good brother."

I snorted. "You wouldn't say that if you could see the murderous thoughts running through my mind involving Rafe."

She grinned up at me. "I'm sure he's had the same about you. Maybe even worse."

When the song ended, Rafe whispered something in Maeve's ear. She beamed and nodded furiously. Another song started and even though it was a more upbeat tempo, Maeve remained dancing with Rafe.

Caterina squeezed my hand. "Maybe there will be another Kavanaugh and Neretti alliance in the future."

I shook my head. "As capo, your brother's marriage will need to be with one of the Italian families. He needs peace among them."

Caterina frowned. "Pity. They look so good together."

Although I hated to admit it, Caterina was right. I couldn't remember the last time I'd seen such a genuine smile on Maeve's face. I still thought Rafe was a bastard but the way he treated my sister had raised him slightly in my esteem.

As his hand trailed down her back, that esteem dimmed.

Caterina must've noticed I tensed because she held her hand out to me. "Let's dance."

"I can still shoot daggers at him from the dance floor," I argued.

She grinned. "But at least your hands will be occupied on me and not on my brother's neck."

I threw my head back with a laugh before I pulled her against me. The music had picked up and we began a jig. Caterina's expression turned from amusement to panic. "I don't know the steps."

"Just go with it."

While she might've been clueless, she made fast work of learning the steps. "Look at you," I called over the music.

"I feel like I'm in that dance scene in *Titanic*," Caterina mused as we whirled around the dance floor.

I suppose she had a point. Of course, I wasn't doing any fancy foot stepping like that bloke, Jack, did. I would leave that up to some of my cousins who knew all that Riverdance nonsense.

We danced and danced until my hair was soaked through, and sweat ran like salty rivers down my back. I'd long since stripped out of my jacket, pulled down my suspenders, and unbuttoned my shirt. My brothers and most of the other men had done the same.

I'd danced with Mam and Maeve along with several of my other cousins and wives of my men. We'd sung Irish songs at the top of our lungs.

But I kept coming back to Caterina.

I loved the way she felt in my arms. God, I couldn't wait until the day I could feel her naked curves. To feel her silky skin beneath my fingers.

At midnight, I cut off the band. Although most of us could've gone on, I didn't want any shite from the neighbor's about the noise. While the band packed up, Caterina rested her head against my shoulder.

"Tired, Kitten?"

She yawned before murmuring, "Exhausted."

"Want me to carry you to bed?"

A drowsy grin curved on her lips as she looked up at me. "You would really do that?"

"I'd do anything for you."

"Anything to get into my pants."

I threw back my head with a laugh. "At the moment, you aren't wearing any."

"Fine. My panties."

Groaning, I replied, "You love to torture me, don't you, Kitten?"

Poison and Wine

With a wicked grin, she stood up from her chair to stand beside me. "It's the gift that keeps on giving."

Chapter Twenty-Two: Callum

The days after my wedding reception turned into weeks, and before I knew it, Caterina and I were celebrating our one month anniversary. Of course, you wouldn't know I was married considering I was sporting daily blue balls and hadn't jerked off as much before bed since I was fifteen.

Somehow marrying a nun had bestowed a vow of chastity on me. I wanted to be patient with Caterina, but if my celibacy stretched on much longer, I was going to snap.

Thankfully, I was keeping busy with the upcoming opening of the Kavanaugh's first Boston owned club, *Bandia*, which meant goddess in Irish.

Currently, I found myself in my office buried under a mound of last minute paperwork. We had a soft opening in a week, but from the looks of all the multicolored papers to sign off on, you would think it wasn't for another month.

Just as I was about to text Caterina that I would be late for dinner, Dare burst through my office door. "This better be important," I growled.

"The alarm for the 15th Street warehouse just went off. I tried calling Sean, but he's not answering."

"Fuck," I muttered as I sprang out of my chair.

As we started for the elevator, Dare asked, "Do you think this is retribution from Alessio?"

After punching the down button, I jerked a hand through my hair. The elevator doors opened up, and we got on. "It makes the most sense. It's been quiet on all the other fronts since word of our marriage came out."

Just like Seamus had foreseen, the alliance of the Neretti's and Kavanaugh's had been a success. Even with the violent animosity from Alessio, it was well-received. Several families we'd lost after my father's murder had reached out as well as a lessening of our threat from the Bratva.

Once we made our way through the lobby, an SUV sat out front waiting for us. During the drive, I tried calling Sean again as well as some of the other soldiers who had been patrolling the warehouse.

With a frown, I turned to Dare. "Nothing."

"Fuck."

When we finally arrived, the warehouse was engulfed in flames despite the hard work of multiple fire crews on the scene. After exiting the car, Dare and I made our way toward the front of the warehouse where Quinn stood talking to Frank O'Dell, the Fire Marshall.

With a grim face, Frank extended his hand. "As soon as I heard it was one of yours, I came right down."

"I appreciate that, Frank."

Gazing up at the roaring blaze, I shook my head. "Have you found anything?"

He nodded. "I had my men take the device away as soon as possible before the cops could get a hold of it. I'll have my best guys on it."

"Thank you."

Everyone in the city could be bought, and Frank was one of them. Of course, it made good financial sense to have members of the fire department in your pocket, especially when situations like these flared up.

At that moment, two firefighters came around the side of the building carrying a black body bag. My heart sank into my stomach.

"Fuck," I muttered under my breath.

Dare shook his head grimly. "I guess that's why we couldn't get Sean on the phone."

"Are we sure it's him?" Quinn asked.

When the taller fireman held out a wedding band, I took it. As I turned the silver piece in my hand, the names engraved in the inside caught the light.

Sean <3 Bridget.

"It's him," I choked out.

After shoving the band in my pocket, I asked, "Were there any more potential casualties?"

"Sean was on guard until midnight," Quinn replied.

"But I couldn't get in touch with Neil or Philip," I said.

"I imagine they were asleep since Neil had duty on the 19th street warehouse last night, and Philip was on here."

I nodded. When I realized what lay before me, my chest clenched. The worst part of losing anyone from a soldier on up to an officer was having to report their death to the family. In this case, I had to go to a young wife and tell her that her husband was never coming back home.

"I have to go to Bridget's," I pronounced.

Quinn's expression saddened. "Do you want me to come with you?"

"No. I'll handle it. You guys stay here and find out all you can."

With dread filling me, I started for the car. Caterina's face flashed before mine as I climbed into the SUV. I wondered what her reaction would be if it was one of my brothers coming to tell her I'd been lost in the field.

Would she be sad?

Would she feel relief?

Would she shed a tear for me?

Considering Sean and Bridget had been together since they were teenagers, I knew I couldn't make comparisons between us. They'd been married for five years and had a three-year-old-son. They'd built a life together where Caterina and I were merely starting.

After making the trip across town, we pulled up outside of Sean's house. I'd called her parents to meet me there. I knew she would need support from her family when I told her the news.

As I started up the walk, the front door flung open, and Bridget ran out onto the porch.

I stopped at the bottom step and glanced up at her.

That was all it took.

Just one look from me and she started to scream.

Telling Bridget was worse than any emotional hell I'd predicted. After staying as long as what would've been considered respectful, I broke away from the trauma. I thought if I stayed one more minute inside that house with the wailing women and traumatized men I would lose my mind.

I desperately wanted away from all that grief and sadness. I wanted the safety of home, but more than anything, I wanted Caterina.

As I trudged through the doorway, Owen met me in the hall. At the sight of my face, he grimaced. "I'm so sorry, boss. Sean was a hell of a guy."

"That he was, Owen," I replied as I made my way over to the liquor cabinet.

After pouring myself a full tumbler of whiskey, I turned around to find Caterina curled up on the couch.

I glanced at Owen with a questioning look. He sighed. "She didn't want to go to bed until you came home. I thought it was best that you told her what happened."

I nodded. "Thank you."

"If you're good, I'll head out."

"Good night, Owen."

"Good night, boss."

Once I heard the elevator doors close on Owen, my hand reached out to touch Caterina. My fingers slid through the silky strands of her hair before I brushed my knuckles against her jaw. Despite my touch, she didn't stir.

With a sigh, I eased down in one of the chairs in front of the window. For a while I just sat there, staring into the night. Even after draining my whiskey, I remained looking out the window in a grief-induced fog.

It was only Caterina's voice that startled me out of my stupor.

"Hey," she whispered drowsily.

"Hey, Kitten."

"Are you hungry? I had Lorna leave you a plate in the warmer."

The only thing that could possibly be a ray of sunshine on this dark day was my beautiful wife with her caring heart.

"Thank you, but I'm not hungry." I motioned upstairs with my glass. "You should get to bed."

With a sheepish look, she said, "When you didn't come home, I thought I'd wait for you. I guess I was sleepier than I thought."

"It's all right, Kitten."

After surveying my face, her dark brows furrowed. "What's wrong?"

"I lost one of my best men today."

"Oh, Callum, I'm so sorry."

Caterina rose off the couch and then knelt beside my chair. She took my free hand in hers and squeezed it. Instead of being irritated by her nearness, her presence somehow soothed me. The cries of anguish playing on repeat in my mind quieted.

"What happened?" she asked.

Normally, I remained tight-lipped about my business around Caterina. But there was something about the empathy that shone in her eyes that made me want to open up to her.

"There was an attack on one of our warehouses, and Sean was in charge of protecting it."

"Tell me about him," she urged.

A part of me wanted her to leave me alone. To stop trying to get me to open up. But then there was another part that wanted to unburden myself.

"Sean had been with the family since Belfast. I danced with his wife at their wedding, and they asked me to be the godfather to their son."

I tossed back the whiskey that remained in my glass. "Tonight I had to stare into the eyes of my godson and tell him his Da was never coming home again."

When I dared to look into Caterina's eyes, tears pooled in them. Without a word, she slid her free arm around my shoulder, drawing me against her.

Although every fiber of my being fought against taking any comfort, my grief outweighed my reason. When I pulled her up from the floor and onto my lap, I'm sure my father was cackling in hell at the weakness in me.

Poison and Wine

Pinching my eyes shut, I nestled my head into Caterina's neck. My nose pressed against her soft skin, inhaling her sweet smell. All the while, she ran wide circles across my back with her hand.

"Talk to me, Callum," she whispered into the heavy silence around us. When I peered up at her, she brought her hand to my cheek. "Tell me what it is you can't bring yourself to say."

At that moment, there was no one in the world, not my brothers or even my mam, who I would've bore my soul to but Caterina. "I can't get the sound of their cries out of my head," I croaked.

"I'm so sorry. I can't imagine how horrible that was for them... and for you."

"My business took a husband away from his wife and a father away from his son."

Caterina paused in rubbing my face. "Sean knew the risks of the job. You didn't force him to do anything."

"His blood is still on my hands," I argued.

She shook her head. "You didn't pull the trigger."

"Every order I give is pulling a trigger in one way or the other."

"I wish I could give you an absolution. Anything to take the pain away."

"Aye, I wish you could, too."

To my surprise, Caterina pulled away from me and rose to her feet. She held her hand out. "Come."

Instead of protesting, I eased out of the chair and placed my hand in hers. Defeated, I let her guide me down the long hallway to our bedroom.

Once we were inside, Caterina pulled me over to her nightstand. At the sight of the flickering candles, I eyed her warily.

Caterina took a long match and handed it to me. After making the sign of the cross, she sank to her knees. When I remained frozen, staring at the candles, she glanced up at me. "Light a candle for Sean and say a prayer."

"I don't know if I believe in all that anymore."

"Then just sit with me while I do it."

As my mind battled against it, my heart won out, and I sank down beside her. Caterina closed her eyes and began murmuring the Prayer for the Dead. The same one Kellan insisted on reciting each and every time we took someone out.

While she spoke, I leaned forward and lit another candle. Images of Sean filled my mind as I made the sign of the cross and then bowed my head. When she finished, I said, *"Ar dheis De' go raibh a anam."*

"What does that mean?" Caterina questioned softly.

I cleared my throat. "May his soul be on God's right hand."

"That's beautiful."

"If anyone deserves heaven, it's Sean," I replied as I rose to my feet.

After rising up, Caterina asked, "Is there anything else I can do?"

The deviant part of me wanted to tell her to strip off her clothes, so I could fuck the grief out of my system.

But I could never do that.

Even though my beautiful virgin's earnest expression told me she was willing to do anything to take the pain away. Maybe even let me take her.

"Let me hold you."

Her eyes flared at my response. "Okay," she replied in a whisper.

Before I could start removing my shirt, her fingers came to my cuff. When I furrowed my brows at her, she replied, "Just let me take care of you."

She then unbuttoned the silver cufflink before moving on to remove the other hand. In silence, I watched as she slid the cufflinks into the pocket of her silky robe.

After bringing her hands to my neck, she slowly began unbuttoning my shirt. With each button she undid, I found my chest rising and falling faster and faster. My heart threatened to beat out of my chest at just her simple touch.

But it was so much more than that. It was the tremble of her fingers. The pink color of her cheeks. Her rapid pulse beating in her neck. The way she nibbled nervously on her full bottom lip. The way her breasts strained against her nightgown.

Once she reached my waist, she pulled my shirt out of my pants. Leaning up on her tiptoes, she eased it off of my arms and let it drop to the floor.

Her gaze dipped slowly down my chest. At her sharp intake of breath, I willed my cock not to rear its head.

This wasn't supposed to be about fucking. It was supposed to be about letting my wife care for my emotional needs.

When her trembling fingers rested on my belt buckle, I took her hands in mine. "I can take it from here, Kitten." Jerking my chin at the bed, I said, "Go ahead and lie down."

After I'd stripped down to my briefs, I pulled the covers back and got inside the bed. With her eyes locked on mine, Caterina slid through the sheets until her body reached mine. I held my arm up to let her burrow against my side.

When she laid her head on my chest, the tension coiling through my body evaporated.

After lying for a few moments in silence, Caterina propped her chin on my chest to peer up at me. "When did you get your first tattoo?"

"I was fifteen."

"That's awfully young."

"It's when I killed my first man."

Caterina tensed. "You were just a baby."

A chuckle reverberated through my chest. "I'd hardly consider myself a baby. I was a man since I'd already fucked for the first time by then."

"Sex doesn't make you a man or woman," she huffed.

"It does in my world."

"Do you even remember the woman?" Caterina asked softly.

"Of course, I do."

"Were you in love with her?"

"Aye, with her tits and arse."

Caterina rolled her eyes before pinching my side. "I was being serious."

"So was I," I countered with a grin.

Wrinkling her nose at me, she pronounced, "You're disgusting."

"I know, love."

"Have you ever cared about a woman beyond the physical side of her?"

Although I hated myself for it, I echoed my father's words when I replied, "Loving a woman is a weakness."

Caterina stared at me in horror. "You don't honestly believe that, do you?" she challenged me.

I lifted one of my shoulders in a shrug. "I haven't been proven otherwise yet."

"But you love your mother and your sister."

"Aye. But that's not the same as loving a woman."

"You've really never been in love?"

"No, Kitten. I haven't."

Her brows furrowed as her fingertip traced one of the tattoos on my chest. "But why does love have to be a weakness?"

"Because love fucks with your head. In my line of work, a fucked up head means people die. A person could even sign his own death warrant from being distracted."

Her finger paused its tracing as she shot me a pointed look. "If you've never been in love, how do you know it messes with your head?"

"Because I've seen it happen to other people."

"Maybe you've just seen it in the wrong people," she murmured.

"And you're the love expert?" I argued.

Caterina scowled. "You know I've never been in love."

"It sounds like neither one of us can really speak on it."

"Unlike you, I don't believe love could ever be a weakness."

As I stared into the intensity of her gaze, I saw what she wasn't saying. Caterina believed, despite the burning red flags surrounding me, that she could come to love me.

But more than that, she thought *I* could come to love *her*.

While I wanted to tell her it would never happen, I kept my mouth shut. Maybe there was a small part of me that wanted to believe in miracles. If anyone could deliver one, it was Caterina.

"We should get some sleep."

Although it looked like she wanted to say more, Caterina nodded. After she laid her head back down on my chest, I tangled my fingers through the long dark strands of her hair. When her breathing became slow and deep, I kissed the top of her head.

"Maybe you'll make me a believer, Kitten," I whispered into the dark.

Chapter Twenty-Three: Caterina

In the days after Callum and I fell asleep in each other's arms, I expected it to bring us closer. But something about being so emotionally vulnerable in front of me had closed him off. He'd barely mumbled more than a greeting to me this week, not to mention he'd come home after midnight every single night.

After the first night he'd come in and ignored me, I'd stopped waiting up on the couch for him. Instead, I stayed awake reading in bed until I heard his footsteps on the stairs. Then I would snap the light off and pretend to be sleeping.

I wasn't sure why I cared that he had shut me out. It wasn't like I entered our marriage desperately in love with him.

But I knew if we were to ever consummate our marriage, I would have to feel something for him. I couldn't just sleep with him out of duty and obligation.

The sinful part of me was only too eager to find out anything and everything about sex.

This morning after waking up to an empty bed, I threw on a robe over my pajamas and headed downstairs. As usual all the Kavanaugh brothers were around the table, as well as Seamus. Although the others were talking, Callum's attention was focused on his iPad.

I took the seat to the right of him. As I reached over to grab a piece of toast, he glanced up. "Good morning," I said.

"Morning."

After setting down a platter of eggs, Lorna smiled at me. "Caterina, I was thinking we could cook the corned beef for the boys tonight."

When I opened my mouth to agree with her, Callum shook his head. "We'll all be home late, so don't expect us for dinner."

I jerked my gaze from Lorna's to stare at him. "You're *all* going to be late?"

It was unusual for all the brothers to be gone. While they might trickle in at different times, they were all usually around for dinner. I'd especially needed their companionship the past week with Callum's physical and emotional absence.

Callum's pointed look reminded me not to question him about business. When he didn't answer me, Dare replied, "Tonight's the opening for our new club."

My brows shot up in surprise. "You guys own a club?"

"Yes," Callum replied as he forcefully speared his eggs.

"What kind of club?"

"A nightclub."

I sat a little straighter in my chair. "I've never been to a nightclub."

"That doesn't surprise me, Sister Sassy," Dare mused with a grin.

After playfully kicking his foot under the table, I turned back to Callum, "Before I was in the order, I always wanted to go to one."

"That's good to know," he replied to his iPad, rather than looking at me.

With a huff, I crossed my arms over my chest. "Why aren't you inviting me to come with you?"

"Because you don't need to be there," Callum gritted out.

"But don't most wives attend business parties?"

"They do," Dare replied, as he shot Callum a crooked grin. Callum scowled back at him.

"Then why can't I?"

Callum cocked a brow at me. "With your background, I didn't think it would be something you would enjoy."

"*Now* you care about my background? It certainly didn't seem to bother you when you were kidnapping me from the Sacred Heart."

"You're never going to let me forget that, are you?"

"Because you kidnapped me!"

"It was a necessary detainment," he grumbled.

"Fine. You can let me come to the club to make up for kidnapping me."

"I won't be guilted or bribed into letting you come, Kitten."

"Come on, Cal. Let the girl come with us," Dare said. After waggling his brows, he added, "Get her a hot little number to wear, and she'll be some killer arm candy for you."

While I blushed at his words, Callum grunted. "She's not a piece of meat for me to parade around."

"No, I'm your prisoner," I replied more to my plate than him.

"Since we arrived, have I kept you under lock and key?"

"You might as well have considering you've only let me go shopping or for a walk under armed guard."

"I've also let you volunteer everyday at St. Francis's."

"The operative word is *let*. People let prisoners do things."

"There's too many vices at a club for an innocent like you," Callum replied around the mouth of his coffee cup.

"Our reception had alcohol and dancing. What's so different about this?"

Dare snorted. "At the reception, there was no risk of people fucking out in the open or someone grabbing your tits or arse."

At my gasp of horror, Callum slammed his hand down on the table. "Never speak that way in front of Caterina!"

With a roll of his blue eyes, Dare replied, "My apologies."

"It's okay," I replied. Turning to Callum, I added, "In spite of what Dare said could happen, I still want to go."

Callum slowly shook his head. "You'll be the death of me, woman."

"Let her go, Cal," Quinn urged.

Glowering at him, Callum replied, "Not you, too. I expect as much from Dare, but you're supposed to be the fucking voice of reason."

"How much trouble can she possibly get into with the four of us there along with our men?"

Callum turned his red-hot stare to me. "Don't ever underestimate this one. Remember?"

As I rolled my eyes, Quinn chuckled. "She really has been cooped up here like a prisoner. She deserves to cut loose and have some fun."

With a beaming smile, I replied, "Thank you." Quinn winked at me before going back to his eggs.

Callum pinched the bridge of his nose. Leaning forward in my chair, I peered imploringly at him. "Please let me go. You can consider it a belated 21st birthday gift since I just celebrated it the day before you kidnapped me. Well, it was sorta the day of since it had just turned midnight."

He turned his head to me. "I almost kidnapped you on your birthday?"

When I nodded, he sighed. "Fine. You can accompany me tonight to the opening of the club."

At my happy shriek, he merely rolled his eyes and went back to his iPad. "I'll need to go shopping for a dress."

"Owen can take you," he mumbled without looking at me.

"What time do I need to be ready tonight?"

"We'll leave at seven. There will be press and some preliminary events before we open at eight."

He then turned his attention back to his iPad and didn't speak to me again for the rest of breakfast.

But I didn't care anymore. Tonight I would make sure he wouldn't be able to look at anything or anyone else but me.

After the men left for the morning, the bodyguard Callum had assigned me, Owen, accompanied me to one of the high-end boutiques. With a beefy, bodybuilder physique, Owen appeared in his mid-thirties, and he was a man of few words. He didn't even converse with the driver. Instead, he stared out the window on high alert.

He kept the same steely reserve when we entered the boutique as if at any moment he expected an assassin to pop out from a rack of clothes.

Jessica, a saleslady I'd worked with before, immediately came over to help me. "Mrs. Kavanaugh, it's lovely seeing you again. What are you looking for today?"

"I need a dress that will give any man with a pulse a hard reaction."

While she laughed, Owen's face remained impassive. "I think I have several numbers that might work," Jessica replied before leading me over to the racks.

After pulling several dresses, Jessica set me up in the dressing room. I slipped on the first one—a form fitting red dress with thin spaghetti straps and a bodice encrusted in silver sparkles that barely covered my boobs.

When I came out to get a better look in front of the tri-fold mirror, Owen's eyes bulged out of his head. "Do you like it?"

"I'm not at liberty to say, Mrs. Kavanaugh."

"Why not?"

In a strangled voice, he replied, "Because your husband would kill me."

Tilting my head, I replied, "From your response, I imagine you like it, but you're too afraid to say."

His expression became ashen. "Ma'am, please. I like my head where it belongs on my shoulders."

My teasing expression faded. "You're serious."

"Yes, ma'am."

"You really think my husband would kill you simply for telling me you liked my dress?"

"Mr. Kavanaugh spoke to all of us bodyguards about what respecting you entailed and what would happen if we didn't."

I blinked at him. I couldn't believe Callum cared that his bodyguards might look at me. It wasn't like we were in a real marriage. At the same time, I didn't want Owen to suffer.

"Then I'm sorry I asked you. I don't want you to get in any trouble."

Owen nodded. "Thank you, ma'am."

Without another word, I slipped back into the dressing room. Taking my phone out of my purse, I dialed Callum.

"Hello, Kitten," he mumbled after he answered on the second ring.

Without even a hello, I demanded, "Did you threaten the bodyguards that you would kill them if they looked at me?"

"No."

"Well, Owen seems to think that."

"I threatened them if they leered at you in any way."

"Callum, that's insane."

"You are my wife, and you belong to me. If they disrespect you, then they disrespect me."

"I currently have a three-hundred-pound bodyguard practically peeing his pants because I dared to ask him if he liked my dress."

A low growl came through the phone. "He's close to where you are naked?"

I rolled my eyes. "I have on my underwear."

"I don't care."

"He's not right outside. He's staying a respectful distance away."

"Good. He's a valuable soldier. I would hate to have to lose him."

"Could you please be a little less psychotic?"

"Show me the dress."

"Excuse me?"

"I want to see what you're wearing."

"Um, okay." I put him on speaker phone and then quickly snapped a picture.

After texting him the picture, he snarled, "Motherfucker!"

"What's the problem?"

"The problem, my dear wife, is you appear to be missing half your dress considering how much leg you're showing. For fuck's sake, if I were to see it from behind, I'd wager your arse would be hanging out."

I scowled at the phone. "I don't think it shows that much. I'm tall, so everything tends to be shorter on me."

"You've only been out of the order a few weeks, and you're already dressing like a fallen woman."

With a gasp, I replied, "I know you didn't just bring up the order." Although there were times I swore Callum knew me far too well, there was no way he could have a grasp on the level of guilt I carried about leaving the order.

"Perhaps reminding you of it will help you make better choices."

"You know what? Since I'm married to a fallen Irish mobster, perhaps I should dress the part," I hissed.

"I'm done speaking to you about this. Pick another dress."

And then he had the audacity to hang up on me. "Two can play at this game," I muttered.

At a knock on the dressing room door, I called, "Yes?"

Jessica replied, "I was just checking to see how things were coming along."

With a smile, I opened the door. "I'll take this one."

Chapter Twenty-Four: Caterina

Just before seven, I stood before the full-length mirror in the bedroom. As I stared at my reflection, it was like seeing a stranger before me. I barely recognized the woman in the skin tight dress, the flowing wavy locks, and heavy makeup.

Guilt, my almost constant companion since leaving the order, rippled through me.

A month ago I would've been in my plain blue skirt and white blouse. My hair would've been swept into a ponytail. My time would've been consumed by caring for others unlike today where it was focused on frivolous things like shopping for a dress to make my husband desire me.

Callum was right. I had turned into a fallen woman.

Unable to bear my reflection any longer, I stepped away from the mirror. Just as I reached around to unzip my dress, a knock at the door startled me. "Yes?"

Seamus stepped inside. At the sight of me, his eyes bulged somewhat comically out of their sockets. "I, uh..." He swallowed hard. "Callum asked me to tell you it was time to go."

I held my hand up. "Don't worry. I'm not leaving the house in this scrap of a dress because I'm not going to the club."

Shaking his head, he closed the door behind him. "But you were so adamant about going at breakfast this morning."

"I know. I was."

"So what changed your mind?"

"You wouldn't understand."

He crossed his arms over his broad chest. "Try me."

"This dress...it makes me feel guilty about leaving the order. I feel like I've lost myself."

I swallowed down the tears threatening to fall. "I feel like I've lost my faith."

Seamus apprised me silently. After a few moments passed, he stepped towards me. "The vast majority of Catholics don't hold positions in the clergy. Does that mean their faith and their works matter less than those of nuns and priests?"

"No. Of course not."

"Then why do you doubt the commitment to your faith simply because your life has changed?"

I sighed exasperatedly "I don't know—I just do."

"A wise person once said that the love of a man and woman is holy. And that just because you love a man, it doesn't mean you love God less."

At what must've been my shock about him alluding to me loving Callum, he smiled. "I said that just to show you that marriage can be honorable."

"It's a very wise sentiment."

"Aye, I thought as much."

"Who was it that said it?"

Seamus winked at me. "Mother Superior in *The Sound of Music*."

A laugh burst from my lips. "I thought it sounded familiar."

"I imagined you might appreciate the reference."

"I'm surprised you know it."

"It was one of my late wife's favorite movies."

My heart ached for the anguish in his eyes. "I'm very sorry for your loss. And for the loss of your son," I said.

"Thank you, lass. I didn't tell you all of that to make you sad."

"I know. And you didn't."

"Did you at least change your mind about seeing a marriage as honorable as being a nun?"

"Yes, I can see it as honorable." I motioned to my dress. "But this?"

With a chuckle, Seamus said, "That dress is sin."

I rolled my eyes. "I knew it."

"But it's a necessary sin."

"I don't think I was schooled on that in my classes at the order."

As a smirk curved on his lips, Seamus asked, "Are you wearing that dress to entice me?"

A shriek of horror escaped my lips. "Absolutely not!"

"Are you wearing it to entice the men at the club?"

When I shook my head furiously from side to side, Seamus leaned closer to me. "Caterina, are you wearing that dress to entice your husband?"

"Yes," I whispered.

He smiled. "Then it's a necessary sin."

I nodded. "I think I get it now."

"Good."

"Caterina, let's go!" Callum barked from downstairs.

Seamus grinned. "Go on and knock him dead."

"Are you sure?"

He nodded. "More than anything else, go and have some fun. You're young, and after all you've been through in the last few years, you deserve to be carefree."

Although I still wasn't totally convinced, I decided it was worth a try. After bestowing a quick kiss on Seamus's cheek, I replied, "Thank you."

Raised voices filled my ears as I made my way down the hallway. "Caterina!" Callum shouted.

"I'm here!" I called from the top of the staircase.

When I stepped into the foyer, talking silenced. I bit down on my lip not to laugh from the expressions on their faces. Although it was nice seeing the effect the dress had on Quinn, Dare, and Kellan, my attention focused only on Callum.

After reaching the last step, Callum barreled through his brothers to stand before me. "What the fuck, Caterina?" Callum demanded.

"Is there a problem?" I asked with doe-eyed innocence.

"I told you under no circumstances were you to get that dress!"

"Yes, I'm aware of that."

"And you chose to defy me?" he growled.

"After all the dresses I tried on, this was my favorite."

Although Callum shook with rage, I wasn't afraid. Reaching out, I patted his arm. "Don't worry. I have a coverup."

He eyed me curiously. "You do?"

"Just let me grab it out of the closet."

When I walked away, I felt Callum's eyes boring into my back or more precisely into my butt. I grabbed a sheer, silver shawl out of the closet.

After I'd slid it onto my arms, I turned around. "See?"

While Dare threw back his head with a laugh, Quinn and Kellan hid their laughter behind their hands. "That doesn't cover shit," Callum growled.

"Oh, okay. Then I won't worry about it." I stripped it off my arms and threw it back into the closet. "Ready?"

When his blue eyes turned black, I took a step back and debated whether I'd perhaps gone too far. "Leave us," he instructed in a low voice.

"We'll meet you there," Quinn replied.

As I watched their retreating forms, I swallowed hard, fighting the urge to run after them. Like a wolf stalking its prey, Callum began to circle me, his steps echoing off the marble floor. In that moment, I knew I'd made a very big mistake.

Chapter Twenty-Five: Callum

Since the night I'd fallen asleep with Caterina in my arms, I'd been in an emotional tailspin. Not only was I dealing with my grief over Sean's loss, but my head was completely fucked up over my growing feelings for Caterina.

In the early days of our relationship, my primary feelings for Caterina had been lust and desire along with a need to protect her. But after that night, my feelings had become much, much more.

Something about lying with her in my arms had splintered the emotional dam I had erected. In those moments, she'd been everything I'd wanted in a wife.

At first, I thought putting distance between us was the answer. I stopped coming home for dinner and spent more and more time at the office. It wasn't totally a ruse since I was finishing up work on the opening for Bandia.

I soon found that distance didn't help.

I still thought about her constantly.

While she didn't know it, I remained in contact with Owen and Shane about what she was doing. Not that I distrusted her. No, I just wanted to know what she was doing.

I was fucking hopeless.

And then she had to go and weasel her way into attending the opening of the club, which was the last fucking thing I wanted her to do. Outside of our reception, it would be the first time she was on display as my wife. Caterina thought I just didn't want to spend time with her, but that wasn't the truth.

I didn't want her to go because I wanted to protect her. Now that I felt even more for her, I worried for her safety.

Once her face was splashed across media sites, all my enemies would have a face to go with the name. I knew it was inevitable that people would know who she was. They would no longer be satisfied with just hearing that I'd married Alessio Neretti's daughter. They would want to see her at my side.

And for the first time in my fucking life, I was afraid.

I was fucking afraid I might not be able to protect my wife from all the wolves circling us.

To protect Caterina, I needed her to follow my instructions. I needed her to bury her defiance because that would only cause trouble for her in the long run. She needed to listen to me and respect my wishes.

But of course, my little hellcat couldn't do that.

Tonight she'd flaunted her disobedience in a dress that could make a man with the strongest resolve come in his pants. Part of me refusing the dress was because I didn't want to murder every son of a bitch who looked at her with lust in his eyes.

But the other part of me didn't want her drawing so much attention. The wolves were looking for any reason to attack.

As I stared her down, I began to pace around her. I tried swallowing my growing anger. "Have I not been kind to you, Caterina?"

"Yes," she replied.

"Have I not indulged you with your wishes to go to university and have a career?"

"Yes."

"Compared to what your fate could have been had another man kidnapped you and forced you into marriage, you've practically won the bleedin' lottery, right?"

She eyed me sullenly. "I suppose so."

"You *suppose?*"

Caterina appeared to be fighting not to lash out at me. Finally, she responded, "Yes, I have."

"Then why must you continue to provoke me by not doing as I ask?"

"It's just a dress, Callum," she protested softly.

"It's more than a fucking dress!" I bellowed.

She held up her hands. "Look, I didn't do it to make you angry or to defy you."

Like hell she didn't. I chuckled darkly. "Don't lie."

"I'm not."

"You knew I didn't want you to wear this dress, yet you wore it anyway. That, Kitten, is defying me."

"But that's not—"

"Stop fucking arguing with me."

At my menacing glare, she cowered back slightly. "I need to know why you go out of your way to disregard my instructions. I need a wife who understands that sometimes my commands are in her best interests."

"You sure don't act like you want me to be your wife," she countered.

"Excuse me?"

Caterina threw up her hands. "You want to know why I bought the dress even though you told me not to?"

"Why?"

"I wanted you to notice me!"

My eyes popped wide. "Notice you?"

She dropped her gaze to her strappy red heels. "Since the night we slept in each other's arms, you've been ignoring me. You barely look at me, least of all talk to me."

After she swallowed hard, she dared to look up at me. "I thought by wearing this dress you'd notice me again."

Fucking hell. How could my bride be so fucking naive? "You don't think I've noticed you?" I questioned, my voice becoming impossibly deep.

"Yes," she whispered.

Slowly, I shook my head. "I notice *everything* about you, Kitten."

She frowned. "Then why haven't you come home at night to be with me? And why don't you talk to me anymore?"

I placed my hand on my hips and countered, "Because you've got me by the balls."

Of course my innocent wife would blush at the mention of my balls. "W-What?"

I chuckled darkly. "You're in my head and under my skin. I want to possess you mind, body, and soul."

I pushed a strand of hair out of her face. "And feeling that way about you fucks with my head.

"Because you don't want to care so much for me?" she questioned softly.

With a shake of my head, I replied, "Because I don't want anything to happen to you."

"I don't understand."

"The moment you became my wife you gained a target on your back. You could argue as Alessio Neretti's daughter, you were born with one. Enemies of your father or enemies of mine would use you to get to us."

Her brows rose in surprise. "And that's why you've been staying away? Because you're worried about protecting me?"

"Aye. And because I'm a man who doesn't do well with expressing feelings."

She scowled at me. "I'm well aware of your aversion to feelings."

"I swear that if anyone can get me to change, it's you, Kitten."

Tilting her head at me, Caterina said, "I'll let you off the hook this time only if you promise to communicate with me."

With a grunt, I replied, "I'm not making any promises."

"Callum," she implored.

"Fine. I'll communicate with you if you'll do what I ask of you." When she opened her mouth to protest, I shook my head. "Like I said before, it's for your protection."

"I'll try," she relented.

I motioned to the door. "We better go."

"You're not going to make me change?"

"Would you?"

"Yes." At what must've been my surprise, she added, "But I wouldn't like it."

I threw my head back with a laugh. "Oh Kitten, you're going to be the death of me." Her sly grin hit me right in the pants. I took her hand in mine and led her out to the waiting SUV.

It only took ten minutes to arrive at the club. When we exited the SUV, the bright camera flashes momentarily blinded me. If there was one thing I loathed, it was having to make nice with the press.

But we needed a positive public profile not just for our legitimate business ventures, but to hide the darker shit we were involved in.

Turning back to the SUV, I offered my hand to Caterina. As she stepped out, her eyes skittered over the crowd with an almost deer in the headlights look.

Leaning over, I whispered in her ear, "Don't worry. I'll do all the talking. Just put one foot in front of the other."

Swallowing hard, she gave a slight nod. After assessing the journalists waiting on us, I steered Caterina over to the one who worked for the entertainment section of the Globe. My assistant had reminded me earlier in the day who Delia Hunter was, and that I should be sure to make nice with her.

Giving her my best smile, I said, "Good evening, Delia."

"Callum, you've managed quite a turnout tonight. What do you think makes Bandia Boston's new hotspot?"

"Well, I suppose it doesn't hurt that it's owned by four handsome men with sexy Irish accents?" I teased.

Delia tittered at my joke. "I would say that's a huge selling point."

"As far as standing out from other clubs, we also brought in some design aspects that incorporate the mythology of our ancestry."

"I have to say the architecture is stunning."

"Thank you."

Delia's gaze cut from mine over to Caterina who shifted nervously in her heels. "Speaking of stunning, who is this absolutely stunning woman on your arm?"

I gave her a genuine smile. "This is my wife, Caterina."

Delia's eyes widened. "Your wife? This news is sure to elicit heartbreak all over the city considering your previous eligible bachelor status."

Caterina eyed me curiously before replying, "I didn't know I snagged one of Boston's most eligible bachelors," she teased with a smile.

At Delia's confused look, Caterina replied, "I'm from New York."

"Oh, I see. Allow me to say your beauty will certainly make the city shine brighter."

Caterina's cheeks flushed at the compliment. Before she could say thank you, I replied, "She's certainly made my life shine brighter."

I grinned at the perfect 'o' of surprise that my compliment formed on Caterina's red lips. Delia gave Caterina an envious glance before saying, "Once again, good luck on the opening of the club."

"Thank you," I replied.

I then steered Caterina through the rest of the crowd. As we started into the club, she peered up at me. "You really laid it on thick with that reporter, huh?"

"Who says I wasn't telling the truth?"

"*I've* made your life shine brighter, or my beauty?" Caterina questioned suspiciously.

I chuckled. "Aye, Kitten, every part of you has made my life brighter."

"That means a lot." With a teasing glint in her eyes, she added, "Especially considering your eligible bachelor status. I'm surprised you never managed to tell me that tidbit."

I flashed her a wicked grin. "It didn't make sense to tell you when I was kidnapping you." Tilting my head, I asked, "If I had, would you still have shot me?"

"Absolutely."

I snorted. "I'm only an eligible bachelor to the ignorant outsiders. The ones who think I'm just a wealthy businessman and have no idea about all my dark dealings."

"Like how you kidnap potential nuns from religious orders and force them to be your bride?" she teased with a smile.

I scowled at her. "I'd hardly call that one of my dark dealings. It was a necessary evil."

She rolled her eyes. "Keep telling yourself that."

With my hand resting against the small of her back, I guided Caterina to a roped off VIP section. Once we were inside, I found

Dare talking with two scantily dressed women. He managed to tear his attention away from them long enough to wave at us.

After waving back, Caterina peered around. Since I was sure she was looking for Quinn or Kellan, I replied, "They're working the floor."

"Quinn is socializing with people?" Caterina questioned incredulously.

I laughed. "Let me rephrase that. Kellan is talking up people while Quinn is keeping people in line with his death glares."

She grinned. "That makes more sense."

After I motioned for Caterina to have a seat in the booth, I slid in next to her. Dare once again tore his attention away from the women to shoot Caterina a wicked smile. "What's your poison, Sister?"

Shifting anxiously in her seat, Caterina replied, "I'm not sure."

"You've really never had any alcohol?" I asked.

"I'm Italian, so obviously I've had wine."

I snorted. "That's it?"

"Some champagne. But nothing too hardcore."

"Aye, yes, you're practically a liquor virgin," Dare mused.

"Watch it," I warned.

With a wink, Dare replied, "Obviously you have to have to drink an Irish whiskey. For your genteel palette, I could recommend starting with Redbreast 12."

After wagging his brows he added, "And I'm not being cheeky by choosing one with breast in the name."

While Caterina giggled, I shot him a murderous look before waving our private waiter over. "Bring us a shot of Redbreast 12 and a bottle of the Teeling 34-Year-Old Vintage Reserve."

Dare whistled. "You have expensive taste this evening."

Shrugging I replied, "We need good whiskey to celebrate."

Caterina glanced between us. "How expensive?"

"About four thousand dollars a bottle."

Dare and I chuckled at the level of horror on Caterina's face. "Don't worry, Kitten. I'm good for it."

She slowly shook her head. "It's positively sinful. Do you know the amount of good that would've done for the order?"

"Would it ease your conscience if I promised to donate the same amount to the church?"

With a scowl, she countered, "It's not my conscience that you should be worried about."

"Fine. First thing in the morning, I'll make sure to donate four thousand to the Sacred Heart."

Before she could argue with me, the waiter reappeared with our whiskey. When Caterina took her glass, she eyed the dark liquid warily. "Are you sure this is what I should drink?"

"Yes," Dare and I replied in unison.

"Fine." With a hesitant smile, Caterina said, "Bottoms up."

Leaning forward in my seat, I watched with amusement as Caterina took a giant gulp of the whiskey. As a shudder ran through her body, she sputtered and gasped.

Waving her hand in front of her face, her eyes watered before spilling over her cheeks. "That. Was. Horrible!" she screeched.

I threw my head back with a laugh as Dare snickered. Our reaction earned us a glare from Caterina. "I should've mentioned it's really an acquired taste."

Narrowing her eyes at me, Caterina replied, "I'd rather never taste it again."

"Trust me, you'll enjoy the buzz if you do," Dare said.

"She's not getting buzzed," I countered.

"And why not?"

I jabbed a finger at Dare. "Because I said so."

With defiance sparkling in her eyes, Caterina brought the glass to her lips again and took another hearty gulp. While Dare snorted at her behavior, I merely shook my head. "Oh, Kitten, it's going to be a long night."

Chapter Twenty-Six: Caterina

While I sat in the VIP booth at Bandia, I'd never felt more out of my element in all my life. What I thought would be a fun evening was anything but. I didn't like the fake smiles and small talk of the club goers. Those who came by to congratulate Callum barely acknowledged me.

No one seemed interested in trying to get to know me. I suppose to them I appeared as the epitome of a trophy wife. Just some vapid social climber who had latched onto Callum because of his money and standing.

"What's wrong, Sister Sassy?" Dare asked.

I smiled at him. "What happened to your admirers?"

He waved a hand dismissively. "I banged them in my office and sent them on their way."

My eyes widened at his admission. "T-Them?" I sputtered.

"Don't tell me you want the details?" he teased.

Heat rose on my cheeks as I stared down at my whiskey glass. "No. I don't."

"I answered your question, so now you can answer mine." His index finger touched my chin before raising my gaze to his. "What's wrong?"

With a shrug, I replied, "It's nothing really."

"Out with it," he ordered.

"Everyone is just so...fake."

"Yeah, the sheer amount of fake tits and bad BBLs I've seen tonight is astounding."

Laughing, I replied, "That's not the fake I was talking about."

He grinned. "I imagined as much."

"Don't tell Callum, but I really wish I hadn't come."

Dare shook his head. "No, no. We can't have you feeling that way. You need another whiskey to loosen you up."

Nibbling my lip, I replied, "I don't know."

"Trust me." He waved the waiter over again.

"I still haven't finished this one," I protested.

"Then do it."

Just as I brought the drink to my lips, a commotion drew my attention over to the edge of the VIP area. A buxom blonde in a slinky dress had her arms wrapped around Callum.

"Oh my God, Cal, it's been forever. You don't know how much I've missed you."

Instead of untangling himself from the woman and telling her to get lost since he was a married man, Callum merely smiled. "It's good to see you again, too, Jocelyn."

Desiring some liquid courage, I threw back the remainder of the whiskey just at the moment Jocelyn's hand slid down Callum's chest to rest on his dick. "I've missed this even more," she practically purred.

The alcohol spewed from my lips as a red rage crisscrossed my vision. Although Callum had shoved Jocelyn's hand away, I couldn't believe he'd allowed her to touch him to start with.

"Caterina, don't," Dare warned.

"She's molesting my husband," I shot back.

"Her father is a city councilman. Callum is just playing the game."

"That doesn't mean *I* have to go along with it." Shooting out of my chair, I stalked over to them.

"Oh fuck, this is about to get ugly," Dare muttered as he fell in step behind me.

Without even thinking, I knocked Callum away from Jocelyn. "What the hell do you think you're doing?" I demanded.

While Callum had the nerve to smirk at me, Jocelyn got into my face. Her blue eyes narrowed to fury filled slits. "I don't know what your problem is, bitch."

"*Bitch?*" I questioned incredulously.

"That's what I said. I don't know who you think you are coming over and interrupting me and my man like that."

"*Your* man?" I flashed my ring in her face. "Last time I checked, he was my *husband*."

While Jocelyn's eyes popped wide at my declaration, I turned my fury on Callum who had the audacity to be staring at me with a grin.

"And *you* can go fuck yourself!" I shouted before I whirled around and fled from the VIP section.

Tears blurred my eyes as I pushed and shoved my way through the crowd. I didn't make it too far until a pair of strong arms slithered around my waist and jerked me back against a hard body.

"Let me go!" I shouted before smacking at the arms around me.

Alcohol laced breath scorched against my ear. "You're not going anywhere until I get a piece of your sweet ass."

"Stop it!" I shrieked.

"Mmm, I'm going to love hearing you scream my name tonight." His hand slid up my ribcage to cup my breast. "Say it, bitch. Say Blake is going to rock my world."

I kept fighting against him to no avail while trying to fight my rising panic. He had to be in the military because he knew to block each of my self-defense moves.

Surely one of the bouncers had to be around, not to mention Quinn and Kellan were supposed to be working the main floor.

Blake's grip suddenly jerked free, sending me staggering to regain my footing. When I whirled around to see what had happened, Callum had the man by the throat. Pure menace was written over his expression.

"How dare you put your fucking hands on something that belongs to me."

Blake shook his head furiously back and forth as his face turned crimson. "Don't you dare fucking lie to me when I saw it with my own fucking eyes!" Callum blared.

As Callum's grip on Blake's neck tightened, Blake sank to his knees. The lethally cruel expression on Callum's face would give me nightmares in the nights to come.

I didn't like seeing him this way.

I didn't like believing he could be that violent.

That deadly.

"Callum, stop!" I cried, as I tried pulling his hand off the man's throat.

"Stay out of this," he snarled.

"You're going to kill him if you don't stop."

"That's what happens when you disrespect me in my club."

Glancing around, miraculously no one had their eyes on us. They remained dancing and talking. Considering how dark it was, you would've had to be right beside us to truly see what was transpiring. Of course, a dead body on the ground would be harder to conceal.

"But everyone will see."

As my words started to break through to him, Quinn and Kellan appeared. It was only their combined strength that pulled Callum off of Blake. A guttural gasping noise came from Blake's lips before he collapsed to the ground.

Quinn and Kellan snapped into action by getting him to his feet. With him pressed between the two brothers, it looked like the three were dancing.

To distract anyone from Callum's rage, I slid my arms around his's neck and dragged his forehead down to rest against mine. His hands reached out to grip my waist before molding me against him. His broad chest heaved against me as he worked to get his fury under control.

Although I was still frightened of his behavior, I couldn't abandon him when he needed me. "Look at me," I commanded.

His blue eyes locked with mine. "Just breathe," I murmured.

The murderous gleam in his expression began to fade. When he finally regarded me without brutality, I sighed. The remorse that glittered in his eyes broke my heart.

"I'm sorry you had to see me like that, Kitten."

"I won't lie that you scared the shit out of me."

He smirked. "Apparently so since it made you curse."

I shook my head. "I'm serious, Callum."

Regret flooded his face. "I know. And I'm sorry." He brushed his knuckles along my chin. "I wouldn't have you fear me for anything in the world."

"Deep down I know that's who you are, but I don't like seeing it. Just like I know it's who my brothers are.

He stared intently at me. "I've never lost my mind like that over any other woman," he admitted.

"You haven't?"

"Besides the fact he was molesting you, no one is to *ever* touch you."

I rolled my eyes. "Quit acting like a neanderthal."

"You're mine, Kitten."

Jerking my chin up, I countered, "I belong to no man."

Callum's hand came to grip my chin under my neck. "You. Are. Mine."

When his expression turned over to smoldering lust, it sent a pulsing ache between my legs. Heat flared over my body under his scrutiny. While we stared into each other's eyes, Callum's hands slid from my waist down to cup my ass.

At my gasp, he slammed his lips against mine. When he thrust his tongue into mouth, I moaned. As he continued his assault on my mouth, his hands pushed my center against the growing hardness in his pants. Gripping his shoulders, I held on for dear life.

As his lips left my mouth, my eyes remained closed as he kissed a trail over my jawline. When he got my ear, he sucked my earlobe causing me to shudder.

At the graze of his teeth, my eyes popped open just as he bit the sensitive flesh. Pleasure shot through me as he continued to bite and lick down my neck.

Taking one of my legs, Callum hooked it over his hip. My dress was so short that it caused the hem to ride up almost to expose my panties.

The new angle pressed his erection against my core. As he continued thrusting against me, my nipples peaked at the feeling while my thong grew damper by the minute.

In that heady, passionate moment, I wanted nothing more than for him to take me. Even though we were in a club surrounded by people, I wanted him to make me his.

I wanted to feel the length of him within me.

I wanted to truly be his.

When Callum started to pull away from me, I gripped the front of his shirt. "Don't stop," I moaned into his mouth.

A chuckle rumbled through his chest. "Trust me, Kitten. The last thing on this fucking earth I want to do it is stop."

When my eyes popped open, I glanced past us to see Quinn staring down at the floor. As I fought to catch my breath, Callum eased my leg down. I quickly pushed the hemline of the dress back down my thighs.

Callum's warm breath tickled against my earlobe. "I have to go handle some business bullshit."

When I nodded, he said, "Quinn's going to escort you to the VIP section."

"Okay."

When he pulled back to look at me, a sexy smirk curved on his lips. "I hope we can finish what we started later.

A shiver ran through me at his words. "Maybe."

He groaned. "You're killing me, Kitten."

I merely grinned back at him. After Callum turned and made his way through the crowd, Quinn finally brought his eyes to meet mine.

I couldn't help the mortification that warmed my cheeks considering what he saw me and Callum doing. Even though we were married, embarrassment still flooded me.

"Come on, lass. I need a drink." A teasing glint flashed in his eyes. "And from the looks of it, you do, too."

At my sharp intake of breath, Quinn chuckled before tucking me to his side. When I reached the VIP section, I thankfully found Jocelyn was gone.

At the sight of me, Dare's eyes popped comically wide. "Sister Sassy, were you and my brother bumping uglies on the dance floor?"

Instead of recoiling in horror, a laugh burst from my lips at Dare's absurd reference. "No comment."

While I might not have been blushing, Kellan was. Dare handed him and myself a drink. Waggling his brows, he said, "I think it's time we did some shots!"

Chapter Twenty-Seven: Callum

While I originally thought my business would only take me away from Caterina for a few minutes, it stretched on and on.

Important people to greet.

Crowd control issues from the bouncers.

Just when I thought I was finished, something else would come up.

Of course, one matter remained chained up in the freezer. Although Quinn and Kellan had worked Blake over, it was up to me to finish him.

A quick background check had revealed Blake had a history of sexual assault not only in Boston, but Farmington and Brookline. He'd done time for raping a coed.

Owen stood outside keeping watch. He nodded at me as I started inside the walk-in freezer. Blake's bruised and battered body shivered in the far corner beside two stacks of frozen hors d'oeuvres.

At the sight of me, he tried fighting against the chains.

I tsked at him. "You've been a very bad boy, Blake."

His eyes peeled back in fear. "S-Sorry. Won't do it again," he mumbled through his split lip.

"You know, I'd love to say I believe you. That my wife was such a vision that it just made you so crazy you couldn't help but touch her."

I shook my head. "But I've seen your record. You can't keep your hands to yourself or your dick in your pants."

Blake had the good sense to keep his mouth shut. There was nothing he could possibly say that would've saved him anyway. Reaching into my suit pocket, I pulled out my knife.

"It would seem that by ending you, I'd be doing the female population of Massachusetts a solid."

At the gleam of my blade in the light, an ear-piercing scream tore from Blake's lips. When I took a step towards him, he began tugging frantically at the chains.

Glancing over my shoulder, I nodded at Owen. Without a word, he closed the freezer door.

I didn't have time to truly toy with him. I wanted to inflict agony for the suffering he had caused others. I knew despite what he had done to her and to other women, Caterina wouldn't agree with what I was about to do.

She would agree he deserved torture but not death. Even though she'd grown up in a mafia family, her heart remained pure. Her faith and her time in the order wouldn't condone it.

As my shoes scraped over the metal grate in the floor, I gave thanks that it would allow the soldiers an easy clean up. I stepped behind Blake to where his back rested against my chest. It was the only way to ensure I didn't end up with blood all over my suit.

After gripping Blake's hair, I jerked his head, exposing his neck.

Whispering into his ear, I said, "You won't ever put your hands on a woman again."

He screamed. But the moment my knife entered his throat, it began to warble and hiss.

Once I'd sliced him from side to side, I tossed him away from me. His body lurched and trembled as the last bits of his essence flowed out onto the freezer floor.

At the squeaking of the door, I turned around to see two soldiers standing behind Owen. I nodded at them. "Make sure there's not an ounce of blood to be found and ditch the chains. I don't want to get fucked over down the road by the health inspector."

"Yes, Mr. Kavanaugh," they replied in unison.

After exiting the freezer, I went to the sink next to the backdoor to wash my hands. I handed off the knife to Owen. "Take care of that for me."

"Yes, sir."

Once my hands were clean, I examined my clothes to make sure I was spotless. Caterina would lose her shit if she saw blood on me. After our dance floor make-out, the last thing I needed was for her to shut me out.

Finally I made my way up the stairs to the VIP section. Surveying the area, I found Kellan talking to a few of his buddies.

"Where's my wife?" I demanded.

"She wanted to dance, so Dare took her downstairs."

Although I didn't like the idea of her dancing without me, I couldn't fault her for growing bored sitting around. I once again made my way downstairs. Gazing around the dimly lit room, I searched for Caterina.

And when I found her, red rage blinded my vision as my wife's voluptuous ass gyrated against my bastard of a brother's crotch.

Not only was the son of bitch not stopping her, but he was grinning at her antics like a fucking Cheshire Cat.

I would enjoy knocking the fucking smile off his face later tonight.

I might punch out a few teeth while I was at it. At the moment, I only had one focus, and that was getting to Caterina.

As I made my way across the dance floor, I started pushing and shoving people. When I stood only a few feet from them, Caterina's gaze locked with mine.

Instead of appearing guilty for her erotic dance with Dare, her eyes popped wide with excitement before she leapt into my arms. "I missed you!" she exclaimed, peppering both my cheeks with kisses. I fought my surprise at how affectionate she was being.

Burying her nose into my neck, she inhaled sharply. "Mm, you smell so good, baby," she crooned.

"*Baby?*" I questioned. I couldn't imagine what the hell had gotten into her using a term of endearment on me. Especially considering what had transpired earlier with me and Jocelyn.

With a giggle, she replied, "Yeah, you're my baby—you big, bad mafia man."

I eased her back in my arms to stare curiously into her flushed face. Fuck me.

My beautiful, young wife was completely banjaxed. She had no clue what she was doing, least of all with who.

"You're banjaxed," I pronounced.

Her nose wrinkled. "What?"

"It means yer feckin' wasted, Kitten."

Wrapping her legs tighter around my waist, she bent her head to whisper in my ear. "I might've had just a little bit to drink."

With a grunt, I countered, "How can you possibly be this inebriated? I was gone for barely an hour."

"Dare dared me to do shots," she replied. Then she giggled. "Dare *dared* sounds funny, doesn't it?"

I glared at Dare over her shoulder. "You did shots with my wife?"

"I didn't expect her to go toe to toe with me." He then winked. "She's a cute little drunk, isn't she?"

As Caterina bounced and jiggled in my arms to the music, I

rolled my eyes. "I was thinking more like an annoying gnat on a summer day."

Caterina jumped down and staggered over to Dare. "More shots!"

"Oh hell no." I shook my head. "No more shots for you. *Ever*."

She pushed her bottom lip out. After smacking my chest, she pronounced, "You're a mean party pooper, Callum."

"That I am." Grabbing her arm, I said, "Come on. It's time to get you home."

"No! I don't want to go," she shrieked, pulling against me.

I shot a look at Dare who had the nerve to grin at me. "I will pay you back for this, brother."

"I look forward to it."

When I grabbed Caterina around the waist, she tried twisting away from me. "Let me go. I want to dance."

"We're going home," I countered before hoisting her up over my shoulder.

Another ear-piercing shriek ricocheted through my ear. "Put me down, Callum!" she commanded.

I smacked her ass. "Retract the claws, Kitten."

"Don't you dare manhandle me." Her fists beat against my lower back. "Put me down, you bastard."

With a chuckle, I mused, "Listen to that language. A month out of the order, and you sound like a sailor down at the Belfast docks."

"I do not!"

"Aye, you do."

With my free hand, I dug my phone out of my pocket and called for my driver. After alerting him, I carried Caterina down the employee hallway to the backdoor. I nodded to the bodyguard at the door and he opened it for me.

Caterina continued to thrash in my arms while wailing about wanting to stay. "If you don't put a cork in it, Kitten, I'll never let you back in my club."

Her angry shouts cut off and were replaced by sniffling. As I slid her back onto her feet, tears welled in her dark eyes.

"Why are you crying?"

Wrapping her arms around herself, she sobbed, "Because you're so mean not letting me come to your club again."

"That's not what I said."

"Yes, it is!" she shrieked.

Be it sober or drunk, this woman was going to be the death of me. I rolled my eyes and vowed once again to beat the hell out of Dare for getting her drunk.

Thankfully, the SUV arrived, and after the driver opened the backdoor, I hoisted Caterina up into the backseat.

As her sobs turned into hiccupping cries, I turned my attention to my phone. I opened our group text to let Quinn and Kellan know I was leaving and to remind the three of them about their closing duties.

After shoving my phone back in my pocket, I cut my eyes over to Caterina. At her heated gaze, I shifted uncomfortably.

While I was thankful she was no longer on a crying jag, I was wary of the sudden lust glittering in her eyes.

Before I could stop her, Caterina lunged across the seat to straddle me. Her dress had ridden so far up her thighs I could see the red scrap of lace covering her pussy. After sliding her arms around my neck, she slammed her lips against mine.

Unlike my sober wife, my drunk wife took what she wanted.

After thrusting her tongue in my mouth, her hips began to roll against my crotch. I could feel her white-hot heat through my slacks, which caused my neglected cock to harden.

Her nails scoured through my hair, causing me to hiss. "I want you, Callum," she purred against my lips.

"Oh, fuck, Kitten," I growled as my hands slipped up her neck. I thrust my erection against her core, causing us both to moan. But then I remembered the woman on my lap was my very drunk, *virgin* bride. I brought my hands to her waist and then pushed her off my cock.

"What are you doing?"

"We're not doing this. Not here and not while you're drunk."

She pouted. "Don't you want me?"

"Aye, Kitten."

"Then why won't you..."

I cupped her face in my hands. "Why won't I fuck you if it's so evident I want you?"

She nodded.

"Because when I finally fuck you, it won't be some frenzied joining in the back of an SUV where I blow my load after two minutes because you've got me so strung out. I'll have you laid out before me on a bed, so I can see and taste every glorious inch of your body. I'll take my time with you, so you'll know pleasure before you know pain. Because that first time is going to hurt no matter how gentle I am."

Caterina reached for my hands. After taking them in hers, she brought them to her breasts. "If you won't fuck me, at least touch me." A pleading look flickered in her dark eyes. "Make me come, Callum."

I shook my head as I pulled my hands away. "You'll still hate me."

"I won't."

"Trust me on this one."

Shifting forward, she once again undulated her hips, rubbing her pussy against my dick. "Don't you want to be the first man to ever make me come?"

I threw my head back as a guttural groan escaped my lips. Surely I was being punished. Apparently, I'd finally found an honorable bone in my body. Unfortunately, it had to be with my wife's virtue.

"I can't do this to you right now."

"Fine. If you won't get me off, I will."

After scrambling off my lap and then over the seat, she collapsed onto the third-row bench. With a defiant look in her eyes, she then hiked the hem of her dress up to her waist.

After bracing her feet on the edge of the seat, she widened her legs giving me a perfect view of her thong clad pussy.

"Caterina, don't," I growled.

Without taking her eyes off of mine, she thrust her whole hand inside her underwear. At her sharp intake of breath, my cock throbbed against my zipper. "You're really going to fuck yourself in front of me, little virgin?"

"I want to come, and you won't help me."

"You're drunk, and I've never made it a practice to take advantage of drunk women."

Caterina's dark eyes blazed as she pulled her hand out of her panties, sending a shuddering breath from me. "I'm glad you decided to finally listen to reason."

The words quickly died on my lips when her fingers came to the waistband of her thong. She ripped it down her thighs before throwing it in my face. The smell of her arousal sent a spasm through me.

"Fucking hell, Kitten. Are you trying to kill me?"

This time when she widened her thighs I got an eyeful of her glistening need. "Christ," I choked out.

Her fingers teased her center. She was giving me a slow death. The way her eyes held mine, her smell, her needy pants.

When Caterina thrust two fingers inside herself, her long moan of pleasure sent me cupping my aching cock. Just as I was about to unzip my pants and start jerking off, I remembered we weren't alone.

I tore my gaze from her pussy to the rear-view mirror where the driver stared wide-eyed into the back seat. "Pull over!" I shouted.

"Sir?"

"You fucking heard me. Pull. Over."

The SUV jerked across two lanes to the honking of horns before whipping into the parking lot of a Taco Bell. Once the car came to a stop, I leaned forward in my seat.

"Take a walk."

"You want me to leave you, sir?"

"No one but me gets to hear or see my wife come. Is that clear?"

He bobbed his head furiously before he fumbled for the door. "Keep your weapon close, and your eyes open," I instructed before he hurried out of the car.

Once he was far enough away, I slid out of my seat and flopped down next to Caterina. Her hips were lifting in time to her plunging fingers.

"Oh, Kitten, you're so wet."

"Mm, hmm."

"Give me a taste."

With a glassy look, she argued, "You said you wouldn't touch me."

"Give me your fingers."

After pulling her fingers out of her pussy, she held them out to me. As I leaned forward, her intoxicating aroma filled my nose. "You smell so fucking good, Kitten."

I sucked her fingers into my mouth. At the taste of her, I closed my eyes. I wanted nothing more in the world to replace her fingers in my mouth with her pussy.

When I opened my eyes, I stared into Caterina's. "Fuck me, I want nothing more right now than to bury myself so very deep inside you."

"Please, Callum."

"Christ, Kitten, I can't. You'll hate me."

"Just make me come. Please."

"I can't," I heaved.

Without taking her eyes off mine, she slowly shook her head from side to side. "I won't hate you. I promise."

"Yeah, you say that now, but I know you. Once you sober up, it'll be months before I ever get a chance to touch you again."

My hands went to my belt. After I undid it, I unzipped my pants. Once I took out my cock, I spit into my hand. Caterina's eyes widened at my actions.

"We'll come together, okay?" I questioned, as I jerked my fist up and down my shaft.

Although she appeared disappointed, Caterina began to finger herself once again. It must've been the alcohol because she was ridiculously good at giving herself pleasure.

Or she'd had some practice before the order.

Whatever the reason it was the sexiest thing I'd ever seen, and that was saying a fucking lot.

"Harder," I growled.

Ordinarily, she hated taking orders from me. But my command seemed to turn her on. Her two fingers plunged in and out of her, filling my ears with the squelching sound of her drenched pussy.

"Pinch your clit."

At her mewl of pleasure, I groaned and jerked my hand harder and faster on my cock. "Are you close, Kitten?"

"Yes, Callum," she panted.

"Come for me," I commanded.

While her fingers continued to furiously fuck her pussy, Caterina's other hand slipped into the front of her dress. After pulling her breast halfway out of the bodice, she began to pinch her nipple. "Oh Christ," I muttered, as I sped up my own hand.

As Caterina's orgasm set off, her cry of pleasure echoed through the SUV. Watching her ride out the high sent me over the edge.

Leaning forward, I shot my release onto Caterina's thighs. Although I might not have been able to touch her tonight, I couldn't resist marking her with ropes of my white, hot cum.

When I finished, I tucked my cock back into my pants. Caterina remained slumped over. Pushing her hair back, I chuckled at the sight of her passed out.

Gripping the hem of her dress, I pulled it down her thighs. Once she was covered, I texted the driver.

Within seconds, he was at the door. "You can take us home now," I instructed.

"Yes, sir."

Poison and Wine

As we started down the road, I rolled down the window to let fresh air into the car. If I continued smelling the remainder of our coupling, I was going to be hard as a rock.

Glancing over, I watched my little hellcat sleep.

If I didn't break down her reserve soon, I was going to end up with a permanent case of blue balls.

Chapter Twenty-Eight: Caterina

As I floated into consciousness, a painful awareness filled me. Someone or something was smashing a hammer into my head. Fluttering my eyelids, I peered around trying to decipher where my assailant was.

And then last night's events came rushing back at me so hard I shuddered.

I had gotten completely and ridiculously drunk. And no one was hitting me–I was experiencing my first hangover.

With a groan, I rolled over to find Callum's side of the bed empty. I glanced across the room at the grandfather clock. It was after nine.

He'd already left for work.

A pang entered my chest that he had left me alone to fend for myself through my first hangover. I don't know why I let it bother me.

Callum was an Irish clan leader. He didn't have time to nurse his wife through a hangover.

Sighing, I rolled back over in bed and threw my hand over my eyes. At the sound of footsteps on the hardwood, I said, "Oh Lorna, please don't turn on the lights. Just let me lay here and suffer."

Her response was to throw open the curtains. With a groan, I threw the covers over my head. "Too bright."

"What's wrong, Kitten? Drink a little too much last night?"

Oh my God.

It was Callum, not Lorna.

He hadn't left me alone. Although pleasure surged through me, I peeked out from the covers to glare at him. "Bastard," I muttered.

He had the audacity to chuckle. "Such language."

"Please just go away and leave me in pain."

He eased down beside me on the bed. "What kind of husband would I be if I didn't take care of my dear hungover wife in her hour of need?"

Although I was thrilled he stayed, I still couldn't help wondering why. As I pulled the covers back down, I stared suspiciously at him. "What's the catch?"

"There's not one."

"I don't believe you."

He held out a mug to me. "This will help you get back on your feet."

I pushed myself up in bed. "What is it?"

"An Irish hangover cure."

As I took the mug from him, I peered down at the steaming, pale contents. When a whiff of the concoction entered my nose, I frowned. "It smells awful."

Callum chuckled. "It tastes awful, too. But it's the only thing that will keep you from being miserable today."

After blowing rivulets across the drink's surface, I leaned forward to sip cautiously. As soon as the contents hit my stomach, I gagged. "Oh God," I muttered.

"Trust me, I know."

He jerked his thumb at the bathroom. "I'm going to grab a shower. You better empty that mug by the time I'm done."

I narrowed my eyes at him. "And what if I don't?"

"Then I'm going to take you over my knee and spank your stubborn arse."

I gasped. "You wouldn't dare!" I winced the moment I shouted as it sent pain echoing through my head.

"Try me, Kitten."

When he turned his back to go into the bathroom, I very maturely stuck out my tongue. Although I was mildly curious about whether or not he would really enact his threat, I decided for my overall well-being it was better to drink the tonic, even though I gagged with each and every sip.

After I was done, I leaned over to set the mug on the nightstand. When I rolled back over, my eyelids felt too heavy. The next thing I knew I was sliding back into sleep.

When I woke again, it no longer felt like I was being assaulted with a hammer. I didn't feel nauseous anymore, nor did my body ache all over. Callum hadn't been lying about the drink. It was a miracle worker.

"Feeling better?" a deep voice questioned.

I opened my eyes to see Callum sitting across from me wearing dress pants and a button-down shirt. He pushed his computer off his lap and rose to his feet. My mouth ran positively dry as I watched him close the distance between us.

"Much better. Thank you for the drink."

He smiled. "I've had to use it more times than I can count."

After pushing myself up in the bed, I frowned. "Why do I feel sticky all over?"

"The drink makes you sweat the alcohol out."

"Oh."

"Do you want me to draw you a bath?"

My heart thrummed wildly in my chest at his kindness. "That would be nice."

He nodded before walking into the bathroom. Since I needed to pee, I threw back the covers and padded across the floor.

When I got inside, Callum was bent over the tub adjusting the taps. A delicious lavender scent floated back to me as foamy bubbles rose in the water.

After sitting down on the toilet, I stared curiously down at my thighs. Furrowing my brows, I ran my fingers over my skin.

"Bath is ready," Callum pronounced from the doorway.

I quickly wiped and flushed before going over to the sink. After washing my hands, I turned back to him. I hiked up my short robe to reveal my legs.

"Did I spill something on me?"

After Callum's gaze dipped down to my thighs, a dark, lustful look entered his eyes. "Do you remember anything about last night besides getting drunk?"

Tilting my head, I concentrated on remembering my time at the club. When I remembered one memory, I narrowed my eyes. "I was ready to slap a woman for laying her hands on you."

He chuckled. "You were."

As I searched my mind, my hand flew to my mouth as I gasped.

"You almost strangled a man to death because he touched me," I whispered.

The amusement faded from Callum's face. "Aye, I did."

I swallowed hard. "You really scared me."

Callum brushed the hair back from my face. "I'd like to say I'm sorry, Kitten, but I'm not. That's who I am."

"I know...and I understand."

His thumb traced over my bottom lip. "You are mine, and no one touches what is mine."

I rolled my eyes. "That's so over the top."

His shoulder lifted apathetically. "It's who I am."

"Then tone it back for me."

"I can't make that promise, Kitten. You drive me crazy."

As the words left his lips, something else dark glittered in his eyes. "Do you remember what happened after we left the club?"

"Not really."

"Try," he encouraged, his voice impossibly deep.

I remembered him carrying me out of the club like I was a sack of potatoes. I remember the car stopping for a bit. And then an illicit reel of images flickered through my mind.

My hips rising and falling as I thrust my fingers deep inside me.

Callum's fist jerking up his shaft.

An orgasm blasting through my core like a runaway train.

Mortification sent warmth across my cheeks and all the way down my neck. Bringing my hands over my mouth, I murmured, "Oh God."

Callum pulled me against him. Taking my hand in his, he rubbed my fingers up my thighs. "Ask me again what this is?"

"What is it?" I whispered.

"My cum."

A shiver shot straight through me before heat coiled in my center. "You..." I couldn't bring myself to say the words.

"*We* came together, Kitten. While I wouldn't lay a finger on you, I couldn't help but mark you as mine."

"Did I beg you to touch me?"

"Aye, you did."

I cocked my brows at him. "Why wouldn't you?"

"You were ridiculously drunk, and I refused to take advantage of you." The corners of his lips pulled up. "But if you were to ask me now to touch you, I wouldn't refuse."

My heartbeat accelerated in my chest. Did I want him to touch me? Considering how long we'd been married, he'd been more than patient with me. Although I didn't think I was ready to fully consummate our union, it couldn't hurt to give in a little.

With my gaze locked on his, I took two steps back from him. My shaky fingers came to the sash on my robe. I loosened it, baring my breasts. Need flashed in Callum's eyes at the sight of my naked chest, but he didn't make a move.

"Will you touch me?" I asked.

A strangled noise came from deep within Callum's chest. "Fuck, Kitten, I thought you'd never ask."

To my surprise, he didn't immediately go for my breasts. Instead, he cupped my face, brushing his thumbs across my jawline. A reverent look entered his eyes.

"For all my sins, I should never have been blessed with such beauty."

My chest heaved under his words and the sincerity with which he said them. "You flatter me," I said softly.

As his hands trailed down my neck, he shook his head. "You are the most beautiful woman I've ever laid eyes on."

A shiver ran down my spine as fingers slid along my collarbone with feather soft touches. I sucked in a breath when his hands dipped down my breastbone to tease along the tops of my breasts. My nipples peaked in anticipation as an ache began to grow between my legs.

Sensing my reaction, Callum's gaze dipped from mine to my breasts. "When Seamus showed me your pictures, the first thing I thought was what a waste of a body on a nun."

I playfully smacked his bicep. "My body has nothing to do with my faith or my desire to serve."

A smirk curved his lips. "Your body has *everything* to do with serving me."

"Keep talking like a caveman, and you'll be back to serving yourself," I countered.

With a chuckle, Callum nipped my bottom lip with his teeth before bringing both hands to my breasts. At my whimper, his amusement continued to rumble through his broad chest.

His calloused fingers weighed and squeezed my hyper sensitive flesh, causing the inferno between my thighs to grow. When he pinched my nipples, I moaned—my fingers pressing into his muscled forearms.

Surprise flooded me with Callum's groan. "You don't know how long I've wanted to touch these."

"Is now when you ruin the moment by telling me I have a fabulous rack?"

He snorted. "I was thinking more of a fabulous pair of tits, but I can live with rack."

At my huff of disgust, he twisted both nipples, which sent a shocking jolt of pleasure through me. My huff turned into a pant of need.

"As much as I've wanted to touch them, I've wanted to do this more," Callum murmured.

When his mouth closed over my nipple, a moan rippled through me. As his tongue swirled around the hardened tip, I jerked my fingers through the strands of his hair. "Mm, Callum," I murmured.

"Do you like that, Kitten?" he questioned, his breath warming my aching breast.

"Yes," I murmured.

He kissed a wet trail over to my other breast. As he suckled and teased my nipple, I feared my nails were going to leave marks on his arms.

"Callum, please," I panted as I scissored my legs to ease the ache.

"Please what, Kitten?"

"I need..." I licked my lips. "More."

"You want my fingers or my mouth."

A flush of embarrassment entered my cheeks. When I didn't answer, he kissed back up my chest to meet my mouth. After a moment of our tongues battling together, he pulled away to surmise me with eyes hazy with lust.

"Do you need my fingers here?"

At the touch of him at my center, my hips bucked involuntarily. "I would say that's a yes," he replied with amusement.

I realized at that moment he was still fully dressed while I was practically naked from the waist up. When he reached for me, I placed my hand on his chest. "Take your clothes off."

"My pleasure," he practically purred.

Like a barbarian, he ripped open his shirt, scattering buttons along the floor. Although it was incredibly sexy, I rolled my eyes. "Did you have to ruin your shirt?"

He flashed me a wicked grin. "Surely you can't fault a man for obeying his wife?"

"Is that what you were doing?"

As he stripped the torn fabric down his arms, he nodded. "I'm so desperate to touch and taste you, I'll do anything you ask of me."

"Anything?" I questioned as his fingers came to work on his belt.

He momentarily paused. "Aye," he replied with heat blazing in his eyes.

I didn't know why the sinful words that formed in my mind flowed so easily from my lips. "Get on your knees."

The shock on Callum's face would've been humorous in any other situation. But then his hands froze on the button of his pants.

Without taking his eyes from mine, he sank slowly to his knees before me, causing my body to tremble.

As he gazed up at me, he cocked his head. "What would you ask of me now, Kitten?"

I truly didn't know. I'd never thought he'd actually take my command seriously. The ache between my thighs had grown almost painful. At the realization I still stood with my robe open to the waist, I closed the gap between us.

"Take off my robe."

He quickly brought his hands to my waist, and his fingers deftly undid the silky sash. Once he opened it, Callum leaned up to gently slide the robe off my shoulders and down my arms.

When it pooled around my feet, I bit down on my lip as I stared at him. His gaze left mine to trail down my body.

When he reached my lace-clad center, he grinned up at me. "I'm glad to see you're not wearing Nun's Knickers anymore."

A nervous laugh burst from my lips. "Excuse me?"

"That's what I named the panties you were wearing the night I took you."

I gasped. "You saw my..." I gulped, "underwear?"

Callum rolled his eyes. "Don't act like I didn't tell you. I had to change you out of your wet nightgown, remember?

"Oh, that's right." I challenged, "Surely you didn't expect me to be wearing something like these in the order." I motioned to my skimpy thong.

"Of course not." His finger dipped into the waistband of the lace, causing me to gasp. "Of course, I'd prefer from now on out, you don't wear any underwear. Period."

"Let me guess. You'd prefer I only wore skirts and dresses."

"That too." He pulled my thong down over my hips and down my thighs.

Once it joined my robe on the floor, he winked at me. "I want easy access to your pussy."

I nibbled on my bottom lip. "Do you always say such things?"

"I do." Winking, he added, "You'll grow to like it."

"We'll see."

As Callum ran his hand over the trimmed pubic hair on my mound, he grinned up at me. "This is unexpected."

I blushed at his meaning. "I got waxed at the spa."

"I like it. I wouldn't have minded a full bush."

"Maybe if you're a good boy, I'll grow it out for you," I teasingly replied.

"Mm, Kitten, your mouth is so sassy today."

Before I could argue that I wasn't sassy, Callum's hand slid between my legs, causing me to gasp. His fingers rubbed along my lips before his thumb found my clit.

As he began to circle and tease it, I gripped his shoulders. My hips began to move of their own accord, desperately seeking out friction.

"Do you like that?" he questioned, his voice deep and husky.

"Mm, hmm," I murmured, as I bit down on my lip.

"I'd have to agree as wet as you are."

When he slipped two fingers inside me, I sucked in a breath. "Is that okay?" he asked as his fingers swirled within me.

I whimpered in response, which caused Callum to chuckle. His thumb continued rubbing my clit while his fingers pumped in and out of me.

I should've been embarrassed by the noise of how wet I was, but all I could focus on was the pleasure. Soon my pants and moans of pleasure joined the squelching sound of his fingers.

As I gripped his shoulders harder, I raised my hips against his pumping fingers. "That's it, Kitten. Take it all," Callum urged.

I'd made myself come with my own fingers, but it was nothing like the feel of Callum's calloused ones. When they curved against my g-spot, I shrieked and clawed at him.

When the first waves of my orgasm hit, it felt like a bomb went off inside me. "Callum!" I cried, as I pinched my eyes shut.

Overwhelmed with feeling and emotion, I let my head fall back as my arms twitched and my legs felt like jelly.

When I came back to myself, Callum had me by the waist and was guiding me back to sit on the top step of the stairs leading into the tub.

As I pushed my hair out of my face, Callum winked at me before sliding the fingers that had been inside me into his mouth. "Mm. You taste amazing."

I flushed both on my cheeks and between my legs at his compliment. "I can't believe you say such things."

He chuckled. "Like I said before, you better get used to them. I'm a very dirty talker."

As he knelt before me again, I brought my hands to his face. "I never imagined it could be that amazing."

Callum gave me a genuine smile as he turned to kiss one of my hands. "Oh, Kitten, I'm only just getting started."

"What else are you going to do to me?" I questioned in a whisper.

"Give you even more pleasure."

My brows shot up. "More than what you just did?"

"Much more."

I sucked in a breath as Callum brought one of my legs up to begin kissing and licking a trail up my calf. After doing the same to the other leg, he placed my calves on his shoulders before his hands gripped my thighs.

After he widened my thighs, his hungry gaze honed in on my center. When he licked his lips, a shudder ran through me.

He gave me a cocky grin before dipping his head. After flattening his tongue against my core, he licked up my seam. A moan erupted from my lips.

His tongue began to lazily trace in and out of my folds before coming back to my clit. He flicked it with his tongue before pressing his lips to my sensitive flesh. When he sucked my clit, I cried out.

If I thought he was masterful with his fingers, I had no idea just how amazing he could be with his tongue and lips.

Callum continued sucking and licking me. He ate me like he was a dying man, and I was his last meal. My hips rose and fell while my fingers trailed through the strands of his hair.

Sweat broke out along my forehead when he thrust his tongue

inside me. "Oh God," I moaned as he swirled it around my slick walls.

His voice vibrated against my center. "I think it's best to leave our savior out of this."

"Don't be blasphemous!"

Callum peered up at me from between my thighs. "You're the one calling out his name when it's *my* tongue fucking you."

As his thumb took up rubbing my clit, my head fell back. "We'll both need to go to confession after this," I panted.

"Forgive me, Father, for I have sinned. I finally got to feast on my wife's pussy."

"Callum," I warned.

He chuckled before thrusting two fingers inside me. Although I wanted to moan another "Oh God", I managed to curse instead, which of course caused Callum to laugh again.

The more he suckled my clit and pumped his fingers in me, the more I cursed.

I pumped my hips against his fingers. Gripping his hair, I jerked him closer to my center. While I should've worried I was smothering him, I didn't even care if he could breathe anymore. I just wanted the pleasure to go on and on. I couldn't believe what I'd been missing all these years.

At the grazing of his teeth against my clit, another orgasm set off like a locomotive charging through me. My thighs, which cushioned Callum's head, trembled and shook. When at last the world stopped spinning, Callum eased my feet down off his shoulders.

My cheeks warmed when he began to lick the wetness off my inner thighs. When he finished, he licked my pussy one last time before rocking back on his feet.

As I gazed down at him, I shuddered at the sight of my arousal coating his lips and chin. With my mind shattered, I not so eloquently said, "That alone was worth leaving the order."

Callum threw back his head as a laugh rumbled through his

chest. After wiping his chin, he winked at me. "I'm so honored to be the one who could corrupt you."

My lazy gaze dropped to his lap where his erection tented his pants. The orgasms I'd received made me brazen because I leaned forward to grip him. "I want to make you come."

Callum groaned. "Those words on your lips are beautiful torture."

"It's the truth."

He cocked his head at me. "What would you like to do to me?"

"I want to touch you and taste you."

Callum's chest rose and fell. With his eyes locked on mine, he rose from the floor to stand before me. "Then take me, Kitten."

I eased off the side of the tub to kneel before him. Although my hands shook, I brought my fingers to the waistband of his pants. Staring up at him, I unbuttoned his fly and after ripping down the waistband of his pants and underwear, I pulled them slowly down his thighs. I sucked in a breath when his erection bobbed before me.

At the thought of taking it in my mouth, least of all my body, I swallowed hard. "You're so big," I eloquently stated.

A laugh bellowed from Callum as he stepped out of his pants and underwear. "While I'm flattered at your assumption, would you truly know?"

I scowled up at him. "Yes, I would."

"Seen many cocks, my sweet virgin?"

"I wasn't in the order my whole life, you know." Lowering my voice, I added, "I've watched porn."

A wicked gleam burned in his eyes as he began to stroke himself. "Did you enjoy it?"

"Some of it."

"Did you watch it while you touched yourself?"

Heat flushed through my cheeks and down my neck. "Maybe."

With his free hand, Callum brought my hand to cover his own on his erection. Slowly, he began to work our hands up and down his length.

"Did you use your fingers or a toy?" he questioned in a hoarse voice.

"Just my fingers. I was too afraid of the maids finding a toy and telling my father."

Callum stilled our movements. "Why the fuck should your father have cared if you were getting yourself off with a toy?"

"Because I could've ruined my virginity for my future husband."

Disgust filled Callum's face. "That's fucked up."

"Everything about being a woman in our world is fucked up."

"It doesn't have to be anymore. Not with me."

I squeezed our hands on his cock, causing him to hiss. "How can I show you my gratitude?"

"You're going the right way."

Callum removed his hand, leaving me to wrap my hand solely around him. Although I didn't know what I was doing, I mimicked what he'd shown me before. I marveled at the silky smoothness of his skin over the hardened flesh.

"How does it feel knowing you can bring me to my knees with just your hand?" he questioned.

"I could do more with my mouth."

He threw his head back with a groan. "Fucking hell, Kitten."

"Would you like me to?"

"I'd fucking *love* for you to do that."

Without any hesitation, I dipped my head and brought his cock to my mouth. Although I still had serious doubts about his size, I suctioned my lips around the tip.

He tasted salty like the sea. I wondered if I'd be okay with more of the taste in my mouth like when he came.

Slowly, I slid him further in, which caused him to groan. "Fuck, Kitten," he grunted.

My hand continued working up and down while my mouth took him deeper and deeper. When he bumped the back of my throat, I gagged. With my eyes watering, I kept bobbing him in and out of my mouth. Callum's hand came to the back of my head. After tangling his fingers through my hair, he began to guide me. I could tell he was restraining himself to truly take my mouth like he wanted.

Staring up at him, I shivered. He was so sexy and manly looming over me. I loved the look of him biting down on his bottom lip as pleasure etched across his face.

More than anything, I loved that *I* was the one responsible for giving him that pleasure.

He stared down at me. "Mm, Kitten, I'm close."

I nodded, but I kept sucking him hard. A shudder went through Callum. "If you don't move, I'm going to come in your mouth," he gritted out.

I hummed my acceptance around his cock. "Fuck!" he barked as his hips bucked forward. At the first warm drops of cum on my tongue, I jerked back in shock. Callum continued to spurt along my lips and chin as I worked him with my hand.

When he finished, he stared down at me with hooded eyes. Now that I was used to his taste, I darted my tongue out to lick him off my lips.

Callum's gaze heated before he reached out to wipe my chin with his thumb. I dipped my head to suck his thumb into my mouth.

When I swirled my tongue around his thumb, he grunted. "Christ, Kitten, you're going to have me hard again."

I grazed his thumb with my teeth before guiding his hand from my mouth. "You're insatiable."

He chuckled as he helped me to my feet. "Even more so since I've had to wait so long to touch and taste you."

My hands came to cup his face. "I can never thank you enough for being so patient with me. You've truly been a saint."

Callum smiled genuinely at me. "I think that's the first and only time I've ever been called a saint."

I laughed. "That doesn't surprise me."

After bestowing a gentle kiss, Callum said, "We need to get you clean."

After turning back to the tub, I dipped a finger in the water. "It's cold now."

"We could always warm it up," he suggested.

"Or maybe we can take a shower together."

He grinned down at me. "I like that idea. Very much."

Just as we started across the marble tiled floor to the shower, a knock came at the bathroom door. "Go away," Callum growled, his voice echoing through the room.

"I wish I could. Dare says it's important," Kellan's muffled voice replied.

With a frustrated grunt, Callum stalked naked over to the door. When he jerked it open a crack, I squealed before diving to snatch my robe off the floor to cover myself "This better be life or fucking death," Callum snarled.

Through the crack, Kellan's face turned crimson. "I'm sorry, Cal. He just told me to find you since one of the shipments came up short. I don't think he realized you'd be..." He swallowed hard.

"Fucking my wife?"

A shriek of horror escaped my lips. "That's not what we were doing!" I protested.

Callum threw a wicked look at me over his shoulder. "I'll forgive your innocence and assure you what we've been doing is certainly considered fucking."

I smacked his arm. Hard. "Respect me enough not to broadcast it to your brother."

"I agree," Kellan said.

Callum turned back to his brother. "I didn't ask you."

Kellan sighed. "Look. Just come downstairs sooner rather than later, okay?"

"He'll be down as soon as he can throw on his clothes," I assured Kellan.

As Kellan hurried away from the door, Callum's head whirled around to pin me with a questioning look. I jerked my chin at him. "I'm taking a shower. *Alone.*"

Amusement swirled in his eyes. "Am I to assume I'm being punished for my comment?"

"Your brother needs you."

"My cock needs you more," he argued.

I shook my head with a laugh. "Go on."

"You're a cruel woman to give me a wee taste and then shut me down again."

"Just for right now." I placed my hands on his chest. "Be a good boy, and I'll reward you."

"I'm holding you to it," I replied.

With a growl, he pushed past me to grab up his clothes. As he hopped into his pants, I headed into the shower. "You'll need another shirt," I called as I turned on the water.

With a grin, he replied, "I'll just go without one."

I frowned. "But then the rest of your brothers will know what we've been doing."

A sinfully erotic look burned in his eyes. "Even if I put on a shirt, they'd still smell you on me."

Shrieking in both horror and mortification, I snatched a hand towel and tossed it at him. "Wash your face."

A devilish chuckle came from deep in his chest. "I'm wearing you as a badge of honor."

He winked and headed out of the bathroom, leaving me alone to die of embarrassment.

Chapter Twenty-Nine: Caterina

I couldn't pinpoint exactly when or how, but I knew without a doubt that I had fallen in love with my husband. We'd barely been married for six weeks, but I knew with everything in me what I felt. It had been coming on so gradually.

Part of me argued that after our antics on the dance floor at *Bandia* and our tub escapade, I had fallen in lust, not love.

But it was moments like the one I currently found myself in that made me realize it was love.

After several times of badgering him, Callum had finally accompanied me to volunteer at St. Francis's. As I swept under the tables in the cafeteria area, he sat with two little girls on his lap reading a story.

While he helped me serve lunch, the two sisters had fallen in love with his accent, and they couldn't get enough of the "funny" way Mr. Callum talked.

I leaned against the broom and my heart beat wildly as I listened to him make silly noises during parts of the story. I wondered what his enemies would say if they could see him entertaining the little girls.

I'm sure they would call it a weakness. That a true clean leader should never exude anything but menace and cruelty.

But to me, it showed his great strength of character. He could be a cruel gangster and a successful businessman, but he was also human. A very caring human.

When Callum glanced up to meet my gaze, he winked, which sent a beaming smile to my lips. I quickly focused back on the dirty floor instead of mooning over my husband.

"It's time to go," the girls' mother said.

At their whine, Callum said, "All right, lovely lassies, you better go with your mother."

"Will you read to us again, Mr. Callum?" the youngest girl asked.

He nodded. "It'd be my pleasure."

To both Callum's and my surprise, she smacked a kiss against his cheek before scrambling out of his lap. For the first time since I'd met him, Callum appeared speechless.

The sight was so endearing my ovaries couldn't help but take notice.

When the other girl abandoned his lap, Callum rose to his feet. It was a rarity when I saw him outside of the house not wearing a suit. Today he had on black jeans and a long-sleeved black Henley, which I'd teased him made him look like a mafia man.

After sauntering over to me, he asked "Need some help?"

"I'm almost done here, but you could grab the mop."

"Be right back."

As Callum started to the kitchen, the little girls called in unison, "Bye, Mr. Callum!"

"Bye, lasses!" he called back.

Once again, my heart started beating wildly in my chest. Whisking the broom around the floor, a beautiful fantasy filled my mind of Callum sitting with our children on his lap. I imagined one with our dark hair and one with his mother and Maeve's auburn hair.

Callum's voice caused me to jump. "What are you smiling about?" he questioned.

Ducking my head, a flush entered my cheeks. "You."

His finger came to tip my chin upward to meet his gaze. "What about me?"

"How good you were with those little girls." While it wasn't totally the truth, it wasn't a lie.

A smirk curved on his lips. "What can I say? I charm the ladies of all ages."

I playfully swatted him with the broom. "Don't make this about your charm."

"I can't help it if it's the truth."

"I'm talking about how I haven't seen you with children before."

"And?"

With a genuine smiled, I replied, "I liked what I saw. A lot."

The cockiness in his expression faded and was replaced by an intensity that sent a shudder through me. "I'd be even better with my own child."

"I know you would." Staring into his eyes, I added, "I'd like to see you with one."

He brushed a strand of hair out of my face. "Does that mean what I think it means?"

Of course, Callum had gone straight for the procreation meant consummation. He'd been more than patient with me. And although he was somewhat satisfied by the handjobs and blowjobs I'd been giving him in the last week, I knew he wanted more.

More than anything, I knew I was ready. In spite of my assurance, a nervous laugh burst from my lips, which caused Callum to furrow his brows.

"I'm sorry. I wasn't laughing at you. It was just nerves."

"There's nothing to be nervous about." Cocking his head at me, he asked, "Haven't I put you at ease?"

Placing my palm against his cheek, I replied, "You've been amazing."

"So what's there to be nervous about?"

"It's a little nerve wracking to ask you to make love to me."

Callum's eyes bulged comically wide. "You're serious?"

I bit down on my lip before smiling slightly. "I am."

He brought his forehead against mine. "Oh, Kitten, you don't know how fucking happy this makes me."

With a giggle, I replied, "I think I can guess."

Callum chuckled, then his expression grew serious. "Tonight?"

When I shook my head, his face fell, and I fought the urge to laugh again. Instead, I replied, "Unless you have something else to do, I was thinking now."

He stared at me in almost disbelief. "*Right* now?"

I couldn't hold back my laughter this time. "Well, not here, but yes."

A shudder rippled through him. "Kitten, you can't say shit like that to me and not expect me to rip your clothes off."

I smacked his arm. "We're in church."

He grinned. "Not exactly. It's not like we'd be fucking on the altar."

A shriek of horror escaped my lips before I brought my hand up to cover his mouth. "If you don't stop, I'm going to have to stop in confession before we can do anything."

Groaning, Callum rolled his eyes. "Fine," he murmured against my hand.

When I removed it, he flashed me a smoldering look. "I'm not sure I can make it back to the house. Can I take you to a hotel?"

"If you do, I want the nicest suite along with the finest champagne."

Callum threw back his head with a laugh. "Now you care about the finer things?"

"Since I've waited twenty-one years to have sex, I think I deserve it. Especially since I didn't get a honeymoon."

His hands came to cup my face. "Kitten, you deserve the world."

After propping the broom against the table, I undid my apron. Slinging it to a chair, I said, "Let's go."

Callum quickly abandoned the mop and bucket and took me by the hand. "If this is the reward I'm going to get for volunteering, I'm going to have to do it more often."

I elbowed him in the ribs. "Stop talking before you ruin this for me."

As we stepped into the sunshine, he grinned down at me. "Once I have you naked beneath me, I plan to do a lot of talking. I plan to tell you each and every pleasurable thing I'm going to do to you and how hot it makes me feel. Then I'm going to tell you what I want you to do to me."

A jolt of lust shot through me. "Maybe I'll have to gag you."

Callum jerked me against him. "Damn, Kitten, I didn't know you had a kinky side."

While he nodded at Owen to open the SUV's backdoor, he brought his lips to mine. Although I should've objected to making out on the sidewalk in front of St. Francis's, I couldn't bring myself to put up a fight.

The sound of my moan echoing through my ears was overtaken by a cracking noise.

Before I could register it, Callum's body pulsed like he'd been touched by a live wire. As he slammed against me, the crackling noises started up again. Horror whirled through me as I recognized what those noises were.

They were bullets.

Someone was shooting at us.

Instead of trying to make it the car, Callum slung my body to the ground before covering it with his. "Stay down!" he croaked as a shaky hand reached into his jacket for his gun.

When I turned my head on the pavement, Owen and Shane crouched by the SUV returning fire. Screams and shouts of panic sliced through the air around me.

When the gunfire silenced, Shane stayed behind the SUV while Owen ran over to us. "Are you all right?" he asked.

Ignoring him, Callum's panicked gaze searched my face and body. "Caterina, were you hit?"

Trembling, I couldn't speak so I resorted to shaking my head. "But there's blood," Callum stated.

"Oh fuck," Owen muttered.

Callum and I both followed his gaze to the blood gushing from the left side of Callum's chest. In that moment, the adrenaline depleted, and Callum's eyes rolled back in his head.

With a shriek, I sat up to catch his head as he pitched to the side.

"Callum? Callum, stay with me!" I cried.

"We have to get him out of here!" Owen called over his shoulder.

Shane abandoned the SUV to rush to our side. I shouted in protest when Shane knocked me away to help Owen lift up Callum. "Grab the door!" Owen instructed.

Considering the hard shakes running through my body, I didn't know if I could stand, least of all move. But I pressed forward to rise to my feet. Lunging, I made my way over to the SUV and threw open the door.

After climbing inside, I slid across the bench seat before turning back in anticipation of Callum. Once they lifted him inside, I once again cradled his head against me.

Owen stripped out of his jacket and pressed it onto Callum's wound. Shame filled me that with all my medical training I hadn't thought to do it. The SUV gunned forward and began racing through the streets.

We sped past the flashing red and blue lights of the police as their sirens screamed into the area.

Tears streamed down my cheeks and dripped onto Callum's face. I reached back into my days as a sister and called out to St. Raphael–the patron saint of healing.

"Please, please heal my husband," I murmured as I ran my hands through his hair.

I couldn't have come this far and experienced such life and love just to have it taken from me.

Chapter Thirty: Callum

As I wavered between consciousness, I began to hear my name being called faintly. My eyelids fluttered. "He's coming around," a strong voice related.

It took me a minute to realize that *I* was the one being referenced. When I opened my eyes, I met Quinn and Dare's frantic faces.

"There you are, brother," Quinn said with a smile.

Everything came rushing back at me so fast I shuddered. We'd been ambushed on the street outside of St. Francis's.

"C-Caterina?" I choked out.

"She's fine. You kept her safe," Dare replied.

I sighed in relief. "And me?"

Quinn's expression remained grim. "We've got two doctors on the way, but I went ahead and gave you a transfusion. From the way it looks to me, a couple of inches to the right, and the bullet would've blown out your artery."

"And I'd already be a goner."

As Dare nodded, Quinn replied, "Yes."

"Fuck," I exhaled.

"But we won't know the full extent until they go in."

"And they're going to do that here?"

"We knew you wouldn't want to risk the hospital."

"Exactly."

After an attack, it was never good being in an uncontrolled location like a hospital. It was why many families had a medical room in their houses where anyone from soldiers to bosses could be patched up. Gunshot wounds at the hospital also alerted the authorities, which was the last thing we needed.

"How is your pain?" Quinn questioned.

"Not great. But not too bad either."

"How long was I out?"

"Not long. We literally just rolled the gurney in here when you woke up. Owen and Shane got you here within ten minutes."

A female's scream in the hallway sent a jolt through me. I'd know that voice anywhere.

It was my Caterina.

Quinn rushed from my bedside to block the doorway.

"Is he in there?" Caterina demanded.

"Yes," Quinn replied.

"Why did we come here? Why aren't you taking him to the hospital?" I knew she had to be in shock to even ask that question. Growing up as a capo's daughter, she would be well-versed with not taking Made Men to hospitals unless there was absolutely no other choice.

"He doesn't need the hospital," Quinn answered quietly.

An agonized shriek came from Caterina. "He's...."

"No, lass, he's not dead."

Caterina's voice wavered as she pounded her fists into Quinn's chest. "But he was wounded. He needs to be at the hospital!"

After Quinn related the reasoning why I was in the basement, Caterina tried pushing past him into the room.

"Stay back," Quinn ordered.

"I need to see him," Caterina pleaded.

"No, lass. You don't need to see this."

"It can't be any worse than what I saw on the street."

"Let her through, Quinn," I croaked.

When he glanced back at me for confirmation, I nodded. Caterina rushed past Quinn and over to my bed. Tears stained her beautiful face.

Trying to lighten the mood, I teasingly asked, "Are those tears in your eyes, Kitten?"

"Yes," she hicupped as she wrapped her arms around her waist.

"Don't tell me you're worried about me?"

"Of course, I'm worried about you! You have a gaping hole in your chest."

"It's more my shoulder," I argued.

"There's blood everywhere, and you're the color of paste," she argued through her sobs.

In that moment, I wished I was a better man. A man who was in control of his emotions and knew how to adequately express them. Instead, I did what I did best, which was to push people away when I couldn't handle the intensity of the moment.

"I thought maybe you'd be happy at the prospect of my imminent demise."

She sucked in an agonized breath. "How could you think that least of all say it?"

"You'd be free to go to your brothers or back to your life in the order."

"What the hell is wrong with you?" she demanded.

With a shrug that caused agony to ripple through my shoulder, I replied, "I was just stating facts."

Caterina's dark eyes narrowed on mine. "Stop pushing me away, Callum. I don't care that you're at death's door."

God, this woman.

While I hated she could see right through my insecurities, it gave me life. "Who says I'm pushing you away," I countered.

"An hour ago I was ready to consummate our marriage. That should tell you that I don't want a life with my brothers or back in the order."

She took my blood-stained hand in hers and brought it to her cheek. "I want a life with you, stubborn bastard that you are."

Her words sent an ache through my chest that wasn't related to my wound. More than anything in the world, I wanted a life with her. I didn't feel that way just because I was staring down at my mortality. I loved every minute of the time I'd had with her, and I wanted more than anything to see things through.

"I am a stubborn, emotionally stunted bastard, aren't I?"

She nodded emphatically before lowering her head to where her breath fanned across my cheek. "But in spite of all that, I love you, Callum."

I'd never heard those words said so genuinely from a woman outside Mam and Maeve. Over the years, women I'd fucked for long periods of time had whispered it thinking it would bind me to them.

But I knew it wasn't true.

Maybe they loved my money or my power or my darkness, but they didn't truly love me.

Caterina didn't care about my money or power, and hating my darkness, she loved me in spite of it.

"Fuck. Why do I have to be dying for you to tell me that," I teased.

Tears streamed down her cheeks. "It's the truth. I swear it on the saints."

Rubbing my blood-stained thumb across her chin, I replied, "I'm not worthy of your love, Kitten."

"Of course, you're worthy of my love. You took a bullet for me! How could I not love you? How can I ever thank you?"

"You don't owe me any thanks, Kitten. If I'd left you well enough alone at the Sacred Heart, you would've never been in danger today."

Her lips hovered over mine. "I'd gladly take the danger if it meant being with you and the life we're building."

She was right. The danger–even getting shot up–had been worth it for her. "If I am dying, I should be making penance for my sins."

I smiled up at her. "For all the terrible things I've done in my life, there's only one I won't ask forgiveness for."

"What's that?" she hiccuped between her cries.

"Don't be daft, Kitten." I winked at her. "It's kidnapping you."

She huffed an exasperated breath at me. "I'm not surprised you won't seek penance for that."

"How could I when the last six weeks with you have been some of the best of my life?"

Her eyes widened. "Really?"

"Aye, Kitten. My only regret is I didn't get to come inside you. It would be comforting to know I might've left a part of me with you in our child."

My comment caused her to sob openly again. At that moment, two of the finest surgeons in the Boston area, who happened to also be on our payroll, entered the room.

"Give me a kiss, my love."

"Please don't leave me," she begged.

"Kitten, I'll fight with everything I have."

She lowered her head to bring her lips to mine. Where she usually tasted sweet, her lips were salty with her tears and sadness. When she pulled away, she stared into my eyes.

Although the pain was intense and I didn't feel like smiling, I curved the corners of my lips up. Since I didn't want to appear weak in front of the doctors, I knew I couldn't say the words out-loud. I couldn't even resort to Irish since they were Irish doctors.

Instead, I embraced my wife's lineage by whispering into her ear, "Ti amo."

Caterina jerked back to stare incredulously into my face. I nodded at her. "Now go."

And for the first time in a very long time, I prayed.

I prayed to see another day with Caterina.

Chapter Thirty-One: Caterina

My fingers trembled over the antique rosary in my hands. It had been a wedding gift from Orla, and one that had been in her family–the Byrne's-for almost a century. With my eyes pinched shut, I whispered prayers of healing in my head.

The silence of the room was punctuated by the pacing of Quinn and Dare. Kellan sat stoically on one side of me with Seamus on the other.

I don't know how long I passed in desperate agony, fearing the worst and hoping for the best. When I thought I would lose it and start screaming, I rose out of my chair to walk the length of the small room that served as a makeshift waiting room.

Standing in the doorway, I peered down the hall where the surgeons were working on Callum. In the shadowy hallway, I made out three other rooms with closed doors.

In all the months I'd lived in Callum's house, I'd never ventured into the basement. As the daughter of a capo, I knew better than to want to explore underground areas. Like in the house I grew up in, there wasn't only a medical/surgical room in which to treat the wounded.

There was also a torture room.

When I was seven, Gianni had dared me to peek inside ours. Scared out of my mind but too stubborn to let him win, I stuck my head in the door. T

o my horror, Leo and Rafe shoved me inside and held it closed. They claimed they were punishing me for snitching to Talia about them looking at porn

In the pitch black, I'd fumbled for the light. When the fluorescents buzzed on, I started screaming.

All these years later the image remained burned into my mind.

As my brothers rushed into the room, they hadn't anticipated my father's latest double crosser to still be strung up by chains. Blood congealed on the floor from the gaping wounds on his chest and neck.

His vacant eyes stared out at me.

The vividness of the memory caused a hard shudder to roll through me. At the feel of a jacket draping over me, I turned and met Seamus's smile.

"So you won't be cold," he replied to what must've been my questioning look.

I gave him a small smile. "Actually I was remembering a memory from my childhood."

Seamus raised an eyebrow. "About your father?"

"Yes." I swallowed hard. "His torture room."

When I glanced past Seamus, I saw Dare and Quinn exchange a

look. "Am I to assume that there's one here behind one of those doors?"

While Quinn retained his usual silence, Dare flashed me a grin. "I plead the fifth."

"I would have imagined as much."

It was then that the door at the end of the hallway swung open. As one of the surgeons stepped out of the room and started for us, my breath hitched.

At the somber look on his face, my knees buckled. I would've dropped to the floor if Dare hadn't caught me.

"I don't like the look on his face," I moaned.

At Dare's snort, I jerked my gaze to his. "Dr. Feany's face always looks like a slapped arse."

"I heard that Darragh," he replied sourly.

I closed the gap between Dr. Feany and myself. "How's my husband?"

"He's one of the luckiest bastards I know."

My breath wheezed out of me. "Callum's alive?"

Dr. Feany nodded. "When we went in to get the bullet out, we found that while it had slightly nicked his axillary artery, it did miss the brachial blood vessels and narrowly missed damaging his glenohumeral joint."

"What the fuck does that mean?" Dare demanded as Quinn nodded

"It could've been a lot worse of a recovery if his rotator cuff had been injured," I replied.

At Dr. Feany's surprised look, I replied, "I'm in my undergraduate for nursing school."

Dr. Feany's sour expression turned somewhat appreciative at my comment. But it faded quickly.

"He still is facing a painful recovery ahead of him along with some intense physical therapy to ensure he fully regains his range of motion."

Seamus snorted. "He's going to love the hell out of that."

Ignoring him, I asked, "Can I see him?"

Nodding, Dr. Feany said, "He's just now come out from the anesthesia. We wanted to make sure everything was good before we came to speak to you."

I broke into a sprint to reach Callum's room. Although I wanted to bust through the door, I eased inside, so I wouldn't disturb him. Callum's eyes remained closed, and I worried about the gray pallor of his skin.

As I made my way over to his bedside, I heard footsteps behind me. Throwing a look over my shoulder, I saw that Quinn, Seamus, and Dare had come inside. I furrowed my brows at them.

"Where's Kellan?" I whispered.

Dare's expression grew grim. "After what happened to Maeve, Kellan isn't able to handle medical shit."

My stomach clenched. Callum hadn't shared with me how horrible the repercussions of the rape had been. Once again, my heart splintered in agony for Kellan.

At Callum's moan, I whirled back around and hurried to his side. "Callum? Are you in pain?"

He grimaced as he shifted in bed. I took his hand in mine and squeezed it. "My love, I'm here."

His eyelids fluttered before opening to pierce me with his ocean blue eyes. "Kitten," he croaked.

"You were moaning. Are you in pain?"

A lazy smile curved his lips. "I was dreaming your mouth was on my cock."

At my horrified shriek, an appreciative chuckle came from the men. After glaring at him, I huffed, "You can dream on."

Callum laughed, causing him to wince. "Are you sure you're not in pain?" I asked.

"No. They gave me the good stuff." His gaze slid from mine over to Seamus. "I need one of you to get in touch with Rafe."

At the mention of my brother's name, my breath hitched.

Although I knew he didn't like me asking about his business, I couldn't help questioning, "Why do you need Rafe?"

Callum drew in a ragged breath. "I want to give him the courtesy of knowing I'm putting out a hit on your father."

His words didn't surprise me at all. I didn't need confirmation to know that today's attack had been from my father. If Callum was out of the way, it would sever the alliance with my brothers. As a widow, my father could marry me off to Carmine or any other man he wanted to.

Seamus eyed me momentarily before taking his phone out of his pocket. I held my hands up. "Don't look at me to defend him. Give me a gun, and I'll end him myself."

Both Dare's and Quinn's eyes bulged while Callum merely chuckled. "You've got the claws out today, haven't you, Kitten?"

"There has never been any love lost between my father and me. Especially not now after he tried to kill the man I love."

Callum gave me a cocky grin. "I like hearing those words from your lips."

While I eased over to kiss him gently, Dare groaned. "Knock it off, Casanova. You've got several weeks of healing ahead of you for that shoulder."

At my blush, Callum only laughed. Crooking his finger at me, I turned my head where he could whisper in my ear.

"I think I could benefit from some sexual healing, don't you?" he replied.

"You just came out of surgery," I countered.

"I still want you."

"Not on your life. I don't want to be the reason you're in pain the rest of your days."

"The longer I go without sex, the more pain I'll have from blue balls."

"Stop talking that way in front of them," I replied as I righted myself.

A wicked gleam burned in his eyes. "Since a bullet can't take me out, I'm sure you'll be the death of me."

As I rolled my eyes, Seamus dialed on his phone. "Speaking of dying, I'm going to go make that call to Rafe."

"Thanks," Callum nodded.

With a wink, Quinn said, "Come on Dare. Let's leave the two lovebirds."

As Callum's brothers exited the room, Dr. Feany entered it. "I see he's back to his old self and barking orders," he mused.

"If he was a normal person and in a hospital, how long would he stay?" I asked.

"Two to three days."

"Does he need to stay down here?"

Dr. Feany nodded. "I wouldn't advise jostling him up the stairs today. We don't want to risk popping open any incisions."

"Then I'll have a rollaway bed delivered, so I can stay with him."

"Are you going to be my nurse, Kitten?" Callum asked.

"I want you to have the same level of care you would have in a hospital," I replied. With a smile, I added, "It'll be good practice for me."

"Will you wear one of those sexy nurse's costumes?"

I rolled my eyes. "Dr. Feany, can you please put him back under for a while to see if he'll wake up less horny this time?"

Dr. Feany's lips actually turned into a small smile. "I could arrange for some laughing gas to knock him out from time to time."

While I laughed, Callum scowled. "I had no idea healing was going to be the 7th ring of hell."

"Good patients get rewarded, so I hope you're going to be a good boy."

Cocking his head at me, Callum asked, "What kind of rewards are we talking about?"

I grinned at him. "The kind I can't discuss in front of Dr. Feany."

Biting down on his lip, Callum replied, "Oh Kitten, I plan on being a very, very good boy."

Chapter Thirty-Two: Callum

From my seat in the deck chair, I watched the waves crashing against the shore. As I listened to the pounding of the surf, I was reminded of Ireland.

Growing up, Mam had taken us out of the city to spend the majority of our summers at our house at Portstewart. The sand and the sea were as much a part of me as the bustling streets of Belfast.

Tearing my gaze from the water, I studied my wife. In the chair next to me, Caterina balanced her computer on her lap and worked on her university studies.

Although she'd been past the admissions deadline and start of the semester, I'd called in a few favors, and she'd been allowed to start. She'd been working overtime to catch herself up.

Today marked one week since I'd been shot.

After spending two days down in the medical room with Caterina hovering over me, my brothers had busted me out. But instead of taking me to our bedroom to continue my recuperation, they loaded me up into one of our bulletproof SUVs. Then Owen, along with Shane and Oran, helped Caterina with our luggage.

My little nursemaid had gotten Seamus to give her the keys to his beach house. Since then, my recovery had come with a beautiful ocean view.

I wish I could say I'd finally gotten Caterina to the beach for a honeymoon, but instead, I was there to save face. I couldn't allow my men to see me recovering.

In the mafia, you could never appear weak. It wasn't just about the Kavanaugh men seeing me. We didn't want anyone outside of Caterina's brothers to know I'd been shot.

To say my wife was a devoted nurse would be an understatement. With my left arm bandaged and in a sling, she did everything from help me to the bathroom, which I teased her by playing helpless and asking her to take out my cock from my briefs, to changing my IV bags. Her medical experience while in the order came in handy.

She'd even arranged for a physical therapist to come to us, so I wouldn't run the risk of being seen. She was a true angel of mercy, and I was loving every minute of it.

Well, except the part where my wife thought I was a fucking invalid and wouldn't let me touch her.

Although she'd led me on with promises of sexual rewards, she jerked the rug out from me when she said that I had to have my stitches out before we could do anything. She wouldn't budge even when I argued that I was already exerting myself in physical therapy, so what would it hurt to finger her perfect pussy?

After closing her laptop, she glanced over at me. "How are you feeling?"

"The same as fifteen minutes ago when you asked me," I teasingly replied.

She frowned. "I can't help worrying about you."

Poison and Wine

I reached over to take her hand in mine. "I know, Kitten. I seriously don't deserve you."

After squeezing my hand, she rose out of her chair. "I'm going to go heat up the dinner Lorna sent."

"Sounds good."

Earlier Kellan had come out with our daily lunch and dinner prepared by Lorna. Tonight was actually the first night one of my brothers hadn't insisted on staying the night with us. Our safety was of concern to them despite having armed guards patrolling the perimeter twenty-four hours a day and having at least two bodyguards stationed at the house.

After a few minutes, Caterina poked her head out of the door. "Dinner's ready."

"Coming, Kitten," I replied.

As I rose out of the chair, I grimaced. The painkillers, coupled with the therapy and antibiotics, were giving me some relief, but this was the worst injury I'd incurred.

Of course, I didn't like letting Caterina see me in pain. Whenever she did, her mother hen instincts kicked into overdrive, sending her hovering over me.

Lorna had prepared a hearty beef stew, and I dug in. I'd emptied my bowl before Caterina sat down, she laughed. "I'm glad to see your appetite is coming back."

When she pushed her portion across to me, I shook my head. "I'm not taking your food, Kitten."

"I insist."

"What kind of man would I be if I took my wife's food?"

"The kind who won't tell Lorna I'm not a fan of her beef stew?" she suggested.

I laughed before and took her bowl. "Your secret is safe with me."

While I gorged myself on the stew, Caterina ate some leftover ziti she'd made for the bodyguards. When we finished, I helped her clean up the kitchen despite her protests.

"You need to be resting," she complained.

"I rest all the fucking time. It's not going to kill me to take a few dishes to the sink."

She huffed out a breath. "You're a stubborn asshole."

I grinned at her. "Aye, that I am."

Using my good arm, I slid it around her waist, drawing her flush against me. When I brought my lips to hers, I tasted the sweetness of the wine she'd had at dinner.

I thrust my tongue into her mouth, causing her to moan. My hand slid up her ribcage to cup her breast. Her nipple pebbled immediately under my touch.

My shoulder might've been in a sling but my cock was working fine.

When I cupped Caterina's arse and rubbed her center against the bulge in my pants, she froze. A flip switched, and she jerked away. She stared up at me with eyes hooded with desire. "We can't risk it," she whispered.

I cupped her face in my hands. "Please, Kitten, don't deny me any longer. Let me make you mine."

As I ran my thumb over her bottom lip, she shuddered. From her expression, I could tell a battle was warring in her mind.

"What if we cause more damage?"

"If it means *finally* burying myself in your pussy, I will risk it."

A lazy smile curved across her lips. "Fine. You win."

"Oh fuck yes."

"Give me five minutes to freshen up."

"Why do I have the feeling that if I let you out of my sight, you're going to change your mind?" I protested.

"I promise."

With a grunt, I eased back and let Caterina hurry down the hall to the bedroom. To calm my strung-out emotions, I went over to pour myself a glass of whiskey. I then checked the doors and nodded to the guard on the front porch before doing the same to the one on the back.

I'd just taken a large swig of liquor when Caterina came around the side of the couch. At the sight of her in white lacy garters and a skimpy white negligee that fit against her like a second skin, the whiskey spewed out of my mouth.

"Fucking hell, Kitten."

With a sexy smirk, she turned slowly allowing me to see what her arse looked like in the lace. While jiggling her ample cheeks, she asked, "Do you like it?"

"I love it."

Cocking my head at her, I asked, "What were you thinking when you packed that sinful little number?"

"That I wanted to *finally* be your wife in all ways."

"Mm, I like your thinking."

She placed her hands on my chest. "How are we going to do this?"

"Well, I'm going to start by licking and sucking your tits until your nipples are rosy red and swollen. Then I'm going to make my way down to your pussy where I'm going to get you so hot and achy that your arousal will be dripping down the inside of your thighs."

A shudder went through her. "Your mouth is—"

"Pure sin."

She nodded. "What I meant was how are we going to do this with your shoulder?"

Caterina had me there. With my injury, there was no way I could support myself on top of her without causing more injury or pain. There was no way in hell I was going to take her virginity doggy style.

I wanted to be able to look into her eyes and gauge how she was feeling.

And then it hit me. "You'll have to ride me."

The look that flared in her eyes had my cock pounding even harder at my zipper. "Okay," she murmured.

When I started to lead her to the bedroom, she jerked on my hand. "Let's do it here in front of the fire."

My brows shot up in surprise. "Really?"

A flush filled her cheeks. "I think it's romantic."

I kissed her tenderly. "Anything for you, Kitten."

Without another word, Caterina went about shutting the blinds and turning off some of the lights while I texted the guards to tell them to give us a little space. After I finished, I eased my sling off and tossed it into one of the chairs.

When we came back together in the center of the living room, shadows from the firelight danced around us. Caterina's hands came to the hem of my shirt.

Gently, she helped me ease it off my right side before taking it off the left. As she dropped it to the floor, I untied the waistband of my gray sweatpants and jerked them down my hips and thighs.

"Of course, you're not wearing underwear," Caterina remarked as I stepped out of my sweatpants.

I winked at her. "I had a feeling I might need easy access to you."

"You were pretty sure of yourself, weren't you?" she teased.

"I knew if my fucking brothers ever left us alone for two minutes, I wouldn't be able to hold back any longer."

Caterina giggled. "I have to agree."

As the enormity of what we were finally about to do hit me, I grew serious. "Most of all, I knew after staring down death, I needed to make you mine."

"Oh Callum," Caterina murmured.

Turning her around, I faced her towards the large mirror on the wall. Our reflections were shadowy from the firelight.

"Watch me," I breathed into her ear. "Watch us."

My hand slid around her ribcage to cup one of her breasts. Kneading it between my fingers, I squeezed and pinched her nipple.

When she started to lower her gaze, I sent a stinging smack against her ass cheek. Heat flared in her expression. "Don't take your eyes off of us, Kitten."

She licked her lips. "All right."

My hand snaked around her waist to dip into the side of the negligee. "Fuck me, Kitten. You're already drenched."

Her arms moved behind her to bring her hands to grip my hips.

With her eyes locked on mine, I thrust two fingers deep inside her pussy.

At her gasp of pleasure, I pushed my erection against her ass. My fingers began to pump in and out of her while my thumb brushed against her clit. Caterina's hips began to move to allow me to finger fuck her deeper.

As her arousal coated my fingers to the knuckles, my tongue licked up the side of her neck and my teeth nicked at her sensitive skin.

At the fluttering of her pussy around my fingers, I said, "You're getting close."

"Mm, yes," she panted, her eyes still locked on mine in the mirror.

"I want you to watch yourself as you come. I want you to see how beautiful you look when your body gives itself over to pleasure."

"Please, Callum," she moaned.

My thumb pressed into her clit as I added a third finger. At the erotic image in the mirror of me finger fucking her drenched pussy, my free hand came to stroke my cock.

Although a few tugs had my shoulder screaming, I couldn't stop. It felt too fucking good.

When Caterina's walls clenched, a scream tore from her lips. I hoped the fucking bodyguards knew their place and didn't come barging in to witness my wife coming.

She kept her eyes on us as long as she could before her head fell back against my shoulder.

I kissed her neck and her cheek as I slid my fingers out of her. With my hands on her waist, I backed her over to the couch.

When I knew she could stand alone, I nodded my head at her. "Strip for me."

As I sat down on the couch, Caterina's tongue darted out to nervously lick her lip. But she didn't fight me. Instead, she kept her eyes on mine as she slowly slid the spaghetti straps down each of her arms.

Tediously, she eased it down her breasts, causing my cock to throb. After shimming it down her thighs, she stepped out of it. When she repeated it for the thong, I began to wonder if my cock might explode.

When her hand came to one of the stockings, I stopped her. "Leave those," I commanded.

"Okay," she whispered.

"I don't think I've ever seen you more beautiful than I do right now in nothing but your garters and a satiated look on your face."

As she sank down onto my lap, she grinned. "You don't have to waste your compliments, Mr. Kavanaugh. I'm a sure thing."

I threw my head back with a laugh. "I'm serious, Kitten."

"Thank you for the compliment."

The amusement in her eyes grew serious just before she kissed me tenderly. "But most of all thank you for loving me."

"I'm the one who should be thanking you."

As her arms encircled my neck, she was careful not to hit the bandages or my left shoulder.

With her lips inches from mine, she said, "Make me yours, Callum."

With a nod, I said, "Sit up."

Caterina rose up on her knees. Taking my cock in my hand, I guided it to her core. Once the tip was inside her, my hands came to her hips.

With my gaze locked on hers, I slowly began pulling her down the length of my cock. As her tight-as-hell walls gripped me in a death vise, Caterina grimaced. "Are you okay, Kitten?"

She bit down on her lip. "It stings, but it's not bad."

"Are you sure?"

Nodding, she replied, "I want to keep going."

It was exquisite torture not thrusting my hips up and impaling her on my dick. But I didn't want to hurt her.

Once I was fully seated inside her, I brushed the silky dark strands from her face. "You're mine," I pronounced.

"I'm yours," she whispered.

"And I'm yours, Kitten. Body and soul."

Gently, I eased her hips back up, causing her to shiver. When I brought her back down on my cock, she whimpered.

"Did I hurt you?"

"It felt good."

"It sure as fuck did."

I then began to work her slowly on and off of me. With a few of my thrusts, Caterina got the rhythm and began to roll her hips against me.

As her tits bounced in my face, I leaned forward to suck a nipple into my mouth. "Callum," Caterina moaned.

While I flicked the bud with my tongue, my hand came to where Caterina and I were joined. When I found her clit, Caterina shrieked and clawed at my back.

I hissed at the combination of pain and pleasure when she hit my left side. My injury might've made me a masochist because I loved the hell out of it.

"Sorry," she panted.

"It's good, Kitten. It's so very good."

I continued to massage her clit with my fingers while Caterina sped up the pace of her hips. As the fire crackled in front of us, the sounds of our skin slapping together and our moans and grunts of pleasure drowned it out.

I couldn't remember how long it had been since I'd been inside a woman. Regardless of the time, it had never felt like this. I'd fucked countless women in my past.

But until today, I'd never made love.

The connection I felt with Caterina was indescribable.

As I moved inside her, I couldn't keep my mouth or hands still. I was kissing her lips, her neck, and her breasts. One of my hands slid up her silky-smooth back to tangle in her long hair while my other hand sent fingers sliding through our silky arousal to tease her clit.

When Caterina's orgasm kicked off, it clamped my dick in a vise.

After a few more pumps, my hips jerked up, setting off ropes of my hot cum deep inside her. I cried out her name as my head fell forward to be cradled between her breasts.

Once I'd come back to myself, my chest rose and fell with harsh breaths as I stared up into Caterina's satisfied face. "You're not my virgin bride anymore," I said with a smile.

"Thank God," she countered with a grin.

"As much as I hate to admit it, it was good we waited."

Her brows shot up in surprise. "Really?"

I nodded. "Because I got to make love to you."

Tears welled in her eyes. "Oh, Callum," she murmured before bringing her lips to mine.

She poured her emotions into the kiss until we were both breathing heavy, and my cock was hard inside her again.

She jerked her lips from mine to stare down at where we were joined. "Already?"

A laugh rumbled through my chest. "What can I say? You make me insatiable."

"But how's your shoulder?"

It fucking hurt, but I sure as hell wasn't going to tell her that. "It's fine."

Caterina crossed her arms over her chest, causing her tits to bounce enticingly. "Don't lie to me," she countered.

Damn. I'd forgotten how well she knew me. "I'll take some pain meds later."

Cocking my head at her, I asked, "Speaking of pain meds, how are you feeling?"

"A little sore."

"Just a little?"

She shifted her hips, causing us both to moan. "I think I can handle another round."

I had a feeling there would be *several* rounds tonight.

Chapter Thirty-Three: Caterina

Four Months Later

Like most mornings since Callum and I had consummated our marriage, I woke up to some form of him between my thighs.

If there was one thing my husband adored, it was morning sex.

Some mornings it was his fingers while others it was his mouth. Within just a few minutes, I'd be wet and achy with need. Before he'd thrust inside me, either his fingers or his tongue had made me come at least once. Then his masterful cock would pound me into another orgasm or two.

This morning his fingers swirled around my clit, causing me to moan. After a few strokes through my lips, his hand disappeared from my pussy. When I mewled in protest, he chuckled against my neck.

"Don't worry, Kitten. I'd never deny you an orgasm."

"You better not," I huffed.

Callum's strong hands came to my waist. Although his shoulder still gave him trouble from time to time, he was finally healed.

We'd certainly been very creative with our sexual positions in those first weeks of his recovery. I'd been bent over more pieces of furniture than I could count and ridden him in and out of the bedroom.

Thankfully, it wasn't too long before he was acquainting me with the missionary position and its variations.

After Callum pulled me up and over to straddle him, he said, "Ride my face." A drowsy, yet incredibly sexy smile curved across his lips. "I want you to come on my tongue."

Nibbling my lip, I began to shimmy up over his abs and chest. "Fuck you're so wet," Callum growled.

When I glanced over my shoulder, a flush entered my cheeks to see the shimmering trail of arousal I'd left on his chest.

Callum brushed his knuckles across my jaw. "Don't be embarrassed, Kitten. I love seeing how much you want me."

Once my knees were on either side of Callum's head, I lowered myself onto his face. "Callum!" I shrieked when his tongue stroked my center. As his hands gripped my hips, he began to move me against his mouth.

After flailing around and tipping forward, Callum's voice hummed against my folds. "Grab the headboard," he instructed.

My hands reached out to grip the intricately carved wood of the headboard. Once I had a tight grasp, I swiveled my hips, grinding my pussy harder against Callum's mouth and tongue.

"Oh God!" I cried.

Callum's fingers came between my legs to spread apart my opening. As his tongue swirled inside me, I shrieked with pleasure. "Yes, oh, oh, yes," I murmured.

He was masterful with his fingers and his cock, but he was so very, very good with his tongue. The flick and jab of it within my slick walls tore a mewl of ecstasy from my lips.

At the crack of his hand against my ass cheek, I squealed as pain and pleasure swirled through me. "Does that feel good, Kitten?" Callum questioned against my clit.

"Mm, so good."

He smacked my other cheek. "Harder," I urged.

As I hissed at the next slap, Callum's hand massaged the stinging globe of my ass. With each smack, I rode Callum's face harder and faster. My undoing came when his teeth grazed my clit.

A scream tore from my lips as a deluge of pleasure gushed out of me and ran down my thighs. With my hands firmly on the headboard, I rode out the orgasm as my walls clenched around Callum's fingers and tongue.

I was still a shaky, blubbering mess of sensory overload when Callum's hands came to my waist. "All right, cowgirl, time to switch it up."

After letting go of the headboard, I pushed the sweat-stained strands of hair out of my face. Then I flipped around to where my ass was in Callum's face, and his straining erection was in mine.

Laying across his chest and abs, I took his cock in my hands. After licking up his length, I suctioned the tip, causing him to groan.

As Callum began licking me back to front, I started bobbing up and down on his dick. "Mm, take me deep, *mo slut salach*."

The first time he'd called me his slut in Irish, I'd almost smacked him.

But then I'd come to like it.

I was a slut for Callum—for him and only him.

Just like enjoying the dirty talk, I'd come a long way since the first time I'd taken him in my mouth. With Callum being such a dirty talker, he'd taught me what he liked, which is why my hand came to cup and massage his balls.

At his grunt, I let his dick fall free of my mouth before I licked and sucked his sac.

"That's it, Kitten."

My hand kept sliding up and down his shaft as I worked his balls. At the slight graze of my teeth against the sensitive flesh, he barked out a cry.

After I brought my mouth back to his cock, Callum's hips began to rise, thrusting his cock deeper and deeper in my mouth. My eyes watered as saliva dripped down the sides of my chin. Even though my jaw ached, I kept sucking him.

After dragging his thumb back and forth through my arousal, he pressed against my puckered hole. When I momentarily tensed, Callum murmured against my folds, "Trust me, Kitten."

I'd come to trust him in all aspects of sex. Callum's thumb slowly dipped inside me, causing me to suck in a breath. As he began to ease it in and out, I moaned at the fullness.

"*Cailín álainn,* you're taking me in this virgin hole so fucking good."

With his arm propped on one of my cheeks, he continued pumping his thumb inside my ass while his other hand slipped two fingers into my core. The fullness caused me to groan around his length.

While his cock fucked my mouth, I rocked my hips back against his hands as his fingers pumped furiously in and out of me. I alternated between harsh pants and moans as it was all just too much.

My body began trembling from the sensory overload of having all my holes filled by Callum.

It was so very good.

I didn't even protest when two fingers replaced Callum's thumb in my ass. At the extra suctioning of my clit, I went over the edge. After he fell from my mouth, I screamed, "Callum, yes! Oh yes!"

He kept fingering me and lapping at my center as I savored my orgasm. Once I came back from my high, I took him back into my mouth.

I wanted nothing more than to taste his pleasure as he exploded on my tongue.

Callum began pumping his hips. As he fucked my mouth hard and deep, his guttural grunts of pleasure filled the room. I gagged and moaned around him as tears streaked down my cheeks.

And as I felt his balls tightening, he cried out, "Caterina!"

Then his hot cum detonated onto my tongue and filled my mouth. After I finished swallowing him down, I licked him clean before flipping over to collapse beside him.

When I glanced up at his satiated face, he grinned. "Good fucking morning, Kitten."

I smiled back at him. "Good morning to you, too."

His hand cupped my cheek. "I wasn't too hard on you last night, was I?"

Heat bloomed between my legs when I thought about how he had taken me across his desk at *Bandia*.

He hadn't been gentle when he'd hiked up my skirt and whirled me around. The lacy thong I'd been wearing had been ripped from my body. Gripping the back of my neck, he'd pushed me face down onto the mahogany desktop. After spreading my legs obscenely wide, he'd slammed into me.

He'd whispered filthy things to me in Irish.

In the brief Irish lessons I'd had with Seamus, I understood Callum's praise of how good I was taking his cock and what a good girl I was to let him ravage my tight, wet cunt.

My nails scoured the top of the desk as I tried keeping my body from sliding off. Callum had kept up his relentless thrusts even after I'd come.

Twice.

When he jerked out of me, leaving his cum dribbling down my thighs, I'd had trouble walking to the car. Like a filthy knight in shining armor, he swept me into his arms and carried me out of his office.

"No. It was wonderful," I assured him.

He searched my face to ensure I wasn't trying to spare his feelings. When he appeared satisfied, he nodded. "Each and every time with you is amazing."

After nibbling my lip, I replied, "Even though I'm still learning what you like?"

"Kitten, your innocence coupled with your eagerness to please is hot as fuck."

"If you say so."

He kissed me tenderly, and I shivered at the taste of myself on his lips. "You won't ever hear any complaints from me."

"Me either."

After eyeing his phone, he grunted. "I have to get a move on."

"Me too. Today's my biology lab."

Callum scowled at the mention of me being on campus. Although four months had passed since he'd been shot, my father and his regime still remained a threat.

Regardless of his efforts, Callum had been unable to kill my father.

He hadn't been seen in New York since the day of Callum's shooting. Rumors from all sides indicated that he'd gone underground. Some said he was working on alliances from Sicily.

With my father still a threat, I'd resorted to as many online classes as possible for the spring semester. The only time I had to go on campus was for the assigned labs for my biology class, which Kellan audited so someone could be at my side at all times.

My professor and the other students would've been shocked to know Kellan was heavily armed beneath his preppy boy appearance.

"It's only one day a week," I protested.

"I still don't like it."

"Kellan is very capable of protecting me."

With a growl, he nipped at my neck–his teeth sliding along my sensitive flesh. As I shivered, he replied, "I still don't fucking like it."

"You're such a caveman," I mused.

He jerked his head up to pin me with a stare. "Just because I want to protect you doesn't make me a caveman."

"It does when you want to chain me to the furniture and keep me locked in the house."

Callum waggled his brows at me. "I like the idea of you tied up."

With an exasperated huff, I replied, "Would you please focus?"

He shot me a wicked grin. "I am focusing. Are you opposed to us using handcuffs and a blindfold?"

"You're impossible," I grunted.

"Actually, I like the idea of you in satin scarves." He brought my hand to his lips. "I don't want to do anything to mar your beautiful skin."

I gave him a pointed look. "I'll let you tie me up if you'll ease up on the protectiveness."

"You drive a hard bargain."

My brows shot up in surprise. "Seriously?"

"I'll try."

"I look forward to it."

He smacked my ass playfully before he got up. "I'm starving. While I grab breakfast, do you want the shower first?"

"Yes, sir."

Callum's blue eyes flashed. "Mm, I like the sound of that word on your lips."

I laughed as I pulled myself off the mattress. "Don't get any more BDSM ideas."

With a wink, he replied, "A man can dream."

Chapter Thirty-Four: Caterina

As I stood underneath the stream of the shower head, I reflected on the past four months. How quickly Autumn had melted into winter, and before I knew it, Callum and I had celebrated six months together.

When I was in the order, time seemed to stretch on endlessly. But now there was so much going on that time practically flew by.

While I lathered up my hair, I smiled at the memories from December.

For the first time in three years, I'd celebrated a traditional Christmas. Well, considering it was an Irish Christmas, it was different from the Christmases I'd grown up with. Orla, Maeve, and

Eamon had flown over, and the house was filled with love and laughter.

The women and I decorated the house within an inch of its life as well as baking sweets constantly. I couldn't remember a time I'd ever been so happy.

In a show of solidarity, my brothers had spent Christmas Day with us, and I'd prepared some of the Italian dishes we'd grown up with.

Since Callum's shooting, my brothers had remained estranged from my parents. The fact that the shooting could've possibly ended my life as well as Callum's had fractured the already precarious relationship. The Neretti family now was split into the camps still supporting my father and the ones who supported Rafe.

Once I finished my shower and got dressed, I made my way downstairs. After receiving another playful smack on the ass by Callum as he came out of the dining room, I headed for the kitchen. I needed to grab something quick if I was going to make it to my class on time.

When I entered the kitchen and smelled the meat frying, my stomach clenched. As bile shot into my throat, I clamped my hand over my mouth. Without enough time to make it to the bathroom, I sprinted around Lorna to throw up in the kitchen sink.

After retching repeatedly, I wiped my mouth and turned on the hot water. Lorna's hand pressed gently on my back.

"Are you all right, lass?"

I shook my head. "I don't know. That came out of nowhere." Glancing at her over my shoulder, I asked, "I must've picked up a bug on campus."

Lorna's eyes narrowed curiously. "When was your last monthly?"

I furrowed my brows. "What does my period have—"

Before I could finish, my stomach lurched again.

As I threw up, I realized how stupid my question was. My period, or lack thereof, had *everything* to do with me being sick.

Once I finished, I dried my lips and face with a paper towel. "I can't believe I didn't realize it."

"What?"

"I haven't gotten my period this month," I whispered.

Lorna's brows furrowed. "How late are you?"

I did the math in my head. When I realized how late I was, I gasped. "Two weeks."

Now it was Lorna's time to gasp. But then a beaming expression lit up her face. "Oh lass, you're up the pole."

I groaned but laughed in spite of myself. "That is the worst expression I've ever heard."

"That might be true, but it's the best news ever." When I didn't respond, she cocked her head. "It is good news, isn't it?"

"Of course."

"Callum needs an heir."

"I know."

She frowned. "Then what's the problem?"

"I guess I'm just surprised."

Lorna shot me an exasperated look. "Considering how many pairs of sheets the two of you go through, it shouldn't be a surprise at all."

Heat burned in my cheeks. "Lorna!" I protested.

She grinned. "It's the truth, isn't it?"

"Yes," I mumbled with embarrassment.

"Then what's the problem?"

"It's just..."

Panicked out-of-control thoughts whirled through my mind.

"It's just fast. We haven't been married long. A year ago I was a sister. I've barely gotten used to the idea of being a wife and now I'm going to be a mother." I swallowed hard. "There's a selfish part of me who wanted more time with just Callum."

"Aw, love, I can understand that. I'm sure it does seem fast." She pushed my hair out of my face. "But if there's one thing I'm certain of, you're going to make an amazing mother."

"You really think so?"

She patted my cheek. "I certainly do."

As Kellan and Quinn came into the kitchen, I put my finger over my lips.

Whispering in my ear, Lorna said, "You want me to make you an appointment today with the Kavanaugh family OB?" At my nod, she turned and left the kitchen.

Kellan sniffed the air before wrinkling his nose. "Why does it smell like puke in here?"

My face flushed and I hurriedly turned back to the sink. As I furiously sprayed cleaner everywhere, I replied, "Sorry. There was some spoiled food I was helping Lorna get rid of."

He nodded and grabbing one of the croissants on the counter. "We better get going if we don't want to be late."

Just before I could argue that I wasn't quite ready, Lorna appeared. "I was able to make that appointment for you this afternoon. I'll text you the details."

Neither Kellan nor Quinn appeared to be paying attention. "Thank you."

She smiled and then in a low voice said, "I want to hear all about it as soon as you're done."

"I will. I promise."

As I grabbed my messenger bag, I couldn't fight the anxiety creeping its way up my spine. I didn't know how I was possibly going to make it through my lab today. I tried burying any thoughts of the pregnancy so Kellan wouldn't be suspicious.

Instead, I put my best college coed face on and prepared to face the day.

After class ended, Kellan walked me to the car. "Want to grab some lunch?" he asked.

We usually had lunch somewhere on campus before heading back to the house. Glancing at my phone, I only had thirty minutes to make it to my appointment.

"Actually, I need to get to the doctor's."

Kellan's brows furrowed. "I didn't know you were sick."

"I'm not."

"Then why do you have to go to the doctor?"

Even though I didn't want to allude to anything to make Kellan suspicious, I knew there was one way to shut him up and get him off the trail.

Tilting my head at him, I replied, "Okay, Mr. Nosy, if you must know, I'm going for my yearly appointment at the gynecologist."

Kellan stared at me, unblinking and unmoving, for a few moments before a red flush crept up his neck and onto his cheeks. "Oh, um, yeah, that's...right."

I bit my lip to keep from laughing in his face. "Sometimes it's just better not to ask, huh?" I teased.

He grimaced. "Fucking yes."

For the rest of the brief walk, he kept his hands stuffed in his pockets and stared straight ahead.

When we reached the car, Owen nodded at Kellan. "Mrs. Kavanaugh informed me of this afternoon's plan. Are you accompanying her to the doctor?"

Red once again flushed over Kellan as he furiously waved his hands. "No, no. I'll have Shane meet me there, so you can wait with her."

Without another glance at me, Kellan hopped into the front seat. When we didn't make any of our usual small talk about class, I caught Owen glancing curiously between me and Kellan. He wasn't used to any silence between us.

Rolling my eyes, I said, "He found out what doctor I'm going to."

Now it was Owen's turn to grimace. "Exactly," Kellan muttered.

As I laughed under my breath, I realized that men being mortified of the gynecologist was hopefully going to buy me more time to keep my secret from Callum.

* * *

Although Kellan was off the hook at being in a gyno's office, Owen was forced to suffer through coming in with me. Apparently being a Kavanaugh meant that there wasn't any waiting because as soon as I checked in, we were whisked back to a room.

"I'll wait out here," Owen muttered. His expression pained further when the nurse asked for a urine sample.

After peeing into the cup in the bathroom, I came back out and climbed onto the examining table. While I was used to getting blood taken at labs or in separate rooms, a phlebotomist rolled her cart right in.

She eyed me curiously, and I'm sure she wondered what made

me a VIP. Once she'd taken my blood, she quickly exited, leaving me alone with my thoughts.

It didn't take too long before a middle-aged doctor with a dark mustache rushed into the room.

"Hello, Mrs. Kavanaugh, I'm Dr. Eilish."

I shook his hand. "It's nice to meet you."

With a smile, he questioned, "Which Kavanaugh brother are you married to?"

"Callum."

My declaration caused him to pale slightly. "Please tell your husband on future visits I'll have my colleague complete your physical examinations."

When I realized his meaning, I rolled my eyes. "Your *female* colleague?" At his nod, I grumbled, "Figures."

Dr. Eilish's smile returned. "It's an honor to deliver the happy news."

"I'm pregnant?"

"Yes. Your HcG levels look strong and—"

"You were already able to test my blood?" With what little medical training I had, I knew it usually took a little longer for those results to come back.

With a knowing look, he replied, "Normally it does, but for special patients, we can speed up the process."

Special patients who were married to Irish gang leaders. "So everything looks good?"

Dr. Eilish nodded. "I want to get you started on prenatal vitamins. If Mr. Kavanaugh would like to accompany you, we can do an ultrasound on your next visit."

Once again, my VIP status was showing since I knew they didn't usually do those until later in pregnancy. "That would be wonderful."

As he started for the door, he said, "Congratulations."

"Thanks."

After he left, I sat in a stupor for a moment. I was pregnant. Callum was going to be a father, and I was going to be a mother.

A very *young* mother.

Despite the anxiety raging around me, I knew I could do it. I had an amazing support system with Lorna and the boys. My long dormant dream of being a mother had come true.

My thoughts went to Callum, and I took my phone from my pocket.

> Just had a quick doctor's appointment. Don't worry, everything was fine. Coming to see you.

I hopped off the table and headed out the door. Owen stood ramrod straight across from me. "Everything go okay?"

Since I couldn't contain myself a minute longer, I blurted, "I'm pregnant!"

Owen stared wide-eyed for a moment before he smiled. "That's wonderful news, Mrs. Kavanaugh."

"Thank you," I replied with a grin. Once again, I checked my phone, but there were no calls or return texts from Callum.

"Let's get you back home."

"Actually, I'd like to tell Callum in person, so please take me to his office," I instructed as we walked into the sunshine.

Owen paled slightly. "Um, I don't think that's possible since he's in back to back meetings today."

"I'm pretty sure he'll give me a few minutes," I teasingly replied.

"No. I better take you home."

My mouth dropped open at his response. Peering suspiciously at him, I commanded, "Take me to Callum's office, Owen."

He grimaced. "I can't do that, ma'am."

"Why not?"

"Because I have strict orders to take you home."

I furrowed my brows at him. "You spoke to Callum?"

"Aye."

Anger and hurt rippled through me that apparently Callum could respond to my bodyguard but not to me. I fully intended to give him a piece of my mind about it.

"I don't care what he said. I'm telling you to take me to Callum's office," I countered.

"With all due respect, Mrs. Kavanaugh, you're not my boss."

Red criss-crossed my vision at his response. "Take me to his office *now*," I bit out.

Owen ran his hand over his face. "I can't do that."

"Why ever not?"

"Because he isn't there."

"Then where is he?"

"I'm not at liberty to say."

With a frustrated grunt, I lifted my phone and pulled up the tracking app that Gianni secretly had installed at the reception.

Initially, I hadn't wanted him to do it, but Gianni had insisted.

Since I didn't even begin to understand the technology behind it, I'd never used it. But like most things in life, there was a first time for everything.

When I read Callum's location, I froze at the description. "He's at a... *strip club?*" I choked out.

"It's not like that, ma'am. The Kavanaugh brothers *own* the club."

I jerked my gaze to Owen's. "My husband is part owner of a strip club and never told me?"

"Aye, but it's a Gentleman's Club," Owen corrected.

"Fuck the semantics, and fuck you!" I spat to which Owen's eyes popped wide.

I couldn't blame him for being shocked at my outburst, but at the same time, I don't know how he expected me to act at the news.

"Please get in the car, Mrs. Kavanaugh."

Ignoring him, I began pacing around the pavement. Bile rose in my throat, which either came from the pregnancy or my overall disgust at my husband.

The husband who currently refused my texts not because he was tied up in an important meeting, but because he was at a strip club.

Worse than that, he *owned* a strip club and had never told me. He knew how I felt about honesty, and he had trampled all over it.

Owen's hand grazed my arm. "Please just let me take you home, ma'am. I'll send him an SOS text, and he'll come right away."

Rage and anguish seethed within me. One thing I was sure of. There was no way in hell I was waiting to confront Callum.

"You seriously won't take me to the club, will you?"

Owen's eyes bulged in horror. "No, ma'am."

"Fine."

As I started to hop into the car, I slipped my hand into Owen's jacket. Before he could react, I snatched one of the guns from his holster. I shoved him away before releasing the safety and aiming it at him.

"You *will* take me to the club," I ordered.

Both disbelief and anger flickered across his face. "Do you really expect me to take you as a threat?"

"Considering I'm manic with pregnancy hormones at the moment coupled with the white-hot rage I feel towards my husband, I sure as hell would. But by all means, you can fuck around and find out."

Owen regarded me like I'd grown another head. "Mrs. Kavanaugh, please reconsider."

"Drive the fucking car, Owen," I commanded.

With a resigned sigh, he ducked his head. "Fine. But you should take the fall when Callum goes ballistic."

"If I haven't managed to kill him, I'll make sure to spare you," I spat.

Chapter Thirty-Five: Callum

I walked through the back door of *Álainn*, meaning beautiful in Irish, which was our upscale family owned strip club. A beefy bouncer nodded his head at me. "Good afternoon, Mr. Kavanaugh."

"Good afternoon, Niall."

Like most of our business, we hired within the clans. There were a few non-clan with us, but they were usually hired as cooks or cleaners.

When it came to our dancers, we didn't like hiring any of the girls with clan affiliation because it just made for bad blood among the men.

Of course, since marrying Caterina, I'd spent as little time as possible in *Álainn*. Instead, I deferred to Quinn and Dare for all things women and alcohol related while Kellan kept track of the books.

Today was the beginning of the month, which meant meetings with my brothers. After sitting down at the conference table in the office, I nodded at them.

"How's it looking, boys?"

Kellan grinned while shoving a red folder at me. "Grand as always."

As I eyed the folder's documents, I replied, "I'm glad to hear it."

"It wouldn't kill you to say thanks, would it?" he teasingly questioned.

While I rolled my eyes at him, Dare countered, "Get fucked, boyo. You're not even old enough to have a drink here. It's Quinn and I that keep this place afloat."

With a scowl, Kellan countered, "I will be of age in three months."

After ruffling Kellan's hair, Quinn countered, "Then keep yer trap shut until then."

I pointed at Quinn. "Speaking of running this place. I've got an audition for you."

A growl reverberated through his chest. "I'm not a fucking plaything you can trot out when it serves your purpose."

I snorted. "As if anyone could ever think of you like that."

"I'm serious, Callum."

"I know. But I need your services."

Since we were one of the finest gentlemen's clubs in Boston, we had to wade through a shit-ton of dancers. As demeaning as it sounds, the first test was appearance.

Did the woman look like she could charm millionaires and billionaires?

If she passed that test, was she a phenomenal dancer who could work the pole?

Considering the amount of colleges in Boston, we had a lot of dancers pass the first and second tests. High-brow coeds who'd spent their childhoods in dance classes usually passed the first two rounds.

But the last one was make or break: they had to give Quinn a lapdance.

We hadn't chosen Quinn because he was allegedly Quasimodo. He was quite the opposite. Like all of us Kavanaugh men, he was a good-looking fucker even with his scars.

When he didn't walk around like the Grim Reaper daring anyone to touch him, women lined up for a piece of him.

He'd become our ringer because of his scary-as-hell demeanor. If a dancer could survive riding Quinn's lap without dying of fright, then she was hired.

At Quinn's continued hesitation, Dare clapped him on the back. "You're the only man I know who begrudges a lap dance from a fine as hell woman."

"Fuck you," he muttered.

"Quinn's not the only one who would."

Dare's brows rose questioningly. "Who else?"

I eased back in my chair with a smile. "Me."

Since I'd returned to the states as a married man, I hadn't received a single lap dance from the girls. Despite my wedding band, I'd still been offered private dances. Many were hoping I'd audition them for a role as my mistress.

But after having a taste of Caterina, no other woman did it for me. I no longer desired random tits in my face or strange pussy grinding against me.

When my phone buzzed, I grimaced at it. "Speak of the devil?" Dare questioned with a grin.

"Yeah, she had a doctor's appointment earlier."

Quinn scowled at me. "Shouldn't you ask the wee lass how it went?"

"She already let me know everything was fine."

When he still gave me a shitty look, I sighed. "Look, she's asking to come see me at the office. There's no way in hell I can tell her where I'm at."

Dare's brows popped. "Sister Sassy doesn't know we own this club?"

Rolling my eyes at him, I replied, "Caterina would lose her mind if she knew about this place. In her book, I already have enough vices on my plate. There would be nothing of my dark soul left to salvage if she found out."

While Dare chuckled, Quinn had the audacity to tsk at me. "You're just digging your grave deeper for when she does find out."

Although I knew Quinn was right, I wouldn't give him the satisfaction. "I believe you have a dancer waiting to ride your dick."

Waggling my brows, I added, "Her pole dance was to some shite Taylor Swift song."

Quinn's growl echoed through the room. "I'll pay you back for this, fucker."

With a grin, I rose out of my chair. "I look forward to it."

Although my phone buzzed again, I didn't look to see if it was once again from Caterina. I walked out of my office to the main floor. Even though it was barely noon, the club was packed. Businessmen in three-piece suits entertained clients as well as the dancers.

Just as I started past a table, an arm shot out to grab me. Before I could knock it away, I saw it belonged to one of the local city councilmen.

He grinned broadly at me. "Callum, good to see you."

"Good to see you too, Lionel." Jerking my thumb at Dare, I said, "Have you met my brother?"

I don't think I've had the pleasure." After Lionel shook Dare's hand, he motioned for us to sit down. "Let me buy you a drink."

"Considering how much you helped me with the liquor licenses for Bandia, it's me who owes you a drink." I slid into the booth and motioned one of the waitresses over. After ordering a bottle of our finest whiskey, I started talking to Lionel.

We'd already downed the bottle of whiskey and called for

another when a dancer, whose name escaped me, came by and plopped down in my lap.

She wrapping her arms around my neck, her bare breasts rubbing against my face. "Would you or your guests like a private dance, Mr. Kavanaugh," she purred.

As I brought my hands to her waist and eased her to her feet, Dare groaned. "Oh fuck, brother, the shit's about to hit the fan."

Furrowing my brows at him, I asked, "What?"

Before he could answer, a stinging slap smacked against my cheek. I shot out of the booth and whirled around to face my assaulter.

To my utter and complete horror, Caterina stood before me. "You fucking bastard!" she shouted before slapping my other cheek.

I held my hands out in front of me. "Kitten, it's not what it looks like."

"Spare me," she spat before shoving me hard.

"I swear it's nothing." Motioning her to the back, I said, "Come with me to my office, and I'll explain."

"Save your bullshit explanations. There's nothing you can say that will make up for the fact you not only deceived me about owning a strip club, but that you just had a half-naked woman on your lap doing God knows what."

"There was nothing happening between us."

Caterina's face turned crimson. "She had her breasts in your face!"

Although the music was blaring and women were pole dancing naked, attention was riveted on Caterina and me. I grabbed her arm and tried moving her away from prying eyes.

She slapped my hand away. "Don't you touch me!" she shrieked.

"Caterina, please, just let me talk to you."

Tears shimmered in her eyes. "I tried talking to you, but you wouldn't answer my calls or texts. I couldn't imagine why you would do that to me, but now I see."

"I'm sorry. I was being a coward because I didn't want you to find out where I was."

Shaking my head, I replied, "You were never supposed to find out about this place."

"So I wouldn't ever have to know you were cheating on me?"

"I swear to God I wasn't cheating on you!"

She jabbed her finger at me. "Don't you dare blaspheme at a time like this."

"I'm sorry, but it's the truth. There isn't another woman in the world for me."

Grabbing her hand, I brought it to my chest and over my heart. "I swear, it's only you."

Tears spilled over her cheeks. "I can't believe anything you have to say anymore."

"Dammit, Caterina, I'm not lying."

She slowly shook her head. "Today was the happiest day of my life, and you've spat and trampled upon it."

I furrowed my brows. "What are you talking about?"

"The doctor's appointment I went to today?" At my nod, she said, "I found out I'm six weeks pregnant."

As I processed Caterina's words, the world around me slowed to a stop.

Fuck me.

Caterina was pregnant.

I was going to be a father.

The pride and pure happiness that surged through me was indescribable. "We're really having a baby?"

Caterina shuttered her eyes as if in pain. "Yes.

My hand brushed across her cheek. "You can't imagine how happy this makes me, Kitten."

Her anguished eyes opened to stare daggers through me. "So was I. But now you've ruined it. Do you have any idea how demoralizing and disgusting it is that I've been reduced to telling you you're going to be a father in a *strip* club? It's one thing having a mafia boss as my baby's father, but it's quite another having one who deals in sex."

"Fuck," I muttered as I ran my hand over my face.

Quinn had been right. My lack of honesty had truly fucked things up. I had no clue how I was going to get myself out of this one. "Kitten, I'm so–"

She held her hand up in front of my face. Normally, I would've lost my shit at someone doing that, but I knew better than to react. "There is nothing you could possibly say right now that will ever make this right."

"At least let me try."

A maniacal laugh tumbled out of her lips. "Do you want to know what's crazy? Your secrecy about this place caused me to pull a gun on Owen."

My eyes bulged. "You held Owen at gunpoint?"

Each and every time I thought I had Caterina figured out, she went and shocked the hell out of me. He had already earned a strong conversation from me for allowing Caterina to come here.

But now I realized why he had disobeyed my orders.

Caterina nodded. "Because he was sworn to obey your orders and to cover your dishonest tracks."

"He was just doing his job."

The unadulterated hate that flashed in Caterina's eyes caused a stab in my chest. "I can't do this with you anymore. I'm going home now."

"I'll take you."

She shook her head wildly back and forth. "I don't want to be anywhere near you."

"Please, Kitten, let me take care of you. Let me show you how sorry I truly am."

She jabbed her finger at me. "Stay the fuck away from me!"

Whirling away, she started sprinting through the club. "Caterina, wait!" I called.

As I started to follow her, a group of businessmen came between us, talking and laughing and ignoring everyone and everything around them.

"Get the fuck out of my way!" I bellowed as I began fighting my way through them.

When I finally busted out of the front door, my gaze spun left and right to try to find her.

At the sound of a scream, my blood ran cold, and I fought to breathe.

Down the street, two men had Caterina. My feet pounded into the pavement as I tried to get to her. Just when I reached them, the men shoved her in a black-paneled van.

As my eyes locked with hers, her scream pierced my heart. "Callum!"

Chapter Thirty-Six: Callum

My wife was gone.

The mother of my child was gone.

My *life* was gone.

I shook my head as I tried shaking myself out of the nightmare I currently found myself in.

Her scream echoed through my ears, piercing my heart. Someone had taken my wife. They'd stolen her right in front of my eyes.

Turning on my heels, I raced back to the club's door. Shouting at the bouncer, I called, "Get my brothers! Now!"

He nodded and spoke into the radio on his shoulder. Before I could even process trying to get her back, I had to know who took her.

It was for emergencies like these that I had injected a tracker in her upper arm. Since I knew she would lose her mind that I was tracking her, I'd done it while she was asleep.

The negative in the situation was if it was any clan or any mafia member who had taken her, they would know to examine Caterina for a tracker and then remove it. I knew we had to start tracking her as soon as possible.

Dare appeared on the sidewalk. "What's wrong?"

"Start following Caterina's tracker," I commanded.

His face grew ashen. "Someone took her?"

After I nodded, he took out his phone and began frantically pushing buttons. "Got her."

He furrowed his brows. "Looks like they're heading towards the North End."

"Little Italy is out that way," I murmured.

Deep within me, I'd known from the moment Caterina had been taken there was no way it was random. Someone wanted to get to me, and they were using her to do it.

Dare glanced up from his phone. "We haven't pissed off any local Famiglia have we?"

I shook my head. "There's only one fucker who would dare to pull this shit."

At the image forming in my mind, I knew I needed to call Rafe. Just as I reached for my phone in my pocket, it rang.

After snatching it out, Rafe's name flashed across the screen. As soon as I accepted the call, I questioned, "Rafe?"

"Why the fuck didn't you text me back?"

"Excuse me?"

"I sent you a couple of SOS texts."

Fuck. I'd ignored the texts earlier in the club thinking that they were from Caterina. "What's wrong?"

"I was calling to warn you. I just found out from an informant at Logan Airport that my father's jet landed there about an hour ago."

"I knew it was him," I hissed.

Silence echoed back on the line before Rafe sucked in a harsh breath. "What do you mean?"

"Some of his men just grabbed Caterina off the street right outside one of our clubs. I thought it was him, but now there's not a question in my mind."

"That fucking bastard!" Rafe growled.

Dare grabbed my shoulder—his face grim. "We just lost the tracker."

"Lost it because of a bad area or it's compromised."

"It's been obliterated."

My chest constricted in a volatile mix of fear and frustration. "Fucking hell!" I bellowed.

"What's happened?" Rafe questioned.

"The tracker I put in Caterina is gone. Before we lost contact, they were heading towards Little Italy. Any idea where he might be taking her?"

"After your shooting, he iced me and the others out of any business dealings. I'm texting Gianni now to hack into his business records to see what he can find in that area."

"I'd appreciate that."

"Look, I'm almost to the hanger now, and I'll be in the air within ten minutes."

Gripping the phone tighter, I snarled, "I can't fucking wait for you!"

"What the fuck are you going to do without an address?"

"The North End is a mile long neighborhood. I'll have my men start branching out from the last ping on the tracker down to the wharf."

"Already on it," Dare replied, furiously texting.

"He could be taking her to the airport," Rafe said.

"You don't think I haven't already thought that? Give me some fucking credit."

"Fine. Will you do one thing for me?" When I didn't answer, Rafe said, "Let me and my brothers be the one to end him."

Deep within me, I understood Rafe's need to be the one to kill his father.

The exact emotions had coursed through me after finding out what had happened to Maeve.

I wanted to be able to give him that privilege, but Alessio burned that bridge when he'd abducted Caterina.

"Until I know what he's done to her, I can't make that promise."

"She's *our* blood to avenge," Rafe growled.

"She's *my* wife. And she's pregnant with *my* child!" I shouted.

Once again, silence echoed over the line. I knew it was the worst way to tell him. But he had to understand everything that was at stake.

Even if it had just been Caterina, I still had the right to take her father out for him kidnapping my wife.

"Do what you have to do," he replied.

"I will."

"We'll be there as soon as we can."

"I'll see you then."

As I hung up, Dare gripped my shoulder. "Caterina's pregnant?"

"She just told me right before she was taken."

I shut my eyes in pain. "It's because of me that those fuckers were able to take her. If she hadn't been so angry at me for the strip club, she wouldn't have run out on her own."

"We'll get her back, Callum," Dare replied reassuringly.

There wasn't a doubt in my fucking mind that we would get her back.

But what sent icy fear through my veins and agony through my chest was what torture she might face until we could get to her. The thoughts of her in pain or frightened had me shaking with rage.

The fact it was her father who took her didn't assuage my fears in the least. Alessio had already fired on her once in Sicily, not to mention risking her life when he put the hit out on me. God only knew what else he was capable of.

A red-faced and flustered looking Quinn appeared with Kellan trailing right behind. Catching them up, I said, "Alessio had his men kidnap Caterina. She's somewhere in the North End, and we have to get her back."

Quinn didn't hesitate. "I'll oversee loading up the van with ammunition."

Without ceasing my frantic pacing, I replied, "Good."

He then sprinted back into the club. Dare nodded at me. "Our men are on the way into the area. Some will hit the streets checking door to door at businesses and others are headed to the wharf to check out the water situation."

Kellan grabbed his phone out of his pocket. "I'll call our contact at Logan and have them ground all private jets for the foreseeable future. Then I'll have Fionn take a contingency down there."

Speaking seemed impossible, so I merely nodded. Although I was never one to let fear overtake me, I couldn't seem to fight the crippling panic spreading through my body. Even with a solid plan, my mind couldn't shut out the dread.

My father's voice echoed through my mind. *You've become weak just as I said you would. Loving a woman has emasculated you! You're going to be the reason she dies. Worst of all, she'll be the reason you die.*

"Don't," Dare murmured.

I whirled around to stare at him. He shook his head. "Don't give in to whatever bullshit your mind is saying."

I didn't get a chance to argue with him. A van screeched around to the corner before coming to a stop. "Get in!" Quinn called.

With a renewed purpose, I climbed into the front seat. Dare and Kellan got in the back. As we started for the North End, Rafe called again.

"What?" I demanded.

"Twenty-three Boston Street."

The air wheezed out of my lungs. "What about it?"

"It's warehouse space my father purchased about two months ago."

After I repeated the address for Dare to track it, Rafe said, "It has a front office along with warehouse space. There's a loading dock with a truck entrance on Ellery Street."

"We're on it." Just as I was about to hang up, I said, "Rafe?"

"Yeah?"

"Thanks."

"You're welcome."

When I hung up, I turned back to Dare. "I'm sure I don't even have to ask if you have the building plan pulled up."

He flashed me a grin. "Of course, I do."

"I just texted our men to converge on that area," Kellan reported.

Pride filled me with how well he was rising to the occasion. While he might've shied away from some of the grittier side of our work, he was really coming through when it came to logistics.

"Great. Now we just have to figure out how to get in there."

Quinn grimaced. "The fact he isn't getting the hell out of Boston doesn't sit well with me."

"It makes perfect sense if he's trying to draw me out."

At my brothers' silence, I said, "He's wanted me dead for a long time. To ensure that it happens, he'll shoot me himself. Then he'll force Caterina into another marital alliance.

"And he's just enough of a bastard to put Caterina in danger," Quinn growled.

"He's a fucking moron to think this wouldn't end badly for him, especially since he's pulled it on our turf," Dare remarked with his head bent over his ipad.

I shook my head. "He wouldn't be willing to stick his neck out this far unless he'd made a powerful alliance, which means we're walking into a possible firestorm."

As we careened into the North End like a bat out of hell, I leaned into the backseat and grabbed two guns out of the arsenal at Quinn's feet. With a nod at my brothers, they did the same. Quinn reached into his suit pocket and produced a Glock.

"Our men have the warehouse surrounded," Dare related.

"How's the opposition looking?"

"Oran says there's a large number along the front and back perimeter." Dare glanced up from his iPad. "He says we're not completely outnumbered."

I nodded. "Send in a contingency in the front to see if they have her in the offices. Minimal heavy range firepower just in case."

"Got it."

"Once we know she's not in the offices, we'll start at the back and work our way through to rendezvous with the front contingency to seal their escape off."

When we wheeled into the warehouse driveway, I heard Kellan murmuring in the back. *"A Thighearna, cuir dochas dlùth, 's olc fad air falbh. Cuairtich orm a Thighearna, cum solas am fagus, agus dorchadas fad air falbh."*

We all momentarily froze at the Irish Circle prayer.

For as long as we lived with Mam, she recited it each and every time we went out with our father. Although I knew we needed more than reciting frenzied prayers, I was willing to say or do anything to get Caterina back safely.

After unlocking the safety on my gun, I said, *"Áimeán."*

And then I went after my wife.

Chapter Thirty-Seven: Caterina

A gony. Anguish. Fear
All of those feelings swirled around in my mind as I slowly came into consciousness. A brass band pounded through my head and the oddest feeling of deja vu overcame me. I'd been unconscious before and woke up with a terrible headache after being kidnapped.

Trepidation sent icy prickles over my body when I realized I wasn't going to open my eyes and see Callum or his brothers. Instead of being spirited away from the Sacred Heart, I'd been taken on the street by two unknown men.

My chest constricted with fear at the thought that these men wouldn't be treating me the way that the Kavanaugh men had.

After sucking in a few breaths, my eyelids fluttered open. My anxious gaze bounced around the room.

Tall ceilings.

Metal walls.

Unmarked boxes.

I was in a warehouse of some kind. The uncomfortable wooden chair I'd been seated in was tucked away in the back behind a large forklift. My arms were pulled around the chair, and when I tried moving them, rope scratched against my wrists.

My hands were tied together. In desperation, I tried to stand up, but I quickly found my legs were bound together.

"Hello, Caterina."

Dread froze my movements. That voice had haunted my nightmares and dreams. Even after all this time had passed, I would know it anywhere.

The sound of shoes clicked across the floor behind me. As I tried regulating my breathing, the figure grew closer to me. The chair began to shake with my trembling.

When he stepped into my line of sight, nausea rolled through me. At the sight of Carmine's face, bile rushed into my mouth.

I didn't bother turning my head. Instead, I vomited at his feet.

As I rubbed my mouth against my shoulder, Carmine sneered at me. "Even after three years in the order, I see you're still a petulant cunt," he hissed.

Despite being scared out of my mind, I had to be strong. I couldn't fall apart. It wasn't just about protecting me. I had to think of my baby.

"What do you want with me?" I demanded.

A maniacal gleam burned in his eyes. "Silly bitch, the same thing I wanted from you three years ago."

I swallowed hard. "Just like then, you can't have me."

"Is that right?"

"In case you missed it, I'm married," I countered.

"Yes, I heard of your wedding to that mick bastard, Kavanaugh."

I bit my tongue to keep from lashing out at him insulting Callum. "If you were aware of my marriage, then why would you kidnap and try to marry me?"

"Because I'm a man who gets what he fucking wants."

Shaking my head, I argued, "Callum and I were married by a priest, and the marriage was consummated."

Carmine backhanded me so hard his ring cut into my cheek, scraping along the flesh. Tears blinded my eyes at the pain. Blood dripped from my face onto my lap. Pinching my eyes shut, I counted my breaths and tried to keep myself from going over the edge.

"Do not remind me that you're no longer pure. The fact you'd spread your legs for that piece of shit almost made me reconsider taking you for a wife. It's only for the alliance with your father that I was willing to overlook it.

As I popped open my eyes, I stared at him in disbelief. Could he be possibly be this deluded.

"What are you even talking about? My father's regime is dying. Everyone knows the true power of the Neretti family lies with Rafe."

Carmine tilted his head at me. "Oh, aren't you the smart one? Let me tell you something. You don't know shit."

"I know that the Kavanaugh's are stronger than they've ever been, not just in Boston, but on the East Coast. Part of their strength comes from being aligned with Rafe."

"Don't worry. Your cunt of a brother is going to get what's coming to him. There's still enough loyal men to take him out along with Leandro and Gianni. It's Step Two of my plan."

Fear gripped me at the thought of any harm coming to my brothers, but I quickly masked it. "It will never happen."

That statement earned me another gash to my cheek. Once my

eyes finished watering, Carmine grabbed me by the shoulders and sneered into my face.

"I'm going to enjoy shutting your smart ass mouth by filling it with my cock."

Glaring up at him, I shouted, "You try it, and you'll end up maimed so badly you'll never be able to use it again!"

After reaching into his suit pocket, Carmine produced a gun. Once he released the safety, he pressed the gleaming metal into my temple.

"You can choose to suck my cock, or I can blow your pretty brains all over the floor."

Before I could open my mouth to protest, a voice stunned me to silence. "You will not speak that way to my daughter, Carmine."

Just like with Carmine, it had been three years since I'd heard that voice.

All my life I had feared it.

As a child, I'd run from it.

The mere sound sent me burrowing under my bed or locking myself into my room. There had never been a single time in my life when it had possessed kindness or love.

When I'd entered the Sacred Heart, I'd hoped I'd never hear it again. After he'd been behind the hit on Callum's life, I prayed I'd never hear it again.

But here it was.

Here *he* was.

As my gaze bounced around the shadowy areas of the warehouse searching for him, Carmine growled, "With all due respect, Alessio, she threatened to bite my cock off."

When he stepped into the light, a cruel smile curved on my father's lips. "Ciao, *mi ragazza vivace.*"

"Don't you dare call me your spirited girl!" I spat.

"It's the truth, isn't it?" he questioned as he moved in front of me. Instead of replying, I merely glared at him.

His eyes narrowed on my face. "Is this your handiwork, or did the soldiers do this?" he questioned Carmine.

"It's mine," he hissed in reply.

"I took you for a smarter man." He tore his gaze from mine over to Carmine. "Only an *uomo pazzo* would mar what was valuable to him."

Satisfaction flooded me at Carmine squirming under my father's remark. "My apologies, Alessio."

After reaching into his pocket, my father produced a knife. Whimpering, I tried inching away from him as best I could.

"This is also no way to treat your future wife," he said as he began to cut through my binds.

At the mention of Carmine's future wife, I recoiled. "I'm a married woman, Father. Although I wasn't married in a church, it was by a priest, and it was consummated," I countered.

Hate simmered within the sneer he shot at me. "Marriages are easily annulled."

When he finished with my hands, he handed the knife to Carmine. It didn't surprise me at all that my father saw it beneath him to kneel before me.

He still saw himself as the all-powerful capo. Carmine's expression told me he felt the same way, but he was left with no choice.

Wincing, I brought my arms around my body from the back of the chair before I rubbed my aching wrists. Once Carmine finished with my legs, I rolled my feet, trying to get some feeling back in them.

Before I could get my bearings, Carmine grabbed me by the waist and dragged me to my feet. Although I swayed, I refused to reach out for Carmine.

He dipped his head to where his rancid cigar breath scorched against my cheek. "I'm afraid we're going to have to skip the nuptials and go straight for the consummation."

I stared past him to my father. "You can't seriously be supporting him in this madness."

"Carmine needs a son and heir. While we work on getting your marriage annulled, he can get you pregnant. Then you'll marry him."

Oh God.

This couldn't be happening. How could both of them be so delusional? The thoughts of enduring Carmine raping me repeatedly sent bile rushing to my throat.

"There's no way you can make any of this legal. Neither Callum nor I would agree to ending our marriage."

My father's brows shot up. "Surely you don't doubt my abilities or the power of my alliances?"

When I didn't respond, he took a handkerchief from his pocket. Although I tried jerking away from him, he brought the fabric to my cheek to clean my wounds.

"Forging signatures is child's play for a man like me. Despite what you think, my name still holds respect and power. There are still judges and law enforcement in my pocket."

He jerked a chin at Carmine. "Not only am I still a very powerful man, so is my underboss. With the marriage of his daughter to the pahkan of the Jersey Bratva's son, we've unified a very strong and lucrative alliance."

I recoiled in horror as I thought about the teenage girl who was once to be my step-daughter. "But Allegra isn't even eighteen yet."

Carmine gave me a shark-like grin. "It doesn't matter if a parent gives consent."

My lips curled in disgust at his response. "She deserves better."

"I'm glad to see you're caring for your future daughter," Carmine retorted.

I tore my gaze from his back to my father. "If you marry me off to him in this harebrained scheme, whatever was fractured between you and Rafe will never be mended."

"I have no use for Rafe or his traitorous brothers..." He pointed to my stomach. "Your son will inherit the Neretti legacy."

My hands protectively flew to cover my abdomen to try and

Poison and Wine

shield my baby from his heinous plot. Trembling wildly, I tried to think of any way out of the current hell I faced.

I hoped and prayed that Callum had managed to track me down, and that he would somehow save me.

Carmine licked his lips while staring down at me. "Can I take her now, Alessio?"

"Be quick about it. After the shipment arrives for Mikita, we're heading to the safe house in New York."

With a lecherous grin, Carmine grabbed my arm and began to drag me away. My stomach churned when I imagined him putting his hands on other parts of my body.

I wanted to save myself, but at the same time, I didn't want any harm to come to my baby.

Although I tried clamping my hand down on my mouth, the panicked scream tore through me and echoed off the walls.

"I'm already pregnant!"

Carmine froze. "You lie."

A part of me wanted to tell him I had. That I could endure him violating me if it meant my baby would remain safe.

But instead, I furiously shook my head. "You can call the Kavanaugh's OBGYN. I was there today. I'm six weeks pregnant."

Carmine whirled us around to where we faced my father. Disgust radiated off of him.

Although it pained me to do so, I sank to my knees. "Please, Father, if you let me go and abandon this terrible idea, I'll ensure that no harm comes to you. On the life of my child, I swear to you that I'll broker a peace between you and Callum. Regardless of how you feel about Rafe and my brothers, there can be a peace and alliance with the Kavanaugh's. Think of the power you'd hold then. You'll truly be unstoppable."

For a moment, he appeared to be weighing my words. I prayed with everything within me that he would accept my offer.

When he closed the gap between us, I held my breath. "I want nothing to do with any alliance that involves that mick son of a bitch you've spread your legs for."

As the hope drained from my body, my chest caved in agony. Tears stung my eyes. "Please, Father."

After grabbing me by the arm, he jerked me to my feet. His cruel sneer caused my stomach to clench. "I suppose we'll just have to ensure you lose the baby, won't we?"

Terror the likes I'd never known cascaded over me as my arms wound around my abdomen. Why had I been so stupid and revealed my pregnancy? I could've endured the rape to ensure my child was safe.

I would've endured *anything*.

But now, my father—my own flesh and blood—was going to kill the child within me.

He shoved me into Carmine's arms. "Take care of it."

"Coward!" I spat.

The words had barely escaped my lips when Carmine's fist connected with my abdomen. A scream tore from me as I sank to my knees.

Desperately, I tried to shield my stomach from Carmine's fists. My defensive exertions left both of us panting.

I prayed for my child's safety.

I prayed for Callum to rescue us.

I prayed for forgiveness for allowing my child to be put in danger.

At Carmine's harsh kick, I groaned as my breath was sucked from my body. Pain, like I had never known, ricocheted through me.

As darkness threatened to sweep me under. I fought to keep my eyes open.

I knew once I was unconscious, there would be no saving my unborn child.

Just when I thought I couldn't hold on a moment longer, an explosion detonated from the far wall.

Time seemed to crawl to a standstill as debris rained down.

Smoke filled the air as Carmine abandoned me to draw his gun out of his jacket. He and my father moved forward to hide behind a few boxes.

As my vision clouded, I desperately peered into the smoke. At the emergence of men, my heart surged.

It was Callum and his brothers.

I was safe.

Chapter Thirty-Eight: Caterina

My eyelids fluttered for several moments before I could finally open them. As I stared up at the tiled ceiling, I realized I wasn't within the confines of my four-poster bed at home.

I was in a hospital.

A deep voice startled me. "Kitten, are you awake?"

When I turned my head on the pillow, I met Callum's concerned stare. Anguish lined his handsome face. His dark hair was unkempt like he'd been running his fingers through it.

"Hey, my love," he croaked in a pained voice.

As I furrowed my brows, I desperately tried processing why I would be in the hospital. Foggy wisps of memories swirled in my mind.

A half-naked woman on Callum's lap.

Running out of a club into the street.

Being hit on the head.

Waking up tied to a chair.

When Carmine's cruel, sneering face appeared in my mind, a shudder ran through my body. "Oh God," I murmured.

Callum leaned forward to take my hand in his. "It's okay. *You're* okay."

I'm okay.

Thank God. But relief was short lived since my agony hadn't just been about me. A sob choked off in my throat. "The baby?"

A beaming smile lit up Callum's handsome face. "She's fine."

"S-She?" My breath hitched in my chest. "It's a girl?"

With a nod, Callum replied, "To ensure the pregnancy was still viable, they did a lot of testing. One of the tests revealed the gender."

"So soon?" I questioned incredulously.

"Aye. They have one now that detects at six weeks. Something about looking for male chromosomes in the DNA to show up, and when it does or doesn't, you know what it is."

He kissed my fingers before staring up at me with such adoration that my chest tightened. "Apparently, our daughter already takes after her mother with how strong she is."

Tears spilled over my cheeks. "She's definitely stubborn like me."

He grinned. "Extremely. I'm sure the two of you will torture me endlessly."

I hiccupped a laugh. "Are you disappointed it's not a boy to carry on the name?"

Callum frowned. "Fuck no."

"But you need an heir," I protested.

"And I'm having one."

"She can't take over the family."

A wicked gleam burned in Callum's baby blues. "Who's to say we won't give her a brother or two? Considering how fertile we seem to be, I don't think it will be a problem."

I rolled my eyes. "If you think you're going to keep me knocked up until you get a son, you're crazy."

"I've got two more chances, right?"

"Exactly. I agreed to only three."

He kissed my fingers again. "I'll hold you to it, Kitten."

"Can I hold you to letting me give our daughter an Italian first name?"

Callum raised his brows at me. "Does that mean our sons get Irish names?"

"Only if they're ones without crazy Irish spellings that they'll have to explain to everyone how to pronounce."

He grinned. "I can work with that."

As I tried pushing myself up in the bed, I winced. "How long have I been out?"

"Fuck, Kitten, I don't know. It seems like forever. They gave you something for the pain that kept you asleep."

"It wasn't anything unsafe for the baby, was it?"

"No, it was fine."

"Thank goodness."

As I thought about my time in the warehouse, my father's face flashed before my mind. "Is he dead?" I questioned softly.

"Aye."

"By your hand?"

Callum shifted in his seat. "Do you really want to know?"

"I do."

He grimaced. "While I wanted his death to come by my hands, I honored Rafe's request."

My hand flew to my mouth in surprise. "Please tell me he didn't."

Callum's brows popped wide. "Would you rather it had been me, Kitten?"

I shook my head. "No. I wouldn't wish it for any of you."

A ragged sigh echoed through Callum's chest. "Although I

wanted my own hands to take Alessio's life, Rafe needed to do it." He gave me a pointed look. "Just as I did."

Although I wanted to disagree, I knew he was right. My father had gone too far for too long. As long as he was allowed to live, Rafe, along with Leandro and Gianni, would've been in danger just as much as I was.

"What about Carmine?"

Pure evil flashed in Callum's blue eyes. "I will take care of him"

A shiver ran down my spine. "He's still alive?"

"He only breathes because I refused to leave your side. Now that you're awake, I'll take care of him."

"Will you torture him?" I whispered.

Tilting his head at me, Callum questioned, "Don't tell me you're asking to spare him?"

"My faith tells me to spare him to spare you. That all life—even one as odious as his—is precious."

I slowly shook my head. "But I'd rather be a sinner. I want you to make him suffer because he was going to rape me." My eyes narrowed. "You should cause him agony because he almost cost us our child's life."

"I plan on torturing him for all of it, Kitten."

"Thank you," I murmured.

Callum leaned over and brought his lips gently to mine. When he pulled away, his intense gaze bore into me. "I love you more than life itself, Kitten."

My heart skipped a beat at his words and the intensity in which he said them. But there was still unresolved hurt with him.

"While I love you more than life itself as well, I hope you know I'm still angry with you."

The corners of his lips turned up. "I'd hoped a near-death experience had softened your heart."

"I'm not joking, Callum."

His expression darkened. "Don't think you're the only one who is angry."

I narrowed my eyes. "Excuse me? Did you find *me* with a half-naked man?"

"Like I told you before, it was business."

Shoving him away, I cried, "Fuck you and your business!"

"I told you yesterday before you ran away, nothing happened between me and that dancer."

"*Stripper.*"

"Semantics."

"I saw the way she looked at you. She wanted you."

"But *I* didn't want *her*."

At the roll of my eyes, he added, "Jesus Christ, Caterina, there isn't a single woman I want on this fucking planet but you."

"Don't take the Lord's name in vain," I chastised.

A low growl came from deep within his chest. "I only want you."

The vast majority of me believed him. Before yesterday, Callum hadn't given me any indication that he was cheating. At the same time, he had deceived me in the worst possible way. We had to reestablish trust.

I shook my head at him. "Trust is the most important aspect in a marriage."

Tears welled in my eyes. "And you broke that by lying to me about where you were and owning a strip club."

Callum's expression grew agonized. "What else can I say or do for you to understand that you're my entire world?"

"It's easy for you to trust my fidelity. I'm constantly shadowed by a bodyguard, or I'm on camera at the house. It isn't fair that you're not under the same scrutiny."

Crossing his arms over his chest with a smirk, Callum countered, "Considering you stalked me down to the club, you know more about my whereabouts than you're letting on."

With a roll of my eyes, I replied, "It's just a basic tracking app."

"I didn't realize you were so techie."

"You know I'm not," I snapped.

"Last time I checked, Gianni had an IT background."

"Yes, he does handle the family's technology."

"*All* his family's," Callum pointedly remarked.

I huffed out a frustrated breath. "Fine. Gianni fixed my phone at the reception, and while you were inebriated, I gave him your phone." I looked at him. "Happy?"

He gave me a crooked grin. "Although I'm glad to hear you admit it, I won't be happy until you are." Squeezing my hand, he said, "Tell me what to do."

I knew what I wanted to ask of him, but it was difficult. I knew how I wanted him to react, and if he didn't, he was going to disappoint me even further.

After drawing in a deep breath, I said, "I don't want you making money off women."

"It's just dancing, Caterina. It's not like we're trafficking or prostituting women."

Gritting my teeth, I replied, "I sure as hell wouldn't be with you if you did."

Callum exhaled. "Let me guess. You don't want me having a part in the club, do you?"

I nodded. "Sell your stake of the club to your brothers."

"You're really serious about this?"

"Absolutely."

As his jaw clenched and unclenched, Callum appeared to be weighing my words. "Fine. To ensure I don't profit anymore on women, I'll give my stake to Quinn."

"What about Dare and Kellan?"

Callum chuckled. "Let's just say I kinda owe Quinn for some extra work he's done for the club."

"As long as your brothers won't be upset about it."

"They won't."

"Just like that?"

"Yes, Kitten. Just like that."

He leaned forward on the bed to where his mouth was inches from mine. "Does that make you happy?"

"A little."

He chuckled. "What else would you have me do to make you *very* happy?"

I grinned. "Some *epic* groveling."

"And what does that entail?"

Tapping my chin, I said, "Hmm, I would say you owe me many, many orgasms, but since that also benefits you, that's a nope."

Callum groaned. "I see you're going to be cruel and demanding."

"Aye, I am," I replied, trying to sound like an Irish wife.

A wicked gleam burned in his blue eyes. "Denying yourself pleasure seems like cutting your nose off to spite your face."

With a wink, I said, "Maybe I'll revisit that one."

Placing his hand on my abdomen, Callum's expression grew earnest. "What can I do for our daughter?"

Tears once again welled in my eyes. "You've already given her the most important thing. A future of her own."

"I'll give her the world." He placed a tender kiss on my lips. "Just as I will you."

And I knew he meant every word. When Callum had kidnapped me from the Sacred Heart, I thought my life was over. Never would I have imagined it was just beginning.

Epilogue: Caterina

Ten Months Later

Although the decor surrounding us was bright and cheery, Callum's dark mood permeated the room. As for me, I couldn't help thinking how comical he appeared in a three piece suit pacing back and forth in front of the rainbow colored examining table.

Wriggling on the crinkling paper was our three-month-old daughter, Julianna.

Callum had kept his word by allowing me to bestow an Italian name on our first born. I had given the Sicilian Giuliana an anglicized spelling. I'd furthered her Irish roots by giving her Maeve as a middle name. I couldn't imagine a stronger role model for my daughter than her aunt.

Stripped out of the designer dress Quinn had bought, Julianna resided only in her diaper. As the nurse slipped the measuring tape through her dark curls, she kicked her legs and cooed.

"She's measuring right on target," the nurse commented.

Callum nodded his head, never taking his eyes off of his daughter. After recording the numbers in a file, the nurse said, "Dr. Sheehan should be right in."

"Thank you," I called as she exited the room.

While I sat in the chair across from the examining table, Callum leaned over Julianna. When his lips brushed against her bare skin, she squealed since she knew what was coming.

He blew the raspberries across her tummy. She giggled and grasped the strands of his hair.

I couldn't help smiling at the sight before me. "Never would I have believed a scene like this would be part of my life when you kidnapped me," I mused.

Callum threw a glance at me over his shoulder. "Even after all this time, you're never going to let me forget that, are you?"

Shaking my head, I laughed. "Never."

Callum turned back to Julianna. "Your mommy is the most stubborn woman I've ever met."

I stood up from the chair to join them. Leaning over Julianna, I added, "And your daddy's biggest weakness is the two of us."

With a grin, Callum replied, "Aye, as much as I don't want to admit it, you're right."

I brought my lips to his for a kiss. When I pulled away, I ran the back of my hand across the hair on his cheek.

"The best thing that ever happened to me was being kidnapped by you."

"The best thing I ever did was kidnap you."

Poison and Wine

Before we could start kissing again, a knock came at the door. "Come in," I called.

Dr. Sheehan stepped in the door with a bright smile. "It's good to see all of you again."

She gave me a knowing look since Callum was in attendance. He'd come to her two-day checkup as well. Even though she'd taken a Hippocratic oath, Callum didn't trust her when it came to Julianna.

"Yes, he's a very involved father," I mused.

Dr. Sheehan smiled. "You're lucky."

Returning her smile, I replied, "I am."

And it was the truth. I'd never imagined Callum being such an involved dad. He'd gone so far as to take a month long paternity leave from his work, so he could stay by our side.

Once he'd gone back to work, he called or texted constantly throughout the day. I tried reminding him he had cameras to check in on us, but he claimed to want to hear my voice. I think it was more about wanting to see a clearer image of Julianna on facetime than the grainy images on the security cameras.

As crazy as he was about her, Julianna was just as crazy about him.

She was a Daddy's Girl through and through, and I teased Callum that some days I felt like she preferred me only as a milk receptacle. He quickly argued that I had him beat considering how much Julianna favored me.

She had both of our dark hair, but her facial features did resemble mine. Of course, it felt a little conceited to say she looked like me and then say what a beautiful baby she was.

So, I bit my tongue and let everyone else remark about her beauty instead.

Once Dr. Sheehan was through with her examination, we came to the part of the appointment I'd been dreading: the vaccinations. While I didn't want my daughter to feel pain, I really feared Callum's reaction when she was hurt.

At the first shot and Juliana's high pitched wail, Callum's hand went for his gun under his jacket. "Callum!" I hissed in horror.

When he met my gaze, he had the audacity not to even appear apologetic. "She hurt her," he gritted out.

I rolled my eyes. "She had to get her vaccines, especially with us traveling overseas."

For Julianna's baptism, we were traveling to Sicily. We'd decided to have her baptized at the church I'd attended as a part of the Sacred Heart.

Most of our family thought we were insane to do it there considering the potential bad memories involved with my kidnapping. Maybe Callum and I weren't sane, because to us, it was a special place.

It was where we first met.

Of course, it was also where I'd shot and bitten him, and he'd drugged me. But without all of our initial trauma, we wouldn't have each other or our beautiful daughter.

Another reason we would be baptizing her there was because I'd asked Sister Lucia to be one of her godmothers along with Maeve. We'd chosen Rafe and Kellan as her godfathers.

Although Quinn and Dare should've been higher on the list, I knew Kellan had the heart and soul needed to watch over Julianna in a spiritual and emotional sense.

As the new capo of the Neretti family, Rafe brought physical protection.

Once Dr. Sheehan was finished, Callum practically shoved her away, so he could get his hands on Juliana. "Oh, my angel, Da is so very, very sorry," Callum murmured as he cradled Julianna against his chest. At her continued wailing, he began cooing to her in Irish.

When Dr. Sheehan shot me a look, I held up my hands. "My sincere apologies. I promise I'll leave him at home for the next set of shots."

Poison and Wine

While she laughed, Callum shook his head. "Like hell. My princess needs me."

Once again, I rolled my eyes. Dr. Sheehan replied, "It's always the hardcore daddies that break down the worst with their wee one's shots."

Since she was one of the doctors connected with the Kavanaugh family, she knew exactly what kind of "hardcore" man Callum was. "You guys have a safe trip, and I hope to not have to see you until the six-month shots."

"Thanks, Dr. Sheehan," I replied while Callum merely grunted. With a frustrated huff, I said, "Come on. Let's get her dressed and out of here before you shoot someone."

He grinned at me. "I'm making no promises."

When we arrived back home, tears once again assaulted my eyes at the glimpse of the moving boxes. At the sight of my face, Callum gave me a reassuring smile. "Kitten, are you ever going to get over this?"

"I can't help it. I'm still so hormonal," I argued.

With Julianna's arrival, it had been decided it was time for Dare to move into his own home after we'd already lost Quinn to his new lady. Although we'd lost two brothers, we would be gaining Orla and Eamon. With me in school full-time, Julianna would need a nanny.

Thankfully, we had to look no further than Callum's mother.

After spending the first month of Julianna's life with us, she decided she couldn't bear to be so far away from her granddaughter.

Eamon was thrilled to be joining his brothers and to begin his initiation into the clan. With their arrival, Maeve would be the only Kavanaugh still in Ireland, but thankfully, there were enough Kavanaugh clan members there to make sure she was safe and protected.

Dare appeared on the landing of the stairs. At the sight of Julianna, his face lit up. "There's my beautiful princess!"

When he reached us, Julianna took one look at him, jutted out a quivering lip, and then burst into tears. Her reaction caused Dare's face to fall.

"What the fuck did I do?"

While Callum chuckled, I shook my head. "It's not your fault, Dare. She just had her shots, so she's not feeling her best."

Dare rubbed Julianna's tear-stained cheek. "Oh, my poor wain," he crooned, which caused Julianna to cry harder.

Not only did Julianna have her father wrapped about her finger, but all of her uncles as well. They loved helping Callum with bath time and bedtime. Her closet was full of ridiculously expensive clothes, not to mention all the toys and books they bought.

It was quite humorous watching them wearing her in the sling, especially when fielding phone calls that involved dark dealings. Like Callum, Dare and Kellan loved having her fall asleep on their chests. While Quinn still shied away from holding her as much as the others, he enjoyed pushing her pram during walks around the neighborhood.

Dare's devotion to Julianna was another reason why I was going to miss him much. Just the thought that he wouldn't be on the floor right above us caused tears to fill my eyes again. It felt like I was saying goodbye to my own brothers.

Although she didn't get to spend as much time with them, Rafe, Leo, and Gianni tried to come down every other weekend.

When Dare shot me a concerned look, I laughed. "I'm fine. I keep getting emotional thinking about you guys moving out."

He grinned his signature cocky grin before throwing his arm around me. "I'm going to miss you, too, Sister Sassy."

I rolled my eyes at him still continuing to call me by my old nickname. "Admit it. You're only going to miss Julianna."

"How could I not miss you?"

Putting my hands on my hips, I countered, "Me or my cooking?"

"You."

I kissed his cheek. "While I don't believe you, I appreciate the sentiment."

"I'm not lying." With a wink, he added, "I still plan on getting my fill of your cooking when I come here for dinner every night."

"I'm glad to hear it."

When Julianna continued fussing in Callum's embrace and rooting around on his chest, I held out my arms. "I think that's my cue to feed her."

Dare wrinkled his nose. "That's my cue to get my boxes and get the hell out of here."

I rolled my eyes. "Like I would just whip my boob out right in front of you."

The only thing that freaked the brothers out was feeding. Nothing made the room clear out faster than for me to start unbuttoning my top. Not that I wasn't modest and wouldn't have wanted to flash them, but it was really quite comical.

I walked into the living room and eased down in one of the chairs. Callum followed closely on my heels, easing Julianna into my arms.

Once she was latched and feeding, he squatted down in front of us. "I'm not going to lie that I'm starting to get slightly jealous of our daughter's unlimited time with your boobs."

With a squeal of horror, I kicked him with my leg. "You're terrible."

He laughed. "I can't help it. I'm wandering through a sexless desert."

I narrowed my eyes at him. "I'm sure if you'd had a third-degree tear to your dick, you wouldn't be ready either."

One thing my husband and mother-in-law had failed to tell me was that Kavanaugh's produced big babies. All of the Kavanaugh brothers had been nine pounds and up, and Maeve had almost been nine. Healing from the tear had been worse than the pain of delivery. I

t's why I hadn't been given the green light for sex at six weeks. While I hadn't had any desire to get physical, I had thrown several mercy blowjobs at Callum.

With a groan, Callum bowed his head to rest his chin on my knees. "I'm sorry I'm a sex-crazed asshole who would die just to be buried inside you again."

He leaned forward to kiss the hand that nuzzled Juliana's head. "I miss you—I miss us."

"I miss us, too," I whispered.

And that was the truth. I'd grown to enjoy the physical side of our relationship almost as much as Callum. I missed waking to his fingers and tongue between my legs. I hadn't even wanted any oral from him because I was still gunshy.

But I'd turned a corner in the last few days. Not only had I finally been given the green light by my doctor, but I'd started to feel more like the old me. I hadn't told Callum yet because I didn't want to promise him something I wasn't sure my body could deliver.

Tilting my head at him, I said, "After I put Julianna down for her nap, maybe we can try."

He jerked his head off my knee, and a laugh burst from my lips at the expectant look on his face. "You're serious?" he questioned.

"I am."

"You're not fucking with me?"

I shot him a wicked grin. "No, but I'd like to *try* fucking with you."

He closed his eyes in exaggerated bliss. "Oh Kitten, that word on your lips."

"I'm going to expect a lot from your lips to get me ready to take you."

He grunted like a caveman, which caused Julianna to turn her head and eye her father suspiciously. When he smiled adoringly at her, she reached out a hand for him, which he took and pretended to gobble up.

It always elicited a giggly response from her. She then kicked her feet and babbled at him.

Rubbing her cheek with my finger, I said, "All right, *piccola stellina*, you need to focus on eating and not on your daddy."

Callum kissed Julianna's head. "I love you to the moon and stars, but hurry up and go to sleep, so Daddy can bury himself inside Mommy."

"You're terrible," I huffed before pushing his head away with my free hand.

With a wicked grin, he winked and heading out of the living room. After Callum left, Julianna returned to nursing, but her eyes began to droop. I kept rocking her in my arms long after she went to sleep.

Callum's whisper caused me to jump. "Quit stalling and put her down."

As I rose to my feet, nervous butterflies filled my stomach. But at the sight of my handsome husband leaning against the doorframe, I knew it was ready.

Epilogue: Callum

In the last three months, there was nothing in the world I loved more than watching my daughter sleep.

To see the peace and contentment etched across her tiny face as she snuggled against me.

To feel the warmth of her body pressed against my chest.

To have my nose overwhelmed with her sweet baby smell.

Whenever I was home, she napped on me. Although we'd been advised to sleep when she slept, I couldn't tear my eyes away from her. She was like her mother in that regard. I wanted my gaze to rest upon her at all times.

But not today.

As soon as Caterina eased Julianna's sleeping form onto the crib mattress, I took her by the hand. When I started pulling her out of our sitting room that had become a makeshift nursery and into our bedroom, Caterina tugged against me.

In a whisper she asked, "Don't you want to wait to make sure she doesn't wake up?"

"She's been in a milk coma for the last ten minutes," I protested quietly.

Although she looked uncertain, Caterina allowed me to shut the bedroom door. "At least turn on the monitor," she instructed as I hurried her over to the bed.

I rolled my eyes. "Do you honestly think we won't hear her in the next room?"

She shot me a wicked grin as she began to unbutton her blouse. "Maybe I'll be too vocal and drown her out."

I groaned as I ripped off my tie. "Considering you both have a set of lungs on you, it is a possibility."

Once I'd shed my tie, I made quick work of my shirt. As I started on my belt, my gaze went to watch Caterina undress. I never grew tired of seeing her naked. Although she worried about her body post Julianna, I loved the extra curves in her hips and breasts.

When she stood before me in just her bra and panties, I couldn't wait a second longer to touch and taste her. After depositing my belt on the floor, I went to her side. As I slipped my hands around her waist, she shivered.

I tilted my head at her. "Are you sure about this?"

She nodded. "I've missed your hands on me."

I brought my lips to kiss the hollow of her throat. "I've missed putting my hands on you, Kitten. More than you'll ever know."

I then kissed up the silky-smooth skin of her neck and over her chin to her velvet lips. As my mouth met hers in a frenzied kiss, my hands slid up her ribcage to cup her breasts. When I squeezed them, she moaned into my mouth.

After undoing her bra, I pulled the straps down her arms. I licked my lips in anticipation, which caused Caterina to laugh. "They aren't that much bigger, are they?"

"You sure as hell won't hear any complaints from me," I mused.

She playfully smacked my arm before I took her naked flesh in my hands. Her breath hitched as I rolled her nipples in my fingers, tweaking the hardening buds. My mouth watered at the thoughts of having them in my mouth once again.

"I need to taste you, Kitten."

When she nodded, I leaned down to suck her nipple into my mouth. Caterina's hands came to fist in my hair as I swirled my tongue over her peaked bud.

"Mm, Callum," Caterina murmured.

As her nipple popped free from my mouth, I kissed a trail over to her other breast. While I sucked and nipped at the hardened bud, a drop of milk landed on my tongue.

Although I should've expected it, it still surprised me. A lesser man might've been turned off by it, but there was nothing that could diminish Caterina's sexiness.

I continued teasing her breasts. My hand slid down Caterina's abdomen. When I reached her center, arousal had already coated her panties.

Touching her over the cotton, I couldn't help but smile. "Three months without sex and you've gone back to your Nun's Knickers."

She huffed out a breath. "Since my pre-baby thongs are too tight, I had to resort to these."

I slipped my hand down inside the waistband. "I'm not complaining. I happen to like these a lot."

When my fingers found her clit, she gasped. "You'd say anything to get me to fuck you, wouldn't you?" she panted.

Those words coming out of her mouth coupled with the feel of her scorching hot pussy caused my cock to jerk painfully in my briefs.

"There is nothing sexier than you with your tits out and a soaked pair of nun's knickers," I replied as I sped up my fingers.

Caterina grinned as her chest rose and fell. Unable to wait any longer, I plunged two fingers inside her slick walls, causing both of us to moan.

Caterina's hips began to rise and fall as I thrust my fingers deep inside her pussy. My mouth found its way back to her breasts and I teased and licked at the hardened nipples.

"Mm, Callum, I'm so close."

Curving my fingers inside of her, I rubbed her G-spot. A cry of immense pleasure erupted from Caterina's lips. As I continued swirling my fingers, her walls began to clench around me.

"Yes, Callum, yes!" Caterina shrieked as she clawed my shoulders.

I welcomed the pain that brought her so much pleasure. While her walls continued trembling, I removed my fingers and brought them to my lips.

As I sucked her taste off of my skin, Caterina sank down on the mattress and ran her hands over her face. "Thank God."

"Isn't it me you should be thanking?" I questioned as I unbuttoned my pants.

She gave me a lazy grin. "You're right. I should give credit where it's due."

Leaning up, she pulled my pants and underwear down over my hips. "After tearing so badly, I was afraid I might not be able to orgasm that hard again," she admitted.

"I'm glad I could put your worries to rest."

She smiled as she wrapped her fingers around my cock. "So am I."

I stilled her movements. At her surprise, I said, "Kitten, as much as I love your hand and blow jobs, I want nothing more than to be buried in your pussy right now."

Fear flashed momentarily in her eyes but she nodded. Before I could ease onto the bed with her, she pressed a hand to my chest. "Condom."

Since I'd never had to suit up to be inside Caterina, a smirk curved on my lips. "We could get started on giving Julianna a sibling," I suggested.

Caterina scowled at me. "If you want to fuck me, you'll wear a condom."

With a laugh, I held up my hands. "It was just a thought."

She shook her head. "It won't be a thought until Julianna's first birthday."

Now it was my turn to scowl. "You expect me to wear condoms for the next seven months?"

"That or go without."

Grunting, I bent over and fished my wallet out of my pants' pocket. After ripping into the foil, I slid the condom down my length. I then climbed on top of Caterina, easing us into the middle of the bed.

At the feel of my cock against her entrance, Caterina tensed. I knew I had to do something to put her at ease.

I decided to take us back to our first time together. I rolled us over, bringing her up to straddle me. "You take control, Kitten."

"Really?"

Nodding, I replied, "I'll take whatever you can give me."

"And if I can't?"

"Then we'll try again another day."

And it was the truth. The last thing in the world I would ever do was hurt her physically. Just the thought sent an ache through my chest.

But like the strong-willed goddess she was, a determined glint flashed in Caterina's eyes as she took my cock in her hand.

Bringing it to her center, we both hissed at the feel.

Then she began to slide inch by glorious inch down my cock. The slow burn had me aching to thrust up my hips, but I knew it would cause her pain.

When I was finally sheathed within her, I shuddered at the feeling. Staring up at her, I asked, "How does it feel?"

She bit down on her lip. "Stretched...but good." She looked at me. "How does it feel for you?"

Shifting my hips, I groaned in ecstasy. "Fucking amazing."

That was an understatement. Nothing felt like being buried deep within Caterina—her walls clenching me in a vise.

The apprehension on Caterina's face evaporated at my comment, and she grinned down at me. "I love you, Callum."

I returned her grin. "I love you more, Kitten."

"Will you fuck me now?"

"My pleasure."

As Caterina began to slowly ride me, I eased my hips slightly up and down. Once she found her stride, she began to speed up her pace. My hands came to grip her hips, and I pushed her on and off of me.

"Yes, fuck, yes," she murmured.

Digging my feet into the mattress, I began to thrust harder inside her. "Are you still okay?" I grunted.

"Mm, hmm." She bit her lip as she stared down at me. "So good, baby."

That was music to my fucking ears. As I fucked her faster, my balls began to slap her ass. Caterina splayed her hands on my chest as hips swiveled on my cock.

Her pants and my grunts of pleasure filled the room. "Oh, oh, oh!" she cried as her walls began to clench around my dick. That was all it took to set me off. It was probably better for her if I didn't last too long.

Once I finished coming, I slowly eased out of her and pulled off the condom. After throwing it into the trash, I joined her back in the bed. I bestowed a passionate kiss on her lips before lying down beside her. "That was amazing."

"It was." She smiled up at me. "It is always with you."

"I feel the same way, Kitten." I leaned in to kiss her again when a wail went off in the sitting room. "I think our cock blocker has woken up."

Caterina swatted my arm. "Don't ever call her that," she huffed, although the corners of her lips did turn up.

I rose off the bed. "I'll throw on some pants and grab her."

Nodding, Caterina said, "I'll go clean up."

As she started for the bathroom, I opened the sitting room door. At the sound of my footsteps, Julianna's waning cries ratcheted up several decibels.

"Da's coming, *mo stoirín*."

When I reached her crib, she held her arms up for me. I quickly picked her up and snuggled her to my chest. I peppered the top of her head with kisses. Her cries quieted to snubs as she burrowed her face into my neck.

I cooed words of comfort to her in Irish. Between Caterina and me, she was sure to be trilingual with Irish and Italian.

When Caterina appeared in the doorway in yoga pants and a t-shirt, adoration filled her face. As she walked over to us, I couldn't keep my eyes off the rise and fall of her hips and the way her top stretched across her tits.

She wagged a finger at me. "You better put those thoughts on the back burner until she goes to bed tonight."

"I have a feeling it'll be longer than that. Mam said she'd probably be fretful today after her shots and not sleep well."

Caterina jutted her chin at me. "Our spoiled girl is back asleep."

I winked at her. "She just needed her da."

Instead of giving me grief, Caterina merely smiled up at me. "Although I should be angry, I love how you spoil and adore her."

"Just like I do you."

Caterina leaned over Julianna to kiss me. "Yes, we're your spoiled and adored girls."

She tenderly ran her fingers through Julianna's silky black curls. "I'm so thankful our daughter has you as a father."

Her words shot straight to my heart. When I'd imagined loving a child, I'd never fathomed just how deep that love would be. I'd known the love of my brothers, my precious Maeve, and my rock of a mother.

By the grace of God, I'd come to know the adoring love of my wife who amazed me each and every day with her capacity to love a miserable bastard like me.

But something long dormant and deep within me came alive the moment I locked eyes with my daughter. She lit a fire within me that I never imagined existed.

In my world where we faced our mortality each and every day, she was a piece of my immortality. Through her, I would continue to live on long after I was gone.

Just like her mother, Julianna was everything good and pure that I wasn't. Until I'd married Caterina, I hadn't given a fuck about the men I killed or the crimes I committed.

But something about her pure soul made me regret it...but not enough to stop the life I'd been born into.

Cocking my brows at Caterina, I countered, "I'm a cold-hearted killer."

"Yes, you are." She gave me a pointed stare. "But when it comes down to it, you have a loving and giving heart."

"Whatever heart I have, it belongs to you and Julianna."

She smiled up at me. "And we happily take it."

Pulling her into my arms, I brought my lips to Caterina's—my beautiful wife, my fiery Kitten, and the sweet wine that made the poison of the underworld worth living.

Author Note

When the idea for a mafia romance series first came to me in October, it was Quinn and Isla's book. During my yearly reread of *Lover Awakened* from the Black Dagger Brotherhood series, a tortured, tattooed, scarred hero came to me. I knew he was to be the enforcer, so I would need to start from the top and work my way down.

Thus, Callum came to me with the kidnapping scene in the religious order.

All the Kavanaugh brothers will have books. I even ended up aging Seamus down because he just appeared so beautifully wounded on the pages that I wanted him to find happiness again after losing his son and wife.

Anyhoo, my ADHD brain says all of this to tell you that YES, **Rafe and Maeve** will have a book. They were never planned—they just decided in the reception scene that they were going to be a couple. I plan to post a deleted scene from Christmas where the two got a little tangled up in the tinsel...well, actually it was the mistletoe, lol.

Book Two, Dust to Dust, is Now Available

After barely dodging death from a car bomb, I shut out everyone but my mafia brothers. With a scarred face and body, I became an even more ruthless enforcer, cruelty and darkness radiating from my ravaged soul. Until a petite goddess with an innocent spirit swayed her hips on my stage, forcing me to let her audition for a dancer at my club. Though I expected her to balk at my marred appearance, I'm shocked to find her eager to touch and seduce me, willing to indulge my monster's cravings if it secures the job.

Isla is everything I'm not—sweet, fragile, and loving. A blinding ray of light in my dark and desolate world. When she is kidnapped from my club, I could demolish anything in my path to hunt down the animal who took her and to reclaim the only brightness left in my world. But even if I rescue her, can a broken enforcer with anger issues be what she needs?

After losing my parents, I clung to the light inside, determined not to succumb to darkness. But with a teenage sister to support and education to pay for, I'm forced to parlay my years of competitive dance for a controversial career as an exotic dancer. At the club owned by the

Book Two, Dust to Dust, is Now Available

ruthless Irish mafia, I cross paths with the physically imposing owner. Though his hardened edges and dangerous aura should have frightened me, I found myself instantly magnetized, helplessly enthralled by his raw, rugged power. Against my better judgment, attraction simmered under my skin, a craving I knew would spell trouble.

Quinn is everything I'm not—brave, courageous, and strong. Every day I try and chisel away at his hardened veneer—to crumble the walls around him, dust to dust. Deep down, I know he is capable of giving love. When I'm abducted from the shadows of the club's parking lot, I pray nightly for Quinn to rescue me. But even if he storms the gates of hell to bring me back, can a broken dancer fighting PTSD be what he needs?

In the merciless underworld, brace yourself for a tempestuous romance pulsating with red-hot danger and forbidden desire.

Also by Katie Ashley

The Proposition Series: She hates her manwhore coworker, but he's the only one willing to offer his DNA to help her dreams of motherhood come true. Of course, he's only willing to conceive the baby naturally by hitting the sheets...or the desk....or the wall.

The Proposition

The Proposal

The Pairing

The Pursuit

The Predicament: A Proposition series novella

The Plan: A Proposition series novella

Runaway Train Rock Star Series:

Music of the Heart: Forced Proximity, Alphahole, Virgin FMC

Beat of the Heart: Secret Baby, Who Hurt You, Second Chance

Music of the Soul: a wedding novella for Music of the Heart

Strings of the Heart: Best Friend's Little Sister, Second Chance, Age-Gap

Melody of the Heart: Second Chance Romance, Small Town Romance

Runaway Train Companion Series: Jacob's Ladder

Jacob's Ladder: Gabe: Single Mom, Small Town, Enemies to Lovers

Jacob's Ladder: Eli: Best Friends to Lovers, Widow, Forced Proximity

The White House Billionaires Series:

Running Mate: Fake fiance, Alphahole, Forced Proximity

Office Mate: Bosshole, Office Romance, Enemies to Lovers

Roommate: Bodyguard Romance, Forced Proximity, Office Romance

Hells Raiders Motorcycle Series

Vicious Cycle

Amazon, B&N, Apple, Kobo, Google Play, B.A.M

Redemption Road

Amazon, B&N, iBooks, Kobo, Google Play, B.A.M

Last Mile: Amazon, B&N, iBooks, Kobo, Google Play, B.A.M

Sports Romance

The Hard Way: College Football Player, Second Chance, Small Town,

The Right Way: College Football Player, Secret Baby, Brother's Baby Mama

Don't Hate the Player: Young Adult, Loss of a Best Friend, Best Friend's Ex

Stand-alones

Reining Her In: Single Dad Small Town, Second Chance

The Actress and the Aristocrat: Grumpy/Sunshine, British Hero, Fake Relationship

Bound to Me: Small town, BDSM, Boss Romance

Drop Dead Sexy: Small Town, UnCozy Mystery with Smut

Search Me: New Adult, Small Town, Second Chance

Young Adult

Jules, The Bounty Hunter

Nets and Lies

The Guardians

Printed in Great Britain
by Amazon